THE SCHOLAR'S WAR

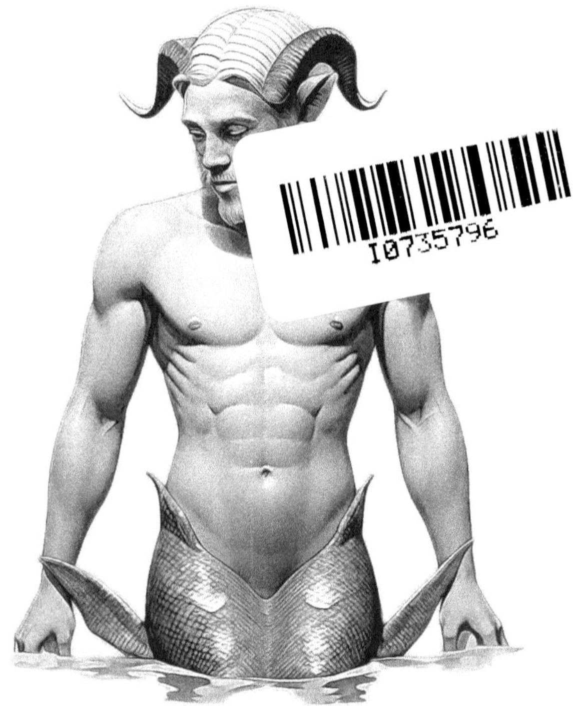

BEN BLAKE

DIVERTIR
PUBLISHING

Salem, NH

THE SCHOLAR'S WAR

Ben Blake

Cover design by Kenneth Tupper

Published by
Divertir Publishing LLC
PO Box 232
North Salem, NH 03073
http://www.divertirpublishing.com/

ISBN-13: 978-1-938888-35-9
ISBN-10: 1-938888-35-9

Library of Congress Control Number: 2024944110

Printed in the United States of America

TABLE OF CONTENTS

Chapter One

A truth of the world: In every place, given time, there will be war.

§ § §

"TELL ME AGAIN what colours look like to you," Mani said.

The young man ducked his head briefly below the water's surface, wetting his skin and eyes. "I could tell you sixty times, and you wouldn't understand. They're different, that's all."

"Different how?"

Slits in the youth's clavicles opened and closed with a *tss-tss* sound, like snakes in the reeds. "Just different. They're one way in fresh water, another way in salt. Hues that are one shade with dawn light above are another shade at sunset. Why do you want to know about colours?"

"Just trying to understand you."

Ripples ran down the young man's scaled lower body, vibrating the water around him until it gave a hum, right at the edge of hearing. Mani had long-ago recognized it as the Sea-Goat's equivalent of a laugh. "You couldn't understand us if we talked until you grew old."

"Well," Mani said, trying to draw the lad into an indiscretion, "you always hide so much, don't you?"

"That's because you wouldn't understand it," the young man retorted. Muscles tightened and he was gone in a glimmer of scales and splashing water.

Mani supposed he should be grateful a Sea-Goat had talked to him at all. Frequently when a scholar rang the bell nobody would come. He'd sit in the sun for an hour before walking back to Aš-alam with dust in his eyes and curses piling up on his tongue.

"There are stories the lagoon fishermen know more about the Sea Goats than we do," Shahan had said once. He was tossing chickpeas into the air and trying to catch them in his mouth. "People are sure of it."

"Well," Mani said, making a mark on his tablet, "people are sure of lots of things."

"I thought we might go and talk to them," the other scholar said. A chickpea ricocheted off his nose and scurried across Mani's clay tablet. "The fishermen, I mean. We could make a few days' trip out of it and travel to the villages."

"I would rather roast my balls in embers," Mani said, "but you go ahead."

Shahan never went to talk to the fishermen, of course. It wasn't a thing scholars did. Their place was in the city, eating from proper plates and talking with other erudite men. It was not clumping down tracks to muddy villages perched on the edge of the marsh, eating half-cooked grain and being stared at by grubby children. Mani wanted answers, but he preferred to seek them in civilized company.

The claim had stayed with him, though. A year or so later he asked one of the Sea-Goats, an older man whose head was crusted like the shell of a turtle. The swimmer sank under the water, looking up at Mani through magnified eyes. Usually that meant they were about to vanish, but this time the Sea-Goat broke surface again and shook water from his head.

"Don't talk to fishers, much." The words sounded pulled from his tongue. "What have they got to say? All they do is paddle about. They don't think."

"And we scholars do?"

The man blinked opaque eyes. "Some think, mostly about the wrong things."

"What are the right things?"

A glimmer and a splash, and the old man was lost in the depths.

§ § §

Aš-alam. The city of the goddess Eala—virgin, mother, whore. Daughter of the Moon and reeds of the river, who brought kingship and ritual to the earth so long ago only the *zami* remember it. The altar in the House of Heaven stood where she had stood. Pilgrims from other lands walked in the gardens, past pools shaded from the sun.

Around that temple, the city thronged. Artisans and labourers, porters with laden donkeys or loads strapped to their own backs, pushing their way through the crowds. Workers and servants, chained slaves, students from the Temples or the schools, census takers and *zami*, the priests and priestesses with their shaved heads and pinched lips. Always *zami*, wherever you went.

Carts inched through the throng, heavy with grain and sacks of vegetables, or cages in which animals squawked and snorted and clucked. Others carried bolts of flax to the weavers, or limestone and cedar brought from the distant west, bound for the builders who exchanged shouts from rooftops. In winter, there were carts piled with baked bricks to be used repairing walls, and clay jars full of bitumen to coat them against the spring flood. Around it all were the signs of smiths and wheelwrights, coopers and carpenters and masons, the men who endlessly built the city and tore it down to rebuild it again, piece by piece.

There were other cities, scattered across the plain like seeds thrown from a farmer's hand. Each had its own god, its own great temple, but none was as large or as grand as the House of Heaven. Priests in those far-off towns followed fashions set here and came to marvel at the temple on its great platform and the ceaseless, towering ambition of the city's other buildings. They sat at the feet of the *zami* of Aš-alam, listened to them speak, and took those words back to their homes. This was the first city, the oldest, the greatest. All others were imitations, lagging a pace behind no matter how they ran to catch up.

Eala had set her feet here, at the edge of the lagoons and waterways that separated the land and sea, the place where three worlds met: heaven, earth, and water. Mani often thought that the memory of her presence remained, like the glister of rain on leaves after the storm has passed.

This was the only place in the world where Sea-Goats would talk to men, however perplexingly. Visitors to Aš-alam sometimes asked why that was important.

"How was Man created?" Mani asked in return.

"Imgar made us to be servants to the gods and set us free when we turned out to be trouble," another man said. He sounded oddly proud of that but then hesitated. "Didn't he?"

"Perhaps," Mani said. "If that's so, then when were the Sea Folk made, and by whom? For what reason?"

Brows furrowed, and then the first man said doubtfully, "Do you mean there are other gods?"

"If I knew all the answers," Mani said, "I wouldn't need to ask questions."

He might be spending too much time with the Sea-Goats. He was nearly as elliptical as they were these days.

Chapter Two

THE BELL WAS half-submerged in water at the end of a pier made of woven bunches of reeds. When the lever was pulled the tocsin rang, the sound muffled as though the clapper was smothered in pillows. Mani had once put his head underwater while a colleague sounded the bell and hadn't thought the sound especially loud. When he came back onto dry land, he found his ears were aching though, a dull pain that didn't go away for a week.

One day when he rang, a young Sea-Goat man arrived, gratifyingly quick for once. He was slim and lithe, as all his people were, and his head was still a smooth grey, unspoiled by long years in the sea. The paler ridges that began above his eyes and curled back over his ears were what had given the swimmers their name. They looked like the horns of a goat, sunk beneath the skin.

"I haven't seen you before," Mani said.

"Nor I you." The young man performed a lazy somersault under the water. "I've always wanted to meet a human."

"Why haven't you?"

"I've only just come to the lagoons," he answered.

That raised the question of where he'd been before. Records at the academy said that many scholars had asked about that before, and such queries always ended with the swimmer streaking away into the deeps. Mani managed to bite his tongue. "I'm Kassu-Mani."

The Sea-Goat flapped his tail, bobbing in the water. "I'm Hanno. Why do you have two names?"

"A lot of my people do," he said. "Some even have three. It's easier if you just call me Mani."

"But why?"

It was hard not to show surprise. Sea-Goats rarely asked questions, and Mani couldn't remember one insisting on an answer. "I suppose I don't know. It's just how we are. I could find out, if you like."

Hanno bobbed under and back up again, water streaming from his hairless head. "It's not important."

"Why did you come here?" Mani asked.

"You rang the bell."

"That isn't what I mean. Why did you come to the lagoon?"

"I was old enough," Hanno said. "I wanted to see humans, too. I've heard all the stories about you."

That was too clear an invitation to miss. "Stories?"

"That you try to make yourselves clever but don't know how," Hanno explained. "You hardly ever dance. You smell of desert winds blowing over the sea, or sometimes of a beach after rain." He shrugged, a curious ripple to his shoulders. "Things everyone knows."

"We don't dance by the lagoon," Mani said, smiling. "We do sometimes in the city, though."

"Not when you move," Hanno said.

Mani didn't really understand that, so he let it go. Smell was interesting though, since to a human nose the Sea-Goats stank of the sea floor and fish drying in the sun. Quite revolting if you stood too close. It made sense that humans smelled strange to the swimmers. As for cleverness, Mani thought it would be easier to learn new things if the Sea-Goats answered with more than riddles. Perhaps this new one might. He was still enigmatic, but less so than others of his kind on first impression.

What Mani wanted to ask was *did you hear these stories growing up*, but the Sea-Goats never answered questions about their home, wherever it was. That was one of the first things a student learned, even before he first spoke to the swimmers. It was the question most certain to send a swimmer plunging down into the green depths, and often it was days afterwards before one would respond to the ringing of the bell.

"Most humans aren't very interesting," Mani said instead. "We work growing food, and we pray. For much of the year there's not much time for anything else."

"You grow grass?"

"A sort of grass," he agreed. "The same way you grow reeds."

Hanno snorted through the slits in his collarbones. "We don't grow it. We just manage where it grows."

"Is there a difference?"

"Reed beds affect water flow," Hanno said. "We shape the marshes and lagoons by what we do. Your farmers don't change the land around them."

"You should go up the river sometime," Mani said. "Take a look at all the canals and reservoirs we've built. Most of that water goes to fields in the dry season. Our farmers affect the land all right."

"Truly?" Hanno asked, and there was a nearly human eagerness in his sibilant voice. Then he deflated. "But the older people say we're not to go into the river. They say it's dangerous."

"Dangerous how?"

"You," Hanno said. He shot Mani a dark look from under the ridges of his brow. "Your people. Men with nets or spears. War, and warriors stabbing and stabbing."

"Fishermen might cause a problem," Mani admitted, "but there aren't any wars in Engiru these days. There were some long ago, when the steppe people came, but we've had none for sixty years."

"You're sure?"

"I'm sure," Mani said.

§ § §

North of Aš-alam lies the river Ranuna behind its great levees, one of two rivers to cross the plain. Beyond those slow brown waters lie the other cities of Engiru: Dar-aš and Tibad, Piqash and Shurraš, Eshkir and Kindar. Further north still is the second of the rivers, the Utuka. Whereas the Ranuna runs slow and brown, the Utuka is fast and clear, its channel bored into the earth as though by the knife cuts of giants.

It is said that in Engiru people take their characteristics from the waters. Men of the south are placid and calm, while those of the north are busy and quick to anger. Quick to violence, as well. Especially the men of Tibad and Labaš. A Sea-Goat who swam so far might find himself fighting for his life in some cleverly contrived arena against a warrior in waist-deep water.

Despite this, priests are the same everywhere. Some are men, others women. All shave their heads, pinch their lips in perpetual disapproval, and believe every aspect of every life is theirs to control. If a man be a king or bricklayer, warlord or farmer, the *zami* will worm their influence into his work and family, never saying it is enough.

Mani was in the scholars' rooms next to the Platform of the New Moon when someone spoke beside him. "I was a year younger than you when I was married," the person said.

Mani looked up. He thought at first that this was another of Shahan's jokes, something that started with a random comment and led quickly to elliptical nonsense. But it wasn't Shahan. The man by the pigeon boxes used to store tablets was older, his hair winged with grey. He had his back half turned, but Mani knew him.

"Darsal?"

"Keep your voice down." The other man didn't take his attention away from the shelves. There was no sound in the hall but his voice and the scritching of the scriveners' quills from their desks at the far wall. "You're twenty-five, am I right?"

"Yes. What does—"

"I was married at twenty-three. The priesthood found me a wife."

Mani frowned. "Why would they bother?"

7

"Think about it. We work in a building on the grounds of the city's third-largest temple. The royal treasurer pays for us, but it's the priests who watch us, and we store our records in the House of Tablets the *zami* built. They like to know what we're doing." Mani could hear the frown in his voice. "They like to know what everyone is doing."

"That's true," Mani said.

"It's about control. That Shusikil and her crones are all around the king and Elders, did you know that?"

The chief priestess's name made Mani shudder. "I knew it. You think they control us by giving us wives?"

"Who knows more about a man's day than his wife?" Darsal asked. A rhetorical question, not worth an answer and not getting one. "They give us women who failed the tests for the clergy. Zealous, but not the cleverest. Women who can't write, that sort of thing." He selected a tablet and pretended to study it. "Why did you want to be a scholar, Mani?"

He stared at the man through the shelving. "So I could talk to the swimmers."

"I know that. But why?"

"Because we don't understand them," Mani said. That didn't seem to be enough. "Look, they know things we don't, yes? How? Where did they learn them? There are answers out in the lagoon, Darsal. I want to know them. I want to learn the age of the world and to set my feet on the soil of their home island. The swimmers know things no human does. Sometimes they share, and once we've learned it, we won't forget. Knowledge is forever."

A chortle, as though that was the funniest joke of the year. "You really haven't lost your enthusiasm, have you?" He tucked the tablet under an arm. "If you want to choose your own bride, Mani, better do it soon."

Mani had mastered his letters when he was seven. That was early even among scholars, mind you. There were six hundred glyphs, and most people baulked just at the thought of learning them all. In truth, most were combinations of simpler characters, so the marks for water and street were combined to give the one for canal. Once you knew the basic sixty you had the language mostly cracked. By nine Mani had been writing essays on the Goddess, on philosophy, and on the nature of divinity and how it pertained to kings. Shortly after that he'd been sent to the Elders' School, and since then he doubted he'd known anyone who couldn't write.

It was the Sea-Goats who'd begun to claim his interest though, to the point where they swallowed everything else. Now it seemed that was all threatened, because a wife found by the priests would be more than a wife—she'd be a snitch too, and everything Mani did would be known in the Temples five minutes after he did it. Darsal was right. The *zami* would try to control him.

Let the priests decide where he went and what questions he asked? Bind him with a wife who couldn't even write? All Mani had was his work. He was an ordinary-looking man, he knew that—no taller than most with his face too bland to be handsome. He had always been clever and always bent that intelligence to the Sea-Goats. He wouldn't let the Temples take it away. A malicious wife was worse than all diseases, the saying went. Mani sat and thought for some time. Then he went to the study he shared with Shahan, because the first thing a man ought to do was warn his friend.

"Force me to marry?" Shahan said. "I'd like to see them try."

"Darsal seemed very sure."

"He always does. He's been a scholar so long he probably thinks the Moon and stars will fall from the sky when he's not here to study them anymore."

"That's not the point," Mani said. "What are you reading, anyway?"

"One of old Lipit's tablets, from sixty years ago. I remember years back I came across a reference to the Sea-Goats' home island. I think it might have been in one of Lipit's."

"You think it *might* have been? He left more than ninety writings in the archive. It'll take you days."

"Does it matter? There's no rush."

"Also," Mani said, "you've got mustard on the tablet."

"See?" Shahan said triumphantly. "The priesthood won't be able to find a woman to put up with me. I'll be blithe and carefree all my life."

Chapter Three

THE PLAIN OF Engiru is completely flat. The annual flood means there are no trees or hedges of thick shrubs. The fields are marked out by irrigation ditches, hundreds of them running this way and that. They gather thickly around the reservoirs and spread more widely elsewhere, crossed by countless narrow bridges of limestone. Each ditch is lined by bricks painted black with bitumen to keep them from crumbling into dust.

It works, for a time. Every few years the bricks must be replaced, in the autumn and winter when the land is parched and the fields lie empty. Shaven-headed *zami* walk the trenches, making notes on clay tablets whenever they see a section that needs repair. Then, while the ditches are dry, men pull down decaying sections and build them back afresh, watched over by those same bald *zami* as they work.

Cities dot the plain, drawing ditches to them in thickening streams. Nestled among them, like a tick on a bull's back, is Labaš.

City of Balih, the god of War and the Wind. Its streets are much the same as those of any other city, its buildings similar, and its people afflicted by the same concerns. The *zami* wear the pinch-lipped expression common across all Engiru, and they shave their heads just as *zami* do in Kindar or Aš-alam. Today, however, they are smiling, taut expressions that look uncomfortable on those narrow faces, as soldiers carry body after body out of the Chamber of Elders behind the main ziggurat and toss them into carts at the foot of the steps.

"They make my flesh creep," Enmer muttered.

His words were hardly loud enough for his own ears to hear, yet one of the *zami* turned his bald head to stare at Enmer as he helped haul another corpse down to the street. Enmer ducked his head and walked a touch faster.

"You fool," Yarim said as they threw the body into a cart. "Do you *want* a curse on your name?"

"He didn't hear me," Enmer said unconvincingly. "Stop worrying."

"I wouldn't worry if I didn't work with a fish-brained *kamal*," Yarim answered. "Anyway, it's not the *zami* that concern me." He nodded his head towards the far side of the stairs, almost imperceptibly. "It's him."

A man stood alone at the top of the steps, watching the bodies as they were brought out. He carried a sickle sword in one hand, curved point resting on the bricks at his feet. Even in the blazing sun, he wore only a kilt, leaving his broad chest to tan and then burn. Black hair curled over his forehead and ears. His left arm was bangled all the way to the elbow, glittering with silver and precious stones. He didn't seem to be looking at anyone. Everyone looked at him, though, mostly when they thought he wasn't watching or when his face was turned to the sky.

Yarim had a bronze club in a sheath on his back, and he knew how to use it. He was inches taller than most men, and his shoulders were like a roof beam. He'd fought in the battle that brought the king to power in Labaš. Not much frightened him, but his eyes were drawn back to that sickle sword, and every time he felt a little shiver of fear.

He and Enmer went back into the Chamber.

Common folks were normally not allowed in here. Except slaves, of course, when they served the Elders their wheat cakes and beer during debates. They never spoke of what they saw and heard though, even years afterwards—the *zami* forbade that. Anyone who uttered a word knew he was doomed to ages in Gizal, the world beneath the world, while flesh rotted slowly from the bones that trapped his soul.

The Elders forbade anyone from entering here, too, but they'd be forbidding no one anything now.

Blood ran down the steps from one tier of seats to the next, to pool in the open space below. The chairs were solid cedar wood. Yarim couldn't resist touching them as he went by, just to see what the wood felt like. He was careful not to touch where blood had spattered, though his hands were red and wet from lifting bodies, so he supposed it didn't matter. There were only ever thirty Elders, one for each day of the month, but they hadn't been the only ones to die.

"There are bodies down by the lower door," Nepada said. The captain pointed to the bottom of the room, as though Yarim and Enmer might not know what *lower* meant. "Slaves, mainly. Get to it."

Enmer grimaced, but Yarim merely gave a nod and moved down the steps. He had to stand aside while two other soldiers brought up a corpse, then continued until his sandals splashed into the blood. He paused to look around. Most of the wax candles were knocked over during the killing, but light still came through the high windows, enough to show slumped forms to his left. He walked carefully over and saw most of the dead were slaves, as Nepada had said, all clad in plain kilts and lying in pooled blood.

One of the corpses was an Elder, or had been. Yarim had seen him a few times, walking in the street with two big men to guard him. A well-fed fellow with a white stripe down each side of his beard, too distinctive to forget, though Yarim couldn't recall his name.

"Get your idle arse over here," he said to Enmer. His friend had hesitated by the last curved row of chairs. "These deaders are soaked, and curse my bones if I'm going to carry them on my own."

They took the Elder first, because he was the biggest of the slain. Blood made their hands slip, so they had to pause halfway up the steps and take handfuls of his clothes for a better grip. That was worse, if anything; the fabric was drenched in blood that hadn't caked and was slimy under their hands. They stopped for a second time just outside the doors. The tall man with the sickle sword was gazing at the sky again.

Someone was climbing the steps behind him, and Enmer abandoned his efforts to find a hold on the dead man and shut his eyes. His lips moved in prayer. Yarim lowered his head but kept his gaze on the approaching woman. She wore a simple white robe and kohl that made her eyes huge, and she should have been beautiful. She should have earned stares and quickened blood as she walked, but instead men turned their eyes away or closed them and murmured words of propitiation until she was gone.

Her head was shaved bald. She still carried an exotic beauty, enough to make Yarim's blood run hot, but it was sweetness in the taste of poison. Yarim knew her, too, and this time he remembered her name.

"High priestess," the man on the steps said. He brought his gaze down from the sky and turned to face her, resting the sickle sword on his shoulder. "You were expected this morning. I began to think you had abandoned our agreement at the last moment."

"I was listening to the voice of the god," she answered. If there was controlled power in the man's voice, there was complete self-assurance in hers. "But I am here now, my king."

The sword point ground on the bricks again. "And what did the god say to you, Kammani?"

"That the time is ripe for a change, and the Council of Elders had outlived their usefulness," she said. "That it is the will of Balih that power pass to the hands of a strong king, unencumbered by the failed traditions of the past."

"How fortunate," he observed.

The woman named Kammani didn't seem to notice the irony. "I will tell the people that you should rule alone. With proper advice from the priesthood, of course, to ensure the continued good graces of Balih."

"In your person?"

"In my person, Sarru-kin. There would be…advantages. Kings and high priestesses must work closely together." She stepped nearer. A tall woman, she still had to tilt her head back to look at him. A fingertip traced a line on his bare chest. "Very closely."

"How fortunate," Sarru-kin said again. He swung the sickle sword back onto his shoulder. "It seems we are agreed. Now, you promised me one thing more."

"I know it," Kammani said. In her place, Yarim thought he would be cringing by now, but the priestess was still serene. "My *zami* hear…a whisper. A rumour, inscribed on a tablet now crumbled from age. It seems there is an island which holds the secret you seek."

"Where is this island?"

"I do not know. But the tablet tells us who to ask." She still held his eyes. "The swimmers. The Sea-Goats of Aš-alam."

Sarru-kin let out a soft breath and turned his face back up to the sky. "Then that is where I will go. The army will march in two days." The sickle sword twirled. "There are cities between here and Aš-alam. If they oppose me, I will soak them in the blood of their own sons, and in Aš-alam I will become immortal."

Chapter Four

THE SPILLED SALT was on the far side of the city, in the north. Mani hadn't been there in some time.

Heat struck him a blow the moment he stepped into the street. Workers had abandoned their scaffolds and now lay dozing in the shade. They were the wise ones today. Shops were shuttered and temple doors closed. The streets were nearly empty. Sweat ran into Mani's eyes, and he wiped it away. More soaked his tunic under the arms.

There was no telling when a priest might appear with a wife for him, though, which meant he had no time to waste. Mani moved into shade when he could, suffered when he had to, and kept going.

Even in the heat of the day, there were some people about, those with business as urgent as his, or who were under orders. In the latter group was a band of debt slaves, two pushing wheelbarrows and the rest laden with trowels and pickaxes. A *zami* walked behind with a bucket of bitumen in one hand, which named the gang as a ditch repair crew. It was late in the year for that, with the Flood due in three months. The work should have been finished by now, but there was always more to do, like a section that collapsed unexpectedly. Better it be fixed now than left until the waters rose.

A man walked down the middle of the street, buffeted at every step by a woman who called him a bastard, cheat, and rooster-cock. He absorbed her blows without comment, his mouth a hard line. That was marriage when it turned out badly. Wed for love, divorce when you've had time to think it over. Mani had heard that a hundred times, and he'd taken it as a warning not to rush into anything. There had been pretty girls here and there, though he was never brave enough to talk to them properly, losing his eloquence in a torrent of um and ah. Because of that, or because of the warning, he'd never rushed into anything.

Until now. He didn't think he had a choice anymore. No shaven-headed fanatic was going to tell *him* what questions he could ask and which answers he could write down.

He really wasn't good with girls, though, and doubts first slowed his steps and then brought him to a halt. Uncertainty made a hole in his stomach, and he only knew one way to fill that.

"Course it's fresh," the vendor told him. "Caught last night in the river. I swear on Eala's virtue."

"The Goddess is a whore as well as a maiden."

"Then I'll swear on her ecstasy too," the man said. "Are you going to buy a fish or not? It's hot as fury out here."

Mani bought a barbel steak, fried with onions and garlic, and sat on a shady wall to munch it. If he was Shahan, he would have wiped greasy fingers on his tunic, but Mani kept a scrap of cloth in his pocket for just such crises. He cleaned his fingers and stood up. The hole in his belly wasn't filled by eating, but he did feel a little braver.

He went on to the Spilled Salt. It stood on a side street not far from the main gates, a square building with steps leading up to a porch flanked by pillars with spirals of black and white cone mosaic. Only two pillars, true, and slender ones at that, but still. Someone who could afford cone mosaic was making a lot of money. It might incline him to be generous or mean of spirit. You really couldn't tell until you went inside and found out.

Across the street was a block of mismatched houses, now being torn down. Well, not right now; the workers were all stretched out in the shade of a remaining wall, arms over their eyes. Someone had told Mani a new Temple was going to be built there, when the clearance crews were done.

Temples everywhere, and *zami* pouring out of them like insects from co-coons. But that wasn't his business today. Mani went up the steps and into the relative cool of the Spilled Salt.

"Scholar!" There was Udar, black hair oiled, his beard trimmed close and curled, sleek as a seal. He threw his arms wide. "I half thought you'd died. Another week and I'd have come to make sure you were all right."

"I don't doubt it," Mani said.

"I swear!" Udar grinned. "I'd have hunted you down like a wolf on a gazelle. I don't like to lose a regular customer. Come, meet my friends."

The tavern wasn't like most of the city's bars. Usually, they were poky places squeezed into a row of houses, like an unwanted guest in the middle of a bench. There was usually no room to wriggle between tables when the chairs were full, so a wise man picked a spot near the door and once in it never moved. The Spilled Salt catered to a more discerning crowd, men with coins to spend and a palate that could tell when the beer mash hadn't fermented long enough. There was space to weave through the tables, which Udar did easily, coming to a bench at the back wall where two men sat.

"Isha, a drink for the scholar." Udar slapped Mani on the back. "These fellows are Ruen and Ramsi. Brothers, as you can see, they're as ugly as each other. Boys, this is Mani. He speaks to the swimmers."

The two men's expressions changed as they reached to clasp arms. Mani knew why. He looked like every other educated man, a little soft around the jaw, his hands unsullied by manual work. Enough for a worker to distrust him, even hold him in a peculiar sort of contempt. But if he spoke to the Sea-Goats, and they let him, then he deserved respect.

"Pleased to meet you," the brothers said in unison. They sat down the same way, arses hitting the bench at the same moment, like marionettes puppeted by the same strings.

"You, too," Mani said. He was about to sit down when Isha came over with a clay mug and set it on the table. He found himself watching as she walked away. She had a fall of hair, black as a raven's dreams, and a nice wiggle to her hips. Not much of those hips, true, and her hair was straight as a knife cut when in true beauties it was curled. Mani shook his head.

"Could we have a word in private?" he asked.

Udar was instantly all solicitation, the perfect host. He led Mani to a corner table well away from the other patrons, who were few enough given the hour. Then he went back for his guest's mug, put it before him, and slid into a chair. He set folded arms on the table. "What can I do for you?"

"Well," Mani said, "you might wish you hadn't asked."

"Nonsense. A friend is a friend, and I owe you a little. People come to a bar where they know scholars drink. They like to listen to their tales, especially about what the swimmers say. Can't get enough of the swimmers. I guess you know that."

He nodded.

"And what have I done to repay you? Nothing. Can't do much, truth be told. What does a scholar need from an innkeep? Beer, that's all, and too much of that can rot any man's brain. I'll allow myself two a night and no more than that for my friends, the clever ones most of all. So ask. Ask."

Mani took a long slug of beer, emptying half the mug. It left froth in his beard, and he wiped it away with the back of his hand. "I, um. That is, I want to uh. Could you…would you—"

"Mani." The landlord's sleek hand covered Mani's own. "Stop fretting yourself. We're friends here. Take a breath and ask."

He took a breath. "Is your daughter still looking for a husband?"

There was a moment in which Udar looked like a man hit over the head with a brick. Then a smile broke, water on cracked ground. "Cripple my father! You want to marry Isha? Truly?"

"Only if you approve," Mani said. "And if she's willing, naturally. I don't want to offend either of you."

"Offend me? By Eala's footfalls, I thought no one would ever ask for her again. Not after…well. To have her wed to a scholar would be a blessing beyond hope. And to a friend, besides." He slapped Mani on the back, and for all that he looked well fed and indolent, the blow hurt. "I will make gifts of thanks in the Immaru Temple at sunrise tomorrow. Great gifts!"

"If she agrees," Mani said. "*Only* if she agrees, Udar. I refuse a forced marriage for myself, and I won't impose it on her. Or any woman."

The innkeep paused. "The *zami*?"

"They want me to marry one of their cast-offs," Mani said. "Or at least I think so. I've had a warning from someone I trust. After that, I'll be able to ask only the questions the priestesses want and write only the answers they choose. A shave-head will be standing behind me every day of my life, even when I'm out at the marsh alone."

"A malicious wife is worse than all diseases," Udar said. His mouth drew down at the corners. "One of those priestesses was in here last week. She wanted to know if I'd agree to have her women in here, talking to the men as they drank. Offered me quarter the value of the business paid every year if I agreed. I turned her down, of course. Men come here at the end of the day for a well-earned drink, not to have priestesses peering over their shoulders."

"They peer over everyone's shoulders."

"It's worse for me," Udar said. "Imagine if the *zami* told you what beer you could serve, who you had to buy from, and at what price. If a man couldn't joke about work or his wife without a shave-head scowling at him. I'd be bankrupt inside a month." He eyed Mani for a moment. "Will they be angry with you?"

"For marrying another woman? I assume so. I'd rather contend with their anger than their interference, and they can't keep me from talking to the Sea-Goats. I'm Guild-approved. That's what matters."

"Don't take it for granted," Udar said darkly. "Their power reaches into every house and field, and they're never satisfied. If they can't tie this string to you, they will look for another."

"Then they will have to do that," Mani replied.

"All right, then. I think it's time you talked to Isha." Udar rose, gripping Mani's shoulder as he stood. "You say you need her agreement, and that's your choice. But know that you have mine." He wove away between the tables, calling Isha's name as he went.

Mani let out a long breath. He'd been more nervous about securing Udar's agreement than he was over Isha, in truth. She was twenty now, or close to it, well past the age when most girls married. Every year, every week made her chances of a good match less. And people knew what had happened. Rumour could be a vicious enemy.

Isha appeared from the doorway beside the bar counter. She stopped to stare across the room at him, and Mani felt nerves twist in his belly again. *More nervous about Udar than about her?* He'd been a fool. She started across the room towards him.

Chapter Five

IS IT TRUE?" Isha asked as she sat. "You want to marry me? Why?"
A simple question, with no easy answer. The truth would likely not do,
except Mani didn't know what Udar had already told her. "The priestesses
are going to insist I wed, and they'll put forward one of their own as my bride.
I can't really refuse. Scholars are supposed to marry. It shows we're serious
about life, as we should be serious about our work."

"So, you're drawn to me because I'm not a *zami*?"

"That's part of it."

"What's the rest?"

"I know you," he said. "I've known you since you were twelve, when you
first started working in the bar. You're clever and brave. Look at how you're
speaking to me now."

"If you can't handle a few questions, you'll never be able to deal with me
in your home."

He shook his head. "That's not what I'm saying. I like sharp wits, Isha. A
dull woman would bore me in a day."

He studied her. She wasn't really a beauty, with her too-straight hair, small
nose, and a figure that didn't curve where a woman's should. Or not much,
anyway. She was pretty, in a sideways sort of way. Then there were her eyes.
Large and dark, and afire with the glint Mani knew as intelligence, which he saw
so rarely even in his colleagues. Most men who talked with the swimmers had
the enthusiasm worn out of them within a few years, ground down by elliptical
answers that made no sense. They turned a little glaze-eyed, like cattle stupefied
by the reek of blood.

Or perhaps it was their wives who did it to them. Their watchful, priestess-
chosen wives. Mani shuddered.

"You know I'm bad luck," Isha said.

Mani shook his head again. "No, you're not. What happened to you was
bad luck, and that's different."

"Once, perhaps. Not twice. It doesn't worry you?"

"Once was happenstance, twice is coincidence. That's all."

"It doesn't worry you?"

"You were betrothed, and your intended lost a hand in a hammer accident.
The second time your husband-to-be died of consumption. It happens, Isha."

"If Eala has cursed me, it could happen to you."

"Well, let's see." He folded his hands on the table between them. "The accident was about a week after your betrothal, I think. The second time he died a fortnight later, is that right?" He waited for her nod. "Then I suggest we have a brief engagement."

Her lips twitched. "Are you quite sure I'm not cursed?"

"As certain as I am of anything," he said. "Although I talk to the Sea-Goats, so my concept of certainty might be a bit vague."

"Do they talk back?"

"Yes. Sometimes I even understand it."

"That must be frustrating. Will you come home and take out your anger on me with a stick?"

He smiled. "I hardly ever beat women."

"You've never been married before."

"True. But all this is just talk, Isha, words for the sake of speaking. Let me ask. Do *you* believe you're cursed?"

Her eyes flickered away from his for the first time. "Perhaps. I don't know the goddess's mind."

"I didn't ask you what Eala thinks."

"I…don't believe I am," Isha said. She still hadn't looked back at him. "You're right. I was just unlucky."

"And at that," he said, "not as unlucky as the poor man who lost a hand, or the one who died."

Another flicker of a smile. "That's true."

"Then what do you want, Isha? You can stay working here, if you like. Your father loves you a great deal. He'd let you stay until you grow grey and withered, like old bones. Or you can try to make a life of your own."

"That's true as well," she admitted. "The question is whether I should choose the life you offer."

He held his peace. There wasn't anything Mani could think of to say. His words had been more fluent with Isha than with any other woman he could remember, but there were limits, and he thought silence was his best friend just now. If Isha turned him down, he supposed he'd go to the nearest Scented House and hope to find a woman who could read and write, or at least think for herself, and be satisfied with that. He was *not* going to let a priestess command him in his own home or his work. Not ever that.

"If you had spoken of love," Isha said, "I'd have known it for a lie, and you a liar. I would have rejected you then. I'll be happy to be the wife of a *lamadu*. A scholar's house is better than I could have hoped to find. I might even be respected in society, innkeep's daughter or not."

"A scholar's duty is to speak the truths he finds, however difficult or unpopular they are," Mani said. "We're not usually respected much. Not in polite society, anyway. We upset too many people."

He was smiling though, and blessings be to Eala, so was she. Isha reached across the table to put a hand over his two clasped ones, and across the room Udar let out a shout of delight.

§ § §

They were married the next day, in a little temple in the west of the city just as the sun rose to bathe it in light. Mani recited the words of a bridegroom and forgot them as they left his mouth. The priestess at the altar turned to Isha.

Bridegroom, dear to my heart,
Goodly is your beauty, honeysweet,
Lion, dear to my heart,
Goodly is your beauty, honeysweet.

You, because you love me,
Pray give me your caresses,
My lord, my protector,
My husband, who gladdens Eala's heart,
Pray give me your caresses.

They were marrying because circumstance had brought them to it, each for their own reasons. Even so, Isha's voice made the words ring with love, or something that would pass for it. It was unsettling, in a way Mani didn't understand. He had no time to think about it.

"Veil," the priestess prompted.

The seats behind were filled—well, two rows of them were. Neither bride nor groom had many friends. Udar had come, and with him some of the regulars from the Spilled Salt, most of whom Mani recognised but couldn't name. Ruen and Ramsi he could name, the brothers crammed into knee-length tunics in the yellow of marriage. In a cluster on the other side sat half a dozen scholars, including some of the seniors. Darsal was there, along with Hitti, who was so old he walked with two sticks but still managed to hobble to the swamp to ring the bell that called swimmers. Tash-Yal had come, dragging himself away from the charts and graphs that covered a dozen desks as he struggled to collate the Sea-Goats' abstract comments into something that made sense. Shahan was also there, wearing a black tunic only bordered in yellow, looking like a crow in a cornfield and shaking his head at Mani's foolishness.

The shaven-headed priestess poked him in the arm and said, "The veil?"

Mani gave a start. He reached behind him, and Udar put a veil in his hands, a light and flimsy thing that would fall apart the moment it was washed. That didn't matter—Isha only had to wear it for a week. He placed it on her head and let the gauze fall over her face. She smiled at him, and he found himself smiling back.

"You are married in the sight of Eala," the priestess said. She was a big woman with a big voice, less like a woman's and more like a bulky charcoal burner. "There is yet room for repentance. Remove the veil before seven days have passed and the marriage is dissolved. Wear it and the seal shall be set upon your union, and Eala will bless you in this world."

Mani looked at his wife. She didn't blink or look away. After a moment he felt her hand creep into his, cautious as a mouse crossing a newly cut field, and she said, "Shall we?"

They went out into the street, a party of a dozen and a half dressed in yellow that shone in the sun. It was still early, but people were about their business, hoping to finish before the sun rose too far and heat became a lion that mauled. Some paused to call congratulations and toss whatever they had into the air; petals or seeds for some, just a handful of dust for others. Mani and Isha walked through a constant shower, sage leaves and dust settling on their shoulders as they went.

It was some distance to the Spilled Salt, where Udar had laid out a wedding breakfast. They followed the street towards the middle of the city, past grain warehouses and homes shoehorned into the spaces between them, past temples with pillared porticoes, past smithies and cobblers and rug makers. A tailor came out of his shop to give them a few yards of cloth he said was no use to him, so he'd make a wedding gift of it. At the corner an apothecary gave them a glass bottle an inch high, filled with powder that he said would ensure a child within one year. The apothecary winked.

They turned onto a wider street, heading now into the shade of a massive platform of bricks. A smaller storey stood upon that, then a third, and finally the Immaru Temple, the place of light, raised so high above the city that the sun's rays fell on it every moment from dawn until dusk. The place where Eala had set her feet when she descended from Heaven, and the centre of the world. A scaffold covered half of one side, with workers like dots hanging from the poles and rigging. They cheered as the little procession went by.

"I hope they don't throw their hammers in the air," Isha whispered.

Mani chuckled. "That would be bad. Let's settle for the cheers."

A moment after he said it the whooping quieted ahead of them. Mani peered and saw people backing to the sides of the avenue, bowing as they went.

He couldn't see why. Then the crowd parted, and he did, just as Isha pulled him to a halt and began to go down into a bow of her own.

"No," the man emerging from the throng said. "Not today, young woman. A bride should bow to no one on her wedding day." He took her hand, kissed the palm, and then he turned to Mani with his hand extended. Mani gripped the forearm and felt strong fingers clutch back.

"Congratulations," said the king of Aš-alam.

"Er," Mani managed.

The king wasn't alone. Three portly fellows in expensive tunics walked close to him, Elders of the Council ready to give advice to the man they'd elected king two years ago. They were matched by an equal number of shaven-headed priestesses, all of them old and skinny as starving dogs. They might have been cut from the same cloth on the same day. Six muscular men with maces walked in a loose circle around them all, bare-chested and grim-faced. They weren't needed to protect the king from the people, but other cities had sent assassins before, in more warlike times. There had been peace for decades, but habits die hard.

"I have no flowers to throw for you," Ra'im said. Something had been sewn into the curls of his beard, tiny glimmers amid all the black. "Will you accept a gift from me, to spare me shame?"

"You're very kind," Mani said. He started to bow, and Isha caught him before he got very far.

"Quite right!" The king was laughing. "A groom shouldn't bow on his wedding day either. Here." He pulled a ring from his baby finger. "Take this. Any jeweller should give you a good price for it."

"Thank you," Mani said.

One of the priestesses took a pace forward. "You're Kassu-Mani. The scholar." Her voice was harsh, like gravel scraping against stone. "Aren't you?"

Mani did bow then, just a small dip of his head. "I'm honoured that you know of me, *zami.*"

"And you're married." The crone cast a flat look at Isha. "How…provident. We were going to—"

Another of the women pulled at her arm, and the hag broke off. The action drew Mani's eyes to the second priestess, and he knew her.

There were stories about Shusikil. Tales of what she had done to rise to the top of the *zami*, and her place one step to the side of the king. Not a step behind. The chief priestess walked alongside the king by right, and when a king died hers was one of the votes cast to decide who would next wear the crown. Some of the older scholars claimed that Shusikil had not chosen Ra'im.

She was tall, thin as a stick, her cheeks hollow and black eyes burning. "No wedding was listed for you."

The king's gaze sharpened at that, as he caught the same implication Mani saw. The *zami* really had been watching him, planning to find him a bride of their own. Perhaps they'd already done so. If he hadn't forestalled them, he would have been wed to a failed acolyte by the time the Flood came. He didn't have to look around to know that Shahan was shaking his head.

"No," Isha said, before Mani could reply. "We met again yesterday, after weeks apart, and decided we couldn't wait. Our fervour overtook us."

Shahan spluttered. Shusikil's narrow face tightened, but she was given no chance to speak either.

"Was this a sudden wedding?" Ra'im asked. "That really is provident. We might take it for granted that the *zami* will be pleased to see a man and woman so quick to take their oaths before the goddess. Isn't that right, Shusikil?"

There was a glint of amusement in his eyes, a flicker of a smile on his lips, as he turned to her. Mani was certain the king knew exactly why the wedding had been so quick. Put on the spot, the crone could only grind her teeth and mutter something that might have been agreement but was a long way short of gracious. It didn't matter. She could make a cage, but Mani was a fox the priestesses couldn't catch.

"Congratulations again," the king said. With that, he moved past them towards the great double doors in the side of the ziggurat of Immaru. The swarm of advisors and guards walked with him, already chattering as they went.

"The rumour comes from two sources," someone said.

"They are both reliable?"

"One is especially so. He is in Labaš itself, and says he watched Sarru-kin's army leave."

"His target?" Ra'im asked.

"My lord, we can't be sure. Perhaps Kindar, perhaps Ashkir. Both lie along the same road from Labaš."

"We can't form an army in time to help. Very well, send an emissary to our royal brother of Ashkir. He probably knows already but warn him anyway. Then send another messenger to…"

The group passed from hearing. Mani realised his wife was looking at him through her veil.

"It's not our business," he said. "We study the Sea-Goats, not war, and Labaš is a long way from here."

A long way indeed, across the wide Ranuna and past most of the cities of Engiru. Still, it was a shock to hear of an army on the march after so many years of peace. War in one place might lead to war in another. It had happened before, a local skirmish drawing in one city after another until the land was in ruins from river to river and the irrigation ditches went unrepaired.

Well, there was no sense borrowing trouble. Now it was Mani making a cage for a fox he hadn't caught yet. He smiled at Isha. *My wife, and isn't that strange?* "Shall we go on?"

They did, passing out of the shadow of the ziggurat of Immaru and back into morning sunlight. Even so, all during the wedding breakfast Mani couldn't shake off the feeling that clouds had thrown their shadows over the day, and he found it harder and harder to smile.

CHAPTER SIX

"M OST INITIATES LOSE their enthusiasm quite soon," the scholar said. He was short, with a tubby tummy and graying hair that stuck up around his head like a deformed helmet. Isha couldn't remember his name. "Mani didn't. Shahan, either. It's good to see."

"Shahan could use a little more earnestness," Hitti said. He said it with a cut of his eyes towards the man in question, who raised his cup in a mocking salute and then stuck his tongue out. "Last month he tried to persuade a Sea-Goat to eat grain bars."

There were grins and a couple of polite chuckles. The *lamadu* didn't seem to indulge in open emotion, or even to relax, as far as Isha could see.

She sat on a bar stool, the counter at her back and her new husband at her side. Isha could see him from the side of her eye, leaning with one elbow on the bar and a cup not far from his hand. He hadn't touched the wine. She didn't need a better look to know that he was tight as a sealed barrel, stiff with tension and nerves.

Behind her Udar was busy serving drinks. Ramsi and Ruen were there too, hurrying to fill cups and cut bread or fruit. The three of them hardly fit behind the counter. Isha didn't think the Spilled Salt had ever been this busy in the morning. On the far side of the bar room the usual early customers chewed, sipped, and threw perplexed glances at the wedding party, crammed into a corner at the back.

"You lot have tried the same tricks for years," Shahan said. He burped, bringing a hand to his mouth too late. "Sorry. Anyway, I thought I'd try something different."

"We all do the same things because they work," Hitti snapped.

"Oh, surely," Shahan grinned. "That's why you've learned so much, of course. All you need is a sailor and a ship, and you'll be off to the Sea-Goats' home island, won't you?"

Hitti and the mad-haired man glared at him. Some of the others allowed themselves more of those discreet chuckles, and one lifted a cup to Shahan. That must be a custom among these men. On any normal day, a drinker who kept lifting his wine would find it knocked out of his hand by an accidental shoulder before the second sip.

"Does anyone know where the swimmers live?" Isha asked.

She had to turn to Mani to ask, lowering her voice so only he could hear.

When she saw him fully, she could tell he was terrified, a man who has taken a leap and didn't know where he would land. His skin had a pallor that she associated with too much wine or not enough food.

"We never figured that out." His eyes darted to her and away, like frightened fish. "We've known for a long time that their home is an island, but it's only four years ago that we found it's in fresh water."

Isha looked at the scholars. "Which one of them discovered that?"

"I did," he said.

She looked at him and then away, no words on her tongue to form a reply.

"Any sailor would leap at the chance to take scholars to the Sea-Goats' island," another man said. Younger than some of the others, but older than Mani and Shahan. Isha thought he was about forty, though he looked tired around the eyes. "But we don't know enough yet. Learning is a slow thing, Shahan, when it comes to the Sea-Goats. Risks are dangerous. You ought to know that by now."

"Risks usually are dangerous," the young man said. His smile flashed. "You ought to know that by now."

"Listen, pup, you haven't—"

"Look," Hitti said.

He was staring past the others, towards the door. Isha turned her head and saw two *zami*, one tall and the other fat as a goose, both twisting to look at the wedding party as they came in. She looked the other way and there was her father, stock still and glaring. There was nothing he could do. Priestesses could go where they wished. These two went to the counter and sat on high stools, hard faces set.

"Dust eat the pair of them," Shahan said too loudly. "Look, Tash-Yal said that Mani and I haven't lost our enthusiasm. He's right, you know. I want to learn things. The Sea-Goats can mumble and frustrate better than anyone, but I'm not going to give up."

"Meaning that I have?" the tired man retorted, firing up at once.

"What about you?" Isha murmured, for her husband only. "What keeps you fascinated with the swimmers, Mani?"

"Knowledge," he answered, without a moment's pause. "They could tell us so much, about everything, and they *won't*. They must be teased and tricked. They're like sphinxes, protecting what they know, and we can't force them to tell so we must outwit them, outthink them. I want to learn everything they know so I understand how important it is." He drew a breath. "That's why."

It was the most animated Isha had seen him. A glimpse into the soul of the man. It both drew her and made her uneasy. "That's close to obsession, husband."

He twitched a shoulder in a half-shrug. "I know it is."

All right. He was bewitched by the Sea-Goats, as helpless as a shepherd possessed by a demon. There were worse things a husband could be. "There's another question."

"What question?"

Isha wondered if he'd be angry that she had an opinion, after no study of the Sea-Goats at all. Maybe he would, but he was her husband now, and he'd said he wanted a clever wife. "Why are they here at all?"

"Who, the swimmers? Because they like fresh water. The lagoon is the only coastal place for a thousand miles where—"

"No," Isha said. "That's not the point. Why would they be anywhere on the coast? Why leave their island at all? You said their home is in fresh water, Mani, so why aren't they there?"

He looked at her. No anger in him, but his brows drew slowly down, and after a moment he bit his lower lip.

"You hadn't thought of that," she said. "I'm sorry. I know it's your work, and you know so much more than I do."

"I know enough to recognise insight when I hear it," he said. "But speak softly. Some of the older men would spit dust and gravel if they heard you say something like that."

"It's not a stupid question?"

"I once heard," Mani said, "that there are no stupid questions, only people too stupid to ask. I don't know the answer, though."

"Well," she said, "the stories say they were here when Eala founded Aš-alam, I think. So, whatever they came for, it was before the city began. That's a long time for one reason to hold."

"Yes." His face had become an agile thing, alive with interest. "They might have come even before the fishermen did, when there was no one here at all. I wonder…" He broke off and then chuckled the little scholar's chuckle. "Listen to me. It's my wedding day—our wedding day—and I stand here yammering about the Sea-Goats."

He changed when something engrossed him. When his curiosity was caught, and he forgot he was an awkward man with a new wife at his side. Isha gave him a gentle push. "Go talk to your friends, husband. You have a new idea to offer them."

"I can't take credit for that!"

"Will they accept the idea of a woman, untrained?" Another push. "Go on. I'll be here when you're done."

"Scholars' talks are never done," he grumbled. He went to the tables and squeezed into a chair by the wall, his cup of wine untouched on the bar counter.

Isha looked at him, through the gauze veil. *My husband.* Not an especially tall man, not deep in the chest or muscled in the arms. His beard was neatly trimmed, his features interesting more than handsome. She'd seen him before, sharing a jug of ale with one or another of his colleagues, and yet she'd never really seen him.

A man you could pass in the street and never notice. Yet he was here, and he was hers, odd as that seemed, and perhaps the Goddess hadn't cursed Isha after all.

"I heard some of that," Udar said behind her.

"Eavesdropper," she said. "You have no respect."

"What, a father shouldn't worry for his daughter? I passed you to another man to care for today, Isha. That doesn't mean I'll stop making sure you're safe from harm." He put Mani's wine cup under the counter, ready for the next customer. "I heard some of what you said. About the swimmers coming for a reason we've long forgotten."

"I'm not sure that's quite what I said."

"Close enough. A mystery to stand with the Goddess herself, isn't it?"

He spoke with an eye on the two crones further along the bar. Neither paid him any attention. They were staring at the scholars, not blinking. Shahan said something and the scholars laughed in a little ripple, as though the amusement was too shy to come into plain sight.

"He's a good man," Udar said quietly. "I would have kicked him down the steps for asking, otherwise."

Mani was leaning forward now, speaking with light in his eyes as his colleagues listened. Telling them her thought, as though it was his own, and Isha said, "I hope you're right, Papa. My life-thread is twined with his now, and there's no taking it back."

Chapter Seven

THOUGHT YOU'D BE sleeping in," Shahan said the next morning. It was two hours after dawn. Yesterday's wedding breakfast had gone on well into the afternoon, and the stream of well-wishers kept bringing gifts. Small things, for the most part, salt cellars and cutlery, or knick-knacks Mani accepted with a smile and an inward vow to throw away as soon as possible.

He now owned seven carved cats in ghastly colours. Perhaps he could give them away in his turn. He did not intend to fill his house with hideous cats.

No need to say his home felt odd now, heavy with the presence of a stranger. "I just thought I'd come in, and I can't afford to miss days. We're not paid a daemon's wage."

Shahan made a face. "Don't I know it."

As a married man, Mani would be paid more. Quite a lot more, in fact, though he hadn't checked the numbers. Marriage had always been something he thought he could leave while he focused on his work for another year…and another, and another. Time had passed without him really noticing. He didn't have much to show for it. A small home not too far from a river garden, enough clothes that he could always wear clean in the morning, and a pile of baffling Sea-Goat comments big enough to cover every desk in the library.

Now he had a wife as well. He supposed that would change his life. Maybe for the better in the end, but he and Isha had spent their wedding night lying sleeplessly beside each other, afraid to reach out and touch.

"Is there anything new?" he asked.

"Nothing. All the scholars spent yesterday at your wedding, and the evening sleeping off too much beer. Tash-Yal's not in yet, and I can't remember him being late before."

"Neither can I," Mani said. He slid onto the bench beside his desk. "In that case, I'm going to review the notes I made last time I was out at the marsh, when I spoke to Hanno. The new one."

"You're such a bore," Shahan said. "You just got married, by Eala's blessed feet. Go home and spend time with your wife. If the *zami* ask I'll tell them you're out at the bell."

There was no way for Mani to say he didn't really want to spend time with his wife. He didn't want to think about it either, so he said, "If you did and they checked, we'd both be in serious trouble. I've upset the priestesses already, if you remember. I can do without making more enemies among them."

31

Shahan sighed theatrically. "Well, if you're staying, I did hear some interesting gossip this morning."

"Did you?" Mani asked, not much interested. He pulled a tablet over and picked up a reed stylus.

"About the king of Labaš," Shahan said, and Mani looked up at him. "I heard he had all the Elders killed. He says Balih has chosen him to rule alone."

"Without a Council?"

"That's what I hear."

"It's just rumour," Mani said after a moment. He wasn't so sure. There had been that snippet of conversation in the street as the king and his advisors moved away. The army of Labaš was on the march, heading to nobody knew where.

Labaš was a long way away. He'd said as much to Isha. Almost all the cities of the plain lay between the two rivers, slow Ranuna and quick-flowing Utuka, among them Labaš. It was further north than most, and as far from Aš-alam as you could get. Aš-alam lay south of the Ranuna. Most of Engiru was between them. The warlord king would have to conquer his way across the entire land before he could threaten Aš-alam.

"Would the priestesses stand for that?" he asked, after thinking it through. "A god-touched king would weaken them, and the *zami* don't like to surrender their power."

"Ahem," Shahan said.

Mani sighed. "Yes, I know you don't believe it, but I do. The priestesses were going to force me to marry and use my wife to control my work. Anyway, this news of Labaš is different. They wouldn't give away their influence over a whole city without a fight."

"*Ahem,*" Shahan said.

Mani started to glower, then realised his friend wasn't looking at him, but past him. He turned on his seat.

There were two priestesses in the doorway. One of them was young, with a cascade of ebony hair and large dark eyes. She might have been pretty if not for a nose that would have done for chopping through reed beds. Young or not, she had the pinch-lipped look that all priestesses seemed to wear out of habit.

The woman beside her had worn the look for decades, and Mani had seen her before, at the side of the king.

"Good morning, *ama-su,*" he said. He thought his cheeks might be flushed. "What can we do for you?"

"You can stop spouting nonsense for a start," Shusikil said. The chief of the *zami* spoke in a hiss, like a snake spitting venom. "The Temples serve Eala. Her, and no other. We don't care about your work. Our interest is Heaven, not power in the mortal world."

"Of course," he said. "Of course."

"Now leave us, Kassu-Mani. Tauth and I wish to speak with your colleague."

Mani glanced at Shahan at the bench behind his own desk. His friend's expression was frozen. *There sits a man faced with a truth he didn't believe in.* It might be that Mani's precipitate action in finding himself a wife had stirred the *zami* to move quickly to snare Shahan. If that was so, it was too late to help. Mani rose.

"I think I'll go to the lagoon after all," he said.

The crone nodded. "Very wise."

Mani found a blank tablet and left, tucking the stylus into a pocket of his tunic. He went ten feet down the corridor and paused, knowing it was risky and the two priestesses would insist on penance from him if he were caught. Still, he had to know. He stood silently and listened.

"—young women," Shusikil was saying. "You visit the Scented Houses once a week at least. It's time you put such careless behaviour aside."

"The Temples have no cause to chastise me," Shahan replied. "I pay my tithes on time."

"Proper worship of Eala comes through the children we raise. No tribute of coins compares to that."

"But I—"

"Tauth has failed her tests for the priesthood." The hag spoke over Shahan without effort. "Not through lack of zealotry. She just struggles with her letters, and every *zami* must keep good records. But she can serve Eala well outside the Temples, as the wife of a good citizen."

Mani had heard enough. He turned and went down the corridor and out into the rising heat of morning. Sweat popped on his brow that had nothing to do with the sun.

The *zami* had been ready to act. Mani thought Tauth had been meant for him, and today was the day she would have been offered. He had no evidence for that. No scholar should reach a conclusion without data, and yet Mani was certain.

He'd been one sunrise from marriage to an illiterate failed priestess. How bad that would have been he didn't know, but surely it wouldn't have been easy, especially when he thought about Tauth's axe of a nose and the bold eyes above it.

He had to give thanks for this. To Eala, ironically. A donation of coins at a temple, probably a chicken for sacrifice too. More importantly, he needed to thank Darsal for the warning, and that was a gift which needed thought.

"I'm sorry, Shahan." His friend would hate being made to marry. Of all men, the laughing, irresponsible Shahan would hate it the most. "I'm sorry."

He had been warned. Mani shook his head and set off down the street.

CHAPTER EIGHT

A PAIR OF vultures flanked the gate, each one set on a tower of mudbricks. Someone entering Kindar had to pass between them, under the glare of stone eyes above cruel beaks. They had been set there by the goddess Sabit to mark the city's victory over its neighbour Iraš, when the dead lay in a carpet half a mile wide. So the legend said.

Iraš was long lost, its bricks worn to nothing by the Flood. Now the vultures that stood in its memory were broken, one of them chipped and its eyes smashed, the other toppled to the ground. It lay in two pieces, face buried in the dirt. Soldiers were sprawled around it, except for a path cleared in the middle. One of the bodies was very large.

The battle had not been without its losses. That giant had laid six men in the dust before Yarim came up to him. Maybe the giant was tired by then, but Yarim was a big man too, and the giant was slow bringing his mace up and around. Yarim ducked inside the blow and struck the huge man on his hip, smashing bone. The giant fell with a shout, and when Yarim fell back to gather his breath he saw Sarru-kin there, watching, the sickle sword spinning its point in the earth.

The king was still there, black hair curled and sewn with threads of silver so it glimmered in the sun. His army stood around, Yarim in the front rank with the scarlet token of a captain hung on his belt. So many of the top captains had been killed in Sarru-kin's seizure of power that one kill at the right time could gain a man rank. It put Yarim closer to the Mad King than he'd like. He just hoped it didn't show.

After a time, there was a commotion at the gate, and a score of soldiers came through. They were Labaš men. The fighting was done here, all resistance broken. They came down the slope from the gate to the plain, led by a woman with a shaven head almost as tall as Sarru-kin. The sun was high, but Kammani wore no hat to shield her. She strode up to the king and gestured, and the soldiers threw a man into the dust.

He stood at once. His tunic was bloody and torn, but it was silk. One sandal was missing. A few silver threads shone in his unkempt hair. Yarim knew who he was.

Sarru-kin tilted his head back, looking over the other man's head, or else at the sky. "You are beaten. How should I treat you?"

"Like a king," said Luduzi, lord of Kindar. "How else?"

"A king who leads his city to disaster is no worthy king."

"I led nothing to disaster," Luduzi said. "You came here with war and an army we could not match. Well done, you've conquered. Do you think you can hold what you've won?"

"I have been promised so," Sarru-kin answered. "The great god Balih intends to impose his authority on the lesser deities of Engiru. I am his chosen means of achieving that."

Luduzi smiled a leopard's smile. "Did he tell you so?"

"He did. Yes," Sarru-kin said. He stroked the blade of his sickle sword. "I know you spoke the words, brave one. But they were Balih's first."

Yarim didn't understand that. He looked at the two men, standing in the dirt with their eyes locked together. It was impossible to miss who was the victor and who the vanquished, but they stood the same way, straight and proud. Kings, both of them.

Sarru-kin tipped his head again, as though listening to voices from the sky. "Swear fealty to me and Balih. This is his city now."

"This is the city of Sabit," the other man said. "Your god holds no sway here. The goddess will remember it."

"On your knees," Sarru-kin said. His voice was still calm, a man detached. "Beg for your life before me."

"I will not," Luduzi said.

They took Luduzi, cut out his eyes, and burned them on an altar to Balih they built under the gate of Kindar. After that, they locked the blind king in a cage and hung him from the wall to die. It took two days. He never cried out, never made a sound as far as Yarim knew.

Soldiers of Kindar were invited to join the conquering army and take Balih as their new god. Balih as worshipped through his chosen envoy on earth, Sarru-kin of Labaš. Kammani smiled her sweet poison smile as she accepted the oaths. The recruits were ordered to smash the Temple of Sabit and replace it with a new shrine, built of bricks taken from the top of the wall. Yarim and Enmer had the duty of watching over them as they worked.

"I don't like this," Enmer said.

"Shut up."

"It's wrong. The goddess will be furious."

"Shut up or I'll never speak with you again," Yarim said. "Talk like that is dangerous, do you understand? We're Sarru-kin's men now. Not Balih's, not men of Labaš. Just the kings."

Sarru-kin appeared when the work was done to stand by Kammani while she consecrated the new temple. There the soldiers of Kindar swore loyalty to Sarru-kin, almost all of them. The few who did not were dragged to the side and beaten to death. Yarim dispatched one himself, teeth gritted.

Three days later the army marched towards Tibad.

Chapter Nine

YOU KNOW SOME of the stars are not stars."

"Yes," Mani said. "Planets."

"Name one."

"Nergal," he said. "The harbinger of drought and summer heat, and the wilderness of war."

"That's all you know," the Sea-Goat asked.

Mani was sitting on a bench, near the end of a jetty that poked out of the reeds. He'd forgotten his hat, and the sun beat on his head. After every two answers the Sea-Goat sank into the water and swam under the pier, to emerge on the other side.

"Do you know more?" Mani asked.

"Nergal is red because she was flayed."

Mani didn't really know what to say to that, so he made no answer. The Sea-Goat submerged and rose again, this time on the same side of the jetty. Opaque eyes blinked. Mani waited, but Sea-Goats could out-wait anyone, and finally Mani spoke.

"Flayed?"

"By the star bird."

"How?"

"That's the wrong question," the Sea-Goat said.

"What's the right one?"

"*Why,*" the Sea-Goat said. His tail swished, and he was gone in a swirl of bubbles.

Mani sighed and made notes on his tablet. It hadn't been a bad exchange, despite the abrupt end. He hadn't heard of star birds before, or a planet being skinned like a turkey for the table. There might be something in the records, a mention of these things made fifty or a hundred years ago, but he'd never come across it before.

Talk of war seemed to be everywhere. First the king, then Shahan, and now Nergal intruded into Mani's life. He made another mark, frowned, and blotted it out with his thumb. Writing *stair* instead of *star.* He must be more tired than he thought.

No sleep on his wedding night. He'd imagined a hot-limbed woman and a time of sensual discovery, not hours of lying stiff on his back while the air grew thick and the mattress harder.

He started back. The path went by a hut with its single sentry and then popped out of a wall of reeds with a clutch of shacks in the distance. Mani turned the other way, towards the road and the mound beyond where Aš-alam stood. Even from this distance he could see the glisten of fresh bitumen on the brick walls. Nothing was left to do to prepare for the Flood, but the Temple teams still found tasks for the debt slaves, digging out channels and building up banks. Some years the Flood was bigger than others. You could never be too prepared.

Once on the main road he began to cross over ditches, deep cuts lined with mudbricks. Only dust lay at the bottom. He met people too, most of them heading out with empty water pails or home with full ones. Another day in Aš-alam, the same as any other. Except he was married, and that changed everything.

Married to a wife he didn't dare touch in the calm of the night. He had no idea how to deal with that. At least Isha wasn't a *zami*, and she didn't have a ploughshare for a nose. That had to be good.

He got back to find the office empty and Shahan gone.

"He went out," Tash-Yal said when Mani found him. The older scholar was bent over a trestle table filled with clay tablets, some alone, others standing in little stacks. He'd hammered tacks into the wood and coloured cords ran between them, connecting this pile to that. "Earlier."

"Of course it was earlier. He couldn't have gone out later, could he?"

"Quite right," Tash-Yal said. His nose was two inches from a tablet, and his bald head gleamed. "Quite right."

"Did he leave with anyone?"

Tash-Yal's eyes flickered. "Two women. I didn't see who they were. Didn't look too closely."

"Of course you didn't," Mani said. With *zami* it was prudent not to look closely, or if you did, to pretend you hadn't. Well, then. Shahan left with a hag and the woman with a ploughshare nose, Tauth. When he came back Tauth was likely to be his wife. No more talk of trips to speak with fishermen, no more tossing chickpeas into the air and catching them in his mouth.

Mani left the tablet on his desk and went to find his wife.

§ § §

The Spilled Salt was empty, except for an old man dozing in a chair by the door. Two flies crawled on the lip of the half-empty cup on his table. Mani wondered how long it had stood there.

"Scholar!" Udar cried. He rose from a chair at the far end of the bar, arms flung wide. "Second-son!"

"Don't call me—"

"And why shouldn't I? My son-in-law talks to the swimmers. A man can be proud of that."

Best to change the subject. "I thought you had servants to run the bar when it's quiet."

"Well, I do, but I must pay them. It's cheaper if I do it. There's no work for a man anyway. Old Teod there is the only customer I've had, and he's made one cup of beer last half the morning."

"Can't you tell him to leave?"

"What, and have an empty bar? That's bad luck for an innkeep."

"You bar owners are really superstitious."

"Maybe," Udar said, "but on the other hand, we don't waffle instead of getting to the point."

His gaze was sharp, and Mani started to smile despite himself. Then something came home to him, and the smile died unformed. "Isha is here, isn't she?"

"Of course she is. Where else would a new bride go for advice, except to her father?"

"All of a sudden," Mani said, "I have the feeling I might be in trouble here."

Udar clapped him on the shoulder. "No trouble, scholar. I called you second-son when you walked in, didn't I? But you chose trouble when you married my girl, and if you didn't know that you're not half as clever as I thought you were."

This time he did smile. "No, I knew that. But trouble from her, not from you."

"Never. Come, sit with me."

They sat at the end of the counter, across the room from Teod and his congealing beer. The worst heat had passed, and hammers rang through the open back door, the construction crew back at work smashing old bricks into dust to make way for a new Temple. From the front came the sounds of creaking wheels, barking dogs, and voices raised in greeting or complaint. The noises of everyday life, faint and far away.

"You're not experienced with women," Udar said.

Mani shook his head. "No. Only in the Scented Houses, really."

"Well, that's good experience, but it only teaches a man about a woman's body. They're all the same, really, just as men are. All the same bits in the same places, am I right?"

"I'm not sure about the *zami,*" Mani said.

"I won't argue with that! You'd have to be a fool to want a peek under those grey robes anyway. But my point is that bodies are one thing, and souls are very different. Do you know what Isha wanted last night?"

"To be alone."

"No, scholar. She wanted you to tell her she was beautiful, and your body yearned for hers. She wouldn't have believed you, but she would have wanted to, and for that night she would have thought it might be true. She wanted you to touch her."

"But she lay down straight as a rod."

"She couldn't touch *you*, scholar! You had to act first. She was lying there waiting for you to move, and you didn't."

He thought about that, chin on his hand the way he did when he was poring over tablets. "I need to go to her."

"Yes, you do. But you ought to know two things first. One is that a marriage is void if the bride removes her veil in the first seven days, or if the marriage isn't consummated by then."

He nodded.

"Isha won't take off the veil. You can rest easy on that." Udar leaned forward. "But the second thing is that the priestesses will look for any reason they can find to take you away from her. Won't they?"

"Yes," he said. "I understand, Udar."

The innkeep nodded towards a door in the side wall. "Through there is the parlour. From it go left to the yard. You'll find your wife sorting her belongings."

He found her in the shade of a lemon tree, flowers and fruit peering out from under the leaves. Isha smiled behind her veil when she saw him. The smile was weak at the edges, like an unfinished thought.

"I'm sorry," Mani said.

Her hands twisted the grey bag between her feet. "For what?"

"For leaving you alone last night."

She looked down and didn't speak for a moment. The neck of the bag was a knot in her fingers. "I wasn't alone."

"I was in the bed," he said, "but you were still alone."

"Is that how our life will be? Have I married a man who will treat me like a servant, and give me nothing?"

Mani didn't say anything.

"I've got some clothes in here." Isha hefted the bag, "A few knick knacks. Nothing else. It isn't much to show for twenty years life."

"I doubt I have much more."

She looked back at him, with that faint smile still on her lips. "We could build more together, if you want to."

"Yes," he said. "I want to."

"Can we go home now?"

He held out a hand, and she took it.

§ § §

Quarter of an hour later Mani held open the door of his house—their house—for her to enter. He shut the bolt and turned to find Isha standing by the divan, her back to him.

"I'll prepare supper," he said.

"No need," Isha said. "I can do it later. Are the tablets from the Sea Folk?"

There wasn't much decoration in the room. A mural painted on one wall showed Eala descending to earth, her arms raised high and one foot stretched to touch the ground. That wasn't Mani's. It had been there when he moved in, and he'd left it in case the priestesses came knocking. The other decorations were his own, and most were clay tablets inscribed with a few words, hanging from pegs in the plaster.

"Yes," he said. "They all are."

She went to the nearest and tilted her head, a shore bird trying to see beneath the surface of still water. "'The seed is good, whether you eat or not.' Is that something the swimmers say?"

"Something one of them said," Mani told her. "I'd asked about learning among the Sea-Goats. I wanted to know how they're taught, if they even are. It ended up with me explaining how I was educated here in Aš-alam, and the swimmer said that to me."

"What did he mean?"

"That learning is valuable no matter what you do with it," Mani said. "I think. It's hard to be sure."

"And this one? 'Pleasure is in the fish.' What does that mean?"

"I don't have the least idea."

She turned. He could see her face through the veil and thought she was flushed. "It's hard for you to admit you don't understand, isn't it?"

He nodded. "I want to know everything, Isha. How the world began, right to how it will end. The Sea-Goats know something of that. But all their secrets are on their island, and we can't get to it."

"You think so?"

"Eala came here," he said. "To where Aš-alam stands now, where she placed her feet on the world for the first time. Why here? What do you find here and nowhere else in the world?"

"The swimmers."

"The swimmers. What are they to make a goddess come to them?"

"I can't explain those things," she said. "But there are other things I might teach you."

He didn't speak. Isha reached up, unhitched her veil, and let it fall. She took a step towards him. She really was flushed, he saw. He was the only person allowed to see her face for another six days.

"Isha…"

"You can teach me, too," she said. "No more nights afraid to touch or speak. Agreed?"

He swallowed. "Agreed."

"I will cook supper," she said. "You tell me of the Sea-Goats, husband. Talk to me of what you've learned, what you think and believe. Let me know you."

"Isha, tonight we—"

"Let tonight wait," she broke in. "Tell me, Mani."

He caught her hand as she turned towards the kitchen. "I will. And Isha, I won't let the *zami* make us part."

CHAPTER TEN

THEY TRIED THE next morning, when Isha was buying vegetables at the market while the day was still cool.

"Those don't look fresh," she said.

The trader shrugged. "The Flood was a year ago. We irrigate, but the results are never as good." Shrug. "This is as fresh as anyone can grow."

"I will test that," she told him.

Another shrug. It only made her smile.

She felt…different, after last night. She kept smiling, for one thing, though that was hard to see behind her veil. At first, she'd wanted to go see her father, but maybe that wasn't suitable behaviour for a new wife. Especially one who'd experienced the marriage bed for the first time.

Well, the marriage divan, she supposed. Then the bed, after midnight when she woke from a doze to find Mani shifting beside her. He still found it hard to relax with her. That would change in time for both of them. It was already changing for her. Strange that what was once so frightening now seemed such a silly thing to fear.

Stranger yet, she found the shrugging stallholder was right. After an hour she'd found no better vegetables than his in the market, fresh or not. The reservoirs were nearly empty now, and the sun a pitiless force that burned plants down to the ground if they weren't shaded. Still, she was sure things hadn't been this bad last summer, or the one before.

"Are there pests?" she asked one trader. "Insects, or…flies, or whatever eats crops?"

He rolled his eyes a bit at her ignorance. "There are always pests. Debt slaves are supposed to keep them off, but they're worse than useless. The Temples would do better to hire proper workers."

"There is presumption in telling the Temples what they ought to do," someone said behind Isha.

She knew who it was before she saw. Priestesses, one tall and made of bones, the other tiny and twitching. It was amazing how many *zami* had tics they couldn't control. "Good morning, clerics. I was about to—"

"One moment," the little priestess said. She might look nervous, but her voice was firm as baked clay. "Trader, we will tolerate a great deal, but you come close to open disdain. Perhaps Eala might be assuaged by a gift at the Temple at tomorrow's dawn, do you think?"

He ducked his head. "As you say, lady."

"We will be watching you," the woman warned. "Now, mistress Isha, if you would walk with us?"

It was phrased as a request, but that didn't fool Isha. She went with the two priestesses across the market, to a side street cut between two narrow houses. The roadway was worn, untended for a long time. Isha wasn't about to follow two *zami* into that. She'd grown up in a tavern, never far from tales of unlit alleys and a person alone. She came to a halt and the women looked at her.

"I have a fear of quiet places," she said. "A city woman's foolish nerves, no doubt. I hope you will forgive me."

She saw in their eyes that they knew what she was doing. Isha was as cautious as anyone about going into back streets, though she wasn't really afraid of them. Not in daytime, anyway. She didn't want to enter one now, with priestesses who had come to find her—and she thought she knew why. She put up a hand to check her veil was still secure.

"You can take that off," someone said from deeper in the alley. "There will be no blame."

Isha had to move a little before she could see the other woman clearly. Then she bowed her head, as one did to the great. "*Ama-su.* I'm honoured, of course."

"You should be." Shusikil stepped forward, a scarecrow shaved bald, with eyes like drips of bitumen. "I can lift your curse, woman."

"My—"

"Your betrothed died or were maimed," the head priestess cut in. "A clear sign that Eala has withdrawn her blessing from you. In the land of gods, you are less than human, hardly more than an animal. Do you wish for an eternity like that?"

Isha swallowed. "No."

"Then I will intervene on your behalf," Shusikil said, "and all you must do is remove your veil."

Isha had thought it might be this, even before she saw the leader of the *zami* had come to speak to her. There was no other reason for priestesses to stop her in the market. "Why would I do that?"

"To save your soul."

"The Temples teach that our souls are weighed according to the good and evil we do," she answered. "I'm sure I remember that from the catechism. Priestesses can't change Fate with a few prayers."

The black eyes flashed. "You don't know what we can do. Let us be honest. Yours is not a marriage of love."

"Yet the *zami* teach that love can grow in barren ground," Isha said. "That's in the catechism too. I always believed that one."

A slip, and Shusikil was on it in an eyeblink. "There are others you do not believe?"

Isha didn't reply, and after a moment the crone sighed. "You are clever, Isha. See? I am honest with you. I swear by Eala's footfalls you have nothing to fear from us. We are not your enemy."

"I'm not afraid."

"But you are. Of your husband? Of a life spent with a man you never learn to love? A woman deserves better."

"I am happy," she said. The words brought back memory of last night, and she felt herself blush.

"You could be happier. We could find you a new husband. A better man, with servants and a fine house."

"You offer me a bribe," she said.

The bony crone's expression turned dark. It was one of the others who spoke though, the little one with the facial tic. "Watch your tongue! I met your husband two days ago and found him arrogant. You should take care not to run the same risks he faces."

Shusikil held up a hand. The fury in her face was still there, hidden now under a smile. "Peace, Lamsi. She really is clever. Not wise, but we must accept she has wits."

Not wise? Isha almost said it out loud, affronted, but managed to bite the words back. She wasn't going to play this game. Not the way the priestesses wanted it played.

"Take off your veil," Shusikil said. "I promise you a husband you like, a life you can enjoy."

"I have those things," she said, wondering if she did.

"For today," Shusikil said. Her cheek shivered. "Who can say about tomorrow? Has he consummated the marriage yet?"

Now Isha really did flush. "Yes."

"It can be checked."

"Then check," she snapped.

"Perhaps we will," Shusikil said. "And perhaps we will offer Mani another wife. He uses the Scented Houses—did you know that? The women there are skilled. Some can make the nights dance with delight and turn men's brains to suet. There are girls with pouting lips, hips that sway, and breasts as full and high as hills. What do you think Mani will say when we take them to him?"

Her mouth was dry. "He will say he's married. Cripple my father, he will! I trust my husband, *zami.*"

"After two days of marriage?"

"Trust too can grow on barren ground," she said.

Shusikil's smile could cut meat. "Perhaps we really will cripple your father."

"*What?*"

"Think about your choices," the head *zami* said. "They become fewer, and less tempting, very fast."

They left Isha shaking, relief and fear washing through her heart. That last had been a threat, spoken in a lower voice but still unmistakable. She didn't doubt it was genuine. The *zami* weren't renowned for wasting words or speaking those they didn't mean.

They might tempt Mani with a sultry beauty from the Scented Houses, all sway and pouting lips. Men with clubs might set upon Udar in a back street as he was buying casks for the tavern and leave him with twisted legs that would never heal straight. Isha's hands trembled.

"What am I going to do?" she whispered. People walked wide of her, faces by chance turned away so they didn't see.

§ § §

She went home, of course.

That was what Isha had always done when she found trouble. Go home, find her father, find comfort, and usually find answers too. Udar had always been her haven, her dry place above the Flood. Where other children remembered a mother's face, a tender touch, Isha had only her father, and he had always been enough.

The Spilled Salt was closed. Not a surprise, this early in the day. Isha went around the side, to the little door tucked behind a corner of the wall. Across the street workers had begun their hammering in the middle of a cloud of brick dust, smashing away the last courses of buildings no one needed anymore.

Isha let herself in. She locked the door behind herself, went through a little parlour, and came out at the back of the bar room. Someone was ferreting around under the bar, and she began to smile. Then he stood up and it was only Ruen.

"He's out," the young man said. He dusted his hands on each other, got a grip on a barrel, and lifted it into place, shoulder muscles bulging. "Went out to buy brandy."

"When will he be back?"

That earned a shrug. "When he's bought it, I suppose."

Isha was unsettled and afraid, and it was disconcerting to see Ruen without his brother. He and Ramsi were hardly ever apart, brothers alike as two fleas. Maybe that was why she rested her elbows on the counter and said, "I need some advice, Ruen."

He blinked. "All right."

She spoke, and as the words piled up a frown appeared on Ruen's brow. It came in stages, like the Flood rising in a slow year, so each morning it seemed to have barely moved from the day before. He was big but not stupid, and she thought the scowl was for the priestesses, dislike rather than confusion. When she finished, he took a rag and absently wiped the bar with it, exactly as her father would have done.

"Not sure what you want to hear," he said.

Trust can grow on barren ground, she'd said. Spoke it to the face of Shusikil, the bony chief of the *zami* herself. "I suppose I want to know if I can trust him."

"Who, your father?"

"Of course not," she said with some asperity. "I meant Mani."

Could she really trust him? He seemed a decent man, uncertain of himself around women and much too fascinated by the swimmers, but still presentable enough. He didn't seem strong though. A strong man would not have lain beside her all through their wedding night, trying to find the courage to touch her skin. Isha wasn't sure she wanted to complain about that. Still, was he strong? Would he defy the *zami* for her, or would he smile and give in, tempted by the promise of a scented woman and all the delights she could give?

I am cursed, something murmured in the back of her mind, and she tossed her head to shake the voice loose.

"I can't help with that," Ruen said. The cloth wiped, back and forth.

"I know," She pinched the bridge of her nose through the veil. "Only I can answer it."

He shrugged. "Maybe not. There are people who offer answers, if you know who to ask."

For a moment Isha didn't understand what he meant. When she did, she flicked glances left and right and leaned forward to whisper. "A seer? Are you insane?"

He grinned at her. "Seers survive, you know. Some *nabu* even come into the city, now and then. Might be I can find one."

"That's dangerous, Ruen."

"For the Seer," he said and chuckled.

She wasn't sure Ruen was afraid of anything, or Ramsi either. They'd worked at the bar since they were striplings, and even then they'd been big enough to throw any drunk through the door. Isha had never suspected they might know the dark side of the city outside the Spilled Salt. They seemed too clean for that. They did what Udar asked and kept the bar safe, and that was all she'd ever thought of them.

"For you, too," she said. "No, listen for a moment, please. Don't put yourself at risk for me. There's a curse on me, Ruen. I've lost two husbands-to-be to accidents, and now I may lose a husband as well. That sort of bad luck can rub off."

"Oh, Isha." He stopped wiping with the cloth and put his hand over hers instead. "The only person who carries that curse is you."

That was not entirely comforting.

§ § §

A troubled mind makes you sick, the saying went, and Isha's mind was plagued.

Mani was clever, as all the scholars had to be. They were drawn from the best students, those who mastered their letters and still wanted more, who asked questions and were never satisfied with the answers. Most of all they needed to be patient. Sea-Goats never gave straight answers, they evaded and confused, and more than one scholar gave up asking and became a bricklayer, or a scribe.

So, clever and patient.

He was kind, too. Last night he had been gentle, almost too much so, holding her like a rare glass chalice in his hands. There had still been pain. There always was the first time, for every woman. Mani had kissed her when she cried out, and she'd dug her fingers into his back and pulled him deeper, as though to say *this is what we chose, what we wanted, now let it be done.*

Clever and patient, kind and gentle. He would stand by her—she was sure of it. Nearly sure, anyway. She had thought, when he came to ask her to marry him and they talked over a table at the tavern, that she could trust him. She'd never thought the *zami* would try to bribe them to part. What would he do when they offered him a hot-limbed beauty from the Scented Houses and freedom from all this worry? Would he reach out and pull away Isha's veil in the street?

She thought on that as she walked. When she came under the shade of the city walls, she was no closer to an answer, and her head was aching. Whether that was from thinking, or worry, or just the blasting heat of the sun, she didn't know.

Once through the gate the first person she saw was the priestess from earlier, the tiny twitching one. The woman was speaking with a merchant, but his eyes flicked to Isha, just for an instant. It was enough. Too much coincidence for that particular *zami* to be here now.

They were watching her.

CHAPTER ELEVEN

"YES," SARRU-KIN said. "Yarim killed their general."

Yarim made sure not to look at the king. Around him other guards stared straight ahead, eyes blank, every one a captain in the growing army. Yarim stood so close to a pillar that he felt the cones of the mosaic against his back.

The hall was beautiful, which gave him plenty to look at. A lion made of brown and red tiles, prowling out of a corner. The doors were inlaid with silver. One whole wall was taken up with lines of white that swirled and curled until at last they coalesced into a woman. She wasn't much more than an outline, the suggestion of a form emerging from the ether. One of the soldiers claimed it was meant to be what a woman was if you took the flesh away and left only what a woman actually was.

That sounded like nonsense to Yarim. He didn't understand art. Boys from the back streets usually didn't, because they never saw it, and it didn't matter anyway. The important things were food, respect, and avoiding the muddy water in drying puddles after the Flood. Sometimes the poor boys made it into the army, two good meals a day and enough respect for anyone, but they still didn't learn anything about art.

Yarim looked anyway, because to do otherwise was to risk watching the king.

"I assume he felt proud," Sarru-kin said. He was seated in a gilded chair, sickle sword in hand and someone else sitting on a step at his feet. Another woman, this one with her flesh still on. For the moment. "What true man would not? To end a life, to watch the blood spurt and see the eyes fade…there is a power in that. It is almost godlike."

Silence for a moment. "No, Azaq, not like that. Yarim is skilled, a good soldier, but still a mortal. He has tasted from the cup of godhood, but he is not like me. I have made that cup my own."

The woman on the wall was Ikuga, goddess of the air and marriage. Patron of Tibad. Her virtues had not helped the city to stand against Sarru-kin's army. Blood had splashed her feet, or the lines that swirled where her feet would be. The fighting had reached even here, in the heart of Tibad's streets and temples. By the inlaid doors a stone cat, unimaginably precious, had been cracked by the blows of maces.

At Kindar Sarru-kin had blinded the king and left him to die in the sun. Word of that had run ahead. In Tibad nobles and lords fought like rats in a drain rather than be taken alive.

"True," the king said. He spun the sickle sword on its point. "True. I am not yet immortal. But that is in hand, Azaq, and when I am, even the gods will tremble before me."

The doors opened. Yarim turned, spear coming down, but he stopped almost at once. It was only Kammani, and if Sarru-kin trusted anyone, he trusted her. The king stopped talking as she strode towards him, robe swishing on the tiles. Moisture gleaned on her bald head. Her eyes darted to Yarim, and he felt the contact like a shock.

What a woman was, he thought, not very coherently. *Like the lines on the wall. The essence of a female.*

It was female like a she-eagle, like a mountain lioness. One who scorns the thought of children and stalks the peaks, hunting for a victim. Poison in a cup.

"My king," Kammani said. She sank to her knees at the foot of the steps, head bowed.

"High priestess," Sarru-kin said. "Stand. Azaq and I have been talking."

Her back was to Yarim as she rose, but in the pause he read her expression. "Your sword?"

"The being who lives in my sword," the king corrected. "He is a *sukkal*, a messenger of the gods. Of course you know that."

"Of course," she said.

"We spoke of war, and how it makes a man proud. I do not know what makes a woman proud. Do you, Kammani?"

"Bearing sons," she answered. "Doing glory to the gods. Myself, I feel pride in serving you, my lord."

He nodded. "So do all who serve me. Look at Yarim there, by the pillar. He chased down the commander of their army yesterday and slew him under the gates of his own city. Such courage, in a low-born man. Do you not think so?"

The tall priestess half turned, and Yarim felt her eyes again, a weight on his flesh. He refused to acknowledge the glance, though. "I do. Ordinary men become heroes in your service."

"And what have you done in it, Kammani?"

The vague tone was gone, replaced by a question thrown like a dart, a spinning knife. That was the reality of what Sarru-kin was. His pale eyes were suddenly sharp. Yarim thought the king might be crazed, but mad or sane, the blades were always there, never more than a beat away.

"There's very little to be found in the House of Tablets here," Kammani said. Her poise never wavered, however Sarru-kin's tone might change. "Tibad has less on the Sea-Goats than we do in Labaš. What my priestesses did find is as you might expect. Vague phrases, elliptical nonsense. Except for one tablet, found near the end."

"Which says what?"

"The same as the one at home," she answered. "That the swimmers keep the secret of immortality on their home island, far out in the ocean. The tablet here speaks of an isle surrounded by fresh water, in the middle of a salt sea."

"Life-giving water," Sarru-kin said, "amid a sea which would kill you to drink from it. Yes, Azaq, it is interesting."

Yarim stared at the woman on the wall.

"What do you think, Kammani?" The king twirled his sickle sword. "Should I make myself immortal?"

"You are the king."

"Yes, but kings have died before. One might point out that all have died before."

She shrugged. "The priestesses of Labaš follow you in all things, my lord. You have made Balih god over the patrons of Kindar and Tibad. The goddess Ikuga bends knee to him now."

"So, you support me in the name of the god, then. Not for myself."

There was a trap here, but Kammani was equal to it. "Both. We support the god, as we are sworn to. We also swore allegiance to you. We will follow you to this island, my king."

"Good," he said. The sword's point grounded on the tiles. "Good. You may leave me. Be ready to march in three days."

"March to where?"

"Piqash," he said, "and then Aš-alam and immortality. However, we must be quick. The Flood is near. If the rains come early, we might be caught on this side of the Ranuna, and my victories and all my soldiers will count for nothing."

"We will be ready," Kammani said. "I must take the oaths of those soldiers who will swear loyalty to you, my king. May I take your man Yarim with me? A captain's presence would assist me."

Sarru-kin waved a hand to signal assent. Kammani beckoned to Yarim, and he followed her down the hall, by which time the king had begun speaking again. "Yes, my heart. Yes. The Flood comes, but not too soon, I think."

He was talking to the sword again. Yarim tried not to shiver.

He put it out of his mind, because Kammani was hardly less dangerous than the Mad King. *Poison in a cup,* he thought, not for the first time. He had to be alert. Hopefully all she wanted from him was to stand nearby while she accepted oaths from the beaten men of Tibad. There shouldn't be a great deal of danger in that.

She turned left at the entrance to the Temple, away from the parade ground where the prisoners were held. "Where are we—"

"Patience," Kammani said. Sweat had begun to glisten on her bald head again, out in the sun. She strode on regardless, not seeming to care. He couldn't help watching her hips move under her gown. She was peril, she was venom, but she was still a woman.

They went up the steps of the main Temple. Ikuga's place, replete with murals of swirling lines that coalesced into figures of people or animals, all of them moving. It was said in Tibad that the goddess could make any living thing from the air, and that creature kept all the motion and freedom of the wind. The walls depicted rams running, fish flapping in nets, and oxen labouring in fields. All shown with grace, as smooth as a cool northern wind.

On the first level of the platform, they went right, along the wall of the second tier. Priestesses passed them with downcast eyes. It was impossible to tell which worshipped Ikuga and which followed Balih. Probably it didn't matter; they were all worshippers of Sarru-kin now, whatever name was on their lips when they prayed. Kammani made sure of that. She went into a doorway, having to duck under the lintel to pass through, then down a passage to a room at the far end. At her motion Yarim shut the door.

He looked around at a table laid with brushes and paints, and a divan with a mirror—a mirror—behind it. "This isn't the barracks."

"No," she said. "Did you really kill Sipad-Ana?"

He frowned, forgetting for a moment who that was. "The general. Yes, I did."

"And did you feel full of power and life, as Sarru-kin said?"

"You heard that?"

"Is it true?"

"I felt alive," he conceded. "But not because I killed him. More because he didn't kill me."

"Ah. Then it isn't killing which fills you with joy. It's living." She poured a cup of wine and turned to face him. "You're a clever man."

"I'm a soldier, priestess. Only that."

"Not anymore. You've put yourself high in Sarru-kin's eyes. Captains can be a threat to a king."

He swallowed. "Not this captain."

She handed him the wine and poured another for herself. "Does that matter? A clever man must see not. A king might choose to see danger where none exists. Especially this king."

This was growing dangerous. Yarim put down his cup untasted, glad to see his hand didn't tremble. "I should go."

"Did you know there is a new faction among the *zami* here in Tibad?" She drank off half her wine. "They say the goddess made the first people from the air. It makes Ikuga the creator of humankind."

"The creator?"

"It's a new thing, and heretical. Orthodoxy says the first people were created by the god Ekur, after he raised the land from the oceans. All the cities agree on that, whichever god is their patron. For Tibad to break with tradition would be dangerous, at another time."

He wasn't keeping up with this. "Another time?"

"If it were not for Sarru-kin. Nobody will be worrying about an infraction of orthodoxy now."

She drank the last of the wine and dropped the cup. It bounced on the floor, unheeded. Then her hands went to the shoulders of her dress, and she wriggled. The fabric slithered into a puddle at her feet.

"Sarru-kin is mad," she said.

Yarim stared at her. Naked, she looked like a cat, gracile and sleek. His tongue didn't want to work.

"The king's not mad," he managed.

"He slaughtered the Elders and wants to live forever." She went to a bowl, picked out a cloth, and began to wash. Water glistened on her skin. "What would you call it?"

"I am loyal to him," Yarim said. It was still hard to find words. Kammani walked across the room, washing with the towel. He was reminded of a cat again, cleaning itself with its paws.

"Of course you are. But is he loyal to you?" She reached to wash her shoulders and her breasts rose. "And for how long? He is insane, Yarim." She turned towards him, cloth moving across the flat of her belly. "Madness can be steered, but not forever."

He couldn't speak.

"You like what you see," Kammani said. She swayed towards him, a smile on her lips. "So do I."

"What…you see?"

"You're a fine-looking man. Brave too, as Sipad-Ana will tell the shades of the dead in the Land of No Return."

Yarim licked his lips.

"People think priestesses are cold," Kammani said. "They say there's nothing in the *zami* but rules and lust for power. I'm not cold, Yarim. I am hot, and my lusts are of a different kind. Do you want me?"

It was hard to breathe. She was very close to him, so close he could see the tiny hairs on her skin. Her eyes were vast and fixed on his.

"You…lie with Sarru-kin," he managed.

She smiled a slow smile. "Sarru-kin has never touched me. His preference is for the cowed, the beaten. Did you recognise the woman on the steps at his feet? She is Puabi. This morning, she was queen of Tibad."

He swallowed. That was what could happen, when Fate crossed your path with that of the Mad King. Sarru-kin was mad, Kammani was right about that. He was insane, and he would eat up cities and lives before he was done. Anyone who stood in his way, anyone who he saw as a threat or who tried to thwart him, would be cut down. Even his allies, his generals, were not safe. There was more danger for them. One misstep could kill.

Kammani was hot-limbed beautiful. She reached out and ran a fingernail down his throat.

Yarim's hands were on her hips before he realised he had moved. She took a step and was pressed against him, her tongue on his teeth and then the roof of his mouth. They bumped into a table, and Yarim realised he'd pushed her against it. Kammani leaned backwards, drawing him down as her legs went around his waist.

"He will kill us if he finds out," Yarim said later.

She was lying under him, on the divan. "He won't find out. He only sees what helps him."

Yarim looked down at her. Sweat trickled into his eyes. Kammani wiped it away with one finger and a shudder ran through him. She smiled, tongue flicking over her lips. "He will go to find immortality and leave a kingdom behind to be ruled."

She reached up to catch handfuls of his hair. For a moment Yarim just looked at her, and then she pushed her hips into his, and he didn't think anymore.

Chapter Twelve

THE REEDS HAD begun to turn brown, even those that stood at the edge of the marsh. Only those with their feet in the water were still green. The land was a brick in a furnace, baking harder every day.

"Scholar Kassu-Mani," the Sea-Goat said as he surfaced. Air hissed from the slits in his collarbones. "You come again."

"I do that," he said.

It was the new swimmer who had answered the bell, the one called Hanno. A man, like all the others. No scholar had ever met a female Sea-Goat, and no one knew why.

"I expect you have more questions."

"Always," Mani agreed. "If you'll honour me by answering them."

"I might." The youth turned a backwards circle in the water and blew air as he came up. "Did it ever occur to you that we might be curious about your people too, scholar?"

He blinked. "But you never ask questions. Yours now is the first I've ever heard from a Sea-Goat."

"We can learn just by watching. So the old ones say. Or by seeing what you ask, and what you don't."

"What we don't? That makes me wonder if we're missing something obvious."

Hanno rippled down the length of his body, making the water around him thrum. Droplets danced on the surface. He was laughing, and it made Mani feel like a schoolchild again, mocked when he failed to understand a problem in algebra.

There was no point asking what was being missed. The more direct a question, the more chance the swimmer would dive and be gone, talking over for another day. Go softly and choose questions that seem to ask one thing while actually aiming for another. So Mani had been taught, and so he'd learned, in hours here at the water's edge.

"Tell me of the stars," he said.

Hanno bobbed left and right. "Tell you what?"

"Something I don't know."

"Hmm." The Sea-Goats sank a little, so the waters almost closed on the top of his head, and then rose again. "They're far away. Even the closest is too far to reach in a lifetime."

"Can they be reached at all?"

Sink, rise. "Any sea can be sailed."

This was cedar wood and clear water, treasure beyond hope. Mani made hasty notes on his tablet. "There's a sea?"

"Of sorts."

"And you sailed it," Mani said as he realised shock made him forget caution. "Or your people did."

Hanno went under, deep enough that he was only a shape in the gloom. He was down so long that Mani almost began to stand, sure the day's talk was over. Instinct made him stay put, though. After a long time, Hanno swished back up, breaking the surface in a spray of water and then sinking back.

"You remembered your hat," the Sea-Goat said.

"My hat?"

"Last time you forgot it. Dassare told me."

Mani knew when he was being manoeuvred away from a subject. It happened on the rare times when a swimmer was annoyed but not angry enough to swish his tail and be gone. Hanno wasn't as quick to anger as the others, probably because he was young. That was interesting in itself, actually. It implied Sea-Goats were born and grew much as humans did. Mani had been foolish not to realise that before.

We can learn just by watching, he thought with an inward smile. Or even just by listening.

Following that thought, he decided to take a little risk. "You trust us more than the other Sea-Goats."

"No. I distrust you less."

"Is there a difference?"

The water vibrated in another laugh. "The older ones tell me yes. Experience."

"Oh," Mani said. "Experience of us."

"Yes. Of you."

"Are we so bad?"

"You forget what you know and then ask us to tell you," Hanno said. "You comfort yourselves with lies and then confuse them with the truth. You make the old ones weary."

"And you?"

Sink, rise. "I thought the stories couldn't be true. Now you're starting to tire me, too."

He ducked his head and curled over, and his tail popped out of the water and smacked back down. When the water settled Mani was soaked and the swimmer was gone. Mani had turned his tablet over to keep the writing side dry, though, and he had what he needed. More than he'd ever found before, in fact. There was a sea that lay between the stars, and ships which sailed it. There wasn't even a whisper of that in the archives, not a hint that Mani had seen, and he would have. Something that large could not be hidden.

More importantly, there had been a time when people knew the answers to questions which now puzzled them. *You forget what you know and then ask us to tell you.* What had been forgotten, and who had once known it?

He had work to do in the House of Tablets.

§ § §

"There's nothing in the records," he said, four hours later.

Shahan sat back in his chair. "Seems not."

"How can that be?"

"You know how," Shahan answered. "Nobody has ever heard the answers you were given today. You hit on something special out there, you lucky dog."

"Why lucky? I did what we all try to do, and I did it well."

"You think there was no luck?"

"Well," he admitted, "maybe a little. I suppose Eala might have been guiding my tongue today."

"Yes, and the gecko wears a tiara," Shahan laughed. "Come on, Mani. Have you gone all religious on me?"

"Hardly." He eyed the other man. "Some of the other scholars will say I made this up."

"Why would they?"

"Because I found out their island lies in fresh water," Mani said, "and now I've learned about a sea between the stars. The two biggest discoveries for decades, and both made by me."

"Pity you can't discover humility," Shahan sniggered.

"How do you find your new wife?"

The smile vanished. "Thanks a lot."

"Poke at me, I'll poke at you."

"Yeah. Well, Tauth's not so bad. Once you get over the nose." Shahan grimaced. "Her veil flaps like a shirt on a line with that beak pushing it out. Still, it could be worse. She's good in bed."

Mani raised his eyebrows.

"Well, she is. She makes the best glazed fruit I've ever tasted. She's decent enough."

He didn't speak.

"Well," Shahan admitted, "she does want me to ask the Sea-Goats all sorts of questions. About a dozen so far, and she says she has more."

"What questions?"

"If they saw Eala when she came to earth. Which god created them and when. All sorts of pointless things. Ask anything as bluntly as that and the swimmers will be gone in one splash."

"So, you won't ask?"

"Well," Shahan's grin was back, "I'll tell her I did."

"What if she checks the records?"

"So, I'll lie in the records," Shahan said. "Really, Mani, you're making this more of a problem than it needs to be."

Mani laid a tablet down. "You will not lie in your reports. I won't allow it."

"What?"

"This is my life. Trying to tease answers from the swimmers. It's all I have." It wasn't anymore, not really, but he pushed that thought away. A wife of three days didn't count. "I'll not let you belittle it with lies and deceits that will perplex scholars a hundred years from now, all because you didn't have the sense to listen when I warned you, or the guts to stand up for yourself."

"How can you—"

"I mean it, Shahan."

They locked eyes for a moment, then the other man looked away, shuffling his feet. "Yes, well. I suppose it was a stupid idea at that."

"Not least," Mani said, picking up the tablet, "because Tash-Yal would notice it in about a week."

"Yes, that's true." Shahan scuffed at the floor. "Him and his endless cross-references. He's got a hundred patterns, and none of them make us any the wiser."

"In two centuries, we've hardly learned anything that makes us any wiser."

"Also true, except for a few days. Like today." Shahan went to a slot in the racks, and from behind a tablet he pulled out a pot. "Beer?"

"You keep beer in the library?"

"Obviously. Don't complain, you'll sound like my wife." He cracked the seal and took a pull of beer. "That's good stuff. All right, then. The stars are islands in a great ocean, and there are ships which sail that sea."

"Yes."

"The Sea-Goats know about those ships."

"Yes."

"Then they might have sailed them. Perhaps they come from one of those other stars."

"Speculation," Mani disagreed. He'd thought the same, in truth, but he wasn't about to put a guess in the records. "I know about the cities in the west, past the forests. It doesn't mean I've seen them."

"Why would you want to?" Shahan pulled on the beer again. "There's one thing we can reasonably infer. Your swimmer said there are things we once knew but have forgotten, and he said it in the conversation in which he dropped this gem about star-seas. It might imply that we once knew it too."

"I thought of that," Mani said. "I think we can fairly link the two. But if we knew, how did we forget?"

"And when did we forget?" Shahan asked.

"Who keeps us from remembering?"

They grinned at each other in the gloomy library, two children who have just discovered a new toy. Then Shahan drained his pot of beer and stood with a discreet burp. "I'd better get going. Oh, and by the way, how's *your* new wife?"

"Surprising," Mani said after a moment.

"Is that all?"

He nodded towards the door. "Get on your way. I'm not going to regal you with saucy stories."

"But I love them," Shahan laughed. He clapped Mani on the back and went into the network of passages that ran between the racks. Mani heard his sandals fade until a door opened and closed, and the hall was silent.

Well. Mani would have bet half his wages that Shahan would be miserably unhappy with his wife. The end of carefree days, the beginning of a lifetime's serious study and discipline. Instead, Shahan was delighted. Drop some men in ox dung and they'd come up smelling of cool air.

He checked the tablets he'd written. He needed three of them to put down all he'd learned, and what could be inferred from it. Inferred with reasonable certainty, of course. He wasn't a drunk in a bar, trading wild speculations with no evidence at all. He would leave them in the foyer of the House of Tablets for the other scholars to see when they came in tomorrow morning. Mani could see the eyebrows lifting, lips forming questions about whether this could possibly be real.

He imagined Tash-Yal would grip handfuls of his own hair and tug at them, trying to frighten his brain into making sense of it all. Then the old man would copy the notes and add them to his bewildering array of references, each linked to others by pins and lines of red cord. They would probably make no difference; the array would still be baffling. Or they might, just perhaps, be what unlocked the whole mystery.

That was the dream, the hope which kept learned men heading to the marsh, however many confusing answers they received. They kept at it, year after year, sifting through the cryptic comments of the Sea-Goats in search of the dropped word that might actually mean something.

Who keeps us from remembering?

The memory of Shusikil wormed into his mind, stretched skin around an eel's smile. Mani shook it away. He picked the tablets up and headed for the foyer. He was halfway there when he heard the door open and close, and he stopped.

He and Shahan had been the last two here. That meant someone had entered, not left, and if it wasn't a scholar it had to be a priestess. Mani cleared his throat, and against all sense he asked, "Shahan?"

After a moment his own name was spoken, in a voice full of tears. He stopped where he was, not sure why a *zami* would be crying. It was only then that he recognised the voice and remembered he was married, and it was his wife in the vestibule calling his name.

He hurried forward, trying to rid himself of a feeling of guilt. The tablets went on a table, and he popped into the foyer. "Isha?" She was in the middle of the open space, flanked on each side by a line of columns. When she saw him, Isha gave a cry and flew into his arms. Mani rocked with the impact, but his arms went around her, one hand moving to stroke her black hair. "Isha, what—"

"He's dead! They killed him!"

"What? Who killed—"

"I saw him, Mani! I saw him!"

"Isha," he said. He made his voice deliberately calm, and it got through to her, at least a little. Her words cut off and she raised her head to look at him. He met her with a smile. "Breathe. Be calm."

"But they murdered him."

"Calm," he repeated.

She nodded and took such a deep breath that she sucked her veil between her lips. It blew out and she took another.

"Tell me who's dead," Mani said. It was harder to sound cool now. He pictured Shahan dead in the street, or Udar sprawled at the foot of a scaffold, and took his own deep breath.

"Ruen. They killed him."

"Who's Ru—wait. The man who works for your father?"

"I spoke with him yesterday. Now he's dead."

"Wait," Mani said, for the second time. "Are you saying he's dead because you spoke to him?"

The tears began again. "I—I think so. He was going to find a Seer for me."

"You wanted one of those charlatans?"

Her jaw hardened like clay in a furnace. "Some of them speak truth, husband. You know that. Don't call me a fool for not knowing the difference. I do."

"I didn't mean—"

"Shusikil spoke to me in the market yesterday."

Mani hissed through his teeth. "Tell me what happened."

She did so, from the moment the twitcher and the bag of bones had come up behind her in the market. Mani felt himself start to scowl and made an effort to relax his face. It didn't do much good.

"They offered you another *husband*?"

"And you another wife," she said. "A harlot from the Scented Houses, who will please you from sundown to sunup and never tell you no."

"And cook me breakfast as well, I expect," Mani said blackly. He was surprised when that made Isha laugh. Through tracks of tears her laughter was beautiful, and that thought surprised him even more.

He listened to the rest. Isha had gone to see her father, of course. He was starting to learn that she always would, even ten years into their marriage, if Fate spared them and they stayed together. She'd spoken to Ruen instead, and the big youth had gone out, and then…

"A repair team found him in an irrigation ditch," Isha said. "His throat was full of mud. He choked to death, Mani."

He felt himself scowl. "The ditches are dry."

"The only way to find mud is to make it," Isha agreed. "Who would have done that to Ruen?"

"*Zami,*" he growled.

She pushed away from him, eyes hard to read through the veil. "Will you leave me for their Scented woman?"

"Do you want me to?"

"Answer me." Her fingers tightened on his arm. "Answer, Mani. Will you walk with me into the street and pull down my veil?"

"No," he said, shocked. "How can you think that?"

"Because I'm cursed," Isha said. "Cursed by Eala, so that marriage brings bad luck around me like summer lightning. I warned you about that."

She had, but Mani hadn't believed it then and didn't believe it now. "This isn't a curse from the goddess. This is the priestesses causing trouble, that's all. What about you, Isha? Will you stay with me?"

"I'll stay," she said. "We'll dance and drink ocean water together." Her smile returned, shining through tears, but it didn't last long. She was afraid, Mani realised, of the priestesses and of him, too. He didn't know how to deal with that. Kiss her, maybe, but he didn't have the nerve to try.

"I'll stay," she said again. "But I really am cursed, Mani." She waited until his eyes met hers again, and then said, "I can't find my father."

CHAPTER THIRTEEN

THE CITY WAS full of alleys. Sometimes Udar thought it was more alleys than anything else. Buildings went up and were torn down, all without planning. Udar found himself edging between a wall he didn't remember and a scaffold on the other side, which was when a man stepped out in front of him.

A man with a cudgel. Udar stopped.

"Are you planning to bludgeon a pig with that?" he asked.

"You kill pigs with knives," the man said. He was built like a boar himself, thick-bodied with muscle. "A cut across the throat."

"So you do," Udar said. "Don't I deserve the knife?"

"You catch on fast."

"You have no idea," Udar said, and with the words he was moving.

There was only one reason why a street tough would step out in front of a man in a deserted alley. Only one reason why he'd talk to a victim, too, and that was if there was a second man on the other side. Someone behind Udar. He had listened for footfalls, and when he heard a creak of sandal leather close behind, he snapped into action.

These men would be formidable, but Udar ran a tavern.

He ducked as he turned, slipping sideways at the same time. The truncheon whistled down where his head had been and struck his shoulder. Pain exploded at once. Udar ignored it, sank lower, and drove a punch into the second man's stomach. His fist found cords of muscle and stopped. The assailant whuffed a little but that was all.

The first man arrived then, cudgel like a hammer into Udar's kidneys. He staggered sideways, and the other tough caught him again, on the same shoulder as before. This time Udar's arm flashed in agony all the way down to the fingers. He could still move them, though, and now he'd had time to reach under his tunic. He brought his arm up in a swift movement, and the second bully boy doubled over it with a gasp. Blood ran out of his mouth. Udar pushed him towards the other man and used the time that bought to transfer the knife to his other hand.

The first tough paused, measuring him.

"Not as easy as you thought, is it?" Udar gasped.

The goon shifted his feet. He never took his eyes from Udar. The innkeep waited, trying to stay calm. They circled the other man's body until his breathing stopped. After a moment the tough came in again, crouched this time, cudgel lower than before.

The man had courage, and his thick body was all muscle. Udar was older, sheathed in a layer of fat, as a prosperous man should be. Under it was the man who carried barrels all day. He waited for the cudgel and then brought his poor left arm up to block it, taking the blow on the bicep. At the same time, he stepped in and thrust with the knife. The thug had already begun to turn, twisting away from the blade, but Udar had expected that. He followed the movement and stabbed the man in the side, under the ribs, then dragged the blade out and stabbed again.

The truncheon hit him on the side of the head, but not so hard this time. If that had been the first blow, Udar would have been laid out like a dead fish with his brains spattered on the ground. Now it only made him stumble. He caught his balance, half turned, and then rammed his knife into the assailant's throat and tore it out sideways. Blood spouted, a great black tide of it. Udar was splashed all down his right side as the man went down, bouncing off Udar as he fell. His hands scrabbled at his throat as though trying to push the flesh back in. When he hit the floor, his head cracked and the hands stopped moving. Udar leaned back against the scaffold, breathing hard.

He wondered who had sent the men. Someone who didn't know him well, didn't realise that a tavern keeper wasn't the soft jovial man patrons saw at the bar. A fool, in short. Then Udar realised he didn't have to wonder—he knew who had done this, and he pushed off the scaffold with a grunt.

§ § §

Quarter of an hour later he pushed open the door of the Spilled Salt, took one step, and stopped.

"Master Udar." The slender man had risen from a table right by the door. He carried a tablet on the crook of one arm, and his tunic must have cost what the tavern made in a week. "I have waited for you."

"Waited for me?" his tongue said. Udar's attention was on the second man, standing behind the chair. Tall, with sloped shoulders and muscles that bunched and relaxed when he moved, and a sword slung on his back. A soldier, or Udar was a bullgoose fool. He would fight street thugs at the drop of a feather, but not a soldier. Not unless it meant his life, and it probably would. Further away Isha and her new husband were seated at a table near the bar counter, Ramsi with them. The young man's eyes were red. No time to wonder why.

"I am Damqa," tunic-man told him. "I work in the House of Statutes, in the service of the Throne."

An advisor to the King, then. It was said they owed their loyalty to the position and not the man. Udar nodded. "All right. I don't know what this is about, but I need medical help. Can we talk about this in the parlour?"

"No," Damqa said. "We speak in public. I understand you committed an assault this afternoon."

"I was the victim of one."

"We were told differently."

Udar managed a smile. "By whom?"

Isha and Mani were at the bar, with Ramsi behind it. Isha had come to her feet, hands to her mouth at the sight of her father's bruises. None of them came over. The soldier shifted his feet.

"That need not concern you," Damqa said.

"Let's talk about that," Udar said. "Do you mind if I sit? I'm in some pain." He dropped into a chair at the table Damqa had risen from. "Ramsi, send for the chirurgeon. Tell him it's urgent."

"Yes, boss."

"And bring me a pot. I'm thirsty. And a cloth." He sat straighter, leaning to the right to keep weight off his injured side. "Now, King's man. Who told you about the fight?"

"It's not your business."

"Oh, but it is. After that fight I walked straight home. Apparently, in that time someone found the bodies, informed the House of Statutes, and still left you time to reach the Spilled Salt before me. Isn't the House of Statutes on the far side of the city?"

"Yes, but—"

"So, did someone grow wings and fly there, do you think? Or did someone tell you before the fight actually happened?"

"You think you're being set up," Damqa said.

"I was attacked by two street toughs in an alley," Udar told him. "They were waiting for me, which means they knew my route home from the warehouse. Someone sent them. The same someone who tipped you off before it happened."

"And who would that be?"

"The *zami*," Udar said.

Damqa snorted. "That's ridiculous."

"See the man at the bar? He's a scholar. The woman beside him is his new wife, and my daughter." He lifted his good arm to beckon them over. "The priestesses wanted him to marry one of them. Control the scholars, you know. Instead, he married my Isha."

"And?"

"They want her to take off the veil," Udar said.

"They told me they'd find me another husband," Isha said as she came up. "A rich man with servants. They said they'd offer Mani a wife from the Scented Houses. And they threatened to cripple my father."

"They said that right out?"

"Plain as day. They killed someone already." She looked at Udar, her lips tight. "Ruen was found in a ditch, Papa, drowned in mud. I'm sorry."

"*Ruen*?"

"My fault," said his daughter, his only child. "I spoke to him when you weren't here. Next day he was dead."

"Drowned in mud? That doesn't make sense."

Mani nodded. "The ditches are dry as dust. The reservoirs are empty. Someone would have to bring water to make mud and pour it into Ruen's mouth."

"So, someone held him down," Udar said. "And Ruen was strong, so probably it was two. Unfortunate, King's man, isn't it?"

Damqa's eyes darted from face to face, searching for a lie. A door banged as Ramsi came back in, a cloth in one hand and a jug in the other. As he set them down Udar put a hand over the younger man's own.

"I'm sorry, lad," he said. "Not much I can do except say that. But you have friends here, and we'll get through this. All right?"

"Right," Ramsi said. Grieving or not, he never had words to spare. He went back to the table, shoulders down.

"Look, King's man." Udar struggled to unstop the jar, trying not to use his injured arm, until Mani leaned over to pull it for him. "Thanks. It's crazy to start a fight with two street thugs. That's a quick way to get your head broken open. I know, we deal with them here every night. I don't go looking for trouble."

"What you're saying is dangerous," Damqa said. He'd dropped his voice to little more than a murmur. "Only fools stand in the way of the *zami*. Why would you do so, scholar?"

"I was warned," Mani said. "Someone I trust told me a priestess wife would try to control my work. I didn't want that to happen."

"So, you defied them?"

"I married. The *zami* tell us it's a man's duty to marry and beget children. I obeyed them."

"Playing word games with the Temples is dangerous, too."

Mani shrugged. "Once the Temples are involved in your lives, everything is dangerous."

He was clever, this scholar who had asked for Isha's hand. Udar had never much cared for cleverness, but Mani wasn't arrogant about it and never rubbed ignorance into another man's face. For the first time, Udar saw him with another educated man, intellect matched to intellect. Mani's eyes were bright and wary. His mind was racing, and Udar knew it might have to if he was to survive.

Mani was too slight to lift barrels, too soft about the jaw to make a fighter, but maybe cleverness itself could be tough.

"I will inform the King," Damqa said at last. "It may be there has been a… misunderstanding."

"There's been a conspiracy," Udar corrected. "Someone tried to trick you. Tell the King that."

"I can't," Damqa said, with a tip of his head towards Mani. "He knows why. Come on, Thros."

He went out, the soldier striding at his heels. When the door swung shut Udar looked at his second-son.

"If he speaks badly of the Temples, it will be remembered," Mani explained. "Even if the King agrees with him. Damqa is a civil servant in the end, and not a powerful one, or he wouldn't have been given this duty. He can't afford to make enemies. You know the palace is a slippery place."

"What happened to you?" Isha burst out. The veil did nothing to hide her huge eyes. "You look half dead, Papa."

There was no point trying to keep secrets now, so Udar told her. Halfway through the telling someone dragged a stool up next to him and cut through his tunic with a knife, and Udar barely glanced at him. Ramsi was close by in case of danger, but it wasn't that. Udar knew this man, even glimpsed from the tail of his eye like the shadow of rain.

"Usually when I come here it's to care for men who got the wrong side of you," Kurunaka said. The chirurgeon wiped a cloth over Udar's bruises, and Udar hissed through his teeth. "I must say, this is a refreshing change."

That made Mani snort in amusement. Bloody clever men and their bloody witty jokes.

"It was the *zami*," Isha said when her father was done. "You're right. There's not much doubt."

"No doubt," Mani said.

Udar nodded. That was how he saw it, too. "Why did they kill Ruen?"

"He was going to find me a Seer," Isha told him.

"They wouldn't murder a man for that." Mani spoke softly, but there was conviction in the words. "Not like this. They were sending a message. They want us to know how far they will go."

"To separate us?"

He shrugged. "To them it's about control. They've been thwarted, so now they want to impose their authority."

"Wait," Udar said. "Isha, do you want to take off the veil?"

"No!" she said sharply, and then he thought she blushed a bit. "I mean, no. I really will be cursed if that happens. Anyway, I like Mani."

Udar looked at the scholar, and after a moment Mani shook his head. "They can't make you, then."

"They can," Isha said. Worry chased across her face. "Poison in a water cup. An arrow from a rooftop. If they can't force us directly, then can threaten you, Papa. I think they'll try."

She was beautiful to him. Always had been, since she was a little thing he could hold in one hand. Udar knew his daughter was plain, by most measures. Her gifts were quickness and clear thought, and a tongue to speak with. She hadn't learned tact, though. "You're as refreshing as rainfall on parched ground."

"Should I lie to you, Papa?"

"No," he sighed. "Just try a little gentleness, will you?"

"I'll leave that for palace intrigues," she said. "I don't have much of it. I do have intelligence, and strength cannot keep pace with cleverness, they say. The Temples have muscle, I have wits. That's where our hope lies."

"We could stay here," Mani suggested.

She rounded on him for that. "And let the *zami* chase us out of our home? Imagine what claims they might make if we did that before the seven days are up. No. We stay where we are."

"Then your Papa can stay with us."

"No," Udar said. "I'm needed here. If word gets around that I'm not sleeping at the Spilled Salt, it will be raided six times a night."

"The same is true," Kurunaka murmured, "if word spreads that you are not able to defend yourself. Due to broken ribs, perhaps. Can you raise your arm? No, with the elbow bent."

Udar did so, wincing. "Even so, I stay here." He gritted his teeth as Kurunaka dug fingers into his side. "What will the Temples do next?"

"Offer me a Scented House woman, for a start," Mani said. "Persuade me instead of Isha. When that fails?" He shrugged. "Kill her, probably."

"That's what I thought," Udar said. Isha put her hands over her mouth. "But they only have until the seventh day, when the veil comes off anyway."

"That's right."

"I'll give up the tavern if that's what it takes to keep Isha safe," Udar said. "Do I have to, Mani? Are you my second-son forever?"

"Yes," the scholar said.

Isha spoke through her hands. "You can't keep me safe. What happens when you go to the Sea-Goats, Mani? I'm in that house alone."

"I won't leave you there," Mani said. He was very calm, and Udar realised the other man had already thought about this. "I'll take you to the marsh with me. You know how to write, Isha. We'll take tablets and you can make notes."

"The *zami* won't like that."

"Imagine how little I care," Mani said.

Chapter Fourteen

"FIRST THING," MANI said. "Don't speak. Not this time. Every apprentice goes out to the marsh with a full scholar at first. Usually, it's the fourth or fifth time before we're allowed to speak."

"Why?" Isha asked.

"The Sea-Goats don't really trust us. They'll talk to a scholar if they know him, not otherwise, and they take any excuse to vanish. Glimmer and splash and they're gone."

A small line formed between her eyes as she frowned. "Why don't they trust you?"

"Good question," he said. "If we knew that, we might have the key to unlocking their secrets. There's one other thing. Make whatever notes you want as I talk. My memory is good, so I'll remember most of it anyway. I only need a word or two written down to jog my thoughts."

"All right."

He pushed open the door and led her into the Scholar's Guild. The air was cooler at once. The streets were baking already, at mid-morning, and the marsh in afternoon would be brutal. There was no way around it. He wouldn't leave her here for the priestesses.

"Shahan will have been out this morning," he said, crossing the hall. "It's Darsal this evening and me now. When the Flood comes, we won't be able to talk to them at all, so it's best to do it now." Movement made him turn. "Hello, Tash-Yal. Is your referencing finished already?

"Oh. Mani." The other scholar seemed to scowl at the end of his own nose. "I was just…taking a walk."

"A walk? You?"

"I just," Tash-Yal began. He broke off, shrugged at the floor, and hurried off down the corridor.

Isha looked at Mani through her veil. "What was that about?"

"I've no idea," he said. "Tash-Yal hardly ever goes out, even to visit the swimmers. He's turned his room into a web of crossing lines. You can only get in by ducking through the cords. Hitti put his back out and won't go there now."

"Put the priestesses in there," she said. They entered the corridor to his room. "By the time they get out we'll be raising our children."

He laughed, surprised by her wit. Then he sobered as what she'd said came home to him. "Our children?"

"People have them," Isha said. "Especially married people. Didn't you know that, husband?"

"I'd heard about it," he said gently. "Shall we leave it for now? We have enough to deal with."

"That's the truth," she said. Her eyes were smiling as Mani pushed open his door and stepped through.

"Scholar Kassu-Mani," the priestess said. She rose from behind Mani's desk from his chair. Dried skin stretched over a too-tall frame. "I expected you earlier."

He stared at her, shocked. "What are you—"

"This Guild is run under the patronage of the Temples," Shusikil said. "I have the right."

"The Guild is under the auspices of the King," Mani said.

"The *zami* are permitted to walk where they wish," a second priestess put in. She was seated by the window, a muscle twitching under her eye. "You have no power to deny us entry."

"No," Mani agreed. "You have the right to see my work, not to intrude upon it."

"How do we intrude?"

He reached behind Isha to close the door.

"Shall we speak frankly?" he asked. "You're in my study, uninvited. I call that intrusion. You've had one man killed and another attacked. I might be for-given if I don't trust you."

"Had men attacked?" Shusikil asked. "I'm afraid I don't understand. Men do drown in the ditches, after all." Her gaze whipped to Isha. "You're still wearing your veil."

"You're still nosing into my life," Isha snapped back.

"All right," Mani said. He knew now why Tash-Yal had been scurrying out like a beaten hound. "What can I do for you, *zami*?"

"It's what we can do for you," the twitchy one said. Her gaze shifted past him.

Mani turned to see a third woman push off from the wall behind the door. She was as tall as he was, maybe an inch taller, with a cascade of hair so black it shimmered almost purple. When she stepped forward, her hips swayed and her body rippled.

"Scholar," she said. "I haven't seen you for weeks."

Too many surprises. Mani's voice was gone again. He didn't move as the woman laid a hand on his arm.

"Elessa is willing to be your wife," Lamsi said. "More than willing, in fact. She's positively eager. What was it you said, Elessa?"

"That I will make him happy every day of his life," the sultry woman breathed in Mani's ear. Her hand tightened on his forearm. "And every night. In whatever way he pleases. You know it's a promise I can keep, Mani."

A second hand closed on his other wrist, and Isha said, "You *know* this woman?"

Perhaps it was her touch, or the sound of her voice breaking the spell that had seized him. Mani could think again, and his tongue began to move. "She works in the Scented House down by the Ox Gate. I've visited her before. Yes, Isha, I know her."

"Then you know what she can offer," Shusikil said. A smile formed on the angles of her face.

"Yes," Mani said. "Physical pleasures. The pride of walking with a hot limbed beauty on my arm. I know what she can't offer, too."

The smile flickered. "Oh?"

"You can't read, Elessa," he said. "You can't write. You have no education except what you've learned in snippets on the pillows. What did they offer you to do this?"

"A better life than I have," she said. Her voice was smoke and scent, intoxicating. "Lamsi didn't have to offer twice. I always liked you, Mani."

"Am I cursed?" Isha murmured. It was so soft Mani hardly heard it, but Shusikil's lips thinned as she stared at the younger woman. Mani put a hand on his wife's, a silent comfort.

"That's not all," Mani said to Elessa. "They will have wanted something in return."

"I would ask the questions they told me to ask," the beauty said. "You'd then ask the Sea-Goats the same things. It's not much."

"Control over my work is not much?" He shook his head. "You never struck me as the kind of woman to do the *zamis'* bidding, Elessa."

The beauty shrugged, making her body ripple again. It was hard to drag his eyes from that. "Offer me the right price and I'll do what the buyer wants. Aren't you tempted, Mani? You don't have to pay a single coin, and you get me in your bed every night. I know you'd like that."

"But the price is having you in my house every day," he said, "and I would *not* like that."

She took a half pace back and her hand came off his arm. Mani saw hurt in her eyes and was sorry for it, but bluntness was the least of his concerns just now. He turned back to the two priestesses.

"Understand one thing," he said. "I will not put aside my wife. Not for anything offered by gods or mortals, or even by you, *zami*. Give it up."

"There are other things we can still try," Lamsi snapped. A muscle jumped in her cheek with every word. "This is the fifth day. There are another two before she may remove the veil."

"Why does it matter so much? Not all scholars are married to priestesses. Why must I be?"

"You defied us," Shusikil said. "That can't be permitted. Scholars must know where control lies."

He sighed. "Only the Sea-Goats control conversations by the marsh. If you don't understand that, *zami*, you're fools. I think you should go now. Close the door when you leave."

They went, glowering and grim. Shusikil stalked by like an angry heron, though any shore bird had more meat on its bones than she did. As for Elessa, she sashayed through the door with a glance of mingled regret and promise. No hard feeling there then, Mani thought. He would be welcome if ever he went back to the Scented House again.

Surprising thought, that. He'd assumed he would always go back, if less often now that he had a wife. Odd to find himself doubting it.

"Did you mean that?" Isha asked. Her hand was still on his arm. "About gods and mortals?"

He nodded. "Yes. I didn't marry you as a joke. You've been hurt, and now you believe you're cursed. I wouldn't want to add to that, Isha."

She studied his face for a moment, fingers tightening on his wrist. He thought she began to smile, but under the veil it was hard to be sure. Then she let go and broke eye contact. "We've wasted a lot of time already. Where are these tablets?"

"Here," he said. He scooped three of them from a shelf in the corner. "I prepared them last night. If you keep them out of the sun the clay stays damp for a long time."

She took them from him. Again, he thought she might have smiled. "Then let's go to the marsh."

§ § §

The heat was brutal. Mani put his hat on and handed one to Isha. She looked strange wearing it and her plain robe. From twenty feet away she might have been a man.

Closer to the marsh the air was cooler. A little, anyway, and even a slight difference was a relief. Mani walked along the pier to ring the bell, then came back and sat with Isha. Behind them the guard dozed in his hut.

"Why is it underwater?" she asked.

"The bell? It doesn't really ring. The clapper bangs on the waist, like a blacksmith's hammer on an anvil. The swimmers hear it, but we can't."

She looked around. "I thought there'd be shelter. Shade from the sun at least."

"No luxuries for the scholars," Mani answered. "The Temples would scream fury if the King tried to pay for that. They don't really want us here at all."

"Why is that?"

"I don't know," Mani said. "None of us do. They don't want us here, but they let us come anyway. The swimmers want to talk but never like to answer. It doesn't make sense."

"The Temples often don't," she said. "Mani, do you believe? In Eala and the gods, I mean."

He hesitated. "I'm not sure. I think we might have created the gods, not the other way around. The clergy of Tibad claim that Ikuga made the first people out of the air. That's a new thing, a new myth, and it makes me wonder if the old ones were invented the same way. But then again, how else could humans have appeared, if we weren't made by gods?"

"You want to understand everything, don't you?"

"Yes. All the questions, every mystery in the world."

"Then you would be a god yourself, Mani."

He shrugged, discomforted by that. "Yes, maybe. What do you believe?"

"I think the gods aren't real," she said. "There's too much suffering for that to be true. If they were real, they'd stop the pain, wouldn't they?"

He nodded. It was an old argument, but different coming from her. Isha had lost two fiancés before him, one maimed, the other dead. She'd thought herself cursed—still did, in fact. When you drank superstition with your mother's milk, it settled deep inside you.

Inside Mani, too. He wasn't immune. His head didn't believe in Eala but oh, his heart longed to.

A splash came from the lagoon, and he smiled. "We have a visitor. Remember not to speak. Hold your questions until later."

He went down the pier. A figure was darting through the green water below, little more than a flash of movement. Mani realised with surprise that the Sea-Goat was playing, a solo game that didn't seem much more than weaving through knots of reeds. He'd never seen a swimmer play before, any more than they had seen Mani dance.

He filed the observation away in his memory. After a moment the blur took form and a head broke the surface, hairless and smooth. Mani bowed from the waist. "Good afternoon, Hanno."

"Scholar," the young swimmer greeted. "Don't you ever miss a meeting?"

"Not that I remember. I enjoy your company too much."

Hanno's body shook from shoulders to tail, and the water vibrated in a laugh. "You're funny. I like you, too."

"I saw you playing down there."

"That? It's just practise. For when hunters come."

He thought about that. "Sharks?"

"Yes. The *dakua*, shadows in the dark. And octopi, far from land. They reach up a tentacle and a swimmer is gone, just like that, dragged down to the Deep. You might break free if you have a good knife, or a spear. But the best thing is to avoid being caught, so we learn to be fast."

This was more treasure. Mani couldn't believe his luck in finding this young Sea-Goat, so much more open than the rest. "And at your home island?"

Hanno ducked under and came up again, water streaming over his eyes. He didn't want to answer that, obviously. His gaze went past Mani and he said, "You brought someone this time."

"Yes. To take notes for me."

"You never needed that before."

"No. Don't get used to it. By next week I'll be making my own squiggles in clay again."

"Who is he?"

"She," Mani said, thinking nothing of it. "Her name is Isha. She's my wife."

Hanno froze. He might have been carved from driftwood. The water around him went still, though his tail must have been moving down below or he would have sunk. Mani hadn't seen a swimmer do that before. His first thought was that he'd made a mistake.

"She isn't," Hanno said at last. "No."

"She is."

"No. No. She can't be."

"She is," he said again, perplexed. "I promise you. We were married last week. I brought her with me today to keep her safe."

Now the water thrashed, though Hanno stayed rigid in the middle of it. "She isn't safe?"

Fate is a dog that walks behind you, Mani thought. If he'd misstepped there was no help for it now. "The priestesses want to make us part. They might kill to achieve that."

The swimmer's voice climbed to the edge of a screech. "Your wife is in *danger*? And you brought her here?"

"Yes. I thought—"

He was talking to himself. A huge fount of water, and Hanno was gone. Mani frowned at the lagoon as the ripples spread and faded, trying to work out what had just happened.

"Is that normal?" Isha asked behind him.

"No," he said. He was still staring at the widening circles where Hanno had been. "It's not normal at all."

Chapter Fifteen

IT SEEMED TO Yarim that his life was made of marching by day, and Kammani by night.

The army was huge now, swollen further by recruits from fallen Tibad. Swear loyalty or die; it was a savage choice they were given, and one most found easy enough. Three thousand men had followed Sarru-kin out of Labaš. Now seven thousand marched on Piqash, spread out across the land like a swarm. There wasn't an army in Engiru that could stand against them. Especially with Sarru-kin at their head.

"There's something about him," Enmer had said, the first night out from Tibad. "It sets him apart."

"Yes. He's king."

"Something more than that."

"Maybe he's half immortal already," Yarim teased, "just by the force of his will."

He had meant it as a joke, but his friend only eyed him over a cup of beer. "Maybe he is."

Many men thought that way. Yarim heard it over and again, from the mouths of men of Kindar and Tibad as well as from home. They said Sarru-kin could make the beasts of the field follow him and charm the stones themselves. Bridges appeared where he needed them. Enemies looked into his eyes and became allies, if not friends. Who could be friends with a man so much more than merely mortal?

Yarim had joined the army for regular food and some respect. Now he spent his days slogging through parched fields, with the sun a brand in the sky and the world a-shimmer with heat. Sometimes he rode with the chariots, creaking along amidst all the spearmen. When he did that, he sometimes wore his captain's bronze helmet, so he could get used to the soldiers ducking their heads when they came to speak with him.

"That suits you," one of the other captains once said. Zammash was a rare thing these days, a man who'd been a commander before Sarru-kin came to power. "Hope you can lead as well as you pose, though."

Zammash tapped his driver, and the chariot wheeled away before Yarim could splutter a reply. *Posing?* His own driver didn't react, but he must have heard, and he'd tell the story. That had been an insult, a blow dealt by an experienced man to a newcomer. It would have to be dealt with, if it happened again. But not now.

Then there were nights with Kammani in her tent, with wine, fruits, and the sheer, intoxicating presence of her.

Yarim had given up hope of secrecy. There was no chance of it, when he went every night to Kammani's great tent in the middle of the camp. Soldiers gossiped worse than girls or debt slaves. They took Yarim's orders now with a knowing light in their eyes, and murmurs that began just before he was out of earshot. That didn't matter, so long as they obeyed.

Sarru-kin did matter, rather a lot. Yarim still couldn't help going to Kammani. He was risking his life, but days would seem hollow without her at the end of them, and he could not stop. Sarru-kin was important, but Kammani mattered even more in the end.

"Does he frighten you?" she asked one night. She was pouring wine at a table, wearing a robe as thin as dreams. It clung to the curves of her from nape to knees. She turned and handed him a cup, looking at him from under long black lashes.

"Of course he does," Yarim said. He was nearly sure she was putting something in his wine. She alone couldn't be enough to do this to his mind, his heart, and his body. "He frightens us all."

"Not me," she said. "I'm beyond his reach."

"I'm not sure anything is," he said.

Kammani smiled and put a hand on his bare stomach. The touch was light, but Yarim's breath caught. "Drink your wine."

He downed half of it and dropped the cup on the floor. It bounced, spilling red wine. By then Yarim had caught the priestess by hip and neck and pulled her to him. Kammani laughed in her throat. She wriggled and the robe slithered down her body.

"Quickly," she said in his ear. "The first time."

Quickly. Yes. He lifted her to a table, and she wrapped her legs around him. Then he was inside her. She bit him where his neck met the shoulder, and Yarim felt blood flow. He snarled, hands on her buttocks as he pulled her onto him and Kammani started to gasp.

It was the same, always. *Something in the wine.* Excitement and passion like nothing before. A tide of it. There had never been a woman like her, never a body like hers, golden, firm, and curved. There was thirst in her, a hunger, driving Yarim to a need of his own. Once there he couldn't stop, or even think. He rode her time and again, or she rode him, and either way he ended drained and weak on the bed while she washed her body with a cloth and blood dried on Yarim's skin.

"Good," she said later. A smile played around her lips. She was touching him with her fingernails, teasing. "You can have more wine, if you like. Or more me. Shall I give you a choice?"

"I choose both," he said. His breath was fast. "Both."

"Good decision," she said. She pushed him over on his back and poised herself over his hips. "Me, then wine."

"Kammani," he said, reaching for her.

§ § §

The next morning, they marched again.

Yarim should have been tired. There was very little sleep with Kammani, and that shot through with memories and her musk in his nose. He should have been exhausted, staggering with exertion, but he wasn't. Perhaps he was in pain but didn't feel it, too drowned in his lust for her to notice.

Or perhaps there was something in the wine.

"You lucky dog," Enmer said.

Yarim made a warding sign. "We'll reach Piqash today. Don't speak of luck before a battle, you fool."

"What else should I call it?"

He shuddered, thinking of what Sarru-kin would say when the story reached him. "Don't call it anything."

Spearing a priestess was bad enough. Doing the chief *zami*, well…that was excuse enough for the king to have Yarim killed. Sarru-kin didn't care for Kammani, but he did care for his pride. It was worth the risk. It must be, for Yarim to keep going back to gorge himself at the same table. Then there was the other prize, the one Kammani had spoken of from the start. Who would be king when Sarru-kin went over the ocean to find the immortality he dreamed of?

"You will have a wife from the noble families," Kammani had said during the night. "A pretty woman, with wide hips to give you sons. And you'll have me." A finger traced along his skin, and he shuddered, biting down a cry. "Whenever you want me."

Name a dream and it would never come to pass. Yarim didn't want to speak of it, didn't want Enmer or anyone else to speak of it. Let the words lie silent on their tongues, and perhaps Fate and the gods would be kind and let it happen as Kammani promised.

Son of a dog, he was hot.

On they went, seven thousand of them spread across the land like a tide of insects, come to consume the crop. Dust stirred by their feet rose into a cloud that clogged the throat but did at least offer some shade. Yarim tied a cloth across his mouth, but there was nothing he could do to protect his eyes, which soon began to sting. He wished he had a bride's veil. He'd endure the taunts of comrades if only he could stop the itching.

They saw nobody. No farmers, no debt slaves working on the last repairs to ditches. Word had run ahead that the Mad King was coming. In a normal war the army of Piqash would have come to meet them, but Tibad had done so and been crushed. Piqash wouldn't make the same mistake. Sarru-kin's army was too big to face in the open.

This was not a normal war, nor Sarru-kin a normal king.

The soldiers came to ditches and scrambled across them, leaving the bridges for chariots. The channels held no water but were full of brick dust. Yarim helped transfer a chariot across, in a line of big men passing it from hand to hand, and emerged filmed with grey like the rest. Many of the men had unease in their eyes, which he saw and understood. The summer was old, the land dryer than long-dead bone. These were the days before the Flood, when only black-feathered vultures fed well. The last days before the water rose.

It might be rising now, trembling at the top of the levees that held back the Ranuna. One more hour and it would spill over, pouring into the parched and cracked land where Sarru-kin's army now marched. The soldiers would walk on because they had nowhere else to go. The water would be up to their ankles by nightfall, when they reached the walls of Piqash. No man would lie down unless on a dike, or the backs of two mules. He would wake to a world submerged to his knees, then his thighs, and the knowledge it would stay like that for a month.

In Piqash, safe behind its banks of earth and bitumen-painted walls, the king and his people would laugh and laugh.

It was with the thought that Yarim realised he could see Piqash, a jag on the horizon made vague by dust. Three miles away, perhaps. Even if the Flood came now, this minute, they would still reach the city. Reaching it was different from capturing it, he knew that, but still. They would be there.

"I didn't really think this was possible," he said. It was breaking his own rule not to speak of dangerous things, but the words spilled out anyway. "Not back home in Labaš."

"Neither did I," Enmer said. "But Sarru-kin knew it was."

Yarim thought of Kammani, and the risk he was taking. "Sarru-kin seems to know lots of things."

"Halfway immortal already," Enmer said.

That had been a joke, or meant as one. Now Yarim wished he'd never spoken the words. Still, even in his fear of the Mad King, he felt a stir of desire at the thought of Kammani. By the small hours of this morning, he'd been slumped on the bed, hardly able to breathe anymore, as though all the life force had been sucked out of him and only a shell remained. He'd been conscious of Kammani though, washing from a bowl across the tent, and the memory of droplets beading on her skin quickened his breath in the baleful heat of the day.

Two miles from Piqash.

The ditches were wider now, and ten feet deep. Men had to lower each other to the bottom and then boost up the other side, reaching for hands to haul them up. Still the land was deserted. If he were defending, Yarim would have ordered the bridges broken to slow chariots, and then sent companies of archers to rain ruin on the spearmen as they struggled in the moats. That would have meant damaging the irrigation, and no king ever ordered that. Not even a mad one. So, the army crossed untroubled, forming ranks again as they moved on.

"Drink," Yarim called to his men. Infantry today, a full company of sixty-four, but only half from Labaš. All the units were mixed now, and he didn't like it. "Not too much. It might be your last chance."

"Or their last drink ever," Enmer murmured.

"If you bring the eyes of Fate onto us today," Yarim said, "I will slice your stomach from side to side and leave you for carrion." Enmer only snorted.

One mile to Piqash.

A rattling made him look around, and there were the chariots. Fifty of them, suddenly all together in a double line, three men in each. They came down the road in plumes of dust, hiding all but their shapes except for the first, and riding there was a man they all knew.

"Ho, Yarim!" the Mad King cried. His armour shone. He must have only just put it on, to keep it clean of grime. "Do you know Piqash has five gates?"

"Does it?" he shouted back.

"This road runs to the Mitu Gate. The Gate of the Dead. Don't you think that's funny?"

He managed a laugh. "Does it earn its name today?"

"He can't help it," Sarru-kin said. He spun his sickle sword on the floor of the chariot car. "He's like the rest of them, nothing but a mortal brain. No, Yarim, it will earn nothing. East of it is the Scorpion Gate. Bring your company there now, at the run. Begin!"

"Now?" he called back. The word was lost in a sudden creak of wheels and neigh of horses, as the drivers lashed them to a gallop. Yarim lifted a hand to wave away billows of dust.

"He isn't," Enmer said.

"I think he is." Yarim paused to spit filth out of his throat. "He's going to attack this Scorpion Gate. Chariots against walls and doors. Burn my eyes!" He lifted his voice. "We run, boys! Forget about good order. Let the other units chase us, but we'll be first to the king!"

<h1 style="text-align:center">CHAPTER SIXTEEN</h1>

Chapter Sixteen

T HE GATE WAS open when they reached it.
Defenders boiled around it, hundreds of them crammed into the street
and on the walls. The doors to the overlooking tower were shut. Someone
had found a ram, and it battered away with dull booms, but the door held.

The chariots stood outside, empty except for a dozen drivers. They sat with
their feet propped on the cars as Yarim and his men dashed past, breath rasping
in their throats. Under the gatehouse they went, and there they found fighting
at the end of the street where it began to run into the city. Sixty or seventy men,
packed shoulder to shoulder behind their shields, with Sarru-kin shining in the
centre like water on glass.

"How?" Enmer shouted. "How did he know?"

A traitor, perhaps. Or else Sarru-kin was halfway immortal already and listening to the secrets of the gods. Perhaps he'd spoken a word and the gates had
swung open while seraphs sang in the sky. It didn't matter. Sixty men of Labaš
and three times as many of Piqash, so there was no time to think. Yarim called
for the first gaggle of runners to form a line and led it straight into the heart of
the fighting, just to the side of the Mad King.

After that there was just the crush of bodies and gasp of breath, sweat and
the stink of fear. Yarim's sandals skidded on dirt, and later on blood. Men who
found themselves facing him saw his size and scrambled to get away, not always
fast enough. Yarim killed two men, both clad in armour of leather that didn't do
much to stop the point of his spear. Commoners then, men pressed into desperate
service as the enemy approached. No glory in killing the likes of them.

Yarim had been a commoner, once.

There was glory in the simple act of survival. One more breath to take under
the sun. It might be the last, if a spear thrust out of the melee at the wrong moment
or an arrow plunged down unseen. But Yarim took it, and then another, and one
more, and at last found himself panting in the bloody street as fresher companies
pushed the defence back.

"You did well," Sarru-kin said. He strolled towards Yarim, four huge soldiers
around him like the corners of a square. "Now that we have broken in, the fight
will not last long."

Yarim stared at him, still gasping. Battle was hard on the body and harder still
on the heart. You lived at vast effort, always one moment from a blade in the vitals
and your blood spilling out. Yet Sarru-kin wasn't even out of breath. His armour

was smeared with dust, but there wasn't a scratch on it. The king grounded his sickle sword and spun it around, a habit that had begun to make Yarim itch inside.

"Did you know?" He hadn't intended to ask, but words were falling off his tongue today. "That the gate would fall, I mean. You must have. How?"

"Azaq told me," Sarru-kin said. He lifted the sword and turned it to catch the sunlight. "Ati me peta babka."

Gatekeeper, open your gate for me. That made no sense, but not much did with the Mad King. Yarim's breath was easier now. He straightened as more soldiers ran past to join the fray. Sarru-kin was right, the battle was just a matter of time from here.

He looked at the four guards. One of them stared back and flexed his biceps, like the muscles in a bull's back.

A party of *zami* came through the gate, walking in a cluster with Kammani at the centre. She was a head taller than anyone else, obvious even if you didn't know her. Her skin shone golden, as Sarru-kin glowed silver in his armour. Neither of them seemed truly mortal, not all of this world. Yarim couldn't help watching as she strode by, though she never gave him so much as a glance or a twitch of her eyes. Nothing to betray what they shared and planned.

The lesser priestesses glanced at him, heads turning like a flock of grebes by the river. Kammani spoke a word and they turned back. The damage was done by then, though, the secret out for those who would see it. Yarim didn't doubt that the Mad King would.

Sarru-kin's attention wasn't on them. A soldier ran up from deeper in the city, sweat streaking the dirt on his face. "My lord!"

"Report," Sarru-kin said.

"Sire, the enemy king has taken refuge in the Temple. We think most of the nobles are in there, too, with their guards."

Sarru-kin twirled the sickle sword. "Who allowed this? Who was in command of the forces there?"

"Idinnam, sire."

"He will open his own throat for me before nightfall," Sarru-kin said. He swung Azaq, and the messenger crumpled like a shot bird. "Yes, my dear. He had to die. Are you ready, Yarim?"

He swallowed. "What?"

"I wish to see how well this craven king has dug himself in," Sarru-kin said. "You will command Idinnam's company now. It is one of the best, all experienced men. Will you follow me to the Temple? And beyond?"

Yarim looked at the body on the floor. One more of the captains who'd preceded Sarru-kin was gone, then. Zammash might be the last. Yarim breathed deep, smelling blood and dust.

"Always," he said. Kammani was out of sight. "Always, my king."

§ § §

King Tarah-ti was dug in like a *sikku* rat in its hole. He must have planned for this. The Temple had been turned into a refuge, most of its doors bricked up and the rest barred and wedged shut. Windows higher up were now narrow slots, just wide enough for an archer to shoot through but too narrow for a man to squeeze. Yarim stood with his king in a street opposite, studying the scene.

"We can force our way in," he ventured.

"Yes," Sarru-kin said.

A body at his feet. Idinnam hadn't cut his own throat. He'd started to draw his sword, ready to fight for his life, but only bared two inches of blade before two of Sarru-kin's enormous guards were on him. One lunged with a dagger while the other brought a mace down, hard. Now blood and brains mixed in the street, trickling around the king's sandals.

"Yes, my dear," Sarru-kin said. "Time is the key. The Flood comes, and the ruin of everything if we don't hurry."

Yarim said nothing. There was a tone you learned to recognise around the Mad King, one that meant he was talking to his sword. It made Yarim think of what he felt for Kammani. Love, perhaps. Certainly passion. He shifted his feet, careful not to step in brains.

"What would you do?" Sarru-kin asked.

Not the tone of speaking to the sword. Yarim hesitated, palms damp. "I would go on to Aš-alam."

"Why?"

He shrugged. "You can come back here when you're immortal. Tarah-ti will have plenty of food stored in there, but it won't last forever."

Sarru-kin looked at him and twirled the sickle sword.

CHAPTER SEVENTEEN

THE STREETS WERE crowded when they got back to Aš-alam. It only took moments to find out why.

"The Mad King took Tibad?" Mani asked. "Already?"

"Smashed its army outside the walls," the soldier told him. "That was four days ago. If he moved as fast as he did after taking Kindar, he'll be on the road again by now."

"For where?"

"Piqash," the man answered, "if he's coming here."

There were a lot of soldiers in sight. Keeping the peace, Mani supposed. It wouldn't take much for people to panic with news like this. He knew where the cities lay, kept a map of the plain in his head, and he could draw a line from Labaš to Kindar and then Piqash. It was almost straight, and if you drew the line longer it would point right at Aš-alam.

"Why would he come here?" Mani wondered.

The soldier had already moved away, and it was Isha who answered. "The Sea-Goats. Why else?"

He frowned at her.

"There's no other reason," she said. "The cities are all much the same. Each claims patronage of a different god, but nothing else changes. The ditches need upkeep, bitumen must be bought for the bricks, and the priestesses strut around looking down their noses at everyone. It's the same everywhere, except for Aš-alam." She saw his expression and smiled behind her yellow veil. "You wanted a wife who could read and write. That means you get one who can think. Didn't you know that?"

"I think I just learned it again," he said. Her smile turned into a laugh.

"Here's another thing to think about," she said. "The Mad King isn't stopping to make sure he controls the cities he takes. He conquers and rushes on, always to the south. Towards us. He doesn't want Kindar, or Tibad. Whatever he wants is here, husband, in Aš-alam."

"Yes," he said.

His tone was so thoughtful that Isha laughed again. She sobered quickly this time though. "Piqash is five days march from here. If the Mad King takes it, they'll be no time for us to prepare soldiers. I think Ra'im might call the adult men for training."

"We already have soldiers," Mani began, but he stopped there as his thoughts

85

caught up. Rumour claimed that Sarru-kin was enlisting defeated soldiers in his own army. Enough merchants and messengers had brought that news to make it nearly certain to be true. That meant the Mad King would arrive with twice the number of men Aš-alam could muster, maybe three times. The existing army wouldn't be enough to stop him.

"We need the Flood," he said.

Isha nodded. "Yes. The water might rise tomorrow, or not for ten days. Sarru-kin might be at the river by then." She hesitated. "Are scholars subject to the summons to train with soldiers?"

"What? No. Scholars and scribes are exempt. Most of the numbers will come from debt slaves. If they fight their service is annulled and they'll be free again."

"My father used to be a captain," she said. "He'll have to go back to the army, won't he?"

"He's past fighting age, though. The king can't force him to fight."

"Thank the Goddess," she said.

It was surprising what you forgot when you were newly married. There were so many considerations Mani had never needed to think about before. In his own home he'd always done as he pleased, without thought for anyone else. He'd known that a married man had to think of his wife, but he hadn't reckoned with a father-in-law, too. Stupid of him, really.

"I need to go to him," she said.

This time he'd expected it. "We'll put our notes into the Hall of Tablets and then go straight to him." He saw her expression and added, "I can't go before. Failing to record a conversation immediately is grounds for expulsion from the Guild, and the *zami* will snatch at an excuse like that."

"And I can't go alone, in case I fall into a reservoir and break my head," she said. "But I need to go."

He looked around. "Soldier!"

Several men looked around, including a muscular fellow with a sword at his hip. Mani beckoned him over and he came, a smaller man with a pointed beard in his wake. "What?"

"A coin for each of you if you take my wife somewhere," Mani said. "The Spilled Salt. I'm sure you know it."

"Might have had a drink or two in there before," the big man said.

"Make sure she gets there safe."

"Who's after her?"

"You don't want to know," Mani said. He put another silver into the man's hand. "On your honour?"

"On our honour," the soldier said.

Mani turned to his wife. "I'll be there as soon as I can. Stay in the tavern until I arrive."

"I promise," Isha said. She hesitated, and then kissed him quickly on the cheek. Before he could respond she was away, the two soldiers hurrying to stay on her heels. Mani turned and walked into the Guild. It was cooler at once, and the hubbub outside died away to nothing. He went down the corridor to the House of Tablets, where his sandals clicked and clacked on the bricks as he walked past the stacks. He reached the desks in the middle, sat down, and only then realised two men were by the window looking at him.

"Sorry," he said.

Shahan waved that away. "Did you just get back? Have you heard the news?"

"Sarru-kin took Tibad," he said. "I know."

"Ra'im made the call for soldiers," Shahan said.

He was jolted. "Already?"

"The Mad King is marching on Piqash." Shahan grinned. "It's very exciting, don't you think? Ra'im couldn't wait."

"I didn't think he'd move as fast as this," Mani muttered.

"Then you're a fool," the other man said. It was Hitti, stooped over two canes and bald as a turtle. His voice was thin as the wind but still clear. "Ra'im is not. He can read the signs."

That was true. The king had always been clever, back to when he was a youth studying history at the Temple school. That was why he'd been nominated for the kingship. He wasn't going to be caught unprepared when the signs were so clear. It was just the speed of it, the decisiveness, that unsettled Mani.

"He's never struck so hard before," he said.

"He never needed to," Hitti retorted. "There's been no war in Engiru for fifty years. None involving Aš-alam for closer to a hundred. Now there's a threat, and Ra'im acts."

"Yes," he said. "I need to transcribe these tablets and then get back to Isha. Though actually," he scanned down the notes, "she's made them nearly neat enough already."

"She?" Hitti said.

Mani looked up. The old man's eyes were sharp. "Well, my wife, actually."

"You took your *wife* to the swimmers?"

He started to explain that he had to keep her safe, and realised Hitti wasn't going to listen. "Yes."

The old man came forward in a clatter of sticks. "That was irresponsible! We never take guests to the Sea-Goats!"

"I know," he said.

"We operate under rules hundreds of years old," Hitti said. "You know this,

Mani. I shouldn't have to explain! You have a duty to remember this. And the *zami*…the *zami* will be livid."

Mani fiddled with the stylus in his hand. "I do not care what the *zami* think."

"You should."

He didn't bother to reply. His stylus scritched, leaving neat lines and angles in the clay. Shadows on the tablet shifted and he knew Shahan and Hitti had just exchanged glances.

"As the sun rises, decisions are made," Shahan quoted. "Sometimes tom fool stupid ones. What ague caught your brain to make you do a thing like that, Mani?"

"No ague," he said.

His old friend sighed. "Did it at least make a difference? Taking your wife, I mean. Did the swimmers even notice?"

"That is not the point!" Hitti snapped.

"I'm just interested," Shahan said. "I mean, anything that drags a straight answer out of them is good, right? I'd juggle half a dozen fruit knives if I thought it would help."

"Stick to chickpeas," Mani said.

"So, did it help?"

He sighed and put the stylus down. "No. It didn't help. I'm not actually sure what happened."

Hitti closed his eyes. "What did they do?"

"It was Hanno, the new one. He thought Isha was a man at first. Then he refused to believe she was my wife, and when he did…" Mani shrugged. "He vanished. Great big splash and he was gone."

"You might have done a lot of damage today," Hitti said in his distant-wind voice. "The Goddess only knows how long it will take to repair it."

He turned and hobbled away, leaving Mani to grimace at his tablet. Hitti was most likely right. If Mani had been thinking he would have told the swimmer that Isha was a servant, a man even. The conversation was meant to be between scholar and Sea-Goat, nobody else. Mani had allowed Isha to become important to the talk, and now the swimmers might not speak to anyone for a month. Or longer. It had happened before.

"Don't worry about it," Shahan said. "The voice of the frog makes the marsh, and that won't change. A day or two and everything will be back to normal."

"The *zami* are trying to force me to abandon my wife and marry a Scented Woman," Mani said. "One man has died over this already. Now I might have put a split between scholars and swimmers that will last months. And moreover, there's a Mad King rushing down on us with a massive army on his heels, and Ra'im just issued a call-up of adult men." He made a final mark and set the tablet aside. "Nothing will be normal for a long time."

Shahan shrugged and sat down, propping his sandals on the table. "The *zami* missed you, my friend, but they caught me. Now I'm married to a failed acolyte whose brains don't match her zeal. She complains when I leave chickpeas on the floor and keeps nagging me to ask questions of the swimmers who I might not even see for some time now. Also, the Mad King matters as much to me as he does to you. Do you hear me complaining?"

"No. But then, I hear your Temple wife is great in bed."

"Oh, she is, she is. In the dark I can't even see her nose. Come on, Mani." The other man swatted him on the shoulder. "Don't be so hard on yourself. Have some fun. Go to a Scented House, drink a cup of beer, and enjoy the day."

"If I wanted a Scented Woman, I would have let the priestesses marry me to Elessa," he said.

Shahan's eyes went wide. "They offered you *Elessa*? And you turned them down? You must be crazed."

"Maybe I am." He stood and picked up the two tablets he'd written. "But I've spent nearly a week trying to convince Isha that she's not cursed. What will she think if I abandon her?"

"You've begun to care for her," Shahan said. When Mani only shrugged, he added, "Maybe she is cursed. Did you think of that?"

Mani was suddenly tired of this. "Warn Darsal about the swimmers before he goes out to the pier this evening. If there's a problem let me know, please. It's my fault if anything happens, so I'll try to fix it. And Shahan?"

The other scholar looked up at him.

"Curses can be lifted," Mani said.

CHAPTER EIGHTEEN

THE STREETS WERE crammed. Everyone had come out to talk and to listen to rumours, and talk about them, too. Debt slaves stood with artisans, housewives with merchants, children with soldiers. Even the construction teams hung from their scaffolds to exchange news with people on the street. They still whistled whenever a pretty girl walked by, though.

Even the threat of war couldn't change that.

Mani wove through it all, trying to keep an eye out for any priestess who came too close—or anyone who did. A knife in the street might be the next thing they tried, and it needn't be a *zami* who made the thrust. Udar had nearly died that way. The crowd was too dense though, and Mani couldn't avoid being bumped and barged as he worked his way along.

"Watch it, mister."

"You whine like a dog," Mani said. The words were thrown over his shoulder because he was already past and moving away. He heard a splutter, but then the speaker was lost in the throng.

Mani had done what he could to be safe. He'd left the Guild through a window, crossed a courtyard, and hauled himself over a wall and into the alley beyond. The wall was five feet high, and Mani had hardly been able to climb it. He was a scholar, not a farmer, and not used to physical exertion. Udar would laugh until he split if he heard about it.

Mani did not plan to tell him.

"The King has to summon men to the army," someone said. "There won't be time to train them if he doesn't."

"And who will mend the ditches?"

"They're already repaired," the first man answered blithely.

They were never fully repaired. Always there was another course of bricks to replace, or silt to dig out of a reservoir. Branches to cut and reeds to tie in bundles for a roof to stop water evaporating away in the sun. The work would be nearly done, nearly complete, and then the Flood would come and fill the caverns and ditches with water. By the time it was gone the bricks would be crumbling, the channels blocked with mud, and everything had to be done again.

He turned right, down a snaky street so narrow that you could step from your doorway to one opposite without setting foot on the road itself. If a Temple-sent assassin found him here then Mani was done for, no question. Any other route took him past the Immaru Temple, which loomed over the rooftops one street to his left, and that was worse. Twitcher and Bones might not be there, peering down at the crowds for a sight of him, but Mani had become nervous now. He had to weigh one chance against another and choose which risk to take, and he didn't think he was very good at it.

"I'm a scholar," he muttered as he sidled round a corner. "Not a schemer of intrigues."

He emerged from the alley into a wider street, with the north gate just visible over the crowd. Halfway to it he worked his way to the other side of the road and reached the steps of the Spilled Salt. Nobody had tried to kill him or even shouted his name. Either his care was paying off, or he was jumping at shadows. He jumped up the steps and burst into the tavern to find it crammed to bursting. Someone swore as Mani knocked his arm.

"Sorry," he said, and hurried on before the drinker could complain. People were jammed tighter than reeds in a bundle, and Mani had to wriggle his way around the walls to make any progress at all. Halfway around he spotted Ramsi working the bar, and a bit further on he caught sight of Isha at a corner table. His heart seemed to lift inside him.

She shouldn't be in such plain view, but never mind that. She was all right—worried, by her drawn expression, but all right. Mani shuffled sideways past a final drinker and came up by her stool.

"My dear," he said, "you really should have stayed upstairs."

She cried his name and clutched at him. "Mani, the priestesses! They're—"

"Good afternoon, scholar," a cold voice said. He turned to find them there yet again, Lamsi with her tics and Shusikil as cold as dead bones, rising from stools set against the wall.

§ § §

Mani cursed inside. "Why are you here, *zami?*"

"A priestess may go where she wishes," Shusikil said.

"I'm surprised Udar let you in."

"My father isn't here," Isha said. "He went to pick up some fish and hasn't come back. I'm worried."

Neither of the priestesses changed expression. Lamsi's eye flickered, but it always did that. There was no point asking what had happened to Udar. If they knew they'd lie, and if they didn't it was pointless, and either way they would be offended.

Flanking them were two big men, bare chested with maces on their backs. Offending the priestesses now wouldn't be a good idea, and Mani realised he didn't much care.

"I think I know the answer to this," he said, "but what do you want with me, *zami?*"

"Set aside your wife," Lamsi said.

"Elessa is still willing to marry you," Shusikil added. "You know she can bring you pleasure of the kind a man desires. We'll give you a house, on Maqatu Street by the west wall. Four bedrooms, and a garden for your children to play in. Nobles live in that street, scholar."

"What would I talk to them about?" Mani asked. "You see, *zami*, you're wrong. Elessa can't give me all the pleasures I desire. I want a wife I can talk to. Someone who can write, and most of all think."

"You have that with the scholars."

"That's not enough." He was tired of this. "*Zami*, I swore an oath. I won't throw that away as though it's of no account. Vows spoken before Eala are sacred, isn't that right?"

"You presume to lecture us on the teachings of Eala?" Lamsi spat.

"I tell you something you already know," Mani said. "You've abandoned it in your desire to control, that's all."

"Insolence will not help you, scholar."

"What will you do that you haven't already done? Attack us in the street? Bribe us?"

The bar was full of people and the chatter of voices. The two shoulder thumpers made enough of a wall that there was distance when Shusikil said, "The Temple's memory is long. We can wait years, scholar, for our revenge. You will never know what we might do, or when the blow will come. Poison in a cup." White lips curled at the corners. "A club in a dark street, or a throat filled with mud, and no one any the wiser."

"I wouldn't be sure about that," Isha said. "People know more than you give them credit for."

For Shusikil, Isha might not have existed. Her hot eyes never left Mani. "Or we will expel you from the Guild."

"You don't have that power. The king runs the Guild."

"To whom does the king listen? Who advises him?" She laughed, a brief cackle like breaking reeds. "Not you, scholar. But the *zami* are always there. Ra'im has bigger problems than you."

True. All true, and Mani had known the priestesses to cost men their jobs. The Guilds were run by the king, paid for by him and the Council, but the *zami* reached fingers into them all. If you crossed them, you lost your job. With your income gone you might end as a debt slave, working on the ditches, and even after that work would be hard to find. Mani and Isha were safe from that because her father would employ them in the Spilled Salt, and one day it would be theirs.

The threat made him furious. Years talking to swimmers had taught Mani to hide his feelings, to breathe until anger had passed. This time he had to bite the inside of his cheek to keep from swearing, and in his head, he cursed all priestesses to suffer forever in the ashes.

"You sons of dogs," Isha said.

The two priestesses ignored her. Shusikil pulled a bag from her belt and set it clinking on the counter.

"Lapis and silver," she said. "Yours, along with the house on Maqatu Street, if you take Elessa there as your bride. You will be wealthy, a man of standing. Your children may grow up to wed nobility, perhaps even join the five Great Houses of Aš-alam. It will be a life made of dreams."

"Or you can be expelled from the Guild," Lamsi said with a twitch. "You'll find work as a drudge in the fields, or serving drinks at the bar here, and never speak to a Sea-Goat again. Who will you think and write with then? What will your children grow to be, with a drudge for a father?"

"Make your choice," Shusikil said.

Chapter Nineteen

MANI BOWED HIS head. He couldn't imagine never speaking to a swimmer again. He'd wanted to do that since childhood, never really desired anything else. Not even a wife, until recently. His life was built around eking knowledge from the elusive folk of the marsh, taking two scraps of comment and using them to build an edifice that collapsed a year later. He could accept that, because one day someone would set foot on the Sea-Goats' island, and the answers would become as clear as light on water. It needn't even be Mani. He could not live with the loss of all that.

Yet Isha believed she was cursed, and if she lost the husband she had finally found, it would scar her forever.

"I choose Isha," he said, and realised the words fell into a silence sweeping across the bar. He turned.

There were soldiers at the door. Four of them, two on each side with their swords drawn. Another man was just mounting the last step, and drinkers in the tavern were going to one knee, mugs forgotten in their fists. Mani recognised him. The king.

"What is *he* doing here?" Shusikil asked. Her voice rang in sudden silence.

Mani didn't know. Then he saw the men behind Ra'im and recognised Udar, and his brain just gave up in confusion. He went to a knee and bowed his head. Aš-alam was small enough that sometimes your path crossed the king's, as it had the day Mani and Isha were married, but you still showed respect. Everyone was kneeling now except Ramsi, open-mouthed behind the bar, and the two priestesses. They only bent their necks, and that barely, as Ra'im came to a halt in front of them.

"Scholar," he said. There was a circlet in his hair, almost hidden by black curls except for rogue gleams of silver. "Have the Sea-Goats shared anything valuable of late?"

"Uh," Mani said. He took hold of himself with an effort. "I mean, no, my lord. Not really. Some news about the stars."

"Truly? What did they say?"

"They told me the stars are like islands in a vast sea, and the sea can be sailed," Mani replied. Whenever he discussed the swimmers, he lost all hesitancy and became more fluent than ever. "I believe they sailed it themselves. They may not be from our world at all."

"Fascinating, if true," Ra'im said. "It makes me proud of our city, that we can talk to the Sea-Goats. We're the only ones, aren't we? Nobody from Piqash or Eshkir can do this. Aš-alam is special."

"It is," Mani agreed.

"The goddess placed her feet here first," Ra'im said. "It was to our ancestors that she spoke her laws, which we've kept ever since. Laws like marriage, for example. The tenets say," he turned to the *zami*, "that we should hold the wedding vows sacred, don't they?"

Lamsi's cheek and eye twitched like nervous fleas. "Yes."

"And yet, you're trying to put this man and his wife apart," Ra'im said. "You want—*I am talking*—you want to throw aside their vows as though they mean less than nothing. That alone is shameful. But to do it to a scholar, one of the men whose work makes us the envy of all the cities of Engiru…" He shook his head. Behind him Udar was trying to fight a grin. "Nahal, what should I be doing now?"

"You should be preparing the city for attack," the second man said. He had the most magnificent beard Mani had ever seen, curled black and glistening with oil. Mani knew him, now that his brain had started to work. Nahal was an Elder, confidante of the king and Overseer of the Army. "Sarru-kin and his forces could be here in two weeks."

"There's something else, too. I'm sure I remember something else."

"The Flood, my lord."

"The Flood," Ra'im agreed. "Nothing is more important than that. The *zami* should be focused on it like a hawk on a mouse. Instead, I find them here, meddling in the personal lives of innocent citizens. I am disgusted, Nahal. Aren't you?"

"I'm appalled," the Elder said. His beard wagged up and down as he nodded. "Appalled."

"Marriage is Temple business," Shusikil said. Her voice was its usual croak, unaffected by nerves. "Not the king's. With respect, my lord, you overstep your bounds."

"My bounds," Ra'im repeated. "I see. And yet the scholars are funded from the king's purse, are they not?"

The bony woman's face was stone. "Yes."

"Then in this case I do have responsibility. Hear me, then. Scholar Kassu-Mani and his wife Isha are to be left alone. No *zami* will attempt to persuade them to part, or bribe them, or threaten them. Is that clear?"

"We have the right—"

"I asked," the king said, "if that was clear."

A moment, and then Shusikil bowed her twitching head. "It is, my lord."

"Good. I only hope neither of them meets with an…accident. A man drowned in mud in a dry ditch this week, I am told. Astonishing bad luck, wouldn't you say? I would have to make a thorough investigation if such misfortune befell a scholar."

Neither priestess spoke. Their expressions were blank, but fury blazed in their eyes.

"Then I will hope to be allowed to concentrate on more important matters," Ra'im said. "The Flood and the Mad King. Udar, I will expect you at the palace four mornings from now. Good day to you all."

He turned and went out, followed by Nahal and the four soldiers. He only took two, normally. Mani supposed that was a sign of the times. Enemies had used assassins before and would again. The Mad King might already have sent them. It was hard to know what to think.

Shusikil threw Mani a glare with blades in it, and then she and Lamsi strode away. The crowd had begun to stand again by then, people turning to look at Mani and the others as they did so, and the priestesses had to struggle through bodies to reach the doors. That wouldn't improve their mood.

"What just happened?" Mani asked the air.

"Papa made an offer," Isha said. She sounded awed and livid, both. "Didn't you, Papa? You weren't out buying fish, and you didn't meet the king by accident. You planned this."

Udar nodded. "They weren't going to leave you alone, Isha."

"Wait," Mani said. "Wait. What offer?"

"He's put himself forward as a captain when Ra'im calls the levy," Isha said. "Men over thirty are excused, which means Papa didn't need to do it. But he thinks the new soldiers will need veterans to lead them."

"They will," Udar said.

"But not you!" she flashed at him. "Not you, and not for me!"

He didn't look away from her rage. "It seemed best. I don't want to find my daughter at the bottom of a dry ditch with her throat stuffed with mud. I had a way to stop the *zami*, so I did."

"And you? What if you're the one in a ditch?"

"Better me than you. It was my choice, Isha. Besides, nothing is certain yet. There might not even be a levy."

That made Mani frown. "Why?"

"The Flood," Udar said. "If it comes early, Sarru-kin's soldiers will be caught by the rising waters. Many men will drown, and the army will disintegrate. On the other hand, if the Flood comes early and the ditches aren't fully repaired, we won't gather enough water to see us through the growing season. This time next year people will starve in their hundreds. So, what does the king do?"

"He waits," Mani said. He'd understood while Udar was still speaking. "To see what happens at Piqash."

"Where Sarru-kin is due in two days," the older man agreed. "It will take another two for news to travel to us. That's why Ra'im wants me at the palace four days from now."

"Indecision," Isha said, biting the words, "is not the best way to deal with the Mad King."

"I'm not sure there's a good way," Mani put in. "Or a good way out of any of this. Udar, second-father." He hesitated. "Thank you. I don't know how to say it better."

"You said it well enough," Udar answered. "You know, I could really use a cup of beer. Will you join me?"

Mani nodded. He felt Isha take his hand and draw him to the bar counter.

"You turned them down," she said. Her dark eyes were very wide. "You chose me, over everything they offered you."

He looked at her, this wife he'd found who bewildered the Sea-Goats. A clever woman who'd seen what her father had done before Mani understood it. "You're not cursed, Isha."

"What?"

"The *zami* peddle lies," he said. "That's one of them. Whoever Eala was, whatever the reason she chose Aš-alam, she wasn't as full of hate and bile as the priestesses. I won't be part of it."

She smiled after a moment, a little uncertainly, but still a smile, and she kissed him on the nose.

"It's over," she said.

CHAPTER TWENTY

A TRAITOR, AT the Scorpion Gate," Ra'im said. "Sarru-kin will have lost very few men. Very little time, either." His mouth twisted. "I'd hoped he would lose a lot of both at Piqash."

"The news is certain?" Udar asked.

"From a source I trust," Mannipa said. He'd been an Elder when Udar served in the army before, and he hadn't been young then. He must be seventy now, but he stood as straight as ever. Slanting brows hid his eyes in shadows. "We can rely on it."

Not much room for hope then. Udar asked the next, obvious question. "And the river?"

"Has begun to rise at last," the king answered. "Late, but not unusually so. The *zami* tell us the water rose one-inch last night."

An inch. There wasn't much room for hope in that, either. Sarru-kin was in Piqash, less than a mile from the Ranuna's high levees. He would know already that the river had started to surge, and he'd be ready for it. The man was mad, but he wasn't a fool.

Udar looked at Nahal.

"Sarru-kin is staging," the Overseer of the Army said. His beard really was tremendous. It deserved a rank of its own. "Our last word had him ready to move within a day. His men have collected every farmer's raft for miles around."

Not a fool, indeed.

They were in the king's palace, one of the lesser halls. Not the throne room, or a reception chamber. Just a modest side room, home to a few chairs and divans with a window that gave onto a garden. The trees offered sparse shade, their leaves thinned by months of drought.

A modest side room, but the divans were inlaid with silver, and a ruby gleamed on each arm. The walls were all carved, one with an eight-pointed star that symbolised Eala. It had an eye in the middle, again a ruby. The floor was cedar, brought all the way from the dragon-haunted valleys far up the Ranuna, near the mountains. Rich men paid fortunes for that wood, while poor men paid with their lives. Ra'im had a whole *floor* of it, in an antechamber of no importance at all.

"He could be across the river in hours, then," Udar said at length. "The Ranuna won't stop him."

"No," Nahal said. "The Mad King will reach us here. In less than a week, I would expect."

"And then?"

"Then we fight, of course. What would you expect?"

"We fight on the walls," Ra'im put in. "Not on the plain. Sarru-kin has too many men, too many chariots. In the open our army would be surrounded and cut apart."

"That did not work for Piqash," Nahal said.

"No. But they were betrayed."

"Anyone can be betrayed," Udar said.

That was the hard truth. However you planned, whatever you decided, everything could be torn to shreds by one rogue with a key to the wrong door. That must be what had happened in Piqash. Ra'im was right, though. To fight the host of Sarru-kin in the open would be suicide. They could only bar the gates, man the walls, and hope the Ranuna would make up for its late flood by flooding fast, to drown the army stranded outside.

Still, Udar wondered. Sarru-kin had known exactly how to take Piqash, just as he'd taken Kindar and Tibad. Either he really was guided by the god of war, or he had been planning this for a very long time. Which meant the question now wasn't how Aš-alam should fight him. It was how they discovered what he had planned for them.

"We're calling the levy, then," Udar said.

"Men are out announcing it in the streets now," Ra'im confirmed. "We'll need your service, Udar, as you promised. Is your oath still good?"

"You're my king, and I gave you my word. Of course it's still good."

"Spoken with a soldier's curt tongue," Ra'im smiled. "And also a decent man's honesty, so I'll overlook your bluntness. You have command of the north wall, Udar, including the River Gate. Recruits will be sent to you as soon as they're armed. Train them well."

"I will."

"We'll keep a room for your family in the Temple," Ra'im went on. He caught Udar's blank look and chuckled. "Oh, you don't know. At Piqash they turned the main Temple into a fortress. The city fell, but king Tarah-ti and his Elders are holed up in there, safe as bats. The Immaru Temple is much larger. We could hold that for a year."

"The windows—"

"Defences are in hand," the fourth man in the room said. He'd been lurking by the door, silent while the others spoke. "Windows can be bricked up, doors barricaded and barred. Inner doorways can be blocked. Anyone who breaks in will find themselves in a sealed room, except for a hole they must crawl through with their head and neck exposed."

"Yasmah-Bau, my Surveyor of Public Works," the king said. "I keep him around for his light wit and deft humour."

Udar snorted laughter. It was good to laugh, amid all this talk of war. After a long moment the corner of Yasmah-Bau's lip curved, very slightly.

"They hung Luduzi of Kindar from his own walls, in a cage," Ra'im said. He wasn't smiling now. Not at all. "With his eyes cut away, they hung him there to die. Sarru-kin should not have done that. He will pay for it, in this life or the next. I don't want that to happen to me, Bau, or my Elders. Fortify the Temple well."

The dry man bowed. "You may rely upon it, my lord."

The Mad King had let defeated soldiers join his army if they swore fealty. That was to push on towards Aš-alam. There was nowhere to go after here, no more cities as the land dwindled away to desert. If he conquered Aš-alam, he might decide he didn't need more men. What would be done to the captains of the beaten army then?

Udar did not want to find out. Tonight, he'd go to Isha and tell her she had a place in the Immaru Temple, and then he'd make every waking hour about keeping the Mad King out.

Chapter Twenty-One

"ECAUSE YOU LOVE me," Isha said.

Mani stirred. She was behind him, leaning over his shoulder. Her hair tickled his neck. "What?"

"Give me your caresses," she said.

He opened his eyes, all the way awake. "Having a wife brings a new surprise every day. What's this?"

"The wedding promise," she said. He could feel her breath on his ear. Her body was pressed against his back. "Remember? You, because you love me; pray, give me your caresses. My husband, who gladdens Eala's heart; pray, give me your caresses."

He turned his head. Isha looked at him with hair fallen over one eye and a blush on her cheeks, but she didn't drop her eyes.

"The night after we went to the marsh you showed me something," she said. "A trick you learned in the Scented Houses, you told me."

"Yes," he said.

"Could you show me again?"

Mani couldn't help laughing. When they were newly wed Isha would never have dared say something so brazen. She'd changed, in a week and a half. Well, so had he. Marriage did that to you.

She bit his ear and Mani's laughter stopped. "Will you show me?"

"Oh, yes," he said, rolling towards her.

Afterwards they lay together, Isha half across Mani's chest with her black hair fallen in front of her eyes. Her skin was hot against his. He closed his eyes and let himself feel that, inhale the scent of her, all the things it was so easy to forget when you watched. He remembered doing the same in the Scented House—with Elessa once, actually. It might have been a different man, living a different life to this.

"What are you thinking?" she asked.

He couldn't mention Elessa. "You've changed me, this last week and a half."

"Have I?"

"I think you know," Mani said. "This, for a start. The first night you and I lay next to each other like a pair of bricks. I didn't know how to speak with you or ask for…love. Now, we're playing Scented House games with hardly a blush."

"Oh, I blushed," she said. "And I will again, but it won't stop me asking. I think I might come to like this."

"You mean you don't already?"

"Shush." She shook her head and hair tickled his mouth. "You've changed me too, Mani. A fortnight ago, I believed I was cursed by the Goddess. Now I'm…not sure."

"And you wouldn't have asked, back then."

"No. I wouldn't." Isha nibbled his ear. "You must have learned other tricks in the Scented Houses."

"Yes," he said.

"Will you show them to me?" Her voice changed, and he thought she was blushing again. "All of them?"

"Now?" he teased. She swished hair across his mouth, and he twisted away, laughing. "All right! I'll show you. Not that I claim any great expertise."

"You could have learned more if you'd agreed to marry Elessa," she said.

"I didn't want Elessa."

"She's as hot-limbed as a woman can be."

Isha was teasing a little, but he thought there was something darker there too—fear perhaps, though the time for it was past. She didn't wear a veil anymore. Their marriage was confirmed. Still, Mani shifted until he could look at her, waiting for her to lift her head.

"So are you," he said.

Isha smiled like sun on water and then dropped her head so hair fell over her eyes again. "When do you speak to the swimmers again?"

"Tomorrow," he said. He'd embarrassed her and let her change the subject without argument. "In the evening."

"Can I come?"

"Do you want to?" he asked, surprised.

"I thought it was interesting," she said. "Hanno was…strange. I can't put my finger on how."

"Nobody can ever put their finger on anything where the Sea-Goats are concerned."

"Perhaps a woman will see something men miss."

"Perhaps," he agreed. It was true. He and Shahan had argued the point years ago, when they were training and were sure it would never matter anyway. Only scholars went to the pier, and scholars were always men. "You certainly got him to react the first time, didn't you?"

"That was just surprise."

"No," Mani said thoughtfully. "No, I don't think it was. Hanno was shocked, that's true, but there's more to it. I wish I could understand what."

He could feel her smile. "Nobody can ever put their finger on anything where Sea-Goats are concerned."

"And that," he said, smiling too, "is why I could never have married Elessa. You have wit. With her I'd have been bored before the veil came off."

"Not at night."

"All right," he said, "but the nights aren't exactly tedious for us, are they?"

"The mornings are quite interesting too," she retorted, and Mani was still laughing when someone started banging on the door.

They looked at each other. These days an unexpected knock could mean anything, and probably meant trouble. News of the Mad King, or a priestess returning with a new threat or promise. Even a summons for scholars to join the army after all, since Sarru-kin's army was so big. After a moment the thumps were repeated. Mani sighed.

"Be careful," Isha said as she slid off him. Eala's Footfalls, even the feel of that made Mani want her all over again. He found yesterday's kilt and belted it on, creases and all.

"Every time," he said, going down the hall. The front door was barred, and he paused with his hand on the latch. "Who is it?"

"Open up. There's a breeze out here, and someone's dog has crapped on your porch, did you know?"

"Shahan?"

"Of course it's Shahan. Open up, you idiot."

Mani opened the door. His friend slid inside before it was all the way back. "You took your time."

"Is there a hurry?"

"I don't like to be on the street too long. I might be dragged into the army before they know who I am. Or they might not care, actually. Besides, are you sure the *zami* have given up on you?"

"Yes," Mani said. He frowned. "I suppose no, in fact."

"There you go, then."

"All right, you're afraid to be outside. What brings you thundering on my door in the morning then?"

"Work," Shahan said. "You're wanted at the Guild. It isn't morning, by the way. Noon was half an hour ago."

"Really?"

"And Tash-Yal found no Sea-Goat to talk with when he went out to the pier today," Shahan said. "In fact, nobody has spoken to a swimmer since you took your wife out there. Quite a coincidence, isn't it?"

Mani didn't answer. It was no coincidence at all, obviously enough. Hanno really had been more than startled when he found out who Isha was. The encounter had changed something and not, it seemed, for the better. Worry wormed into Mani's belly.

"Will they expel you?" Isha asked. He turned to find her standing in the doorway to their bedroom, wearing a dress with her hair pinned back. She looked a respectable matron, not someone who'd just been bare to her skin and playing bed sports.

"I doubt it," Mani said. "That's very rare."

"But for this," Shahan put in, not very helpfully, "you never know."

Isha came down the passage and put a hand on Mani's cheek. "Don't worry. I am with you forever."

There was something in her dark eyes that he didn't recognise, couldn't name. Too many emotions all mixed up together, in her and in him, like mud swirling in water. Words died on his tongue. Mani went to dress and then walked to the Guild in air already cooling as the Flood began to rise.

Chapter Twenty-Two

ALL THE DOORS and windows were open, letting air flow through the Guild. It stirred drowsy heat from corners, shifting dust that hadn't moved for months. Sunshine made brilliant squares on walls and floors. The spirit felt lighter, the day brighter. It was always the same when the Flood came, and with it the cooler mountain air. The oppression of months of unchallenged heat was over once more.

Mani felt it, even through his worry.

They waited for him in the dining hall. Hitti in the middle, with Tash-Yal on one side and Darsal on the other. They were all Mani's friends, or had been. Guests at his wedding. He wasn't sure what they were now. They'd given their lives to studying the Sea-Goats, and if Mani had ruined that, he couldn't expect much from them but rage.

"Sit down," Hitti said.

Mani sat. He felt like a naughty acolyte, sent to a stool facing the wall until he was ready to apologise. Except that this time an apology would not be enough to help him.

"You know that no swimmer has spoken to any scholar since they saw your wife," Hitti said.

Mani nodded.

"I assume you accept that cause and effect implies it was your action which caused this."

"Yes," Mani said. Shahan was gone, he realised. His friend had walked with him to the Guild but then made himself scarce. Well, that was Shahan. Never around when the debt fell due.

"Can you tell us anything?" Hitti asked. "Where the Sea-Goats have gone, perhaps?"

"We talked about that," Darsal said. "The Sea-Goats are still in the marsh. I saw one myself, when I was out there yesterday. He popped up a hundred yards away, saw me, and went under again."

"It was the same for me this morning," Tash-Yal said. Hitti pursed wizened lips but didn't interrupt. "A swimmer looked at me and vanished. What did you *do*, Mani?"

"You know what I did," he answered. "I put it down on my tablets, all of which I'm sure you've read twenty times since."

"Then you missed something."

"I'm not known for missing things," he said. "Or making mistakes in my records. You all know that."

The three men exchanged glances. They did know that. No scholar lasted long if he made that sort of mistake. *A point to me*, Mani thought, and waited. He didn't think they were going to throw him out anymore. They would have done it right away, if that were their plan. They wanted something, so he'd let them get to it in their own time.

"Even so, none of us has spoken to a swimmer for three days," Hitti said. "And the fault for that, as you already accepted, is yours. What are you going to do about it?"

"Hitti, if the Sea-Goats aren't talking to scholars, there isn't much any of us can do."

"Find something," Darsal said. He really was a friend, the man who'd warned Mani that the priestesses were making plans to fix him up with a Temple girl. But he was a scholar first. "You put this wrong, now put it right. Swim out there if you must. Dive down to their towns, if they have any. I don't care. But deal with it."

He sighed. "Where would I have learned to swim?"

"Teach yourself," Tash-Yal said.

"And what if I can't fix it?"

"Then I suggest," Hitti said bluntly, "that you learn to run the tavern your wife used to work at."

They would expel him, then. After everything, when the *zami* had failed, it would be his own colleagues who threw him out. It was hard to believe, but Mani looked at their expressions and knew they meant it. All three of them had a haunted air, the expressions of men who were afraid they would never experience joy again. Like priestesses suddenly deaf to the words of Eala. That was a strange simile to come to mind.

He got to his feet. "Thank you for your time, gentlemen. I will do my best, of course."

"Don't be like that," Darsal began, but Hitti cut him off.

"You have two days," the ancient said. "That will take you past the time when you can be made to join the army, at least. Whatever you've done, I wouldn't send you to your death in battle."

"That's so kind," Mani said. Anger had begun to bubble inside him, and it was all he could do not to kick the chairs over and bellow in these men's faces. He turned and went out, fuming his way back down the corridor and into the main hall, where he found Shahan waiting. The other man held a tablet, but he wasn't paying it any attention.

"What did they—"

Mani brushed past him without a word. None of this was Shahan's fault, but just then Mani didn't feel he could speak to anyone without shouting. He went out into the street, aware at once of a breeze on his face. People waited half the year for the air to feel like that. Down by the marsh it would be wonderful, a lightness to the world that showed in stirring reeds and the chirrup of cicadas.

"How am I supposed to swim to the Sea-Goats?" he asked of no one. He couldn't, of course. Hardly anyone knew how to swim. There was never a reason to learn. He stopped still, thinking.

There had never been reason to take a woman out to the marsh, either. Sometimes there was no reason for a hundred years until, all at once, there was. Once, long ago, there must have been no reason for a man to speak to a Sea-Goat either, but someone had. Once done, people kept doing it. That was how traditions began.

"They kept doing it," Mani said. He smiled to himself. Once you'd begun, you kept going the same way.

He'd turned towards the marsh when he emerged from the Guild. Now he retraced his steps and set out for home, and for Isha. Taking her to the swimmers got him into this. Maybe taking her back would get him out.

§ § §

"This might make it worse," Isha said.

"I'm not sure how it could be worse," Mani replied.

Three days without a word from a Sea-Goat. They had popped their heads out of the water, so they must still be there, but they wouldn't talk. They wouldn't even come to the pier. It had happened before, but nobody had any idea why. This time they did, and they had a man to blame.

"It might make things better too," he said.

She nodded slowly. "I suppose. I admit, I wonder why the swimmers come up to look when someone rings the bell."

"That's what they've always done."

"No. From what you say, they've always either come to talk or ignored it. Not this half and half reaction."

"I don't know what you mean."

"Think, husband. You'd see it, if you weren't so full of anger at your fellow scholars." She put a hand on his arm. "The swimmers come up to look. What are they looking *for?*"

"Me," he said after a moment. "Or rather, us. You."

"Yes. Maybe."

They walked in silence for a while. The fields were empty now, the workers and debt slaves called away to train with the army. As though a few days practice with spears and shield would make them a match for Sarru-kin's battle-hardened soldiers. Many of these men were going to their deaths. Mani supposed that for a debt slave, anything that shortened your service and made you free again was worth the risk.

Dust stirred in cool air, blowing down from the mountains with the Flood. Devils danced across the ground and died.

"I thought you said this was a bad idea," Mani said.

"It is. They gave you two days. Today you should go alone, and if that doesn't work, bring me with you tomorrow."

He rubbed his jaw. "That feels wrong to me. Like a half and half reaction."

"Clever man," she said. "All right, Mani. We'll do it your way. Just remember one thing."

"What?"

"If we end up running the Spilled Salt, you won't know what needs doing," she said, "so that, we'll do *my* way."

He managed a smile.

Isha looked different without the veil. She hadn't left the house without it since their marriage, until two days ago. Her features were softer than he remembered, finer. Odd how he could have forgotten those things when he saw her face unveiled at home.

She moved differently too, her stride firmer, her head up. There was a new confidence in her. Born out of victory over the *zami*, he thought. Maybe the belief that she was cursed had begun to wither, a weed burning away in the sun. He hoped so. Carrying the weight of that had left scars.

They came to the reeds, whispering in a breeze, and beyond it the pier and the bell.

"Do the same as last time," he said. She already held the tablets, a pair of them made with fresh clay. "Don't speak."

She nodded. "Eala's footfalls go with you."

He went down the pier. The rising river had made no difference here yet. Water still covered the bell almost to the top. Mani pulled on the cord, feeling vibrations in the boards under his feet. A moment, and he pulled again, then let go.

He didn't know how to do anything but talk to the swimmers. He seemed to have a talent for that. An odd thing to be good at, but some people never found anything where they excelled, and Mani had always been content. The thought of losing it forever was…hard.

He had Isha now. There was something peculiar there as well, too new and unexpected for him to put his finger on yet. A change in who she was, or how they were together. Hard to pin down. Her being there made it easier to think of losing all this. A little easier, anyway. He still couldn't imagine a life without Sea-Goats in it.

Something popped out of the water.

It was fifty yards away, but that was a Sea-Goat head. It vanished again at once. Ripples spread and faded away.

The sun was growing hot. Cool mountain air helped, but the peak of the day could still burn, and Mani had left his hat at home again. Nothing moved in the water. He started to turn and then stopped.

He would suffer in the ash forever if he lost the Sea-Goats. As a child, he'd read all he could about them, from recent stories to the tales of ancient days more myth than fact. He had read a tale of the days when Sea-Goats had legs as well as tails and came into the city to hold council with kings. Nonsense, of course, but the story caught him, and from then on Mani wanted to know about the swimmers.

He began to pester scholars at the doors of the Guild until they found themselves telling him snippets of this and that, phrases spoken and hints dropped by accident. Hitti had been one of those men, half-amused and half-impressed, not sure whether to take the boy into his confidence or tell him to run on home.

There was nothing Mani had ever wanted to do except be here, on this jetty in the sunshine, waiting to hear what a swimmer might say next. Waiting for the chance to sail with them to their home, and there learn all the answers. How did you live, when the only dream of your life had died?

He looked back at Isha, watching him from the shore, and wondered. *The only dream of your life.* Was that true anymore? He might build a life, something new, made of family and children and time. Maybe he would learn to move on.

The marsh was quiet. Mani sighed and took a step away.

Something exploded out of the lagoon beside the pier, a shape hidden by curtains of flying water. Mani ducked instinctively. By the time he looked around, drenched to the skin, he saw only a fluked tail an instant before it vanished again. He stared.

A head emerged from the water. It was a Sea-Goat, one who had come here dozens of times through the years and never spoken a single useful word. "Hello, scholar."

"Barek," he said. "Thanks for the soaking. It's all right," he added to Isha as she started down the pier. "It's all right. Go back."

"It wasn't me who wetted you," Barek said. He was looking past Mani though, towards the shore. "Is that your wife?"

"Yes."

"Truly?"

"Truly," Mani said.

The swimmer pushed himself higher, so his shoulders and chest emerged. Mani had never seen that before or heard of it. Barek looked at Isha for a long moment and then sank down again. In the sunshine the ridges on his head were as pale as his eyes. There was a smell of sea floor and dead fish, cloying to the nose.

"You've honoured us," Barek said.

Mani couldn't think what to say. Not a word. He might have stood there all day if another figure hadn't erupted from the water, with such force that he stood on his thrashing tail before he fell back. "I told you! Barek, I told you all!"

"You did," the older swimmer said. The other had crashed back into the water in another fountain of spray. "And you were right. But I had to see it to believe."

"They named me a liar." Hanno surfaced again, somersaulting half in and half out of the water. "Scholar, they said I must not have seen what I thought I saw and called me a fool. I would have been cast out if you hadn't come again."

"I know the feeling," Mani said. It was hard not to share some of the young Sea-Goat's joy. "The same would have happened to me."

"Then those who command you are fools."

He smiled. "After today, I think you might be right."

"Hush, Hanno," the older swimmer said. He had still not taken his gaze from Isha. "Will you honour us further, scholar? Will you allow us to speak with your wife, before we speak with you?"

There wasn't any way to refuse. Somehow Isha was important to the Sea-Goats, in a way Mani didn't understand. No, that was wrong. The swimmers had always known the scholars were married, that they raised children. It was bringing Isha here that mattered. Seeing her. What that changed Mani didn't know, but he could see nothing to do but go on.

"Of course," he said. She was close enough to hear and came at once, no sign of unease in her step.

"Wives are life," Barek said. He nudged himself closer to Hanno, bumping the younger male. "Men play, but they become fathers and play must end."

"Are you a father?"

"No," Barek answered. "I wasn't thought worthy. Hanno may be one day, if he is well thought of."

Who were the wives? Females had been mentioned before, but it was rare, very rare. Mani didn't think they'd ever been referred to as wives. Did the Sea-Goats have a marriage ceremony? Did the females bear children as human women did? Wean them, raise them? He couldn't hold back any longer. He opened his mouth to speak.

"Tell us of your children," Hanno chirruped. He sounded like a child, all excitement and no restraint. Barek moaned in his throat and rose even higher than before, tail thrashing. The scent of dead fish was strong again.

Mani hesitated, his words unsaid. The air had changed when Hanno spoke.

He fell into the habit of the scholar—if in doubt, say nothing and wait. Silence can be a tool like any other.

"We don't have any," Isha said. The glance she gave Mani was suddenly shy. He remembered this morning, and three nights ago, and thought he understood why.

"No children? Yet your husband risks you here?"

Her turn to pause. "Is it a risk?"

"It's always dangerous for a wife to leave her home," Barek said. "But you haven't even had children yet. If you died before birthing, your future would die too, and your husband's with you."

"Is that why your wives stay on your home island?" Mani asked. He couldn't stay silent any longer. "To keep them safe?"

"No. Just the women."

He frowned, trying to work that out. "Is there a difference?"

"Of course," Hanno said. His voice was a song, thrumming with rhythm. "Of course. Wives can't swim."

§ § §

"Do you see?" he asked Isha on the road back. Mani was almost dancing, too full of excitement to be still. Rather like Hanno flinging himself out of the water and turning somersaults, thrilled to be vindicated. "Wives can't swim. That implies their women can, until they marry."

"Yes," she said. "I see."

"Or until they have children." He jittered as he walked, blood and thoughts fizzing through him. "I wonder what they do to them. Crop their tails, perhaps."

"Or kill them."

He looked at her, appalled.

"How would you know?" Isha asked. "They don't give straight answers, and what they do say might not mean what we think it does. Remember what Barek said? *If you died before birthing your future would die too.* That suggests that dying after giving birth isn't important. After their wives have offspring, the males might think of their life as complete."

He wanted to deny it, wanted to argue. He couldn't find a way. She really was clever. Mani rubbed his eyes and nodded.

"You'll keep your job," she said, comforting him. "Don't worry. The answers may yet come."

Yes. He could keep going to the pier. The Sea-Goats were still slippery, but not as evasive as before. He'd earned some trust, by accident, but still. Mani found he was smiling.

113

Chapter Twenty-Three

THE STREETS WERE different now.

No teams of debt slaves hauled bricks for the ditches or bitumen for walls. The scaffolding stood empty, except for a few older men with missing fingers and callused hands. Every man of fighting age had been called to the army. It wasn't compulsory. There was a choice.

They had chosen to go. For the debt slaves that was a given. Instead of another five years working off arrears, you could be free for as little as a week's work, and a hero besides. If you lived. The labour slave's life was dangerous, and by the time a man had cleared his slate he might be lame in one leg from falling bricks or have fingers too twisted to write again. Battle was a more intense risk, but a briefer one.

A roll of bone dice. Win and you've won everything. Lose and it didn't matter anymore.

Aš-alam waited for the Mad King.

"He's at the river," a grizzled man told Mani from his perch on a scaffold. He hung there like a scrawny bird, chewing something nameless on one side of his mouth. "Crossin' it, they say."

"Do they, now."

"Be here in two days, if that's true."

"Yes," Mani said, moving on.

Two days, perhaps three, depending how fast the river rose. Usually the Flood came slowly, a few inches a day. Engiru was so flat that even so little meant water flowing across the whole land, marsh to western hills, but there were always little bumps that stayed dry for one more day. Youths would paddle out to them with their slingshots and slaughter rats that had taken refuge there, chittering in their thousands. The poorer half of the city survived on rat stew for a week, and rodents didn't gnaw through the storehouses for another year.

But sometimes the water rose like something out of the old stories, when Mesannipa built his boat with six decks and survived a deluge that covered the world. One morning Aš-alam would wake to find itself an island in a shining sea, all the way to the horizon. In those years slingshots went unused and the rats drowned.

Soldiers might drown too, if it happened that way, but such a Flood came one year in twelve, maybe fifteen. Mani had seen it twice. He didn't think this year would be a third.

"And if it does, Sarru-kin will probably be ready for it," he told Isha. "He seems to have prepared for everything. He might almost have a monstrous ship, like Mesannipa."

"That was always a silly story," Isha said. "Papa told me a ship with six decks would collapse under its own weight."

"I'm not an engineer," Mani answered, "but that sounds right to me."

Labourers still worked in one place, though. The Immaru Temple crawled with them, even at night when torches burned in long rows. Mani saw the glow through his window in the dark and heard the thump of hammers and clatter of the scaffolds going up or coming down. The noble families were still in their own homes, waiting for the noise to die down before they moved to the Temple. It was hard to persuade Isha to go now, to the room Ra'im had set aside, while that was true.

"A wife's place is with her husband," she said when Mani mentioned it, and that was that.

Sometimes he thought the scholars didn't care about all this. Other times he thought they hadn't noticed. All they cared about now, night and day, asleep or awake, was the Sea-Goats.

"It's not my turn," Shahan had said earlier. "But we're all going out whenever we can, now the swimmers are talking to us again."

"Yes," Mani said diplomatically. He didn't mention the person standing with his friend, but then Shahan did anyway.

"Tauth is coming with me," he said. "We figure that if the Sea-Goats are excited by Isha, they'll be excited by Tauth too. I mean, what's not to like?"

The axe-nosed woman smiled like a cat that knew a secret. Well, she might think she did. People who believed they could predict the Sea-Goats were always surprised in the end. Not even scholars knew what they would do next. A failed *zami* was just guessing.

"Good luck," Mani said. He moved aside to let them past, careful not to smile. Tauth might imagine something triumphant in it, a hint that Mani was smug at having beaten the priestesses before. They could take one tic and turn it into a story.

He went down the corridor to the House of Tablets. He found Hitti there, etching letters into a slab, and Darsal eating lentils and mustard. Both beamed when they saw Mani.

"My boy!" Hitti said. He fumbled with a cane as he got to his feet. "Wonderful! What you did…I never thought to see it."

"Most of it is only supposition," Mani said. "We need to learn more before we can confirm it."

"We always need to learn more," the ancient agreed. "But what a start, lad, what a start."

The start had been long ago. Scholars had studied Sea-Goats for hundreds of years, and they probably were studied in return. There had never been much trust, on either side. Humans tried to tease and trick, swimmers evaded and confused. Mani saw a picture in his mind, of a swimmer watching from the reeds as scholars talked by the shore.

"I always thought the females were in the marsh, but hidden," Darsal said. "You proved me wrong yesterday. The ones here are bachelors, some past marriageable age, others too young. A little like a crew of sailors. Some new boys marry and leave the sea. Those who don't, grow old there."

"Perhaps," Hitti said, fussy as old men were. "Perhaps. Though imposing our own social assumptions on Sea-Goats is usually unwise."

"What do you think, Mani?"

They were treating him as an equal. More, as someone to be listened to, whose words held wisdom and insight in equal measure. Part of Mani was pleased by that. He had worked for it, all his life, since he was just a boy full of questions.

Part of him knew it had just been luck. It started with Darsal's warning, the beginning of a cycle of events worthy of the great tales, if they'd happened to a king. Mani had hurried into marriage and then found himself threatened by *zami* for it. To protect his wife, he had taken her to the pier. Only for that. He'd had no idea, not the faintest hint, what it would lead to.

Even so, there was something else. Anger.

"I think you're the two men who threatened to have me expelled," he said, "and it's to your shame that today you act as though it never happened."

Darsal bowed his head in what might be embarrassment. Hitti's eyes went hard, and his cane rattled on the floor as he gripped it tighter. "You've no right to speak to me that way."

"Years ago, I learned that the Sea-Goats' island lies in fresh water," Mani said. "You called that the biggest insight of your lifetime, Hitti, do you remember? I visited four other cities to talk about it, at the Temples' request. I even met Sarrukin, though he was only an Elder then. And yesterday you behaved as though all that was nothing, less than dung on your sandals, to be scraped off and thrown aside rather than be borne another moment."

"Stop it."

"Now I've found out that Sea-Goat wives are not the same as Sea-Goat women," he went on. "I've found that the swimmers in our marsh are bachelors, or something akin to that. No scholar has learned as much in two hundred years. No, right? You had no right to say what you did to me, Hitti, or to threaten me. I expect that from the *zami*. I had hoped that a man of education might have learned better."

"You're right," Darsal said. His voice was hoarse. "You're right, Mani, and I'm sorry. I was afraid. There's been so much lately, with the Mad King and… never mind. It's no excuse. I'm sorry."

He sighed. "Accepted, Darsal. You warned me what the *zami* had planned. I owe you for that."

The other scholar managed a smile.

"For myself," Hitti said. "I have nothing to apologise for. I'm senior scholar, and I did what was best for the Guild. One man's future doesn't matter compared to the work we do."

"Two weeks ago, I might have agreed with you."

"Then what's changed, Mani?"

"I have," he said. He realised as he spoke that it was true. "Marriage has changed me. One man's future always matters, Hitti, and our work is meaningless if we lose ourselves in it so deeply that we forget to care."

"What I care about is us talking to the Sea-Goats again," Hitti said, "and for that I thank you. However, you should never have taken your wife to the marsh. It was the action of a fool. Eala has blessed you and you were lucky. Be glad of your fortune and learn from your mistakes."

"As you have?" Mani asked. "In all your years, what have you learned of the swimmers, senior scholar?"

Hitti glared at him and whirled. Mani thought he would leave, but the old man limped back to the table, sat, and began to etch marks on his tablet. They were deep marks this time, driven in until the clay ridged around the letters. School-children were taught to avoid that, but at this moment Hitti probably didn't care.

Mani and Darsal shared a glance and shrugged at the same moment. Mani couldn't help a smile, and he was glad when it was returned.

§ § §

Word came from the river that afternoon. Sarru-kin's army was crossing the Ranuna on dozens of farmer's rafts, thirty or forty men on each. Even with supplies, that wouldn't take long.

"In the time the news took to reach us, he'll have made it over," Shahan said. He fished in a bag of wheat cakes and came out with half of one, crumbled along one side. "He moves fast."

"We knew that already," Mani said.

They were in the Spilled Salt, run by Ramsi now that Udar was with the army. The man had been with the priestesses yesterday, taking his brother to the Towers of Silence to be laid out for the crows to eat. How that must have been, speaking the phrases of sorrow beside the *zami* who had drowned Ruen in mud, Mani couldn't imagine.

The tavern was almost empty. People were staying home, hoarding their coins. Aš-alam felt like a city already under siege.

118

Hammers still rang out from the Immaru Temple. There were cries from the wall too, where men trained with sword and spear. Real ones—there'd been no time to make wooden fakes. Udar had told Isha it was a balance. If practice was too realistic, men would be injured before the invaders came, but not realistic enough and the same men would die quickly in the battle. Four of his recruits had been wounded too badly to fight. Udar said that was good.

Not for them, it wasn't.

Feet tramped outside in the street. Some of the captains took their men on runs, to build up stamina they said, though Mani didn't think they had enough time for that to matter. The footfalls peaked and then faded. Shahan took a morose sip of beer.

"I forgot to ask," Mani said. "How did it go at the marsh with your wife there to help?"

Shahan made a face. *"Don't ask."*

"That bad?"

"A Sea-Goat came," the other man said. "The one called Arvad, you know? Cranky even for a swimmer."

"I know him."

"He was bouncing in the water like a boy with a sweetcake." Shahan snorted. "I've never seen a Sea-Goat like that. Words fell out of his mouth as fast as he could speak them, and you know what? All he wanted to talk about was you and your wife. Isha, Isha, Isha."

"Didn't he see Tauth?"

"Oh, he saw her. Blinked a couple of times and then went back to talking about you." Shahan drained his mug. "You can buy me another one, if you don't mind. You're the man of the moment, while I am going to have a horrible ear-bashing tonight."

"It's not your fault."

"Thank you for saying that. I *know* it's not my fault, you chattering imbecile, it's yours. You dodged marriage to a Temple wife, and that made them angry, let me tell you. Then you went and cracked some secrets out of the swimmers, and now the *zami* are absolutely livid. You're the toast of educated society, and they can't tie a string to you. Now they're running about like hens in a panic. Who do they shout at about this? My wife. And who does she shout at?"

"Well, you, I suppose."

"You suppose right. Tauth wanted to come with me today because she thought the swimmers might take to her as they took to Isha. It was meant to solve problems, not add to them. You realise Tauth isn't going to touch me in bed for weeks? Not in any of the interesting places." He pushed his mug towards Mani. "Please buy me a beer. I'll need it."

"You're a married man now, and your pay is higher. Buy your own beer." Mani drank off the last of his cup. "I'm sorry things are tough, but I did try to warn you, remember?"

"Thanks," Shahan said sourly. "That really helps."

"Look, just don't go home. Spend the night at a Scented House and it might be better in the morning. Tauth can't stay angry forever."

Shahan looked at him.

CHAPTER TWENTY-FOUR

ISHA SAT WITH her feet in the water, leaning back on palms that rested on the pier.

"My father runs a tavern," she said. "A place where people go to drink. He's done well in life."

"It's hard to imagine," Hanno said. Folded arms rested on the planks of the jetty. Now and then he let himself sink under the water, just enough to wet his skull. "People paying for a drink. Money."

"Sea-Goats don't use money?"

He shook his scaled head. "Why do you call us that? Sea-Goats. You think of us like animals."

"What should we call you?"

The right question, asked in the right neutral tone. Isha would have made an excellent scholar if she'd been born a man.

Further down the pier Mani stood with his stylus poised over a tablet, his third of the morning, and heard Hanno say, "Our name for ourselves is the Puradu. We are the Pure."

"Why that?"

"We are what we are," Hanno said. "All of that, and only that. Nothing else. Ourselves, unspoiled."

"I wish we could be like that."

Out in the marsh a Sea-Goat head popped up, then another, watching the group at the pier.

"Maybe you are," Hanno said. "Maybe humans are just like that. Maybe an unspoiled man is cruel and selfish by nature."

"A lot of us are," Isha agreed. "Men, and women too."

"Yes. You always were."

"How long have you been visiting us?"

"I've only been here three weeks."

"No," she said, laughing. "I meant you, the Sea-G—the Puradu. When did you start to visit mankind?"

"I like it when you laugh," Hanno said. He pushed off the pier and went into a backwards somersault, only half in the water so his tail fluked slapped at the surface as he turned.

That was the third tablet finished. Mani put it down and grabbed the fourth one, the last, as Hanno resurfaced and floated back to the jetty.

"I like it when you do that," Isha said, smiling. "Well? When did your people first visit mine?"

She would have made an excellent scholar, but Isha hadn't been trained. She'd never learned when to pry and when to let an issue pass, so what she did was from instinct alone. This time she was wrong. When a Sea-Goat dodged a question, the right approach was to move on, circle around, and come back to the matter later. That might be after a week, or a month. It might mean the question was taken up by the next scholar to use what had been your office, thirty years later, when the tablets you'd etched were crumbling at the edges and scriveners were ready to copy them out.

"Here, nearly a thousand years ago," Hanno said.

Mani managed to close his mouth.

"You've been in the marsh that long?"

He nodded. "We prefer fresh water. We can travel through salt, but fresh water is…like home. We can't use the rivers here, though. Once there were crocodiles and hippos, hard to avoid in shallow waters. Then humans came and killed most of those creatures, and that made it worse. Now rivers are full of nets, and they're always full of poison."

"Poison?"

He rested his arms on the slats and blinked opaque eyes. The two heads still floated out in the water, watching. "Waste. Filth and garbage. There are a lot of you, and a lot of waste. So, we stay where the water is still fresh."

"Is this the only place?"

"Yes," he said. "Why don't you dance?"

Isha blinked. "We do."

"Not when you move."

"I've heard that before." Mani came along the pier to join them. The rules of this game had changed, and he didn't know why, but he'd take advantage of it. "I didn't understand. Can you explain?"

"You only dance in patterns," Hanno said. "Set forms."

He looked at Isha, who gave a slight shake of her head. "So?"

"That's not dancing. That's just stepping. Forward, back. Forward, back. You don't see it." Hanno ducked under and re-emerged. "Think of seagrass bending with a tide. By morning this way, in afternoon that way. It isn't a dance. It's only movement."

"How do you dance?" Isha asked.

He shrugged. "Differently. Each time is new."

"Nothing is set?"

"No. Water is movement, and it always changes."

"Well, then." Isha stood up and held out a hand. "Husband? Shall we dance?"

"What, here?" he asked, but he knew it was too late. Hanno had gone rigid, the way Sea-Goats did when they were shocked or excited. There was no way to refuse without risking everything Isha had gained, and Mani wasn't about to do *that.* He took Isha's hand.

"I've no idea what to do," he said.

She smiled up at him. "Me neither. Isn't it exciting?"

Mani barked a laugh, and with that she stepped off, the way you did in the Crane Dance. One knee raised and the movement to her left, body angled to the side. Mani followed and nearly tripped over her feet. That made her turn to avoid the edge of the pier, and suddenly they were dancing to no rhythm or form he knew. Hanno slapped his tail on the water and went under, coming up on the other side of the jetty.

"I don't dance," Mani said to Isha.

"I danced at two betrothals to men who never married me," she said. "Don't you dare stop."

He didn't stop. Isha guided their steps along the pier almost to land, then let go of his hands and did a little pirouette to turn him around. There wasn't a dance in Engiru where a woman did that. Mani felt stiff as a wall, out of his depth. They came back along the jetty, Isha now twirling in and out of his arms, and came to a halt where Hanno waited.

Where three Sea-Goats waited, now. The far-off watchers had abandoned their observation and come to join Hanno. Barek had, anyway, bobbing a couple of yards away. The other waited further off, still unwilling to come the last little way, or unable to, maybe. Sun glare made it hard to be sure, but Mani thought he looked like a younger male, not brave enough to cross that final gulf.

"You honour us again," Barek said. "After all these years you surprise me, scholar."

Hanno's head moved but he didn't look around or acknowledge the older swimmer. There might be some tension there. Mani pretended not to notice. "I surprise myself. Every day, since I married Isha."

"Have you stopped playing games with your words when you speak with us, then?"

He hesitated. This was dangerous territory, the kind of topic where a misstep could make the Sea-Goats refuse to talk to a man for years, or a lifetime. It was best avoided, but there had been centuries of avoiding it. Mani looked at Isha.

"Surprise yourself again," she said.

He grinned and sat down on the edge of the pier with his feet in the water. She sat beside him and held his hand. It felt good when she did that.

"We play games because we have to," he said. "I'm not proud of it. But you've played games too, Barek."

Water vibrated in a laugh. "Because we had to, also."

"Why?"

"Why did you?"

"Partly because we've never felt you were honest with us," Mani said. "You avoid too many questions and sometimes swim away when we ask them. We learned to stay on safe subjects and try to tease information from you more subtly."

"Most of you are as subtle as sharks."

He chuckled, thinking of Tash-Yal with his complex web of connections, trying to gain insights through referencing. It was like using algebra to understand love. "That's true."

"What's the rest of the reason?" Hanno asked.

This time it was Barek who pointedly didn't look around. Definite abrasion between these two for some reason. If they were human, Mani would say the older man felt usurped by the younger, who in turn was impatient with the old ways of patience. If they were human. Dealing with Sea-Goats—with Puradu—you could never be sure.

"Sometimes our behaviour is determined by the *zami*," he said. "They tell us what questions to ask, or they try to. Then we—what's the matter?"

Both swimmers had sunk low, almost submerged. They scowled up at Mani while water swirled around them, evidence of beating tails. It was a long time before they spoke.

"The priestesses," Barek said finally. "Have you ever asked a question they gave you, scholar?"

The wrong answer would ruin everything they had gained.

Mani knew that at once, and he also knew the honest answer was the right one. "No. They wanted me to."

"You refused?"

"I married Isha," he said. "They planned to force me to wed a failed priestess, someone full of zeal but without the talent. She would then have told me what to ask. So, I found my own wife."

"And they tried to blackmail us, and threaten us, until we parted," Isha put in. "Which we would not do."

"Why?"

"Because," Mani said, and stopped.

He couldn't say why. It had felt wrong, yes, and he hadn't wanted a *zami* prodding him every morning anyway, but that wasn't it. He'd refused to put Isha aside because she thought she was cursed and had trusted him with so much when she agreed to marry him. Not her heart, perhaps, but her soul. Then, later, he'd found there were other reasons. More…personal ones.

I surprise myself every day, since I married Isha.

"Don't deceive us," Hanno said. He swam back to the pier and rested his arms there again. "Not now."

He sighed. "Some I can't tell you, because I don't understand it myself. It just didn't feel right. My whole life has been coming here to talk to the Sea…the Puradu. I'm dedicated to that, and to learning. I'd betray both things if I let the *zami* control my tongue."

"I can tell you," Isha said. Her hand was still twined around his. "Because neither Mani nor I ever thought to find someone, and then we did. Because we married for convenience and found something more."

A moment, and Hanno asked, "Is that true?"

"No," Mani said. "Maybe. I don't know, Hanno. I'm feeling my way in this. I'll tell you when I can tell myself."

The two swimmers looked at each other. They might not share much liking, but something passed between them that Mani couldn't read before they turned back to the jetty.

"Thank you," Hanno said.

Barek took over. "We will tell you why the Puradu have avoided your questions. Why we've never trusted you."

Mani's heart was beating hard. "Why, then?"

"Because once we did trust you," Hanno said. "It's a thing all young males are told, before we come here to the marsh. Say little, offer nothing. Humans will take what you give and poison it, like coral dying when the water is cold. Watch, and listen, and be content."

"All right," Mani said. From the corner of his eye, he saw Isha's brows draw down in concentration. "Once we betrayed you, then?"

The Puradu exchanged looks again.

"Eala founded your city," Barek said. "Your stories say she came down from Heaven and set her feet here, at the edge of the marsh, and taught humans how to build and become great."

"Yes."

"Eala was a Puradu," Hanno said.

CHAPTER TWENTY-FIVE

MESSENGERS CAME TO the companies, and the army of Labaš stopped for the night on a tiny rise in the ground.

No other dry land was in sight. There was nothing but water, and the ridges of earth that marked drainage ditches. This was the only place where men would be able to lie down to sleep. Yarim could see the sense, looked at like that.

Except the Flood was rising. The delay meant another night before they reached Aš-alam, another camp made in the fields north of the city, and the Flood was rising. Tomorrow this island would be drowned. Every inch of country from here to the marsh would be under water, and the comfort of a dry night now would be lost then.

"This is where he'll fail," Kammani had said that morning. She was sitting on the side of the bed, naked as a babe. "He was always a fool, Yarim. He's powerful and makes men dream of following him, but even Sarru-kin can't persuade the Flood."

Yarim had never thought they would come this far. Leaving Labaš he had believed the path was too long with too many other cities in the way. The army could fight and win once, perhaps twice, but it would have to win four battles at four cities to take Aš-alam. Nothing like it had ever been done. This was the king who had just slaughtered the Council of Elders and most of the army's captains with them. They would march with no leaders but one.

Mad? Yarim had thought Sarru-kin lost in his own insanity.

He still thought that, in fact.

"I don't know," he said slowly. "He's found ways to do things I'd have said were impossible. Bringing defeated soldiers into his own army, for one. He knows things. He knew the Scorpion Gate of Piqash would be open for him."

"He had a traitor inside. There is nothing supernatural about it."

"He still finds a way," Yarim said. "Maybe he will this time, maybe not. But I'm not going to bet against him."

She stood and slinked over to him. Just that was enough to dry his palms, even now. "Zammash wants to be king. If you wait too long, he will be."

"If he doesn't wait long enough, he'll be dead."

That brought a flashing smile, dangerous as daggers. "True. Be patient, then, but not too much. There is a limit to waiting."

§ § §

A plume of water rose half a mile away and moving very fast. That must be a chariot, racing away to Aš-alam with news that the invaders had come to a halt. There was no point chasing. After a few miles it would change with a new chariot, a new driver and team. You couldn't keep up unless you changed to fresh horses as well, and the army of Labaš couldn't. Their enemy would always know where they were.

With that, Yarim began to have a glimmer of understanding, just a hint of what Sarru-kin might try to do.

"Tell the men to eat fast and then rest," he said. "No dice games, no cups of beer. Just food and sleep."

"Why?"

He turned his head to look at the other man. "Because that's the order I gave, Enmer."

His friend muttered something and went to pass the word.

Let him complain. Yarim was a captain now. It was hard for an officer to stay on good terms with the ranks, and for the most part he hadn't even tried. He had to tell the men to march when they were tired, to lead the attack when they wanted to hang back. It wasn't the kind of thing that made a man popular.

He hoped Enmer was still his friend. They went back a long way, to the day they'd both joined the army. Sarru-kin was just an Elder then, the young scion of an old but diminished family. Last of a glorious line and unmarried. Someone to pity, perhaps. There'd been no sign of what he would become, no hint or whisper of madness. Not then.

He sat on the dry earth and ate a supper of goat and leeks, plundered from a village nearby. All the warehouses had been empty since they crossed the river, but sometimes a farmer had tried to hoard a little for himself. It was always worth looking. Yarim sat, and chewed, and thought of Kammani and Sarru-kin, and himself between the two.

He slept for an hour and was awakened by a toe in his side.

"Rested?" the king of Labaš asked.

Yarim sat up. Soldiering gave a man the ability to come awake in an instant. Sometimes it was that or die. "Well enough."

"And your men?"

He shrugged. "Well enough."

"I have orders for you," Sarru-kin said. His four bodyguards stood around him, massive enough to block the falling sun. "You did well at Piqash, and before. I thought I would trust you again."

"Do we attack now?"

The Mad King gave him a slow look. "I hope you have not spoken that thought to others."

"No." The words had come without thought. That might be fatal close to Sarru-kin. "I ordered my men to eat and rest, that's all. To be ready in case my hunch was right."

"It was right. We attack tonight. If we leave at dusk, we can be at the walls of Aš-alam before tomorrow's dawn."

And then what? Yarim wanted to ask. This time he caught his tongue though. There had been a surprise at Piqash, a man inside the walls. Perhaps Sarru-kin knew something here as well and would pull the veil from everyone's eyes when he was ready.

Still, there was one point to make. "That's more than twenty miles, in seven hours of darkness."

"Is it beyond you?"

"No," he said quickly. "No, my lord. But it may be too much for some."

"I have chosen my companies well," Sarru-kin said. He pulled the sickle sword from a scabbard on his back and twirled it. Yarim's breath hitched. All the king did was twirl the blade, but Yarim's eyes were dragged to it, however he tried to pull them away.

"The rest of the army will follow, but we lead," Sarru-kin said. "The horn will sound soon. Be ready."

He was gone then, striding along the front of the camp. Men watched as he passed, making sacred signs in warding or worship, or both. Some likely didn't know. Sarru-kin did that to you, sowed doubt in your mind until you weren't sure what to believe anymore. He listened to advice from his sword, and then knew what he had no right to know.

Maybe there really was a god in the blade. That was stupid, of course…but Yarim wondered.

His company was still waking when Kammani came by, her *zami* a cloud around her.

"The last test," she said. Others were close enough to hear, and her eyes said more than her words. "Win, and he wins everything."

And will be king forever, were the words she didn't say. "He's our king. We follow him, and trust."

"Always?"

Dangerous words, and she was the only one who could speak them aloud and live. Yarim's palms were dry as dust again. "I want you beside me for always. No matter what comes."

Around them men had begun to buckle on leather breastplates, pulling the straps tight on greaves. A lot of the gear had belonged to soldiers in Piqash once, or Kindar, dead men left to be picked over by the birds. Kammani looked at them, and then at Yarim, and smiled a tigress's smile.

"Come back and find me waiting," she said.

It would be a sour thing, to die in the assault on Aš-alam after surviving so much. To be on the brink of glory and have it snatched away. To be dead, food for vultures, while Kammani still sashayed through the world of the living and men followed her with longing eyes. You never knew if the gods had marked you as another body fallen in the dust, or as one who might rise above it. Yarim could imagine his spirit making its way down the twisted paths to the Land of No Return, cursing at how close he had come only to spill out his blood at the last.

He shook the thought away. "Enmer!"

"We're ready," the other man said. Pots were still being jammed into packs, last bites taken of old bread or wheat cakes, but that always happened. Yarim slung his shield over his back.

"Tell them to grab their spears," he said.

§ § §

They marched through half an inch of water as the sun went down.

The night was clear. They usually were, in the days of the Flood. Stars and a half moon lit the endless lake. Anyone watching would see the little army easily. Three foot companies and a hundred chariots, with ripples spreading out on either side of them, hurrying towards Aš-alam. Behind them came the rest of the army, slower units, following in the wake of glory.

Nobody would be watching. Yarim would have thought it unlikely anyway, but Sarru-kin didn't think there was a risk, and that was enough. The Mad King had a knack for being right. The soldiers moved through an abandoned world, ghosts in a desert of water.

Ditches were marked by levees that rose out of the lake. The bridges that crossed them were even easier to see, and the land between as flat as a tabletop. Between channels they trotted, and sometimes sang marching songs, voices hollow in the night.

Balih sees us
Hand and spear
Balih sees us
We draw near

Balih sees us
In his eye

130

As we conquer
Or we die

That was the Labaš way. You won or you fell, with nothing between. Nothing with any glory. Yarim had always been proud of that. No other city in Engiru was as proud, as martial, as Labaš. Then again, no other city had produced a Mad King, who butchered his own Elders and yearned for immortality. Maybe there were other ways.

They funnelled across a wider ditch, the arch of the bridge dry across most of its span. Chariots sped away on either side, to cross other bridges and then rejoin the army and not waste time.

Maybe it was Kammani who had him thinking this way. She hadn't said anything against the army, or Labaš' history of war. She had her own ambitions. She'd found a way inside Yarim's thoughts, inside his heart, and nothing felt the same as before. He didn't think death in a far field was glorious, not now. He thought it was just death, and he wanted to live and be with Kammani, hearing her cry out beneath him in the night.

The moon moved across heaven. There was no one to see the army pass, no farmers left in their huts. Everyone had fled to the city as Sarru-kin approached. It was an advantage to being the Mad King. He had changed the rules of war, and now nobody knew what to expect from him. They were afraid, and frightened men fled. The army marched through the space they left, the chariots creaking along behind.

A driver caught Yarim's company up between ditches, wheels sloshing to above the rim.

"The king says to go faster," the rider said. It was Zammash, commanding the chariots. Of course it was. "Don't be laggard, new captain. Your king wants you first into the fight when weapons are raised."

There was no time to reply before the horses were turned and the chariot receded, back to the line of cars behind the infantry.

Yarim's legs ached. He'd marched most of yesterday and had only a little rest before starting out again at dusk. All of it was through water, each step a little harder than it would be on dry land. None of that mattered. They had to reach Aš-alam before dawn, or else fail, and the gods only knew what failure would do to Sarru-kin. Or what he would do to others, to those he believed had failed him.

Yarim nodded for Enmer to pass the order. The company's trot became a run, from bridge to bridge across the fields of Aš-alam.

Chapter Twenty-Six

A SENSE OF endings. Shahan hadn't been able to shake it all day. *Spend the night at a Scented House,* Mani had said, with all the silliness of an infant. *It might be better in the morning. Tauth can't stay angry forever.*

Well, she was doing a good job of trying. Shahan had suffered an ear-bashing when he got home, and the morning brought stiff silence and a turned back. As though it was his fault the swimmers didn't give a stuffed turd who Tauth was. When she did speak, it was to tell Shahan that he should have taken her to the marsh first.

"But I didn't know," he protested. "None of us knew."

"Kassu-Mani did!"

"Look, can't you just call him Mani? Using his full name is as formal as curling your hair before hauling bricks."

"We are talking of the Sea-Goats, not Kassu-Mani."

"But you mentioned him."

It was no good arguing with Tauth, though. She'd failed the tests, but she was a *zami* to her bones, with zeal for blood. She was pleasant enough when she chose, but still, why couldn't the priestesses have told Shahan he could have Elessa as a wife? They'd suggested her for Mani. Didn't seem fair, really.

So rather than argue, Shahan took himself out of the little house and went to the Spilled Salt, which was still mostly empty. A couple of beers didn't do much to shift his morose mood, and neither did a fried fish with onions bought from a street cart, and deliciously oily. From there his steps took him on to the Scented House near the wall. The one he'd always used, with the best girls and best beer. Everyone knew him there. He wanted familiarity tonight.

He found it at once, when a purring voice said, "And you a married man, scholar. I thought we might not see you again, especially if your Temple wife is as good in bed as they say."

She was tall, with dark hair like curls of night, and he said, "Elessa."

§ § §

Now it was morning, and he dressed as quietly as a mouse on carpet. He stuck a knife behind his belt, inside the tunic, where the handle poked him awkwardly in the ribs.

"Just in case," he'd said when Elessa asked him about it. "The Mad King will be here tomorrow."

"But he can't get into the city."

"That's what they thought in Piqash," Shahan said. "Can we not speak about this? I didn't pay for you so we could talk politics all night."

He looked at her now, sprawled on her bed with moonlight falling over her body. Elessa was extraordinary, even lying still. As beautiful as a goddess, as Eala herself, and yet no maiden, no timid blusher of a woman as Mani's wife seemed to be. She'd woken him twice during the night to excite him again, the second time riding his hips the way he liked it best, her head thrown back and hands on his chest.

Never mind that. Shahan went to the door and put a hand on the knob.

"It's not morning yet," Elessa murmured from the bed. She hadn't opened her eyes, and Shahan would swear he'd not made a sound, but she shifted, and a long leg eased free of the covers. "There's time for us, if you want it."

He thought of several quips, the witty nonsense everyone knew him for, and couldn't summon them to his tongue. "I want it. You, I mean. But I can't stay any longer."

"Your wife?"

"She's a terrible harridan," he said. This time the levity was there. "I'd much rather be married to you."

Elessa opened her eyes. The smile she gave him smoked the air. "Then you should have asked, scholar."

"What would you have said?"

"I might have liked that life." She stretched, languid and cool. "You make me laugh. I always thought I was meant for something, Shahan. Who knows? I may yet be."

"You're already something."

"I know," she said, and Shahan laughed.

He turned the handle and went out, down the stairs to the deserted lower room and out to the porch. The aged guard was asleep in a chair, snoring like a sow with mud in its nose. He didn't stir when Shahan opened the door and clicked it shut again.

The street was cooler in the hour before dawn. The city was silent, when Aš-alam was never wholly quiet. That sense of endings, again. The air had been brittle all through yesterday, and today would be worse. Talk in the streets was that Sarru-kin would arrive with tonight's sunset.

Shahan looked to his left, past the Spilled Salt to the bulk of the Immaru Temple beyond it. He saw the towers with their clusters of scaffold, rooftops and chimneys dark against the sky. Aš-alam, the city of Eala, built with her image always in mind. Lady of Love, daughter of the Moon. The *zami* said she was strongest at night, when the moon shone silver and men and women clung together in their beds.

There was a faint shine to the east, just enough to turn towers and chimneys into silhouettes. Night was ending.

After a moment he turned the other way, towards the city wall. The street was deserted but for him. He stayed to the side, in the shadow of homes and shops, until he came out by the River Gate and saw the guard there, leaning a shoulder against the bricks.

His back was to the street, his eyes close to a slot in the gate through which he could peer outside. Silly, really. Guards on the wall could keep a better watch, but the man was alert, and turned as Shahan came up behind him.

"What're you doing here?" he asked. His voice was a rumble, and one hand strayed towards the hilt of his sword. "Hang on. You're that scholar."

"That's me," Shahan said.

The hand paused, and then left the hilt. "Couldn't sleep?"

"I couldn't sleep," he agreed. "I went to a Scented House, and even that didn't help me rest. Any news?"

"Won't be, yet." The man bent to look through the slot again, just to check. "Mad King won't be here until—"

Shahan pulled the knife from his belt. It had slipped sideways, and the handle caught on cloth the first time. The soldier still had his back turned, and Shahan got his blade free, stepped in, and slapped one hand over the man's mouth. At the same time, he rammed the knife into the other fellow's neck, probably much harder than he needed to. He felt bone crack and gristle part. The guard spasmed once and was abruptly dead weight, a sack of grain tumbling to the ground.

There was blood down Shahan's arm. He hadn't expected that. No time to worry about it. He went to the little guardhouse by the gate, looked inside, and saw a second soldier sleeping on a bench, helmet and sword beside him. Two quick steps and a slash, and the man's eyes opened to see his life spilling on the floor. He tried to scream and could only manage a gurgle. He fell over, hands at his throat as though to hold the blood in.

Shahan stabbed him in the back, under the leather jerkin. Still the man tried to clamber up, so the blade went in again, and this time blood gushed over Shahan's hand. He really wasn't very good at this, didn't know where to strike or how hard. The second man went down at last. His hands clawed at the ground and then went limp.

Shahan went back outside. The eastern sky was paler now, the promise of dawn. He hurried to the gate and pulled back a thick bolt. It screeched a bit, but not enough to be heard, he thought. He was breathing hard, which made it difficult to listen. He put both hands on the bar and waited.

Waited, with two dead men nearby and blood up his arm, on his clothes. Terror rasped in his throat.

Sunlight touched the tower tops, and a horn blew outside.

Shahan hurled his weight against the bar. He wasn't a soldier, or a labourer, and had never used strength to work. Cleverness had always been enough, but brains didn't move a weight. The spar shifted with a creak. He shoved again and it groaned through the bracket.

"What's that?" someone above called, and a moment later a deeper voice came. "Who's down there?"

He had only seconds. Shahan threw everything into a shove, and the bar slid clear of the left-hand gate. He grabbed at the handle and hauled back on it. His sandals scrabbled on the earth. The door swung back, and he ran to get the other.

Someone landed in the gateway behind him. Shahan spun, hand flying for his knife. An instant later he flung himself to the ground as a sword whipped through the place his neck had been to embed itself in the door. Someone kicked him in the ribs, and he doubled up with a gasp.

"Bastard," a deep voice said. The one from the wall, he thought. A boot rammed into his side again and he groaned, trying to roll away. He thought he was going to be sick. He managed to open his eyes and saw Udar, captain at the River Gate. A man who had brought him cups of ale beyond count these last few years.

"You'll be left for the crows for this," Udar spat. He went towards the open door and put his hands on it.

He stiffened. The point of an arrow protruded from his back. Another joined it, and he fell against the door.

Wheels rattled, quite suddenly. Shahan gritted his teeth and rolled away from the road. Then a chariot came through the gate, moving slowly because only one door was open. The warrior riding in back leaned over to slash a blade across Udar's neck, and he slid into the dust.

"You're the one for crows," Shahan gasped. He was alive. He felt wetness and realised he'd pissed himself.

Someone was pushing the other door back. A second chariot came through, to yells of alarm from the wall above. This one carried a man in shining armour, a bearded face Shahan knew. The king of Labaš. Sarru-kin jumped down and came over, walking like a heron, as though willing to allow only his toes to touch the earth where mortals trod.

"You kept your promise," Sarru-kin said. Soldiers were clattering down from the walls as chariots kept coming through the gate. The air was full of shouts. "Will you live, do you think?"

That last was said with an ironic smile. Shahan tried to stand and couldn't even sit up straight. "I'll survive."

"You are luckier than my agent in Piqash. He was killed by his own people just as I arrived." Sarru-kin began to turn away and paused. "You will be paid as agreed."

Shahan nodded. By then the Mad King had drawn his sickle sword and was striding towards the knot of defenders coming down the stairs from the gatehouse. He had to be insane, to challenge them all. Then infantry poured past Shahan, sixty men with spears and shields, and he understood. He let himself fall back to the ground.

"I think you broke my rib," he told Udar's body. Every breath brought a stab of pain. Shahan lay there while chariots and soldiers rushed past him, and twenty yards inside the gate bronze clashed and the battle began.

Chapter Twenty-Seven

MANI CAME AWAKE in a rush, from the pillows to sitting in the time it took his eyes to open. Isha came with him, woken at the same time. Her leg slipped off his thighs. They looked at each other.

"No," Mani said.

She was pale in the darkness. "That was—"

The sound came again, metal crashing on metal, with the hoarse shouts of men behind it. It wasn't far away, a street or two perhaps. Mani stared at Isha a moment longer and then moved, throwing himself from the bed to scrabble in the moonlight for a tunic and kilt. She was already reaching for a dress. "The Immaru Temple isn't far. We can—"

"Forget the Temple," he cut in. "Where will the Mad King's soldiers go? The palace and the main Temple. He won't want what happened in Piqash to happen again here."

"But where else is there?"

"The marsh," Mani said.

"But there's no shelter—"

"There are islands," he cut in. "Most aren't much more than reeds in mud, but there are old fishing huts on some of them. I *told* you to go to the Immaru." Recriminations did no good, but he couldn't help it. "For two days I told you."

"I was wrong," Isha said. Her voice was calm, but he saw her hands tremble as she bent to fasten her sandals. "You can blame me later. Leave it for now. How long would we last on these islands?"

"I remember a murderer who hid in the reeds. A hundred men searched for two days before they found him." He grabbed his heavier tunics, one for each of them. "Sarru-kin's army could hunt for weeks and not find us there."

"He won't look for us, will he?"

"I can't think why he'd want to. Ready?"

She nodded, still pale. They climbed through the bedroom window into a walled garden. A narrow gate at the back gave onto an alley. On the other side danger waited. Mani hesitated with his hand on the latch.

"What?" Isha whispered.

He looked down at her. Once he'd thought she wasn't hot limbed beautiful. That seemed strange now. "Soldiers won't stop to check who we are. If they see us on the street tonight, they'll just kill us."

She swallowed. "Do you think we should stay?"

"No," he said. "The Mad King's army is big, and the men will be tired and bored. That's a bad combination. I don't want to be close to it, and I really don't want you to be. We go."

He pulled open the door. Morning sunlight stabbed his eyes, and he raised a hand to ward it off. From its shelter he saw he was facing a soldier and a drawn blade. The man's expression changed to surprise, quickly masked. "Kassu-Mani? The scholar?"

Mani stared at him and the gleaming bronze blade. Another dozen soldiers stood behind the speaker, ranged across the street like turkeys in a pen. All of them carried spears or swords. Mani's first thought was that Ra'im had sent a squad to escort Mani and Isha to the Temple, but he didn't recognise any of them. That meant they were men of Labaš. He didn't understand.

"Yes?" he said. He moved in front of Isha and tried to make his voice more certain. "Yes, I am."

"I am captain Yarim. You're to come with me." The man's eyes flickered to Isha. "Both of you."

Mani eyed the sword, but after a moment risked a question. "On whose orders?"

"Sarru-kin, king of Labaš," the man said. "Regent of Kindar, Tibad and Piqash, and now of Aš-alam. He's called for you."

"For me?"

"Are you stupid? Of course for you." The man shifted and pressed a foot against the door, so Mani couldn't slam it shut. "The king doesn't like to be kept waiting. Come now, scholar, for your own sake."

§ § §

Half an hour later they stood in an anteroom, hearing shouts and the crash of metal from the streets.

"Did you see the Temple?" Isha murmured.

Mani nodded. The soldiers hadn't brought them past the Immaru, instead taking a back lane that led around, but they'd come close enough to see why. All the Temple's windows were blocked except for narrow slits, and the main door was a mass of brick and wooden bars. The attackers couldn't get close without coming under arrow fire. Mani had seen two bodies lying in the dust, left there by comrades as they fell back.

"I hope Ra'im got there in time," she said.

Mani didn't reply. If he spoke, the words *I told you so* would escape his tongue again, and he didn't want to argue. Not ever, but especially not now. There was an insane conqueror in the palace. Mani needed his attention on that, not on something he couldn't change.

"Why does Sarru-kin want me?" he asked Yarim.

The captain shrugged. He was a big man, black-haired and bearded, with huge shoulders and flat eyes. Mani thought about pressing the point and decided not to. Yarim was much taller and heavier by two stone. He could pick Mani up and beat him against a wall if he chose to.

A knot of priestesses came down the corridor. Mani recognised a stick of bones in the middle and watched Shusikil as she went by. She saw him, but her expression never changed. The *zami* walked down the passage and out into the courtyard, where the murmur of a conversation began just as the doors swung shut.

"They must have seen him," Isha said. "This king, I mean."

That was true, but the women had left no clues as to what dealing with Sarru-kin was like. Mani had his memories, but they were four years old and probably not a good guide. The Mad King was a different man now.

A man appeared by double doors at the far end of the corridor. He beckoned and popped back out of sight.

"It's time," Yarim said. He gave Mani a little push to start him moving. Only the captain and one other man came with him this time. It wasn't as though Mani had anywhere to run to if he fled. He went along, Isha at his side, to the double doors at the end of the hallway.

The chamber beyond was tiled in blue and green, the colours of the river. Reliefs were carved into the walls, the one to the right of people rising from the reeds of the marsh while Eala looked on and smiled. As though she had made them, crafting their bodies from mud and sparks of her own spirit. On the left archways let in light and the reliefs between were separate scenes of daily life and play. There was no furniture, and no people except a pair of soldiers by doors at the far end. No Mad King.

Mani let out a breath. His heart was beating hard. He felt Isha's hand slip into his own, and his instinct was to pull away and not be distracted by her touch. But he didn't. He smiled at her instead, and he wasn't surprised when she swallowed and clutched tighter.

They went down another passage and through a courtyard, planted with acacia trees. More guards eyed them before they were allowed to pass. The Mad King had only been in the city for an hour, maybe even less, yet he had settled here like a bug in a blanket. He had been planning this adventure for a long time, that was obvious now. Perhaps even from when Mani had met him before, in Labaš when Sarru-kin was only an Elder.

They came to the gate of a walled garden and stopped.

"He's in there?" Mani asked.

"That's right." The captain seemed to hesitate. "Be respectful to him. He will not give you another chance."

Chapter Twenty-Eight

THERE WAS SOMETHING in Yarim's tone, and the flick of his eyes through the gateway, that hinted at a lack of loyalty. There was no chance to pursue it now. Instead, Mani turned and went into the garden, Isha following on the narrow path.

Inside, earth had been piled into tiers, held back by walls of stone. Stone, brought from far away just to contain mud! Mani couldn't imagine how much that had cost. Shrubs and blooms flowered on the steps, salvias and pansies in the shade of joshua and juniper. Yellow chamomile erupted in sunbursts. Mani thought of the effort needed to keep this fertile, the water that must be carried from the marsh every day, and shook his head. Maybe it wasn't only this king who was mad. Maybe all kings had to be.

The path rounded a tree and opened into a wider space, centred around a pool where fish swam in the shade. A man stood there, his back turned, a sickle sword held idly in one hand. Mani never doubted it was Sarru-kin.

"Scholar Kassu-Mani," the Mad King said. He twirled the sword so its point spun in the earth. "I expect you never thought to see me again when you parted Labaš four years ago."

"That's true." His palms felt clammy. "You've come a long way in a short time, my lord."

"I am a seeing man in a world of the blind. A hawk among sparrows, if you will. I will do much more than this before I am done."

There was nothing to say to that. Sarru-kin was less hawk than vulture, to Mani's mind, tearing at the bodies of the dead. Those were words left unspoken by any man who wanted to live. Mani held his tongue and went down on one knee, head bowed as you should only do to your own king on formal days. Yarim had advised him to show respect. One moment with the Mad King and Mani knew he hadn't needed the warning.

"You discovered something once," Sarru-kin said. He still had his back turned and still spun the sword in one hand. "That the swimmer' home island is in fresh water, not salt."

"Yes."

"Which suggests it is not out in Ocean, as we always thought."

"Yes."

"What have you learned since?"

"About their home island? Nothing."

The Mad King turned to him. Sarru-kin's face was flushed, his eyes too bright. Mani's first thought was that he was ill. If so, it was an illness of the mind, a fever burning so deep inside him that it could never be removed. The sickle sword spun, grounded for a moment in the earth, then spun again.

"You do not know where it is?"

"No," Mani said, and then added, "my lord."

"You will find out for me."

"What?"

The man's chin came up, and his eyes flashed like stars. "I said you will find out. I wish to go there."

Mani tried not to stare. "But that's impossible. They'd never take you, or any human. The Sea-Goats are always secretive, but about their home they become obsessively so."

"And yet they told you it lies in fresh water."

"Well, yes, but that was a slip. It was never meant—"

"I suspect," Sarru-kin broke in, "that the swimmers are more clever than you think, scholar. What you call a slip may have been intended. Did you never think that they study you as much as you study them?"

Barek had said as much down by the pier. Scholars had always supposed it, all down the years of work. "Yes. That occurred to me."

"They told you a secret. They trust you. If you ask, they may tell you another."

"That's not how it works," Mani said. "No Sea-Goat would admit water is wet if you asked him directly. We must be subtle. We seem to ask one thing while aiming at another, and we listen, always. The information we gain isn't usually what we asked for."

"Has that not changed in the past week, since you took your wife to the marsh?"

Mani's breath seemed to stop. "What?"

"You won their trust when you took them your wife," Sarru-kin said. "Isha, I believe. Is this not true? They have talked to you, these last days, more openly than to any other scholar in the history of Aš-alam. They told you their true name is Puradu, the Pure." He took a step towards Mani. "Will you tell me I am wrong?"

How could he know that? Mani tried to speak and found his mouth as dry as dust before the Flood. He licked lips with a cracked tongue. *How does he know? How?*

"How do you know that?" Isha whispered.

"The same way I gained entry to Piqash without a fight," Sarru-kin answered. "The same way I broke into Aš-alam before your soldiers knew I was here. Can you guess it?"

"You had someone inside," Mani said. He licked his lips again. "Someone to unlock the gate."

"Someone to unlock the gate," the Mad King echoed. He half turned towards the screen of junipers. "Show yourself, servant."

There was movement, and Shahan stepped into view.

Mani's mind reeled. *Shahan*? Always joking, too fond of taverns and Scented women, leaving chickpeas on the tablets he stored in the House. Shahan was in the pay of the Mad King? It didn't seem possible, but there his friend was, one arm in a cotton sling and an abashed smile on his lips, and for Mani something fell into place.

"Four years ago," he said. "When you came with me to Shurraš and Ashkir, and then Labaš. That's when he bought you, isn't it?"

Shahan winced. "That's a bit harsh."

"Isn't it?" Mani shouted.

"That's when he enlisted me," Shahan said. "I never thought…I never expected this, Mani."

"Four years ago, only a madman could have expected this," Isha said.

"Sarru-kin did," Mani countered. He took deep breaths, trying to calm himself. "He hired Shahan, and the nameless man in Piqash, and who knows how many others. How long have you planned this, my lord?"

"All my life," the Mad King said.

"You hid it well. It shows in your face now."

Sarru-kin shrugged. "I am closer now. Halfway to immortality. There is little left to stop me."

"Immortality," Mani repeated. "So that's what you're after. You really are insane." *So much for respect*, part of his mind thought.

Sarru-kin only twirled the sickle sword again. "I am destined for this. A seeing man among the blind. It is no insanity to acknowledge Fate. As you say, it shows in my face. The shadow of the god I will become."

"I can't help you."

"But you will."

"No," Mani said. "I don't mean I won't. I mean you ask the impossible. It's the dream of my life to walk on the Puradu's home island, my lord. I've longed for it, the way warriors long for battle or fields for rain. Despite that, whatever has changed lately, they will never agree to this. They won't listen, and I can't make them."

"But you will," Sarru-kin said again. "Your father died at the River Gate, Isha, when Shahan opened it for me. I do not hesitate to kill. You carry a child, I believe."

For Mani time stopped.

It started again when Isha took two steps and hammered a fist into Shahan's nose. The scholar went down on his backside, an expression of astonishment on his face. By then Mani's muscles had begun to work again, and he caught his wife around the waist, pulling her back. Blood trickled from Shahan's nose as he stared up at them.

"You bitch," he said. He wiped blood away with the back of his hand. "May dust eat you, you bitch."

"You whine like a dog," Mani told him. He felt strange, disconnected. "Is it true, Isha? Are you…is there a baby?"

She turned a shocked face to him, grief and dismay mixed, and Mani knew. He put a hand on her belly, as though he might feel the kick of a foot. "What…how did he know? How did Shahan know before I did?"

"I went to a healer," she admitted. "He gave me wheat and barley, for the test. Healers are governed by the Temples, aren't they?"

He nodded. It was clear now. The healer had told the *zami*, who had told Tauth, who spoke to her husband about it. Shahan knew. Mani's old friend still lay on his elbows, his expression hurt. Isha spat at him.

"Your wife bites like a whelping bitch." It was, predictably, Sarru-kin. "I could find it amusing in another place. But now, scholar, you see I know all your secrets. Will you find me a way to the swimmer's home?"

"They'll never take you." He still had arms around his wife. "Never."

"Find a way," the Mad King said softly.

Mani's jaw was tight. He stared at Sarru-kin and then at Shahan. Isha's body shook against Mani's, either with rage or sorrow. Mani couldn't see her face, but he thought it might be both.

"Find a way," Sarru-kin said.

Mani nodded. There was nothing else he could do. The flush of the Mad King's face seemed to brighten to a glow, the shine of sickness in healthy flesh.

§ § §

"They won't do it," Isha said later. They were back in the street, in the light of early morning. "They won't. Will they?"

The road was all but deserted. A few shoppers skulked along the sides, driven out by need. There was no other reason to come out, not today. On the wall a soldier called to another, his accent harsh on Mani's ear.

"No," he said.

Isha put a hand to her stomach. "But the Mad King is right. You must find a way."

"Yes," he said. He kissed her brow and turned towards the marsh.

Chapter Twenty-Nine

THIS MAN IS a *dakua*," Hanno said. "A killer fish that comes out of the deeps to slaughter. No conscience, just death. Yes?"

"Yes," Mani said.

"He really threatened your wife? And the baby?"

"Yes. Several times."

"Dakua," Hanno said again.

Barek hovered behind the younger swimmer. The bone ridges of the Puradu's heads didn't leave much movement in their brows, but Mani thought he was scowling.

"I didn't know any Puradu had ever spoken to a human of immortality," Hanno said. He was propped against the jetty again, arms on the boards and tail in the water. "How old is this record of yours?"

"Old. I'd never heard of it either. There must be a tablet in Labaš. The gods only know how it got there."

"It's from the first days," Barek said. Water swirled as he moved closer to the pier. "When we were newly come, and the only humans were farmers who scratched a living from earth replenished by the Flood. We spoke more freely then."

Hanno nodded. "There was more trust."

"We hadn't yet been betrayed," Barek said. "Wherever humans are, there you'll find treachery."

Mani said nothing. The Puradu was right—human had deceived them from the day the priestesses first decided to claim Eala as the founder of Aš-alam. That had made the Puradu cautious, reluctant to talk. In turn the scholars became devious, subtle, trying to trick information from sluggish tongues. Evasion and deceit, turn and turn about, for all the years since.

"He wants to live forever," Hanno mused.

Mani sat down, the way he had when Isha was here with him. The way she'd shown him he could, when formality and caution were tossed aside. "You talk as though it's possible."

"It is," Hanno said.

"You're joking."

"No. There is a way."

"Enough," Barek snapped. He swirled closer still. "This cannot be done. The wives would forbid it if they knew."

Hanno looked over his shoulder. "Perhaps. There are no wives here. We must decide as best we can, alone."

"We must do as we've always done. Say little, give nothing. It's worked for hundreds of years."

"We abandoned that when Mani brought his wife to us," Hanno said. His wide mouth curved in a smile at the memory. "It's too late now. We go forward or we go back, but we can't stay as we are."

"You're a youth and new here. Leave the decision to—"

"Everyone here has the same status," Hanno broke in. He turned in the water to face the older male. "That's as we've always done it, and you know that. All are equal, and we decide together."

Barek's glare was venomous. "Then decide to stand back. Human affairs are nothing to do with us."

"He brought his wife to us," Hanno said gently.

"He didn't know what that meant! Did you, scholar?"

"No," Mani admitted. He wanted to lie, anything to make the Puradu decide to take the Mad King away. If they caught him in deceit that would be the end of it all, and Isha would die with their unborn child. All he could do was hope. "I had no idea."

"An unmeant promise still holds," Hanno said. "What's important is that Mani brought Isha to us. His wife, here at the marsh. He trusted us more than his own people, and we owe him for that."

"You're wrong. You—"

"I will argue it when we gather," Hanno said. It was the second time he'd interrupted the other swimmer. Two weeks ago, he would have deferred, Mani was sure. Not now. "I'll say that Mani trusted us with what he treasures, and we should do the same. Either that, or leave the marsh forever, because the distrust of the past has grown so great that we will not breach it to save the life of an unborn."

Barek made a rattling sound in his chest. Anger, Mani thought, though he hadn't heard it before. The Puradu dived in a splash of water and was gone before the water settled, not even a shape in the green depths. Hanno went down too, but only to wet his head. He resurfaced and shook water droplets from his scalp.

"I'm sorry," Mani said.

"For what? Asking help from friends?"

He couldn't help smiling. "I've spent all my life hoping to one day call a Puradu my friend."

"Just as I longed to meet humans and talk with them."

"Is it really possible? Immortality, I mean. Can it be done?"

"The wives say it can," Hanno replied. "There's a yellow flower on the sea floor, north of our home. It only grows in one place, a spread of fissures in the rock. Not many Puradu ever dive so deep. I've seen the flower, from far above, when the water was clear. The wives say if eaten, it will give everlasting life."

"It's real," Mani said, wondering.

"It is," Hanno agreed. "But it's a lure for fools. The sea is deep there, and the broken rock makes savage currents. I wouldn't go down if my lineage depended on it."

"But you'll take the Mad King to it, if you can?"

"If I can," Hanno said. "Be here tomorrow at the same time, scholar, and the day after that, until I meet you. Until then, look after your wife. We care for her. Even Barek."

"I will," Mani said. But he was talking to a tail, then to a widening circle in the water. Hanno was a blur of movement far below, and he was gone.

§ § §

By midday, Mani was standing outside the Immaru Temple, hands raised to show he was unarmed.

"I want you to talk with Ra'im," Sarru-kin had said. "Take him a message. You are wholly my vassal now, are you not?"

No, he was not. Mani was a scholar, a man whose weapons were words and the learning he described with them. He couldn't fight a king. For now, he had to duck his head, obey, and wait for a time when his own blades might have a chance to bite.

Blades of thought and cleverness. A man would laugh at that, if he had laughter in him.

A hand emerged from the barricaded Temple door to beckon him forward. Mani went, watched by Sarru-kin's men on one side and no doubt Ra'im's archers on the other, hidden in narrowed windows with arrows nocked to the string. His skin writhed as he walked, but no arrows flew, and no spears were thrown. He reached the doorway and went inside.

"Stop."

He stopped. Large men came out of the shadows to search him for hidden blades, or a jar of poison that might be hidden in a fold of his long tunic. They didn't find anything. The most dangerous thing Mani carried was his belt, and they let him keep that, perhaps sure he could never use it to strangle the king.

"Come," a voice said. They were men of few words here it seemed. Another big man led Mani down a passage. Every few yards it was partly blocked on one side or the other, providing cover to archers firing towards the entrance. Men with bows sat on upturned boxes or the floor, watching as Mani passed.

At the end of the corridor, it narrowed on both sides, and there a dozen men lounged with spears propped against a wall. They watched as well, and none of them spoke. Men of few words, indeed. Mani was taken up a flight of steps, past a window built over with fresh bricks. He'd never been here before. Only Elders and *zami* had.

Through two chambers, both decorated with murals in colours brighter than sunlight on water. Then another passage, more stairs, and finally a high room whose window looked out over the plaza below. Sitting in shadow beside it was the king.

Mani went to one knee. "My lord."

"Scholar," Ra'im said. He stood and came forward. "How have you come here? The Mad King isn't letting anyone—ah. He sent you, did he?"

"Yes. After he sent me to the marsh. I have a message for you."

"Later," Ra'im said. "Guard, bring food and drink for the scholar. Now, Mani, tell me what's happened since the gate was breached. The message can wait; we've had no news. What is Sarru-kin after?"

"Immortality," Mani said.

He explained, pausing now and then once food had been brought. At some point he noticed that Nahal was in the room as well, listening from beside the door. The Overseer of the Army. Nahal's mouth turned down at the corners, and he never blinked.

"He's insane," Ra'im said at last.

Mani lifted his wine cup and frowned when he found it empty. "That's why they call him the Mad King."

"I suppose it is. So, either the Sea-Goats refuse to take him to their island, or he goes and comes back disappointed. In each case we still must deal with him, don't we?"

"The moment he leaves his army will fall apart," Nahal said from the doorway. His beard was untended, not the magnificence it had been before. "Half his soldiers are from other cities. They won't need much to believe he's not coming back."

"It might not be that simple," Mani said.

They looked at him, and he shrugged. "He might come back. The Puradu won't want him on their island, will they?"

"There is that," the king admitted. "I have two questions for you, scholar. Can he make himself immortal?"

Nahal laughed. Mani didn't, and he saw Ra'im register that even before he replied. "I doubt it."

"You mean it's *possible?*"

"The Puradu say there's a way," Mani said. "But it's impossible. He would have to dive deeper than even they can go, and through bad currents too. I can't see how he could."

"This is Sarru-kin," Nahal said.

He didn't need to explain. The Mad King had already done many things that had been thought impossible. Conquering his way across Engiru in half a summer, for one thing. The capture of Piqash and then Aš-alam with hardly a blow struck, for another. Maybe he could do this as well.

Mani thought of the shine under Sarru-kin's skin and felt cold.

"What was your second question?" he asked.

"Why are you here?" Ra'im asked. "What makes Sarru-kin think you'll go back out to him? Or that I'll let you?"

"He has Isha," Mani said. "And she's carrying a baby."

He hadn't meant to say that. Ra'im's expression changed, and he leaned forward to slap Mani on the shoulder. "Good news, man! The wrong time, and you must be frozen with fear, but still."

Mani half shook his head, unsure what to say.

"Children are a gift from Eala," someone said. He turned his head to see Lamsi in the doorway. Her eyelid twitched. "You should give thanks for her blessing, scholar."

"As I should thank her *zami* for threatening my wife?" he asked. "Or the goddess, for founding the city?"

Her face became rigid. "What do you mean?"

"You know what I mean."

"What is this?" Ra'im asked.

"Eala never founded Aš-alam," Mani said. He was full of anger, at so many things, and Lamsi was in front of him with her serene words and endless twitches. "Did she, *zami*? The Puradu did. When they came here, they found farmers, and they taught us how to build."

"A lie," Lamsi said.

"And yet you're not surprised," Mani said. "The Temples have never liked contact with the Puradu. You've tried to curtail our questions, block us, married us to *zami* so they could control our questions. Because you knew the truth all along, isn't that right? You've been terrified that we might discover the truth."

Lamsi's face spasmed. "The truth is Eala."

Mani shook his head, biting back words that could never be forgiven. Lamsi saw it and pressed on. "Belief is necessary. Don't you see? Faith holds us together, and on this plain, cities die without it. We survive because we work as one. All the cities do! If any city lets its ditches fail, they all fail. The people look to us to lead them. How else would the work be done?"

"The Elders could organise it as well as the Temples do," Mani said, "and you know it."

"What happens when a king falls? What happens during wars? It wouldn't be long before an army smashed the ditches of a rival city, if kings could hurt each other that way." Her lips trembled, like a baby about to cry. "Look at what Sarru-kin has done. It's only the Temples, in every city, which can stand apart from war and keep the ditches safe."

"Enough," Ra'im said. "We can discuss this later. I won't allow us to bicker now. Mani, you said the Mad King had a message for me. What is it?"

For a moment he didn't know what Ra'im was talking about. He had to pull his gaze away from Lamsi before his mind cleared and he remembered. "He demands you surrender and swear fealty to him as overlord. Aš-alam will convert to worship of Balih, under the Temple of Labaš. If you refuse, he'll leave his army here to starve you out."

The king glanced at the door. "Nahal?"

"Not a very tempting offer. He wants to put a rope around our necks, like slaves. Besides, I still say his army will break up as soon as the Mad King sails for the Sea-Goat's island." The Overseer rubbed his chin. "I suggest we simply stay here and wait."

"I agree," Ra'im said. "I'm not about to give up my city to a maniac. Tell him I said no, scholar." He rose to his feet. "And good luck. With everything."

Mani stood too, but before he could speak Lamsi said, "Shusikil never reached here. Have you seen her?"

He glared at the priestess, but that never did any good with the *zami*. "I saw her. She was with Sarru-kin before I was, and then she left."

"Is she working with him?"

"I have no idea," Mani said. "Why don't you go out and ask her yourself?"

It was her turn to glare and to be ignored. Mani bowed to the king and left them. He heard Ra'im demand something and Lamsi answer, her voice shrill, and Mani grinned to himself.

§ § §

"He refused," Sarru-kin said.

Mani held his peace. The Mad King seemed more distant than before. More the god he was trying to be, perhaps, and less a normal man.

"I thought he would accept. Yes, Azaq." He spun the sickle sword. "You said so first. I know, dear one."

"Perhaps you will not make such mistakes," the tall priestess said, "when you have become immortal."

Sarru-kin turned hot eyes to her. There was something in them that made Mani shiver. "Perhaps," Sarru-kin said.

CHAPTER THIRTY

NO PURADU APPEARED the next day.

"One must hope," the tall priestess said when Mani told her, "that your skills of persuasion will work with the swimmers rather better than they appear to have worked with your king."

She wore a gown so thin it hid almost nothing. When she passed by soldiers sweated and their eyes moved, following her like dogs panting for water. Even now, even men of Aš-alam.

Ra'im had not surrendered. He and most of the nobles were still barricaded in the Immaru Temple, waiting for an assault that didn't come. All Sarru-kin's army was inside Aš-alam, drinking in the taverns and picking fights. Mani thought they wouldn't be left idle for long. If the Mad King couldn't go to the island, his rage would turn on an enemy he could reach.

Outside the Flood was higher. It lapped against the mound on which the city stood, still short of the foot of the walls but not by much.

"That priestess frightens me," Mani said to Isha.

"The tall one, always with Sarru-kin?"

"Yes. She smells of madness, just as he does."

"It's desire she reeks of," Isha said. "Desire and need. Next time watch her less and notice the men around her. Their eyes are dragged to her every time she moves."

"I saw," he said.

"Will you come with me this afternoon when we cremate my father?"

He did, of course. Even in normal times Mani would have done so; now, there was no doubt of it. He was not about to let his wife walk the streets without him. If Kammani smelled of desire, then the city stank like a belch from an upset stomach. Fear and uncertainty were enough to unsettle the strongest belly. Besides, there were the Labaš soldiers to consider, drinking and fighting, sometimes leering at women as they passed. Rumour said it had gone past leering, more than once. Too many people in the city, too many tensions, and no chance of either changing before the Flood went down.

Udar should have been burned in the Immaru. He was a man of property, a trader, someone of importance. That was impossible, so he went to the flames on a smaller platform near the wall. Ramsi was there, leaving the doors of the Spilled Salt closed. He spoke some awkward words that Isha accepted with a touch of his arm, and then he was gone, back to the tavern that was Isha's now, to fill it with northern soldiers spending looted coins.

"Your father deserved better," Mani said.

Isha nodded. She was dry-eyed, though he knew her well enough now to realise her tears would come later, when she was alone. Her father had taught her that. Grieve, because the lost deserve it, but never let your sorrow make you weak, and never show it unless you must.

"A lot of the dead deserved better," she said. "Angry shades will be waiting for Sarru-kin when his soul walks the path to the Land of Dust."

"May the day be soon," Mani murmured.

"That's not yours to decide," she said sharply. "Don't take it on yourself to hasten the day, Mani. I've lost a father. I don't want to also lose my husband or my child."

He didn't answer, and her fingers closed on his arm. "Tell me you won't take that on yourself. Please."

"He has an army," Mani said. "I can't oppose him, and I'm not fool enough to try. Except…"

He trailed off, and her grip on his arm tightened. "Except what?"

"They say strength can't keep pace with cleverness," he said, "and my dear, I am clever."

They went home then, to wait for Udar's ashes to be placed in an urn and brought to them. Shahan was waiting on the porch.

§ § §

He felt Isha go tense even before Shahan said, "Can we talk?"

"Go on in," Mani told his wife. Her colour was high, and he squeezed her hand. "It will be all right."

She went, for a wonder. Shahan moved aside to let her pass, which was wise. He had two guards with him, big men as all the northerners seemed to be, but Mani wouldn't have given all three of them much chance with Isha in this mood.

"I could use a cup of water," Shahan said.

Mani shook his head. "You're not coming in the house. You killed her father."

"I didn't strike that blow."

"I'm sure that's a great comfort to his shade," Mani said dryly.

Shahan winced. "Do you have to—"

"Be like this? I think so." Mani heard his voice rising. "You betrayed us. The Mad King has threatened my wife and the baby she carries, because of you. You let him into Aš-alam, and you told him she was pregnant. You told him where we live, didn't you? They say if you become a thief, you become an outcast, and you did much worse than thievery. There's no forgiveness for it." He nodded to the lurking guards. "That's why you need these men, isn't it? Without them it wouldn't be an hour before someone put a knife in your ribs."

"What could I have done, Mani?"

"Left the River Gate shut, for a start."

"I'd taken his money! Sarru-kin kills people who disappoint him. I wouldn't even have lasted that hour."

"He was on the wrong side of the wall."

"You think that would have stopped him? That I'm the only man in Aš-alam who took his coins?"

Probably he wasn't, at that. Sarru-kin had planned this too well for something to be hung on the thread of a single frightened man. It didn't matter. "You should have thought of that before you let him bribe you. It was when we were in Labaš, wasn't it? Four years ago. Did he take you aside and ply you with wine, or were you easier than that?"

"Wine," Shahan said. "And women. A…a Scented Woman, and a priestess."

"Well," he said. "What extravagant fantasies you have, Shahan. Did you make the *zami* keep her robe on?"

Another wince, which Mani thought meant he had. "I made a mistake, all right? We've been friends a long time. I hoped we could—I hope we *can* move past this, Mani."

"We were friends. We're not anymore. I'd be surprised if the scholars let you in the Guild after this."

"They won't," Shahan admitted. "Tash-Yal and Hitti met me at the door this morning and forbade me entry."

"Become a thief," Mani said, "and become an outcast. Was there anything else, Shahan?"

Annoyance flashed across his old friend's face for the first time. "You're clever, Mani. Think about it. Hitti and Tash-Yal won't last long when Sarru-kin gets back from the island."

"He doesn't care about them," Mani said. "Or you, now you've served the purpose he bought you for. I thought you were clever, too, but you're being remarkably stupid."

"He killed Yasmah-Bau this morning."

"What?"

"Had him beheaded in the square, right in front of the Immaru Temple," Shahan said. "Sarru-kin says it was a warning and a threat. That's what he does to people who anger him, or who get in his way."

"I see," he said. "He frightens you, too."

"No. I'm on his side."

"Then you must be threatening me."

"No! But you need to know what you're dealing with. Mani, you can't stand against Sarru-kin. He'll kill you without a thought."

"I'm not standing against anyone," Mani said. "I just want to be left alone with my family."

"That's not an option anymore," Shahan said. "Think about it, Mani. Think whose side you want to be on."

He turned and walked away, on the best parting shot he was likely to manage. It wasn't much of one, even so. Mani watched him go and then went inside to where Isha waited with elbows cupped in her hands, pacing the floor in worry.

"Has he gone?"

"He's gone," Mani said.

"He makes my skin creep."

"It won't be a problem. The older scholars have refused to let him into the Guild Halls."

Some of the tension left her eyes. "What about you?"

"I told him he couldn't come in our house. I said we're not friends anymore." He shrugged. "There's not much more I can do."

"I'm sorry," she said. "That must have been hard."

He laughed, without much humour. "You're sorry? We just saw your father cremated, and you have sympathy for me?"

"I'm your wife. I should be—"

"I think I love you," he said. Isha smiled and took his hand.

§ § §

"We have decided," Hanno said.

He hung in the water, hardly moving. Seven other Puradu were ranged behind him, watching. Mani had never seen so many at once before. He recognised them all. Old Aradus, Shamayim, Kabaal, irascible Barek. All of them wore the rigid expression he knew was the equivalent of a frown. It didn't tell him anything.

"We will take you," Hanno said.

Mani let out a breath. For a moment all he could do was sit on the pier, look down at the water below, and listen to the rush of his blood.

"Two of us have gone to tell the wives," Hanno said. He moved closer, water rippling behind him, and put his hand on top of Mani's. "I know this is hard for you. It's hard for us as well."

"I know," Mani said. He lifted his head and drew another gulp of air. "Thank you. All of you."

Kabaal ducked his encrusted head. "It is a large thing we do, but thank Hanno. He was eloquent in your cause."

"It was earned." The young swimmer shrugged. "The scholar brought us his wife. Now we will show him our wives."

"Thank you," Mani said again. "You have done so much for me. But…I need to ask you for more."

Hanno stilled. "More?"

"If the Mad King goes to your island and eats that flower, he'll be immortal. True?"

"He cannot survive the depths," Kabaal answered. "No human could. Even Puradu avoid those currents."

"He is Sarru-kin. He's done things nobody thought were possible. And I've met him." Mani shivered at the memory. "He makes me afraid. I wonder if there's anything that will stop him."

"Your madman will not survive," Hanno assured him.

"All right. But what if he forces one of you to dive for him?"

"We would not!"

"Even to save my wife? My child?"

Hanno turned to look at the other Puradu. His face was hidden, but Barek and Kabaal looked troubled.

"I need to know everything you can tell me," Mani said. "Everything, except for the wives. I won't ask about them. In Aš-alam we say that strength cannot keep pace with cleverness. I'll add to that and say cleverness cannot keep pace with knowledge. I need to understand, Hanno, to learn everything I can, so we can give the Mad King what he wants and still come out of this alive."

An hour later he leaned back on his hands, head tipped back to stare up at the bronze sky. Mani had remembered his hat, but after so long in the sun his brain felt swollen, the blood thick as bitumen.

"I have an idea," he said, and explained.

The Puradu had been here for so long, since the days when Engiru was just a plain, unnamed, flooded once a year when the Ranuna rose. People lived on reed rafts, built every summer and joined by woven bridges, so they rose with the water and kept food and livestock dry. They had taught those farmers how to build, how to write, and slowly the cities had grown, surrounded by ditches to control and hoard water when it came. In the thronging streets were kings and priestesses, masons and scholars, all striving to make something a little better than it had been before.

In the lagoon, always, had been the Puradu, watching with their eyes just above the water.

Mani finished speaking. Hanno went under and then came up again, standing on his tail so his torso was above the water. Ripples spread around him. "This plan will be dangerous for you. And your wife."

"Yes."

"I don't like that."

"Neither do I, much," he admitted. "But she's in danger whatever I do. This is our best chance to make her safe again. Maybe the only chance."

Hanno looked over his shoulder. Kabaal and Barek nodded, and then the others, and he turned back to Mani.

"We agree," he said. "We will lie for you."

CHAPTER THIRTY-ONE

"THEY AGREED," MANI said.

Sudden light shone from Sarru-kin's face. "I knew they would."

"Did you?" Mani tried to keep skepticism out of his voice. "I didn't."

They were in the throne room this time. Mani had never seen it before and was taken aback by its opulence. The floor was cedar, the walls panelled with the same wood, this time painted in geometric patterns. Lapis was set into the centre of each panel, cut into a flowering design. Cedar slats covered the windows too. In summer they kept out the sun, but now they were open to let cool air waft through the room.

Enough wealth could bring you anything. Cedar grew far up the river, in dangerous lands where fire monsters had once lived. They were gone now, but the distance was still vast, and expeditions cost fortunes to fit out. Kings must have emptied treasuries to embellish this one room.

"They need to know how many people will go," Mani said. "Will we fit in a single ship?"

"Yes. A large one. I have a builder with me."

"You need time to build the ship?"

"Watch your tone," the tall priestess warned.

Sarru-kin waved it away. "I am assured it will not take more than two days. One to build the frame, and another to plait on the reeds and caulk them. The engineers of your own city will be glad to help. Will they not? After all," he smiled, "it brings me closer to leaving here."

Mani said nothing, and the Mad King sighed. "That was a joke."

Kammani chuckled then, as did the guard by the doors. Yarim, if Mani remembered right. The four hulking men around Sarru-kin didn't so much as twitch their lips. Mani supposed they were paid to loom, not laugh.

"There are conditions," Mani said.

Every eye fell on him. He'd known they would, and his heart was beating fast. There was no way around it. He had to play this out as the dice had fallen and pray to Eala for salvation.

"Conditions," Sarru-kin repeated. He pulled the sickle sword from a sheath on his back and held it up in the light.

"Set by the Puradu," Mani said. "Not by me."

"I am the mightiest king Engiru has ever seen. They should be proud to do my bidding."

"Puradu are not of Engiru," Mani said, and thought it prudent to add, "my lord. They don't think the way we do. Human squabbles and ambitions don't matter to them. You could conquer every city on the plain, and all the far west too, and not make any difference to them at all."

"So, these conditions," Sarru-kin tasted the word with a grimace, "are not your own invention?"

Mani shook his head. "I'm not such a fool."

"No. No, you are clever, and that is why you bear watching. True, Azaq." The Mad King turned the sword left and right, watching the blade. "I am stronger than any man has ever been—but there are those who believe strength cannot keep pace with cleverness."

"He's not that clever," Kammani said, "and not that stupid, either. He cares for his wife, my lord."

"So, I can trust him because he fears me? Good." Sarru-kin grounded the tip of the sword. "Very well. But you and your wife will accompany me on this voyage, scholar."

"She has nothing to do with this. There will be dangers. She's safer at home."

"Do not dispute with me," Sarru-kin said. He didn't raise his voice, but the tone changed, and the glow in his eyes brightened to a flame. "Your fish people have their terms, and I have mine. What are their conditions?"

Mani made himself breathe deeply. He had expected this, though he'd hoped he was wrong. Sarru-kin was insane, but he was still human, and his actions could be foreseen. Even so, the thought of Isha on a ship with this lunatic filled Mani with terror. He had to close his eyes to fight down a sickness in his throat.

"The conditions?" Sarru-kin said again.

"There are two," Mani answered. Another breath, and he went on. "First, the Puradu will speak only to myself or my wife. Nobody else. They'll swim alongside the ship, but to anyone but us they might as well be nothing but seaweed."

"As long as they guide me well," Sarru-kin said.

"Which they promise to do, if neither myself nor Isha is harmed. That's the second condition. If we're hurt, if we die, they'll vanish and leave the ship lost in the Ocean with no idea of which way is home. They tell me we'll travel through strange seas. Without them, we'll never see home again."

Sarru-kin stepped towards him. He came up to Mani and stared into his eyes, still spinning the sword in one hand. "Are you sure you did not devise these terms yourself, scholar?"

"I'm not that stupid," he said. Kammani nodded, perhaps in recognition that he had used her words. "And not that clever, maybe."

The Mad King watched Mani, not blinking. The sword spun. At last, Sarru-kin turned away, flipping the weapon into its sheath with a twist of his wrist. "If I wanted to hurt you, it would be better to wait until we have returned, when you are no longer of use. These are terms made by fools. I agree to them, since it costs me nothing."

"Then build your boat," Mani said.

§ § §

"I've never been to sea," Isha said.

Neither had Mani. Hardly anyone had except fishermen and the crews that manned ships on their long journeys east and west to trade. It wasn't a thing people did unless their living took them there. Now that he thought about it, he hadn't even paddled out into the lagoon. In all the years he'd spent studying the Puradu, he'd never once thought to examine the habitat in which they lived.

"Nor I," he said.

They were in the garden, sitting on a bench under the stars. The sky was very clear, and there was no moon. Mani looked at the river of stars and wondered if the Puradu had come from there long ago, when they sailed the sea between worlds.

"People fall sick, don't they?" Isha asked.

"At sea? So I've heard."

"I bet I will," Isha said. "So far I haven't had morning sickness, but on a ship I'm sure I will."

He put an arm around her. "Will that hurt the baby?"

"Not unless I'm *really* sick," she said gloomily. "It's fear that worries me, Mani. A mother-to-be is meant to relax. Instead, I must go on a sea voyage to a faraway island, with a Mad King who's using me to blackmail my husband. I'm so tense it frightens me."

"I am, too." He looked at the stars again. "All my life I dreamed of going to the island where the Puradu live. I thought of what I might learn by looking at their buildings, or sitting in their libraries, if they even have them. I could learn a lot just by seeing what they don't have, as well as what they do." He had to pause to swallow. "Now, I'd give the fingers of one hand not to have to go at all."

"Do you mean that?"

"Yes," he said, and meant it. "Yes, I do. We scholars say you must be a little mad to study the Puradu, a little obsessed. It's true. I have been mad."

"Not like Sarru-kin."

"No, but maybe a bit like the *zami*. I never realised how much madness there is, when you look for it."

"My father always said—"

She broke off. Her father was dead, a truth that sprang at her again when she mentioned his name or thought of him. Mani could see it in the sudden stillness of her face. He'd been through it himself, a long time ago. He tightened his arm around her, just for a second, and Isha's expression softened as the moment passed.

"I'm not going to let him hurt you," Mani said.

Isha smiled. "I know. You'd do anything for the baby."

"And for you."

"As I would, for you," she said. "But he's the Mad King. He rules half the cities of Engiru, and you're a scholar. If Sarru-kin really wants to hurt me, Mani, he will."

"He can't. If he harms you, I'll jump over the side of the ship, and the Puradu will abandon the boat in the middle of the Ocean."

"He'll wait until we're home."

That was what Sarru-kin had said, in the opulence of the throne room. It made Mani shiver. "Strength cannot keep pace with cleverness."

"A saying," Isha said derisively.

"A truth."

She twisted to look at him. Her lips parted and closed again before she spoke. "What are you thinking?"

"Trust me." He thought of the guards posted around the house, and the keenness of ears, and made his voice a whisper. "He won't harm you."

Her fingers touched his face. "Thank you."

"I love you," he said. "It feels strange, saying that. We didn't marry for love or expect to find it."

"Eala made fools of us," she said. "I love you, too. Not because you saved me from the drab life I thought I was fated for. Because you're sweet, and kind, and a good man."

"I used to think you weren't hot-limbed beautiful," he said.

She rested her head on his shoulder. "Mocker."

"No," Mani said. He brushed a hand down her hair. "How long is it—I mean, can we still..."

"Why, husband," Isha said. She tilted her head back to look up at him. "Whatever can you mean?"

He felt himself redden.

"We can love each other for a long time yet," she said. "Until the baby is nearly here. Although my belly might make things a bit awkward before then, if it swells enough. Why?"

"You know why," he said. She drew his head down to kiss him under the light of stars.

Mani lay very still that night, Isha sleeping half beside him and half on his chest. He couldn't sleep, though. His mind was full of thoughts of Sarru-kin and the voyage ahead. There was a way to live forever, and Sarru-kin might find it, however unlikely that seemed. If he did, and came home to Engiru again, what did that mean?

He won't harm you.

Brave words, but empty, unless Mani could make them real. He lay on the mattress and stared at the window, watching the stars wheel through the sky as he waited for the dawn.

CHAPTER THIRTY-TWO

IN LABAŠ, YOU got out of the way of chariots when they rattled down the street or when a lord went walking with his knot of hulking guards. Brats bred in the back alleys moved twice as fast, because guards and drivers never cared if there was one less urchin. Tomorrow there would be two more, slipping out of their mothers into lives of filth. It wasn't worth worrying about them.

Yarim remembered those days. Some of them were still vivid, burned into him like scars from a hot iron. He and other boys had squeezed into doorways and watched the chariots clatter by, wishing they lived the simple, easy lives that wealth bought.

It was said that a palace is a slippery place. It could never be as treacherous as the back alleys, the ditches where sometimes you had to grub for food, or the corners where you slept with one eye open in case someone came past with a knife. Yarim had laughed when he heard people say it. Try living in the gutter for a week and see how perilous you thought palace life was then.

Yarim had seen both things now, gutter life and palace. The only difference was that in the palaces there were always sheets on the bed.

§ § §

"We are surrounded by madmen," Kammani said.

Yarim took the wine she offered him. He could feel his pulse, blood throbbing through his flesh. "The scholar?"

"He doesn't have the sense of a goat. Amazing, how often-clever men have no grasp of simple things. He taunted Sarru-kin, and the king isn't likely to forget that."

She was right, as usual. This Mani was vital to Sarru-kin for the moment, his one chance to reach the swimmers' island and the promise of immortality that waited there—but only for the moment. Once the ship ran its keel onto the coast of Engiru again, there would be no more need of Kassu-Mani, and he'd be as dead as last year's flowers. If the king felt generous it would end there. If not, a wife and unborn child would he tossed in the pyre as well.

"It's not only the men who are mad," Yarim said.

Kammani's eyes smiled over her cup. "No?"

"You are too," he told her. He felt giddy, reckless with wine and desire. "Insane enough to believe you can ride Sarru-kin like a chariot, so long as he goes where

165

you want, and then discard him. I don't know why fear doesn't root you to the spot. Perhaps it's only madness that holds the fear back."

"I'm hurt," she said. "Don't you love me anymore?"

"I love you more than my own life. More than the taste of cool water in the heat of summer. That's why I'm here with you, though I'm afraid of Sarru-kin, and a little of you."

"Then don't think of that." She set her wine cup down and pulled at a clasp on her shoulder. Her robe slithered down her to pool on the floor. Yarim made a strangled sound. "Do something that will make you not think of anything for a while."

Yarim thought of many things when he was trying to hold back a little longer before his climax swept him away. How thirst felt at the end of a long march, with a throat full of dust and blisters on his feet. A beggar he'd once seen in Labaš with two enormous warts on his face and a wound seeping pus on his neck. Anything but Kammani on her knees beneath him, shaven head now forward and now thrown back, skin gleaming. Never a woman like her before. Never another again, beyond doubt. If there even was another woman like her in the world of men. He doubted there was.

"In a week he will be gone," Kammani whispered later, her lips almost touching his ear. She was above him then, straddling his hips, and his flesh thrummed with the rhythm of her. "He'll be gone, and you and I will rule Labaš together for thirty years."

"I'm still the same," he answered, hardly aware of the words. "Still sleeping with one eye open, in fear of a man with a knife."

"I don't understand."

Yarim never explained, because he broke then and cried out as his body spasmed, and Kammani shuddered against him and bit his shoulder. *Never a woman like her.*

He would ride her wherever she took him, like a chariot, and pay the price in the end.

CHAPTER THIRTY-THREE

"HE WAS RIGHT," Mani said. "We really will be ready to sail tomorrow."

One of the men working on the ship grunted. "Maybe. If we're in time for the tide."

"There aren't any tides in the lagoon."

The labourer rolled his eyes and picked up another sheaf of reeds.

"Well, there aren't," Mani muttered.

The truth was Mani knew almost nothing about the sea. Leave that to traders and fishermen. He remembered when Shahan wanted to talk to fishermen along the shores of the marsh, in case they'd gleaned information on the Puradu that scholars had missed. Mani had dismissed the idea. *I would rather roast my balls in embers*, he'd said.

He was paying for such narrow focus. He didn't even know how wide the lagoon was, now that he considered it. He had no idea how ships worked, what the crew did, or how people lived on board. Sarru-kin was forcing him into a venture Mani had never wanted.

Another thing Mani had never known was how quickly you could build a ship. Sarru-kin's was a large one, fifty feet long and two decks tall, with curls at prow and stern. The rear third was just a frame of struts. The middle part was being covered with plaits of reed, woven around the frame, while the front was already being caulked. The smell of tar was strong, even in the breeze.

"The sailors say you never know how a ship will behave until you sail her," Darsal observed. "One can be a whore, the next an angel. They only show you which on the water."

"At least one of us knows something about ships," Mani said. "Do you want to go instead of me?"

"Thank you, no."

"I didn't think so."

"Any idea what that is?" Darsal asked, pointing.

'That' was a half-built platform twenty yards back from the edge of the marsh. The land was slightly higher there, and the Flood only covered it with a few inches of water. Men had hammered posts into it and laid planks across the top. Some still worked, stapling boards together to make sure the surface was as level as they could.

"No idea," Mani said. "Maybe the Mad King wants to keep his feet dry when he comes for the launch."

"He'd still have to come out here first."

"So he rides a chariot."

"Yes, maybe." Darsal half turned to Mani. "I want to apologise to you. I should never have been part of threatening you with expulsion from the Guild. I was afraid we'd never speak to the swimmers again, that's all. It's no excuse. I shouldn't have done it."

Mani sighed. "We're facing bigger problems now, Darsal."

"Even so. I shouldn't—"

"Isha is going to have a baby," Mani broke in. "We married because it was convenient, for both of us, and here we are a few weeks later, expecting a child. We have you to thank for it, do you remember? It was you who warned me the *zami* were planning to foist a wife on me. If not for you, I'd be married to Tauth now, trying to wriggle out of the things she demanded I do. Everything we have is owed, in part, to you. We can't thank you enough."

The older man smiled. "That's generous."

"Bigger problems," Mani said again. "Well, I'm going home. I don't like leaving Isha on her own these days."

"Eala smile on you," Darsal said. "In every way."

Mani clasped his friend's arm and turned for home. He took one step and then halted, because it seemed Eala had stopped smiling on him before she even began.

"What's that thing?" Shahan said. He waved an arm towards the platform being built to one side. "Looks like a dance floor. Hello, Darsal. Are you all still keeping me out of the Guild?"

"That's Hitti's choice," the other man said. "But after what you did, I support him in it."

"No matter what I do next?" Shahan took a handful of chickpeas from a bag and popped them into his mouth. A pace behind him was Tauth, glaring at Mani and Darsal as though they'd insulted her family. "No matter who the king is?"

Nobody answered that. If Sarru-kin ordered that Shahan be allowed back in, the scholars would have a hard time stopping him. There were other ways to ostracise a man, but it would still be a blow. Shahan seemed oblivious, stepping past them to peer at the construction ahead. "Son of a dog, is that the ship? She's a barge. I'll tell you, I won't like travelling on that thing."

"What?" Mani said.

"Didn't I say? I'm coming too. In case Sarru-kin needs another scholar. He's not a trusting man."

"You'll be checking on me," Mani realised.

"Seems so. But I'll also get to see the Sea-Goats' home island, which no other scholar has ever done. How will that change things, Darsal?" Shahan grinned.

"Will the Guild still bar me at the door, even when I've seen something none of you ever will?"

"Not with the Temples against them," Tauth said. Her voice had a whine to it under the words. Probably because of that axe of a nose. "And the High King. They will make a place for you."

"High King," Darsal repeated. "When did he claim that title?"

"He can claim whatever titles he wants," Shahan said. "That's what power gives him."

The words were as brash as ever, but there was a tightness around Shahan's eyes. Mani was close enough to see it, and he knew what it meant. His childhood friend was afraid, terrified even, and not just of the sea. Shahan had put out his hand to take Sarru-kin's money without knowing what it meant, and now he was caught in a storm he'd never imagined. He was trying to walk a thin line between friends and enemies, and he no longer knew which was which.

"We'll be at sea a long time," Shahan said. "It would be easier if we were friends, Mani."

You no longer know which is which. "I have nothing to say to you. Good day, Darsal."

With that Mani walked away. He heard Shahan call his name but didn't turn, and then Tauth said something he didn't catch. There were no more shouts. Mani went down the little slope and into Flood water, soaking his tunic to the knees. He was halfway back to Aš-alam before he let himself wipe away the tear that had come to his eye.

§ § §

Soldiers came for them the next morning, before the sun had touched the edge of the sky.

"This is it," Isha said as they dressed. She spoke softly, wary of the men waiting in the front room. "From now on we walk with snakes, in every moment. Watch your words."

"I always do."

"No," she murmured. She came close to him, dress half tied and one hand on his chest. "Your habit is to speak your mind, husband. I love that about you, but it's not always wise. You have a plan, don't you? So, hold your tongue when you can."

He bent and kissed her hair. "I will."

"For our baby," she said.

For the baby he would do anything. Throw himself on Sarru-kin's sickle sword or take on the whole Labaš army with a single knife. Mani didn't think he'd been unwise when speaking his mind, that was unfair, but he wasn't going to pick a fight about it. He kissed her again and sat down to buckle his sandals.

"We need changes of clothes," he said.

She filled a bag with tunics and dresses and went to the table where she kept the little make-up she used. Her hand hesitated and then she shook her head. "I won't need that."

"You don't need it here," he said.

That won him a smile, though it was tremulous. Mani took her hand and kissed her once more, and this time she clung to him. He could feel her trembling. There was a quiver in his own skin too, for that matter. They stood like that until a soldier banged a fist on the door, and then parted. When they looked at each other they both sighed.

"All right, then," Mani said, opening the door.

Chapter Thirty-Four

THE PATH TO the marsh was knee deep in water and lined with soldiers. A chariot waited for Mani and Isha at the city gates, on the mound that kept the city above the Flood. Mostly, anyway. In bad years water would reach the foot of the walls, which is why bitumen was painted on the lower courses of bricks. This morning it lapped at the ridge of earth that bumped under the gate.

"Another week and there will be water on the walls," Shahan said.

Mani stepped into the chariot car and didn't bother to answer. He saw his one-time friend grimace and ignored that too. Mani reached down to help Isha up beside him. A second car waited for Shahan and Tauth. When they were aboard, the drivers clicked their tongues, and the horses began to walk.

The army watched them go. Faces three deep on each side turned to look as they passed. Mani felt dwarfed, surrounded by men bigger and broader than he was, and he wondered what they were thinking. Did they believe the voyage was doomed? He might, in their place. He might think his king was sailing into nothing, never to be seen again, his pet scholars with him. If he was a man in this army from Kindar, or Piqash, he might pray for it.

"It would be best for the whole plain," Mani murmured, "and all the cities on it, if none of us ever came home."

Isha was turned half away, her hair falling down the side of her face. He could see her lips and read the words she barely spoke. "We walk with snakes, husband. Remember."

She was right. He held his tongue as the chariot rolled on.

When they reached the marsh, Sarru-kin was already there, standing on the wooden platform with his four hulking guards. The tall priestess, Kammani, was there too, standing proud a few yards away. Lesser *zami* waited behind her with a pair of tethered goats. Sarru-kin was going to sacrifice before they sailed, it seemed.

At the end of the pier the ship rested. Mani felt a churn in his stomach and looked away as the chariots came to a halt beside the platform. Water swirled around the wheels and was still.

"Come," a soldier said. It was the captain from before, Yarim. He reached out to help them across the gap. There were scars on his bare arms and a bad one on his thigh, evidence of a soldier's life. Even in times of peace between cities there were outlaws to hunt down, or cattle raiders from the hilly northlands. All the wounds were on his front. Mani remembered Udar telling him once that it was a sign of courage.

He let the man pull him over the gap. Isha followed, and Mani made sure to keep himself between her and the Mad King. It wouldn't do any good if Sarru-kin decided Isha was to die. Mani would stand in front of her anyway, and the child. Sweat made a clammy layer on his skin.

Shahan and Tauth came behind, and after them Shusikil. Her face was stone as always, but her eyes darted to and fro, betraying her unease. No, not that. It was fear she felt, roiling her guts like live snakes. Mani wondered if anyone else noticed.

Tauth saw Shusikil and nodded, very slightly. The bony woman nodded back, hardly moving her bald head. Then Sarru-kin moved towards the front of the platform. He rested one hand on the table set there, fingers curled into a fist.

"Destiny has brought me here," he said. His voice was loud, but there was no sense of him shouting. It was as though the world had become quieter when he started to speak. "Destiny, and you, my soldiers. Only one task now remains—to fulfil that destiny, and become your undying king, equal with the gods, and master of the world.

"In Labaš, the same divine mandate compelled me to remove the Elders. I was told they were no longer needed, so I acted." He twirled the sickle sword he almost always held, perhaps not even aware he did so. "But sanction was still needed and will be for as long as I remain mortal. The *zami* of the Temples of Balih spoke in my favour. Today I ask them to do so again, to bless our voyage and the Fate I seek."

Kammani stepped up beside him. She lifted a pair of bronze knives from the table and handed them to the other priestesses, handle first. The women knelt, shortened the ropes around their animals' necks, and slashed. It was over so fast the goats had no time to bleat. One moment alive, the next down on the boards and kicking as blood drained away. Kammani crouched to examine them. Looking at entrails, maybe, or the pattern blood made as it pooled and ran. Either could be used for divination.

Kammani handed the women cups, which they used to catch a little of the blood. She took them back, sipping first from one and then the other. Her lips wrinkled. Mani wasn't surprised that blood tasted so bad, but he thought Kammani was. He realised she was frowning.

Isha's hand crept into his like a mouse.

Something is wrong.

"The auguries are good," Kammani announced. She stood and came back to the table, opposite Sarru-kin. "Gamil, god of water, and Balih, god of war, have spoken. They say you will set your feet upon this hidden isle, my lord king. The gods told me the same in dreams last night. You will go and return as more than any man has ever been."

The Mad King turned his eyes up to heaven, like a man in prayer. "Balih told you this?"

"He did, my lord."

"Did he say anything of you?"

The answer was perhaps a bit slow in coming, the only hint that this composed woman might not understand. "He did not. But I am of no consequence in this."

"That is true," Sarru-kin said. He was still smiling, still gazing at the sky.

"Something's wrong," Isha whispered.

Unease crept over the back of Mani's neck on a thousand tiny feet, but all he said was, "Walk with snakes, remember?"

She dug her nails into his palm, making him wince.

"My lord?" Kammani said. Yarim shifted his weight. The Mad King said nothing, continuing to stare upwards while he twirled the sickle sword in the air. He'd been supposed to speak by now, Mani realised. His followers were growing edgy. The four guards around Sarru-kin watched for trouble, and nobody moved from their places. In the ranks of men below, waist deep in water, armour creaked and voices murmured like trickling water.

"Did you know that our ancestors once drank blood?" Sarru-kin asked. "All of them did, not just the *zami*. At first, it was to thicken milk into yogurt. Blood from oxen, usually. But they went on doing it even after Eala came here to Aš-alam with the gift of civilisation. Do you know why?"

Kammani rested a hand on the table. Her throat worked. Her other hand joined the first.

"To disguise unpleasant tastes," Sarru-kin told her. "I imagine it was medicines, but it hides poison just as well."

Kammani's skin had taken on a pale sheen. She leaned on the table and panted, staring at the king. Yarim made a convulsive movement, and all four guards swivelled to stare at him, hands drifting to the handles of their maces.

"The thoum plant," Sarru-kin went on. The sickle sword twirled. "Perhaps you know it? It is rare on the plain but more common to the north. It gives a poison that no one can survive. It tastes of copper, so it cannot be taken unknowingly— except if masked in a cup of blood. I smeared thoum on the cups, Kammani. You will be dead before I sail."

She tried to speak and couldn't. Spittle ran down her chin. Her skin had begun to turn yellow.

"You have been useful," the Mad King told her softly. "But the gods speak to me, through Azaq." He smiled at his curved blade. "They do not come to you in dreams. Did you think me a fool? Did you think I would not know you planned to use me for your own ends?"

Yarim twitched again but didn't move. Cords stood out on Kammani's neck as she struggled to speak, but all that emerged was a high moan, like a child's. She fell, crashing into the table and then the boards, to flop down on her back. Her chest heaved, green stuff spattered from her mouth, and then she lay still.

"We sail," Sarru-kin said.

A walkway ran from the platform to the pier. Sarru-kin went down it, pausing for a moment to look at Yarim. A bigger man, the soldier met that stare eye for eye, his skin stretched and taut. Then the four bodyguards came up to flank Sarru-kin and Yarim dropped his gaze. The Mad King smiled and moved on, still spinning the sickle sword in one hand.

"Eala's footfalls," Isha whispered.

Mani swallowed. His legs wanted to flee from here, back home to the city and then as far as they needed to run to make him safe. Except there was nowhere, here on the plain of Engiru or beyond, that was safe enough. Not now. A few yards away Yarim stood like a tree, unmoving.

"If I could spare you this I would," Mani said. The voice didn't sound like his own. "I'm so sorry. But there's nothing I can do."

"Not your fault." Her hand squeezed his. "Not your fault, husband. We must go with him."

"Yes," he said.

They walked towards the jetty, following the Mad King. Mani heard heavy footsteps behind and knew Yarim was coming too. There was something strange there, an oddity in how the soldier reacted to Kammani's death, but Mani was too shocked and afraid to think.

<h1 style="text-align:center">CHAPTER THIRTY-FIVE</h1>

A TURNING POINT. The Temples taught there were times in every life when the course of things changed. Mani supposed he still believed it, whatever reason he had to dislike the *zami* and their schemes. Their lies, too, but they had spoken a truth in this.

He boarded the ship. The reed deck gave under his feet. A soldier watched him, and a barefoot man at the base of the mast turned to look him up and down. A sailor, that one, his hands worn to overlapping calluses by years of work with rope and reed. He would have walked in far lands, seen leopards roam in Daqda and traded for ivory and coconuts in the Stone Town of Kumbi. Mani might see those places himself before this was over. He ought to be excited about that.

The whole ship was shaded by a second deck held up by wooden poles. Probably taken from the scaffolds of Aš-alam, Mani decided. He could see through gaps in the reed ceiling to cabins built on the upper surface. That was where Sarru-kin would sleep, then, and his trusted men. Mani took Isha's arm and led her aft, towards the platform where the steersman sat. Another man with callused hands and a face crinkled from years of squinting at sunlight off waves. He gave Mani a nod and a slight twist of his lips.

"He's not pleased about this voyage," Isha whispered.

His clever, clever wife. "No, he's not."

Men were still coming aboard. Mani tried to count without seeming to and thought Sarru-kin was taking ten or twelve soldiers, apart from his four ever-present guards. That was all, even on such a large ship. None of them knew how long they'd be at sea. It was better to take extra water than extra mouths.

Yarim was one of those soldiers. He stumbled across the deck and up a ladder to the top deck, wordless and pale.

There were unhappy men here. The steersman, Yarim, Mani himself, even Shahan. None of them wanted to be here. They all had different reasons. Yet here they were, swept up in the tail of the comet that was Sarru-kin. A rogue star, burning across the firmament of the world. Comets burned more brightly than the stars around them.

"Until they burn out," he said. Isha studied him, but he shook his head, and she didn't speak.

Holes had been left in the sides of the ship, six on each side, with a bench by each. Some had already been filled by sailors. The rest began to be taken by

Sarru-kin's men, stripped of their armour and weapons. They all unshipped oars and slotted them into place. Sarru-kin went to the steersman and said something.

The twist-lipped man stood and came to the front of the raised deck. "This is for you, soldiers. Remember that you don't know this work. Take advice from the sailors, take your rhythm from the man in front of you, and don't tangle the oars. The man at the back on each side controls the tempo. Tell me now if that isn't clear."

No one spoke. The man nodded to himself. "I am Ludari. On my ship my commands are followed. I'll accept orders from the king, but for everyone else when I speak, I might as well be king myself. You obey me and ask about it later, and by Eala's footfalls that had better be clear, or I'll toss you over the side.

"All right. Get ready to pull on my word."

He went back to his seat. Men were storing sealed flagons in the holds near the bow, and sacks of dried food beside them. The boarding plank was still in place. It wouldn't be for long. Mani could feel his pulse, a beat more rapid than it should be.

"There are no swimmers," Isha said.

He shook his head. "There won't be, with so many people around. Especially on shore. Wait until we're under way."

"What if there are none then?"

"If they don't appear?" He paused, but she deserved the truth, and he couldn't think of a lie. "Then I expect I'll be dead before we leave the river."

Isha looked at the water again.

Ludari shouted an order. The rower at the back of each bank of oarsmen gave a call, and with ragged splashes the blades went into the water. The ship trembled. Mani wasn't sure it had moved until he saw a gap opening between the hull and the jetty. Sailors shouted angrily, and the uneven strokes became more regular.

"We're really going," Isha said.

Mani swallowed. Now that they were moving, he wasn't sure he'd really believed it either, but he didn't want her to see that. She needed reassurance, not more doubt. "I always wanted to see the lands across the ocean. Maybe we can think of it that way."

"We're on a ship commanded by the Mad King," she said. "You must take him to an island nobody has ever seen, led by guides who aren't even human, so he can become an immortal god. If you don't, he's going to kill you, me, and our unborn child. I doubt I can think of it as an adventure."

"Well—"

"I'm afraid, Mani." Her voice was quiet but composed, her face calm. She didn't look afraid. He knew she was, could feel it in her, even before her hand crept back into his. "Two months ago, I was resigned to living my life alone. Then you came and asked to marry me, and now there's a baby growing inside me. I want it, Mani. I want that child in my arms so I can sing him to sleep and clean him when he's dirty, and I have so much to lose now that it makes me shiver when I think about it. I can't stop thinking about it, no matter what I do, because the Mad King is on this boat, and there's nothing I can do to make my family safe, and that kills me."

He had no reply to that. Mani squeezed her hand, she leaned against him, and that was all. It would have to be enough. He caught sight of Shahan from the side of his eye, standing not far away with Tauth a step behind him, as she always was. Mani thought that if Shahan tried to speak to him, he'd punch him or throw him overboard if he could. Maybe the other man sensed that, because Shahan hesitated and then moved away towards the ladders to the top deck.

A cough made him turn his head. Tauth had stayed. "You have a cabin up top. It's two along from ours. I can show you, if you like."

"We'll find it," Mani said briefly.

The long-nosed woman measured him. "Not all the *zami* are liars, scholar. Not all of them are cruel or evil. You're not helping yourself when you behave as though they are."

"The Temples lied," he said. Anger bubbled in him, and he fought it down. Here was a target for his rage, but it was control he needed, and he clung to it. "They told us Eala founded our city, when they knew all along it was the Puradu. All done for power. That's why my wife and I are in this boat. Because of lies a thousand years old."

"That's true." Her voice was nasal, like an old man whose nose has been broken too many times. "But how many priestesses knew? Only one or two at a time. Any more and the truth would have been spoken. A thousand years is a long time to keep a secret."

"Did you know?"

"Of course not. I was never consecrated, remember? I serve the Temples, but I'll never be a *zami.*" She bowed, perhaps in irony. Mani couldn't tell. "But it shouldn't have been done. I don't like deceit, scholar. If I can help you on this voyage, I will. Let me know."

Not in irony, then. Mani watched her leave with no clear idea how to respond. She was right, though, curse her for it. Only a very few priestesses could have known about the great lie. The rest were guilty of interfering, of being power-crazed old crones who stuck their noses into everyone else's business, but they hadn't known.

"We might have one friend on this boat after all," Isha said.

They might. Though how unlikely that the friend would be a woman who served the *zami*. Mani put an arm around Isha's shoulders, and together they watched the water slide by.

§ § §

As dusk approached, the captain ordered the anchor to be dropped off a low island. He leaned on the tiller, and the reed ship began to turn.

Mani was still at the rail. An hour ago, Isha had admitted to exhaustion and gone to bed, refusing to let him follow her. "You can't stick to me like a beetle in my hair, husband. Besides, if Sarru-kin wants to harm me he can. That's the hard truth, isn't it?"

He couldn't deny it.

"But he won't harm me tonight," Isha said. "I'm so afraid I have no spit in my mouth, but the Mad King won't harm me before we reach this fabled island in the ocean. He would lose his control over you, wouldn't he? And you're restless, Mani. I'm so tired I could sleep for a month, and I don't need you tossing to and fro like a fretted foal."

He stayed, watching the sun sink behind the ship. Aš-alam had been lost to sight for some time. There was nothing but still water, distant reeds, and the odd islands like the back of a giant sea beast. Such as the one Ludari had chosen for their night's anchorage. Mani looked for a sign of a hut, or a fishing smack pulled up in the reeds, and couldn't see one.

They might as well be the only people in the world, moving across its face in a fragile vessel of dry grasses.

"I have not seen your swimming people," Sarru-kin said.

Mani hadn't heard him approach. He turned to find the king studying him, sickle sword in hand as always and four men at his back. None of the guards ever seemed to smile or change expression at all. Their eyes had the same gleam as senior *zami* and young women just recruited as acolytes. One might call it zeal. Mani called it fanaticism.

"Do they abandon you?" the Mad King wondered. "Will they let us sail and never appear to guide us? Bad for you, if they do."

He tried to twirl the sword with its point in the deck, only for it to tangle in the reeds. His lips went thin as he pulled it clear. It was just an instant, but Mani saw then the insanity that lived in Sarru-kin, which wouldn't allow him to be baulked in the littlest thing. Madness was too gentle a word for it. There were demons in Sarru-kin's mind, eating whatever reason he'd once had.

"Well?"

"That doesn't make sense," Mani said. "The Puradu wouldn't have needed to let us sail and then betray us. They could just have refused and vanished into the lagoon. In fifty years, they might return when all this is gone. At best you would have been an old, old man, crouched on the shore with that sword in a wizened hand."

"And you would have died."

"Yes, but that doesn't mean anything to them. I told you before the Puradu don't think as we do, remember? I don't know why, or exactly how they think, but it's not as we do. If I hadn't taken my wife to them one day, that's exactly what they would have done."

"Fate smiles on me, then," Sarru-kin said. "As it always smiles on me. Except they are not here, scholar."

"Don't you think so?" Mani said.

He stepped aside, offering the Mad King his place at the rail. After a pause Sarru-kin stepped forward to stare down at the calm water. The sun was very low now. Light flashed back from the surface and turned everything below to gloom and green shadows.

"I see nothing," Sarru-kin said.

"Wait. Let your eyes adjust."

The Mad King bent further over. Mani was seized by a sudden urge to grab his legs and tip him in. Hardly anyone in Engiru could swim. In his armour Sarru-kin would go down like a falling rock, nothing but a trail of bubbles to show where he had fallen.

Except the Mad King had been prepared for everything. Each test had been met and overcome with ease. Who was to say he hadn't taught himself to swim? Besides, the four guards were only feet away, glowering all around but at Mani in particular. If he did grab the king, and somehow pitch him in, and if Sarru-kin did drown, Mani would plunge after him moments later. Their bones might keep each other company on the lagoon floor until the world grew old.

Mani wanted to see his child. More than anything, more even than the answers he'd sought for so long, he wanted that.

"Ah," Sarru-kin said.

There were shapes down there. Bodies about the same size as men that could be a dolphin or a fish but weren't. Mani knew the Puradu well enough to be sure of that. When Sarru-kin pushed away from the rail his face was shining again, his faith in his own divinity restored.

"Tomorrow, then," the Mad King said. "When we reach the open sea. You should sleep, scholar. If you can."

He strode away, surrounded by his guards. Mani looked down at the water.

"Tomorrow," he said.

Chapter Thirty-Six

IT WAS HARD to sleep in the cabin. The bed was made of rushes, covered over with sheepskin. Every time Mani or Isha moved, the mattress shifted strangely under them. He slept in fits, disturbed every few minutes by an odd ripple in the bed, or the call of night birds, or the footstep of a soldier along the deck. Or by his own dark dreams and fears.

He woke early and went on deck to find the ship about to move.

"We'll make the sea today," Ludari said. He was already by the steering handle, feet propped on the bench. Mani wondered if he'd slept there. "High tide is early afternoon. If we miss that we'll have to lay up for a day, and I don't reckon the king would like that."

"I don't either," Mani said.

Ludari gestured. "There's a bowl of fruit there, and honey bread. Reckon you're used to better for breakfast, eh?"

"This will do well enough."

"You don't look like a scholar," Ludari said. He eyed Mani through eyes sunk in webs of crinkles. "I always thought they were soft. You don't look soft to me."

"I think I used to be," Mani said. "A month ago, even."

"Yeah. It's been that sort of time for a lot of us." His lips twisted again. "Have something to eat. We can't have you fainting with hunger, eh?"

Mani took a pear and went to the side. He'd taken two bites when Ludari called an order and the oars bit water, more smoothly than they had yesterday. The big ship stirred, wallowed, and then began to move. She was slow to start and slow to stop, probably more so than smaller ships. Mani wondered if such a large vessel would ride ocean waves or be broken by them, her frame snapped like twigs in the wind.

"Bet Sarru-kin thought of that, too," he murmured. "Probably back in Labaš, years ago, when everyone thought he was normal."

"Talking to yourself, scholar?"

He looked straight down, where the voice had come from, and there was Hanno. The young Puradu swam with one hand on the ship's hull, almost directly under the rail. He'd be invisible to anyone not leaning over a little, which Mani supposed was the point.

"I'm the only one who listens," he said.

"You scholars always know how to do that," Hanno said. "Listen to me, now. We'll be with your ship. People might see us, but we'll keep our distance unless we have something to say. Make sure you come near the rail, alone, a few times each day."

181

"I will."

"We'll have weapons. Tell your Mad King not to be alarmed."

"Weapons?"

"Spears, tridents, and nets, mostly. There are dangers in ocean deeps, Mani. A shark will attack anything if it's hungry enough."

He thought of the *dakua,* a killer fish that rose from the depths to take its prey and then was gone again into the dark. "I'll tell him. I don't know if he'll listen."

"Maybe he won't. Give this instruction to your helmsman. When you leave the estuary, sail due south. There will be a wind behind you."

"That's straight away from land."

"Yes." Hanno smiled. "That's where the ocean is, Mani. Trust me. We won't break faith with you."

"I do trust you," he said.

Hanno lifted a hand in what might have been a salute. He dived and was lost in the ripples spreading from the hull.

Mani finished his pear and threw the core overboard. When he turned it was to find Ludari watching him from the steerman's seat, that twisty set to his lips again. Maybe the man always looked that sour. There was nothing Mani could do about it, so he went over and told him what Hanno had said. Ludari's face was just wrinkles and wear, impossible to read.

"South," the captain said. "Due south."

"Yes."

"And we'll have wind with us, eh?"

"So he says."

Ludari scratched his ear. "You know, we boatmen tell stories of the swimmers. You hardly ever see them, really. When you do, they're just shapes, deep down, like they were yesterday, remember?"

"Yes. Sarru-kin couldn't see them."

"No," Ludari agreed. He flicked Mani a glance, one which weighed whether he could be trusted. Ludari must have decided yes, because he scratched his ear again and went on. "I've seen them close twice. The first time as a raw sailor, about fifteen years old and sure there was adventure behind the next wave. Then again, half a lifetime later, as captain of my own boat. That time he surfaced and spoke to me. Warned me there was flotsam ahead, and he wasn't wrong. I think a ship went down there, and the wreckage might have sunk us too if we hadn't been warned."

"They want to help," Mani said. "That's why they come to the marsh. It's why they helped us build Aš-alam, a thousand years ago."

"Did they, you say?" Ludari shook his head and pulled the steer handle towards him a little. "Well, maybe, but there are other stories, eh? Times when Sea-Folk climbed the rails in the night and slaughtered every man aboard. Times when they led ships onto rocks and plundered the debris, after. They're bad luck. We never fish when they might be in the water, and we never harm them. Don't want to rile them, you see?"

"If they slaughter everyone aboard, who tells the stories?"

The boatman grinned. "I didn't say it made sense, did I? But it doesn't have to. You had an education, right? Then you know superstition doesn't need to be true. Just to be believed."

It was hard not to like Ludari. There was a sort of gritty honesty about him, the directness of a man who knows deceit and can't be bothered with the effort. "Well, usually I'd say you don't need to worry, but on this trip I don't know. We're heading for their sacred ground."

"I know," Ludari said. "We'll put no nets in the water, and we'll speak our prayers to Eala and Gamil. There's not much else we can do." Eyes glimmered sardonically through the crinkles. "It's a dangerous place you've brought us to, scholar."

"Not me," he said.

"I suppose not." Ludari leaned on the handle again. The ship began to turn back the other way, to pass on the left of another islet. "Reckon we'll be lucky to see home again, eh?"

"Yes," Mani said. "Ludari, why did you agree to come, if you think this is so dangerous?"

"To see what's never been seen," the captain answered. "I wanted to go everywhere when I was a boy. Daqda and Kumbi in the west, or Pallavas the other way. Well, I've been there. I used to gawk at the elephants and the tigers, but after a while I stopped noticing them, and you know what? The streets in those cities are just as dirty as in Aš-alam. There are still cripples begging for coins and children sick with rickets."

"So, you want to see a place of true marvels."

"If that's what it is. Most likely, it'll turn out to be no better than anywhere else. Just different." He smiled and squinted at the same time. "And just maybe, it will be the adventure behind the next wave."

"Maybe it will," Mani agreed.

"Be careful of the Mad King," Ludari said. "He'll see you dead as quick as a blink if he's crossed."

He must have decided Mani could be trusted after all. There was nothing else to say though, no words that were safe to speak. Mani took another pear for Isha and went to their cabin to wake her.

§ § §

Just after midday the water through which they rowed began to ripple. There was a wind, the first all day, blowing from the north. Not a strong wind, but it was there. Mani and Ludari shared a glance.

Then the reeds drew back, all at once, and the boat bobbed as it was caught in currents of the Ranuna.

Here the river was huge, five times as wide as at Aš-alam. The far bank might as well be another world, around one of the stars the Puradu claimed was just like the sun. It looked the same, and tiny fishing smacks moved near the distant shore. Isha reached for Mani's hand, but this time it was he who caught her fingers first, his hand that crept into hers like a mouse.

"So much water," he said. "How can there be so much water?"

A sailor behind him choked on a laugh.

The ship turned right, pushed by the Ranuna's endless flow. There ahead of them was the reason for the seaman's laugh. The sea stretched across the world, vast beyond imagining, curving at a horizon impossibly far away. The river's current poured into it, vast and massive, and was swallowed. Brown water grew paler and was lost. The breeze capped every wave with white here and there in an ever-changing pattern.

Mani swallowed.

"Raise sail!" Ludari bellowed.

Sailors standing behind the upper deck hauled on ropes. A sheet of cotton rose from a pile on the floor, pulled by twenty thin cords to the horizontal bar above. A yard, Mani thought it was called. The sail billowed, and then sagged, and the ship wallowed where she sat.

"Damn," Isha said, throwing up over the side. Over Mani too, or at least his arm. He held her shoulders while she heaved and wiped her mouth when it ended. Someone had brought a cup of water, and he held it to her lips while she sipped.

"That only happened because I'm pregnant," she said finally. "It's your fault."

He rested his forehead against her cheek. "Bad baby."

"Yes," Isha said. She guided his hand to her stomach, still as flat as the plain. "Bad baby."

The sail bagged again, and this time stayed full. The boat rose out of the water and men shipped their oars, stowing them along the foot of the rail. For the first time Mani felt a sense of speed, the vessel moving under him, and his stomach stirred uneasily.

Ahead of him, out in the river, two shapes broke the surface for a moment, like jumping fish. A third followed them moments later, and this time something glittered where the figure might have had a hand, if Mani had been close enough to see. It could have been the splash of water.

Or it could have been a blade.

Chapter Thirty-Seven

ISHA WAS ILL all day. Mani stayed with her as much as he could, with a bucket by the bed and a pile of damp cloths on the reed floor. When she dozed, he slipped away to empty the bucket and spend a moment by the rail, hoping a Puradu would appear.

None did, but Sarru-kin was always there.

He would be watching when Mani came on deck, sometimes from his own door further astern, or through a ladder hole from the deck below. The sickle sword was sheathed on his back now. Ludari had told him not to spin the point on his deck for fear of piercing the bitumen that kept water out. The king had listened with a strange expression on his face that made Mani think Ludari may need to hide when they all reached home.

Sarru-kin put the sword away. Since then, his hands had writhed over each other, itching for the handle they couldn't touch. The flush never left his face now. Either the madness had him more firmly, or he really was halfway immortal already.

"How far to your island?" the Mad King asked, just after midday. "How long to reach it?"

"I don't know," Mani answered. "They tell me what I need to know, when I need it. Nothing more."

"Then let us hope what they tell you is true," Sarru-kin said. His hands dry-washed each other, over and again.

The seas were calm, the sky a blaze fluffed with clouds. There was no sign of trouble, but they were still heading due south, a light wind at their backs. Some of the sailors didn't like that.

"We're too far from land," Mani heard one of them tell the captain. "I've been a sailor twenty years and ain't never been this far out. If anything goes wrong, we'll be food for sharks."

Ludari shrugged. "You want to tell the king, you go right ahead and speak to him, eh?"

Nobody spoke to the king. There were his hulking guards to think of, though mostly the fear was just of the king. There was a lot of exchanging glances, each one darker than the last, all behind Sarru-kin's back. Knowing him, he probably saw them and didn't care. Not yet anyway. The sailors might need to find a sanctuary as soon as they reached home again, too.

By evening Isha was a little better. She ate an apple and managed to hold it down, and some sips of water too. After that she fell into a proper sleep. Mani lay beside her, watching through the door as light faded from the day.

Two days since they'd left Aš-alam and one day on the open sea. Still, Mani had no idea where they were going. He'd caught glimpses of Puradu around the ship, breasting the waves and then sinking beneath them again. They could breathe in the deeps, so they must only be showing themselves for his sake, letting the Mad King know they were there. Or they could be playing, he supposed, the way dolphins were said to. He still knew almost nothing about their lives, after all these years.

He couldn't sleep. After an hour Mani rose, slipped into his tunic, and crept out of the cabin. For once Sarru-kin wasn't there. Half-immortal he might be, but he still needed to sleep. Mani went to the water barrel and dipped a cup. He'd found it was best on board a ship to drink in sips and eat small bites to keep his stomach settled. Insofar as it was settled. Fear and uncertainty were a bad mix for a calm belly.

Ludari wasn't on the tiller. The captain needed to sleep, too, however reluctant he was to leave his place on the steering bench. A sailor sat there now, not much more than a shape in the darkness but too big to be Ludari. After a moment, Mani turned and went forward instead to watch the sea from what sailors called the prow. Someone was there already.

Shahan and his wife. In the dark her nose was hidden, and you'd think her beautiful, a slim and rounded figure lit by starlight. Mani stopped, not sure whether to retreat or stay.

"Can you blame him?" Tauth asked.

Shahan's silhouette shifted. "No. I suppose not."

"Mani might soften, in time," she said. "But you did betray him. You betrayed all of us."

"I know," he said.

"Why did you do it?"

"Take Sarru-kin's coin? Because it didn't seem to do any harm. He was a long way away. It never occurred to me that he might roll up to the gates of Aš-alam one day. Scholars don't make a lot of money, you know. Not in the first few years, at least."

"You shouldn't have done it."

"No, I shouldn't have." Moonlight on his face showed a grin, the old expression Mani knew so well. *Who, me?* "But there's always wine to drink, Tauth, and women to seduce. Or pay for—that's good too. Before you, I mean."

"You've been to the Scented Houses since we were married."

"You know about that? Oh."

"Would you have done that to a wife you'd chosen yourself?"

"I don't know. Probably." Shahan's grin flashed again. "There's always more wine and more women, Tauth. I mean, I like you, but I never wanted anyone for my wife."

"I know. I like you too, Shahan." Her face was turned away from Mani, but he heard a change in her tone. "But I serve the Temples before I serve my husband."

"I know," Shahan said. He rolled his eyes, as though to say that was too obvious to be worth a mention.

Tauth's arm moved. Mani thought he saw something flash, and Shahan hunched forward, staring at her with wide eyes. Her hand came back and pushed again. Shahan made a choking sound. Mani watched and couldn't move his feet or make a sound.

"I never wanted to marry either." Tauth's voice wavered. "But you shouldn't have betrayed the city. What can't be forgiven is that you betrayed Eala."

She threw something over the side. It glittered and was lost to the sea. Then she caught Shahan around the throat and chest, and he went backwards into the rail and toppled over it. There was a splash. The ship kept moving, the sail baggy with wind.

Tauth turned, took a step, and saw Mani standing by the ladder.

She stopped. They stood and looked at one another, she in moonlight and he in shadow. Mani remembered to breathe and drew in night air. At last, Tauth moved. She walked past him to the ladder and climbed out of sight, turning towards the stern. He listened to the tread of her footfalls until he couldn't hear them anymore.

Mani looked up at the moon, breathing through his nose. There was a bitter taste in his throat, and his heart ached, but there were no tears. No tears for his friend.

After a long time, he turned and went up the ladder. He walked along the upper deck, rushes crackling under his feet, and found the doorway to his cabin. Isha was still asleep, on her left side by the wall. Mani pulled off his tunic and eased into bed next to her.

A moment, and *then* tears came, so hard he couldn't hold them in or stay silent. A sob broke from his lips, then another. He tried to bite them down and couldn't. He was shaking, he realised, shuddering like a broken-hearted child with salt water on his cheeks.

Then Isha was holding him, his head on her shoulder. Mani let himself weep. The scholar in him whispered the tears weren't all for Shahan, but for himself and his wife, their baby, and all their futures. For the fear and horror Sarru-kin trailed in his wake like dust.

His shaking calmed, bit by bit. He didn't know how long it was before the tears stopped.

"What?" Isha whispered, lips to his ear.

There would always be someone listening on this ship. *We walk with snakes.* Mani turned his head so he spoke into her neck. "Shahan."

Her fingers dug into his back. "Gone?"

His clever wife. Perhaps she'd expected it, even back in Aš-alam. When Shahan was brought on the voyage, she must have known it for certain. Mani had never even considered it. He'd known Shahan would face retribution one day, or else the casual viciousness of the Mad King, but not yet. Not on this boat, and not from Tauth.

He nodded. Isha folded her arms around him, and the tears came again.

§ § §

"We didn't see you this morning."

"No," Mani said.

Hanno ducked underwater and came up again, blinking. "Are you ill? You look not quite here."

Mani thought he should ask about that phrase, but there was no energy in him. "No, I'm not ill."

"Then turn east. A little north of due east, if your helmsman can manage that. Tell him now, and then come back. You should have turned an hour ago."

Mani went to the tiller. Ludari's eyes sank deeper into their nested crinkles as he explained.

"East," the captain said. "That's straight into the current."

"A bit north of east. Can we do it?"

"I can do it," Ludari said, with emphasis. "I'll angle the sail to catch wind. But we'll be slow. Tell your friends that."

When Mani got back to the rail the sea below was empty. He waited, and after a moment Hanno surfaced, reaching to grip the black hull. Amid the swirl of water, Mani saw his other hand with a spear in it. He didn't say anything. There were sharks in the ocean and sharks on the ship, and everyone protected themselves as best they could.

The ship had started to turn. "You did well, scholar."

"He didn't like it," Mani said. "He says the current will slow us down."

"You don't need to worry about the current. Trust me." There was a low hum, nearly too deep to hear, and Mani thought the young swimmer was laughing. He couldn't see the ripples in the ship's wash though. "We saw Shahan last night. In the water."

"Is he all right?" Mani asked before he could stop himself.

"He was bleeding from two stomach wounds in waters filled with sharks," Hanno said. "No, he's not all right. He was dying anyway, so we left him."

188

"You didn't help?"

"There are sharks," Hanno said, as though Mani was being deliberately dim.

That was it, then. There had been a spark of hope when Hanno said they'd seen Shahan, but that had died now. They had swum past him, leaving him to drift in the water as sharks smelled his blood. Mani couldn't imagine what that had been like. It would have been kinder for Shahan to die as Kammani had, choking on poison in the sunshine.

The Puradu were alien. They didn't think as humans did. Mani had never seen that as clearly as he did now.

"I'm sorry," Hanno said. "Should we have saved him?"

Saved him for what? Shahan would have had to come back on board. He'd have accused Tauth, who might have been killed then, too. Shahan would probably still have died. Two stabs to the belly killed most people.

"No," Mani said. "I suppose not."

Hanno peered up at him. "Stay on this course, Mani. Be here tomorrow morning, not long after dawn."

"What will we have to," Mani began, but the Puradu was gone, back under the water where his friends swam. Where sharks swam too, and bloodied bodies tumbled. Nothing to be done about that.

"I hope it was quick for you," he said to the sea. To Shahan's spirit, if it was still nearby. Then he went to find his wife.

Chapter Thirty-Eight

"WHY EAST?" TAUTH asked.

"I don't know," Mani said.

He had no idea how to talk to her, especially with Shusikil glowering at her side. Tauth had murdered his best friend, the companion of so many studies and games. For most of their childhoods it had been Mani and Shahan together, the clever boys, set apart from their peers by wit and understanding. Bullied by some for having wit when others had fists. Everyone always said they were meant for better things, even when they were six years old.

They had gone together to a Scented House when they were sixteen. The first time Mani had been with a woman. Shahan said he'd had a lover before, but Mani thought it was his first time, too. Their hands had both trembled as they handed over coins to a man with a knowing smile. He winked as one of the women took Shahan's hand. For once Shahan had been caught without a quip, his eyes wide and white as he was led upstairs.

Mani always remembered that look. Past the charm, under the easy arrogance, there was an uncertainty no one else saw. Mani himself had only seen it twice, perhaps. Once seen it was impossible to mistake or forget. That was Shahan. Grins and insouciance, and a soft soul beneath.

Gone now. Mani couldn't even claim it was unfair or undeserved. A palace is a slippery place. Shahan had mixed himself into the business of a king, a palace, and missed his footing.

The day was ending. Behind them the sun had begun to turn orange as it sank, and it looked swollen to Mani. Maybe that was because his eyes were red.

"I thought they talked to you," Shusikil said.

"They do." Mani was too tired to listen to this. "Did you have a purpose with me, *zami*, or did you just come to nag?"

The two priestesses fixed him with identical glares. It was a shame Tauth couldn't work her numbers, because she had the *zami* glower down pat already. In twenty years, she would have been a crone to terrify innocents. That nose helped. Mani had seen ravens with smaller beaks.

"What are you going to tell the king," Shusikil said, "about how our city was founded?"

"The truth, I suppose."

"Don't you think that might cause harm?"

"Perhaps. Don't you think that dishonesty does? As a rule, I prefer truth to lies, and it's not just me. I seem to remember that the Temples exhort us to be honest."

"Don't be clever."

"I have no other way to be," Mani said. "I'm flawed, *zami*. I know that. It's only taken my wife a few weeks to come up with a long list of my faults. I am clever though. I'm not going to deny it for you."

"If you tell people that we lied," Tauth said, "then you're telling them their faith is a lie, too. Faith is all the poor have. Many won't believe you. But you'll destroy the ones who do."

"I was poor as a boy. I'd have preferred the truth to a comforting lie."

"Does the truth feed you?"

"Do lies? Stop it, now. I don't know what I'll do if we ever get back to Aš-alam, but it will be guided by my conscience. You might remember what that is, if you try." Mani held up a hand when they tried to interrupt. "Spare me, *zami*. I'm not in the mood to listen to your self-justifications. We have larger problems anyway, don't we?"

"Sarru-kin," Shusikil said, her voice suddenly an undertone. "He's the enemy, Mani, not us. We should work together against him."

"You want me as an ally?" He laughed. "No. No, I don't think so."

"It would make sense. Together we could—"

"Achieve nothing," he broke in. "As we can achieve nothing now. He has his guards and his soldiers, and there's nothing we can do except see where this journey takes us. I won't endanger my wife and child with some idiotic plan you cook up."

"We can—"

"Besides which, I don't trust you. The *zami* lie. Haven't you been listening to me?"

"Will you listen to *me*?" Shusikil shouted.

Too loud. A couple of sailors looked around, and a soldier near the stern as well. Part of Mani wanted to snarl at them, dare them to confront him about what was being said. There was so much fear and sorrow in him now. He just wanted to scream in someone's face until the pressure eased. But he wouldn't. There was Isha and the child.

Isha and the child. Always, there in his mind like a talisman, a gleam in all this darkness.

"No," Mani said. "I won't listen to you. The *zami* have lied to me for too long. You tried to marry me off to one of your own. When I forestalled you, you threatened my wife. You talk piety from the sides of your mouths and make a mockery of it when you act. I don't want any part of you. Stay away from me, priestess."

He went away from them to the stern so he could watch the sun go down.

He wished Isha could watch it with him. She was still sick, able to swallow nothing but water and a few bites of dry biscuit. It wasn't possible for him to stay with her, because he was needed in case the Puradu wanted to talk. He had to stay on deck, which was where the two women had found him. One a priestess, the other a fanatic and a murderer.

"Can you smell anything?" Ludari asked from the tiller.

Mani tried to pull his mind away from the *zami*. "Sea and salt air. Why?"

"Keep thinking I smell something strange. I don't know what. It's nothing I've smelled before."

"Everything here smells strange to me," Mani said. He leaned on the rail a yard from the captain. "I'm no sailor."

Ludari measured him for a moment. "Neither was your friend, eh? The missing one. Do you know anything about that?"

"Nothing," he lied.

Those eyes noticed everything from inside their nests of wrinkles, and Mani didn't think the other man believed him. Ludari didn't push it though. He moved the steer handle a fraction one way, waited, then pulled it halfway back. The boat might have swayed a bit, as far as Mani could tell, but not much more.

"She's a good ship," Ludari said. "I didn't expect that. She's too big and too flat on the bottom for the ocean. A storm would wreck us, eh? The weather's been kind so far."

A pair of human-looking backs broke the water thirty yards away, and without thinking Mani said, "It might not be luck."

"Might not be, at that. Which doesn't make me much easier in my mind."

Mani squinted at the sun. It was very low now, almost touching the sea. He didn't answer.

"Any idea how much further we have to go?"

"No. The Puradu don't tell me everything." He shaded his eyes. "Ludari? Have you ever seen a blue sun?"

The captain stared at him, and then in one movement stood up and twisted to look behind.

The sun was still the same to a casual glance. When you looked closer, there was a bluish light around the rim, like sunlight through rain. Mani lifted a hand and felt his eyes ache. The shadow of his fingers was wrong, too sharp, and the light on the reed hull too bright.

"I never saw that before," Ludari said. "Never."

He sounded shocked to his toes, but one hand never left the tiller. As he spoke he pulled, angling the ship a tiny fraction to one side. It was just instinct, the ground-in habits of a man at sea all his life. It was reassuring, in a way. There was very little here that Mani liked, but that was one thing.

"The air *is* wrong," Ludari said. "I knew it was. I just couldn't work it out. Now I don't have to. This is the doing of the swimmers, isn't it?"

"I think it must be," Mani agreed.

The sun touched the sea, and suddenly the light and shadows were normal again. Maybe because twilight masked the differences. Mani realised his mind was trying to work out the answer, a habit as deeply worn as any of Ludari's, and he chuckled to himself. It felt strange. His last laugh might have been a hundred years ago.

Something else was wrong. He was looking down at his hands, and the shadows there were moving. Ludari had sat back down, though, and the boat was steady. Darkness was gathering like a shroud, but it wasn't complete. Mani craned his head back.

There was a moon above. Not the normal one. This was small and roughly oval, a stretched pearl flying across the sky like a god's flung fire. Mani could see it move, eating the stars ahead as it went. Behind it they winked back to life. It might take an hour for the moon to cross the whole sky, maybe a little more. Mani stared at it, hardly breathing.

"Well," Ludari said. He was looking up too and sounded hoarse. "I never saw that before, either."

The stars were suns like our own, Mani remembered. The Puradu had told him that. The gulfs between were a sea that could be sailed.

They had never said you built a ship in the sky to do it.

"Eala have mercy on us all," he whispered. "We've travelled to a different world."

Ludari jerked so hard the handle was wrenched to the side. He didn't even seem to notice. The ship began to veer north, and Mani reached for the tiller to push it over again. His hand came down on top of Ludari's, and the captain recovered himself with another twitch. "I've got it."

"All right," Mani said. He took his hand back. "I might be wrong. This is new to me as well."

Ludari laughed, a bit unsteadily. "When was the last time you were wrong, scholar? About your work?"

Mani knew he wasn't wrong. He looked at the stars and saw none of the constellations he knew, none of the familiar guides in the sky. Ludari would know that too. Sailors knew the stars better than the bodies of their lovers. "This isn't my work. And my wife would tell you I'm wrong fifteen times a day."

He meant it to lighten the mood and saw Ludari smile under his beard. "Only fifteen? You're a lucky man."

"Yes," Mani said. The last slice of sun disappeared, and he looked at the racing moon above. "The luckiest man in the world."

Chapter Thirty-Nine

A SECOND MOON appeared just before midnight. It was smaller than the first but brighter, shining nearly blue. Mani watched it from the doorway of his cabin with Isha sleeping behind him. A knot of sailors on the deck below muttered and made sacred signs, until someone came and shouted at them to go back to their work.

"Good idea," Mani murmured. A new world was not the place to let the ship sail itself.

He thought he could sit there for a week and not sleep. In the end he dozed, though, waking to see the first moon scything across the sky again. He sat and watched the shadows move until he fell asleep again, head nodding on his chest.

This time he woke to see Sarru-kin staring at the sky.

"The gods may be different here," the Mad King said.

Mani blinked at him. "What?"

"The gods," Sarru-kin said. "Who is to say the gods are the same in this world as in ours? Destiny may take a different shape. Is that not a legitimate concern, scholar?"

"I suppose so." He was trying to wake up. Being in a different world when Sarru-kin woke you ought to be enough to jolt any man to wakefulness, but apparently not. "To you, anyway."

"Of course to me. How could it matter to ordinary men?"

"They might pray and find no god to answer," Mani said.

"A fate that might change the course of the world," Sarru-kin said sardonically. His hands dry-washed each other, still bereft of the sickle sword to spin and twirl.

Mani didn't say anything. Being awake seemed to mean he was prone to speaking when he should be quiet. Isha had warned him about that. It was time he started to listen. Two of Sarru-kin's big guards were in sight, and they wouldn't hesitate to kill him.

"I may keep your wife as a concubine," Sarru-kin said.

Mani's mouth fell open.

"She has a certain attraction. Not at first glance, but when one sees her move. I like interesting people around me." He gestured. "Like yourself, scholar. I sensed something in you when we first met in Labaš, and I was right. You have brought us to another world."

Moon shadows chased each other across the deck.

"Most men are mud," Sarru-kin said. "Mud given shape for a time, and no more. Only some men, a very few, act on the world instead of passing through it. Men like me, scholar, and like you, too. I will live forever, because that is my destiny, but it was you who led me here. I will not forget it or separate you from your child when it is born. I assume you hope for a son?"

"You can't have Isha," Mani said.

Sarru-kin turned his eyes skyward, as though communing with an unseen god. "I can have whatever I choose."

"No," Isha said from the cabin.

Both men turned towards her. Even Sarru-kin looked startled, the first time Mani could remember any expression on him except serenity. Isha was on her feet, belting a robe around herself. She was very pale, but there was a set to her lips Mani recognised.

"I will not be yours," she said. "Not willingly. You can force me, of course. I know that. But you'll always be waiting for the knife in the dark, or a rope around your neck."

"Women are searched before they come to me."

"By guards as clever as I am? Do you think they'd find something if I didn't want it found?"

Mani swallowed. The Mad King stared at Isha with hot eyes, set in a face flushed even by moonlight. His guards moved forward, sensing trouble even if they weren't sure where it was.

"To places!" Ludari bellowed from the stern. "To places, I said. Call the oarsmen to the bench!"

Sarru-kin's head snapped around. "Does he think he gives orders here? Come!" The last was to his guards, who flanked him as he started towards the tiller. One went ahead of the Mad King down the ladder, in case an assassin waited at the bottom. Mani watched them go, his heart thumping. He hadn't stood up during the whole exchange.

"You're braver than a lion." Isha laid a hand on his shoulder. "And as stupid as a goat. What were you doing, speaking to him like that?"

A laugh was torn out of him. It sounded crazed, as insane as the Mad King himself. "*I* was stupid? You just threatened to throttle him in his sleep, and I was stupid?"

She might have flushed. In the sharp-edged moonlight it was hard to tell. "I'm not his. Mani, what's wrong with the light?"

"The moon's different," he said. It was only then that he remembered what Ludari had shouted and knew what it must mean. His hands were still trembling, but he grinned despite himself. "Come with me."

"What?"

"Sarru-kin went to the stern," Mani said. "We'll go the other way. Come with me, Isha."

She did, barefoot on the reed deck. Her colour was still wrong, but she moved without hunching over her stomach now for the first time since they sailed. They hurried past people emerging from cabins, rubbing sleep from their eyes. Some stared at the racing moon with slack jaws. Others didn't notice. The strangest sight they would ever see, and they didn't notice. On the deck below sailors blundered out of their hammocks, still half asleep but trained by habit to know where they were needed and get there just as they woke.

"Mani," Isha said, "what is it?"

"Ludari wants the oarsmen ready," he answered. "A ship only uses oars in dead calm, which this isn't—or in inland waters."

"Like the lagoon," she realised. "We're near land."

"Near enough to see," Mani said.

They burst past the last cabin, and there it was, dead ahead of the big ship. A bank of clouds, lit on top in silver and blue by the moon. Under it was a smudge, a smear that wasn't water and so could only be land. Mani felt his breath grow short. Not from running.

"Eala's footfalls," Isha whispered. "It's real. It's real."

The island of the Puradu. It couldn't be anything else. A place of dreams for scholars in Aš-alam for generations. They had swapped speculations over cups of beer, sneered at one another's ideas and then borrowed them, all with hardly a shred of evidence. Tash-Yal scratched his notes and linked them with threads, trying to make sense of the senseless and failing. So little was known that anyone could make any guess, and no one could prove him wrong.

Scholars worked with tiny details, accidental clues, gleaned over years of patience. You couldn't blame them if their imaginations sometimes ran amok.

Through all the years, century after century, the dream had been to be here, in sight of the Puradu's home.

"This is it," he said.

He was the first scholar to lay eyes on this. Almost certainly he'd be the last. It was his duty now to see as much as he could, remember it, and write it down on a tablet or carve it in stone. Cut it into his skin if he had to—anything that preserved the knowledge to be studied by men back home. It wasn't only his.

More than that, this was where Sarru-kin meant to become a god, and if he did, he might bring terror to Engiru forever.

Something broke water and splashed back, not far to the side. Mani couldn't see if it was a Puradu or a shark.

§ § §

The land drew closer.

Mani began to make out details. There were mountains on the island, three peaks that reared up like towers. Moonlight glimmered blue on their flanks. Between them were valleys the shape of horseshoes, falling to beaches and bays still hidden by the night. Mani stared until his eyes ached, but the details wouldn't come clear.

"Rest," Isha said. "Eat, husband. It will be hours before we make landfall."

She was right, but Mani couldn't relax. He ate two bites of an apple, put it down again, and then nibbled at the edge of a hard biscuit he couldn't swallow. After a cup of water, he went back to the prow to stare at the approaching land once more. This time Sarru-kin was on the deck above, hands writhing over one another. He glanced at Mani but didn't speak.

Tauth was by the rail as well. She kept silent too, for which Mani was just as grateful. He still didn't know what to say to her and had no attention for anything but the island anyway.

Closer yet. He began to pick out acres of trees, running down almost to the shoreline. The peaks rose out of them, bare-shouldered, their shadows stark in the night.

Then the mountains flashed blue at the edges. For a moment Mani thought the island had caught fire, and then he realised it was the light of dawn, blazing from behind the peaks. He scrubbed at his eyes but still saw livid scars when he blinked.

"Scholar."

Mani looked down to see Hanno, swimming alongside the ship. The Puradu dived and came up again, cutting through the waves. "No weapons." Dive, surface. "On shore. Tell them." Dive and surface, spray pouring from him. "No weapons."

"No need," Sarru-kin called down. "I heard."

Hanno turned on his back to stare up at the king. A wave covered him, and this time he didn't come back up.

"Look." Isha's hand closed on Mani's arm. "Look!"

The sun had climbed over the side of the island. Suddenly the sea was washed in bluish light, and the isle too. Mani saw beaches and headlands with rocks for teeth and mountains rising behind. In between were forests, but they were split by lakes like rainbows, green water shimmered by the alien sun. He made out cabins by some of them, sheltered under trees.

"Built for whom?" he wondered.

The oars splashed. Puradu rose and fell ahead of the ship, showing the way in. Ludari shouted something and the port side stopped rowing, starting again at a second yell. The ship spun to the left and straightened again with her nose aimed straight between two promontories. There were rocks on each side now but only open water ahead, and then a bay. Mani knew nothing of sailing, but he knew expertise when he saw it, and he grinned in appreciation.

Right now, almost anything would make him grin.

He looked at the cabins again, trying to pick out any details. They were just houses, though, with doors and windows like any building back home. Something Barak had said came back to Mani then, from one of their talks by the pier. *Wives can't swim.*

Mani had wondered what the Puradu did to them. Cropped their tails, he'd thought. His forehead creased.

"They can walk," he said. "Eala's footfalls, the wives can walk!"

"What?"

Mani didn't answer his wife. He squinted in the strange light, trying to squeeze detail from the lakeside cabins, but it was useless. The ship was too near now anyway, so trees began to obscure huts and pools alike. The vessel nosed between the headlands. Water foamed around rocks on either side. There might be currents here, but Mani didn't feel anything or hear the groan of the timber frame as the ship was pulled two ways. He laughed at himself. He was in a different world, in the blue light of a strange sun, and he was worrying about currents.

Then the rocks were past, and the boat came into a wide bay. Now Mani felt the difference of still water, as waves diminished to ripples. There was a beach ahead and people waiting, some in the water and some under the trees, near where a stream poured across golden sand.

Under the trees. Standing.

The wives.

Chapter Forty

I WON'T BE able to speak with you now."

Hanno was in the water, one hand braced against the ship's hull. Until he spoke Mani hadn't known he was there. "Why?"

"Because you're to go on the land. Inland," the swimmer corrected himself. "I can't go there."

"Even in the river?"

Hanno's brows came down, hiding his eyes. "No one swims in the rivers unless the wives…no. I can't tell you."

"All right," Mani said.

The people under the trees hadn't moved. Shadows were sharper here, the contrast between light and dark clearer to see. Mani couldn't make out anything, even whether they were male or female. They had to be the wives. No other Puradu could walk.

"What will they do with us?" he asked.

The water danced to a hardly-heard hum, so deep that Mani felt it in his teeth. Hanno was laughing, though his face was still grim. "Scholar, I don't know. The wives tell us very little, and this has never happened before. I can't guess what they will do."

"All right," he said again. "Thank you, Hanno, for persuading them to allow us here."

"You trusted us when you brought your wife. You trusted me." Hanno pushed away from the ship, on his back. "You've changed everything, Mani, but you've been my friend. I'm glad I came to the marsh. Be careful where you swim."

"What does—"

The young Puradu had gone under. Mani saw his tail slap water and Hanno vanished into the depths, out in the bay. A moment later ridged heads began to pop up, all around the slowly moving ship. There were spears, nets, and tridents wherever he looked. Some of the Puradu darted to the shallows, where they waited with weapons ready. Their bodies were dark forms in the water, like fish in drying pools.

"Oars in," Ludari shouted from the stern. There was a rattle as the poles were pulled aboard and stowed. The ship slowed, coasting towards the sand. Puradu moved aside for it. Mani thought it would stop too soon, but Ludari knew his business. The boat found a shade more energy and crossed the last feet to bump against the beach.

Nobody jumped ashore. There were no hitching posts, no jetty or wharf to tie against, but that wasn't why. Everyone on deck had turned, pulled around, to look at Sarru-kin.

The Mad King was still on the top deck, hands curled around the rail. His face had been lit by inner light before, but now it shone. Sweat made a sheen on his cheeks. He stayed there for a moment, eyes fixed on the figures under the trees. Then he whirled into sudden motion. He went to the ladder and slid down it, ahead of all his four guards. By the time he reached the prow his soldiers had assembled there, all twelve of them.

"No weapons," Mani reminded them.

They looked at Sarru-kin and waited for his nod. Even then they hesitated, until Yarim said, "Do as the king says."

Yarim had spent almost all the voyage in his cabin. His eyes were still tight, but that was all. He dropped his mace and sword and pulled a knife from his belt. All were thrown to the deck. The others followed his lead, some reluctantly, and he scowled at them. "I'll check every boot for knives before you step on shore. Don't try to fool me."

The soldiers scowled right back, but they dropped their knives. The pile on the deck looked enough to equip a small army. Sarru-kin went to the rail.

"My lord," Mani said. "Your sickle sword."

Sarru-kin's hand went up to touch the hilt above his shoulder. "Azaq goes with me."

He swung over the rail. Handholds were built into the hull, and he clambered down, jumping to the sand. The soldiers followed. They looked odd without weapons, like snails with no shells. Tauth went down, and then Shusikil. Mani watched them, hands tight on the rail.

"It's too late to decide you don't want to," Ludari said. He'd come forward from the tiller, the familiar twist on his lips. "Go on, scholar."

He was right. Mani helped Isha over the rail and followed her down. Sand crunched under his sandals. He breathed in a deep lungful of air, tasting the sweat of forest leaves and sea air mingled together. Something was wrong there. It only took a moment to realise what it was.

"There's no salt," he said. "It's true, then. This island sits in fresh water."

"I smelled brine at sea," Shusikil said.

"Yes. It's only here. Springs, perhaps." Mani gestured at the river. "Maybe all the lakes come from wells. The island might be riddled with them, above the sea and below."

"You may talk later," Sarru-kin said. He'd stopped dry-washing his hands. He looked serene, if flushed. "We are here for a purpose. Who are the people waiting for us, scholar?"

"Let's go and see," Mani said.

§ § §

They went up the beach. The sand was gritty, like bits of broken pottery. Looking at the sand hurt Mani's eyes. The shadows thrown by this strange bluish sun were wrong in a way he couldn't quite pin down. Their edges were sharper, but that wasn't it. The million shadows of grains of sand wouldn't even be visible at home, but here they almost were, and his eyes ached.

He realised he was looking anywhere but at the people under the trees. He was sweating, and his pulse flapped like a landed fish.

"You're a scholar," Mani told himself. His voice was barely a whisper, but Isha reached out and took his hand. That calmed him more than any resolution he could make. He lifted his head.

The group were all women. Not a great surprise. Twenty of them stood in an arc inside the shadow of the trees, just where the sand began to peter out and grass grew in patches. Mani thought they were meant to be evenly spaced, but they'd drawn together into three or four clusters, as though for support. Again, not a great surprise. This meeting had no precedent.

The Puradu women had no more idea how to handle this than Mani did, and they were afraid. He could see it in the way they stood. Or at least, humans who stood that way would be frightened. Maybe Puradu were different. He'd never met one with legs before.

The visitors stopped five yards short of the women. It was only then that Mani realised the Puradu were armed.

A few held spears, short-shafted with barbed tips. They reminded Mani of the harpoons fishermen used in the shallows of the lagoon back home, when they wanted the larger fish that lurked in reed beds. A net was no use there, but keen eyes and a fast strike could feed a family for three days. To see them now was bad. Worse was that ten of the women carried bows, arrows already nocked to strings. One to Mani's right was shaking so that the point of her arrow wobbled from side to side.

They looked human. Tanned and oval-faced, their skin lighter than Mani was used to. There were no ridged heads, and no nictitating eyes. They even had hair. Their skin was light, but even so, they could walk down the street in Aš-alam and never get a second glance.

"Good morning," he said. His throat was so dry it came out as a croak, and he paused to cough. "I am Kassu-Mani, the scholar."

"We know who you are." The speaker was a very tall woman with pale hair in sheets over her shoulders. She wore a tunic that left her arms bare and a skirt that showed her knees. "You brought your wife to talk with our envoys. We should thank you for that."

"I might not have done so," he said, "if I'd known what it would lead me to."

She cocked her head. Her eyes were bitumen black, he saw, dark as damnation. "Really? You would have turned aside from the chance to stand where you are now?"

Mani couldn't answer. The woman smiled, and the severity of her face dissolved into sympathy. "Unfair question. I'm sorry. My name is Nikkal-Adoyah. Welcome, scholar."

"It's an honour," he said. "This is Isha. My wife."

"Welcome," the tall woman said. "I wish the circumstances were different."

"And this is—"

"Enough." The Mad King stepped forward. All the bows came up, every arrow aimed at his chest, and he seemed not to notice. "I am Sarru-kin. I have come to complete my quest."

"We know who you are, too," Nikkal-Adoyah said. Her tone was hard again, the lines of her expression set once more. She wasn't armed, but she faced him without fear. "You were told to bring no weapons."

"Azaq is a god before he is a weapon. Your prohibition did not apply to him."

She eyed him up and down. Nobody would have had the courage to do that for years or lived even if they had. Again, Sarru-kin didn't seem aware of it, though Mani was certain he was. Nikkal-Adoyah breathed through her nose, like a tethered bull.

"You may keep the sickle sword, but at every step you'll have arrows trained on you. If your hand touches that hilt in a way we don't like, you won't live to finish your breath."

"I do not," Sarru-kin answered, still serene, "intend to die."

She nodded. "I know. You want to be immortal. Why?"

"What?"

"I asked you why," she said.

"Because," the Mad King said. A crease appeared between his eyes, and he stopped. Mani had never seen him uncertain before. "Because the worst thing in life is to die."

"Death is necessary."

"For the weak," he said. Confidence had returned. "For the mortal. It is not the only choice."

"It's not a choice at all. Death comes to us."

"Not to gods."

"Gods?" Nikkal-Adoyah repeated. "You fool. There are no gods but those your ancestors invented."

"What?" Yarim burst out. He wasn't the only one. Several of the soldiers shouted denials.

"Don't listen to these lies," Shusikil said. "Eala blesses us. Trust in her."

"All the gods nurture us," Tauth put in. "Even Balih, who glories in war and suffering. The northern tribesmen don't know our gods, and neither do these alien women."

She stared at Mani as she spoke, daring him to contradict her. He didn't intend to. There were more important things here than arguing theology. If they got home alive, then perhaps it would be time to tell the truth about the founding of Aš-alam. Not now.

"Is that what you think?" Nikkal-Adoyah asked. She cocked her head again. "It was we who taught you how to build and irrigate. We taught you everything, long ago."

"Lies," Shusikil said calmly.

She was going to deny it all, then. Shusikil looked stone-faced back at the taller woman, and Nikkal-Adoyah said, "Eala was a Puradu."

Everyone froze.

Mani and Isha had known already. Hanno had told them, back at the marsh. To everyone else it was a new thing, and a shock they couldn't absorb. Faces were slack, others white with shock. Only Shusikil kept her composure, lips thin as knives. "Your words are deceit. Nothing more."

"Humans built their first city on the marsh of Engiru," Nikkal-Adoyah said. "Why there? Why not Piqash, or further north, or halfway around the world? Because the Puradu were there. It is the only answer. You know it."

"You repeat the same lies," Shusikil said.

Mani told himself to be calm, to hold his tongue. There were greater problems here than the *zami*. Even so anger filled him, the frustration of knowing the truth and seeing it denied, as though truth was a worthless thing to be tossed aside, trodden into the dirt.

He bit the inside of his mouth, trying to keep silent, and was saved when Sarru-kin stepped forward and again said, "Enough."

The bows were still trained on him. He ignored them and moved between Shusikil and Nikkal-Adoyah, hands on hips. "I did not come here to listen to you bicker. I came to make myself immortal. Everything else is petty, a distraction for which I have no time. Enough, then. Nikkal-Adoyah. What must I do to live forever?"

"This evening," she replied. "We'll meet you at the north point of the island and tell you what you must do."

"Now would be better," Sarru-kin said softly.

"Evening is better," she retorted. "The waters are calmer then, between tides. For now, you'll be shown to a place you can rest." She began to turn away, throwing the last words over her shoulder. "You'll need to."

Mani had never seen a woman show so much skin. Most of the Puradu women wore skimpy clothes though, sleeveless vests that left arms bare, or short dresses with legs on display. This was just the Puradu way, he knew that, but it was hard to know where to look. However he tried not to see, his eyes fell on flesh.

As Nikkal-Adoyah walked away her legs caught his gaze, and he saw scales there, glittering on the back of her thighs.

CHAPTER FORTY-ONE

"WHERE ARE THE others?" Mani asked.

"Not far from the beach," Yarim said. He looked smaller without his weapons. "The king told me to stay with you."

One of the Puradu looked around at that. She was much smaller than Nikkal-Adoyah but wore the same sort of revealing clothes. A tunic in her case, hanging to her knees but without sleeves. Her red hair lay in cornrows and her eyes were night black, just like the first woman's. "We've been told to keep them separate and away from the pools. They won't be harmed unless they try to approach the water."

"If they do, they will be killed," another woman added.

"But you've brought Isha and me right to a pool," Mani said. "So why are we here?"

"Because we trust you. Both of you."

'Here' was a cabin half a mile inland. It stood at the side of a clear lake, fed by one stream and flowing out into another. Trees grew all around. The sun was different and the light strange, but this felt the oddest of all. Engiru was a flat plain with hardly any trees. Here they grew like walls on the steep slope of a mountain. Mani felt unsteady, as though any movement could make him start to slide all the way back down to the sea.

"You trust us," Mani said. "But you're armed."

She touched the knife at her hip. "Of course. Trust has been betrayed before."

"It won't be this time."

"I know that, but I'll be careful all the same. Mostly because of you," she added, with a nod at Yarim. "Don't be offended. Our children are born here, and we'll protect them."

"I would too," the soldier said. His eyes still carried a shadow, as they had since he watched Kammani die.

"Let's leave that for now. My name's Tanyih. This is Sharabyi." She indicated the second woman, just as small but also armed. "Can we get you something to drink or some food?"

"I'd appreciate that," Isha said. "I've hardly eaten a bite since we boarded the ship."

A few minutes later they were sitting on the grass, food spread in front of them. It was familiar enough, bread and cheese mostly, with meat sliced so thin you could see through it. Isha took a careful bite, swallowed, and waited for a moment. Then she began to eat more quickly. Yarim took his food and sat a couple of yards away, with the group but not really part of it. Sharabyi sat turned so she could see him, one foot on the grass, ready to be on her feet in an instant.

To their right water tumbled over rocks into the pool. On the other side it flowed over a shaped bank of earth and tumbled away, down towards the sea. Archers stood in both places, watching the group eat.

"There's a lot I don't understand," Mani said.

Tanyih nodded. "For us, too."

That made him pause. "Really?"

"We don't know how human women carry babies," Sharabyi said. She was whip-slender, the first Puradu Mani had seen with hair as black as an Engiran. She wore it pulled back into a ponytail, though, a style no woman would dare back home. There was a single iridescent scale under her ear. "Or how you give birth."

Isha paused with bread close to her mouth. "How we—then how do you give birth?"

"In the water," Tanyih said, as though puzzled.

"But how does—" Isha began, before Mani's hand closed on her wrist.

"Let's go slowly," he said. "There's so much we don't know. Be calm. We'll learn the answers."

"No wonder the males at the lagoon liked you," Tanyih said. "Well then, Mani. What do you want to know?"

"Why you can walk," he said.

"That's because of childbirth, too. Puradu women are born just like the men, with tails and gills. We lose them during pregnancy." She pulled her collar down to show a smooth clavicle. "Legs grow inside our tails. During pregnancy, the tails tear and fall away. Then we learn to walk."

"Our skulls change too," Sharabyi chipped in. "We lose the bulges you think of as horns under the skin, and later we grow hair." She grimaced. "It hurts."

Tanyih nodded. "I was helpless for a week while that happened. I couldn't even stand, let alone learn to walk. Our gills vanish at the same time. We're water dwellers until we give birth, and then we live on land."

So many answers, and still the questions piled up on Mani's tongue, like children themselves eager to be born. "Where are the babies?"

"In the water."

"You leave them?"

"They're amphibious," Tanyih reminded him. "They can breathe on land, but they can't walk. We protect the pools, though. Nothing can reach them to harm the little ones. When they're big enough, the young move to lagoons, and then near adulthood they're allowed into the sea for the first time."

Mani frowned. "Then you don't raise your own children?"

"We don't even know who they are. It's probably for the best. I couldn't have dealt with five children anyway."

That stopped Mani, and Isha said, *"Five* children? At once?"

"We only give birth once. Why? How many do humans have?"

"One," Isha replied faintly. "I hope."

"Tell us," Sharabyi said.

"Humans are not nearly as interesting," Isha said.

She explained, and evidently the two Puradu found it more than just interesting. After a while Tanyih said, "And the man lies on top of you? That's how it's done?"

"Well, usually," Isha said. Mani could hear the laughter in her voice and smothered his own chuckle.

"How do Puradu make love?" he asked.

"The males swims in a pool and deliver their seed," Tanyih said. "Later the females swim there, too. Those who have been chosen."

"What? That's it?"

"Better than the sweaty writhing you do," Tanyih said.

"No," Yarim said. He hadn't spoken for so long that Mani had forgotten he was there. "No, it really isn't."

Mani couldn't keep the laugh in this time. Isha grinned, and then they were all laughing, sitting on the grass around their picnic. Sharabyi threw her head back and then winced a little, shading her eyes. "It's getting bright. We should go into the shade."

"Light hurts your eyes," Isha said. It was the tone she used when she'd just realised something. "Because you spend your youth under water?"

"Yes. We're used to seeing the sun through water. When you see it naked your eyes can hurt."

"We feel that here all the time," Mani said. "Your sun is too blue and brighter than at home. Shadows are wrong."

"The males always tell us your world is dimmer," Tanyih said. "Let's pack up. We can resume under the veranda."

They cleared away the lunch things. The two Puradu women moved with a grace that Mani found almost hypnotic, even doing something so mundane. Like snakes, maybe. No, that was wrong. They were like fish, sleek and quick. *They dance when they move*. He was seeing the shadow of what they'd once been, a memory that still lived in their flesh and bones.

They settled around a table in the shade. Again, Yarim stayed a little distance away, seated on the steps down to the grass. Grief was a solid thing in him, tightening his chest until breath choked in his throat. Mani could see that, too. It was strange to see open grief in such a big man, but Yarim was a soldier, and Sarru-kin's man. Violence was what he'd chosen.

"I have questions for you," Mani said to the women. He was aware of the sun crossing overhead, marking time as it slipped past him. "Will you answer them for me?"

Sharabyi smiled. "We're told that humans always had more questions than their tongues could hold. Our ancestors found you clad in animal skins, but your minds already bubbled with thoughts."

"Ask," Tanyih said. "You brought your wife to speak with the males. Puradu haven't been treated with honour like that in centuries. Ask."

"How was Aš-alam founded?"

That was it, asked right out. Mani had spent so many years trying to be subtle that it felt peculiar in his mouth. He'd been trained to think in curves, by education and then experience. A scholar tried to tease out information, tempt a word into dropping from a distracted tongue. He didn't blurt a question out like a fool on the street.

Tanyih leaned back in her chair and crossed those elegant legs. "We were exploring. Males went out to every coast, looking for a place where we could make a home for ourselves. It had to be on the shore, and it had to be fresh water. There aren't many places like that."

"And you found the marsh."

"We found three places. One far to the east of Engiru, in an archipelago where every island has a lagoon. One was freshwater, like yours. A second further south, where a river breaks into channels as it nears the sea and forms a pattern of lagoons that changes every year. The best was the marsh at Engiru, fifty miles of clear water and reeds, fed by not one great river but two. It was perfect. There were villages nearby, houses built of mud and rushes. We asked the fisher folk to be careful not to catch us in their nets. We can cut our way out easily enough, but the barbs can hurt, and the nets must be remade. Better for everyone if we were never snared.

"They asked us who we were, and we told them. They began to make stories about us."

Sharabyi took over. "Do you know how important stories are? An animal who can spin tales isn't an animal at all. He can imagine and dream of different things. Even better things. Women were in the lagoon in those days, and the fisher folk told tales of a Puradu woman who fell in love with a human man and bore him children."

"I've heard those tales," Isha said. On the steps Yarim had turned to listen. "Children hear them, when they're small."

"Stories last a long time," Sharabyi agreed. "We realised what the humans were saying. Some Puradu began to say the fisher folk could be taught something more than they knew. We could show them how to bake mud into bricks and make paint for the new walls to keep water out. We could teach them how to grow crops after the flood had passed. Perhaps much more than this, but something, at least. But nothing like it had ever been done before. There were arguments, some saying we should teach, others saying no. One of the leaders of the teaching faction was called Anath-Eala Sisi."

A swimmer. It was true, then. The goddess, lady of love and fertility, daughter of the Moon and reeds of the river, had been a Puradu. Born in the pools here, raised by older women who guarded the waters while she grew and learned. She'd found her way to the lagoon of Engiru. A restless spirit in her, perhaps, eager to see things for herself. Strong, too, if she led a movement to do something that had never been done before.

Mani could close his eyes and see her, rising out of the past like a shadow from deep water.

"Anath-Eala fell pregnant," Tanyih said. "She should have come home, but she refused. She said if we were to leave a mark on the world then we must become part of it. By then the arguments were so bitter that no one could gather the will to force her, or the strength. Anath-Eala gave birth in the lagoon, in a place kept safe for children, and for the first time in her life she stood on unsteady legs on the dry land."

Isha's hand found its way into Mani's and clutched it.

"She began to teach humans," Tanyih said. "There was still no agreement on it, but she didn't wait. If nobody had the support to send her home, then nobody would be able to stop her teaching either. She showed the fishermen how to plant crops in mud after the Flood and keep them watered as the summer grew hot. She built them pits for the Flood to fill with water, and roofs of reeds to keep the sun off so the water would last. Basic things, at first. But with more food, things began to change."

"Children," Isha said. "There were more children."

"More children survived," Tanyih corrected. "The result was the same. There were too many fisher folk for the little villages to hold. As well, the fishermen didn't have time to do more work on crops. Farming needed full time hands. A new place was needed, somewhere to build homes safe from the Flood with fields all around."

"Anath-Eala helped them build a great mound of earth," Sharabyi took over. "On it they built a wall of bricks with houses inside. When the waters rose, they lapped at the slope and then receded. For the first time humans had mastered the Flood.

"Anath-Eala could never come home. She had no tail, and we had no ships. We'd never needed them. She died in what had become Aš-alam, with her daughters beside her."

"She died there?" Mani repeated.

"Her daughters took her body down into the depths of the marsh and weighted it there." Tanyih took up the story again. "Opinion had already begun to turn against what she'd done. Young males who went swimming up the Ranuna sometimes never came back. It happened too often to be chance, and journeys in the river were forbidden. Women no longer went to Aš-alam. Worse yet, people in the city began to mutter against us. They called us names. *Anzillu. Dalkhu.* You know the words?"

Abominations. Demons. "I know them."

"Then Belessun appeared. A woman from the city. Anath-Eala had been dead for three generations by now, and Belessun said she couldn't have been a Puradu. The founder of the city was a goddess, beautiful, not a scaled monster who stank of the sea floor. She came down from heaven, not up from the waves. People began to believe it."

"We believe what we want to believe," Mani said. "Humans, I mean. We never think the bad man with the knife is going to hurt our loved ones until he does. Then it surprises us."

From the steps Yarim looked at him, brow creased in a frown. Sharabyi let a hand drift down to her belt knife.

"How long did it take?" Isha asked.

"Not long. Once a thing like that begins, it can spread quickly. We began to find ourselves ostracised. Females were sent back to the island. No more young were born in the marsh. The males might have left too, except that Belessun came to the shore to speak with them."

"She had a nerve," Mani said.

"She was desperate. Nobody in Aš-alam knew where to find the bitumen to coat their bricks. They didn't know how to mix it so it could be painted, or how to make axes to chop the great trees upriver, and a dozen other things. Again, there was an argument among the Puradu, with some saying the humans had brought disaster on themselves. Others said Anath-Eala wouldn't have left humans to starve. In the end most Puradu left, but some stayed, to help the innocents of the city survive."

"And they stayed all this time," Isha said. "How long has it been?"

"Almost a thousand years," Tanyih said. "But it ends after tonight. The argument is over at last."

Mani felt as though she'd stabbed him. He looked at her, lips moving, but no words came out.

"I'm sorry," Tanyih said. "For you especially, scholar. You honoured us. We brought your Mad King here for that, because you'd earned the right to be saved. But humans will never come near our birthing pools again. When you leave, we will take this island away, forever."

Chapter Forty-Two

T AKE IT AWAY?" Mani's voice sounded distant, words in wind. "What does that mean?"

"The Puradu will close the door to your world," Sharabyi told him. "We won't accept any risk to our young."

"Close the door?"

"The one you came here through. At dusk, when the stars and sun changed."

"We might even go home," Tanyih put in. "To Nyan Aduno. The world of women, that none of us has ever seen."

"But you can't."

"I'm sorry," Tanyih said gently. "We have to."

They were leaving. There would be no Puradu in the marsh, no scholars walking out to the pier. The idea was too big for Mani to grasp. He tried to cast around for an argument and couldn't find one.

"We told you there have been disagreements," Tanyih said. "We Puradu have never been completely sure about humans. Anath-Eala took things into her own hands. If she hadn't, we might never have taught you anything."

"You hardly did," Mani said. "I mean, I'm glad you showed us so much. But you know far more, don't you?"

"Of course we do."

"Will you tell me?"

The Puradu smiled. "You don't change. The males tell us you've always been the most curious of the scholars. Always trying to tease out one more detail, even now."

"Tell me," he asked.

"We could show you how to smelt iron. A harder metal than bronze, better for points and blades. With it, you can work stone better. There's good ore stone upriver of Aš-alam. We could show you where."

"Could *have*," Sharabyi corrected.

"Yes. It won't happen now."

Mani felt a knife in his chest beginning to twist." What else?"

"Does it matter?"

"Yes." He closed his eyes. "What else?"

"We can move carriages with steam," Tanyih told him. "You burn coal, or charcoal. A bit like solid bitumen. The heat boils water, which turns wheels. You could move loads without oxen."

"A miracle," he said.

"Or we could give you compasses. A needle always points north, so a sailor or navigator knows which way to go."

"Stop," Mani said. "Stop. That's enough."

Lost, now. All lost. He would remember the names and how they worked. When he got back to Aš-alam he'd write it all down, repeat the words to the other scholars, and hope someone made something of them. One day, someday. With enough time.

But he would never build a steam engine or a compass. Never see it built. He thought of Sarru-kin, and rage erupted inside him like a fire, burning his heart and throat. It was all the Mad King's fault. Without him, Mani and Isha would be talking to Puradu at the lagoon, learning more than any scholar before. Ten years from now there might have been horseless wagons in the streets of Aš-alam. Mani would never see them.

"We would have taught you those things before," Tanyih said. "And more, besides, but your *zami* betrayed us. There were some who said then that we could never trust you." She pointed down the mountain to where Sarru-kin waited, out of sight. "I think they were right."

"I can't argue with that," he said. He looked at Isha, seated beside him at the table. She took his hand. All his pains seemed to be lessened whenever she took his hand.

"What will I do?" he asked her.

Isha squeezed his fingers. "Whatever you choose to do."

"But I—"

"No, Mani, listen. You'll be famous when we get home. People in every city will want to speak with you. They'll invite you to discuss what you saw here, and what the Puradu said. You'll be asked to teach classes at the Temple schools. You could make a good living for five years, maybe ten, just from having walked on this island."

"All right," he said, listening.

"Or you could change career. You're a clever man, husband. Nearly as clever as me." He opened his mouth, saw her grin, and couldn't help a chuckle. "Look, you'll still be famous. You could ask Ra'im for almost anything, and if he won't give it then ask in Piqash or Shurraš, or anywhere else."

"Ra'im is a king with no kingdom."

"As long as Sarru-kin lives," she said. "Will he see Engiru again?"

Mani said nothing.

"So ask," Isha said. "Or be an architect. Be a planner, but don't wallow in self-pity, husband. It doesn't suit you."

He sighed. "How did I ever manage without you?"

"Badly. I saw the state of your tunics cupboard when I moved in."

He looked at the floor. Isha was right, and her words had lifted him, but it was still hard. No Puradu.

"Our world will be a poorer place," he said.

Tanyih nodded. "I think we will be lessened, too. There is sorrow in this."

Some sorrow. Mani swallowed. "Maybe we'll build our own doors one day. Come and meet you on your worlds."

"Perhaps you will," she said.

"How do we build—"

"No," Sharabyi interrupted. "We will not tell you. Humans are cruel and they're violent. You've done enough harm on your world. We won't help you make a door to others."

Her hand drifted to the knife at her belt as she spoke. Out of the side of his eye Mani saw Yarim stiffen, and the Puradu women both shifted their eyes to the soldier. After a moment the big man relaxed again. That was good, because the two archers had stepped forward at the same moment, ready to shoot.

It hardly mattered now. The future was gone, replaced by something grey and dull. Mani shook his head, too stunned inside to really care.

"Come," Tanyih said. "We should start out to meet your Mad King."

"He's no king of mine," Mani said.

"He's certainly not ours," she retorted. "But come, scholar. You might see sights to remember."

The words brought him back to the reason they were here on this island on another world. Sarru-kin, the Mad King, and his quest to live forever. To the plan Mani had formed, talking with Hanno and Barek in the lagoon back home. It might work. He would not know until the time came.

He stood up, still holding Isha's hand. "Show them to me."

§ § §

"Star fruit," Tanyih said. "Here, taste it."

Mani turned it over in his hand, a yellowish lump a bit like several bananas stuck together. He took a small bite. It was very sweet, like the glaze on a slice of pear but without the pear. He handed it to Isha. She bit, raised her eyebrows, and swallowed the rest in two bites.

"Pregnant," she said.

Sharabyi laughed. "Humans do that, too? You have cravings when the young grow in you?"

"So I'm led to believe," Isha replied. "I've not noticed any yet, in honesty. I'm not very far along."

215

"This is breadfruit," Tanyih pointed to a tree with reddish leaves. "You must cook the fruits, I'm afraid. But one tree can produce enough to feed a person for half a year."

There were very few trees in Engiru. Only stories of some kept for apples and pears, luxuries brought in by cart from the faraway hills, and a handful on the banks of the marshes where the Flood never reached. The idea of a single orchard that could feed whole families was…peculiar.

Something made a babbling sound in the canopy above. Mani half saw a shape swinging away through the branches.

"You never brought us these trees," he said. "We could have fed so many people."

"No. The Flood would drown them, Mani. Trees must learn to survive inundation, and these never have. Besides, on that wide plain of yours the wind would bend and break them. It's not a place where trees thrive."

"You could have found a way."

"Where we could find a way, we did," Tanyih said gently. "For the most part. There are coconut trees scattered across your world because we set them on the waters by the thousand, long ago. Currents and winds did the rest."

"Did you help anyone else?"

"Once," she told him. "Around the same time that Anath-Eala came to your ancestors. It was on islands to the east of Engiru, in the ocean that covers nearly half your world. There was a freshwater lagoon, like yours, and people who paddled the sea in great canoes with two hulls. They used to call us the Agunua."

"Used to?" he asked.

"They were lost. A volcano erupted—you know about those? A god who broke the earth in fire and fury. There was a great wave. The islands were lost or swept clear of life." Tanyih's head bowed. "Many Puradu were lost. Very few humans survived, and those who did forgot what they had been. Now there are only a few ruins. The people there say giants made them."

"Time turns against us," Sharabyi said. "Come, now. We must walk if we're to reach the north point by evening."

The path was old, worn into the ground so that stones poked through. It wound between trees parted by brooks, splashing their way towards the sea. There hadn't been rain since Mani and the others had arrived, so he wondered. Did water literally bubble out of the ground here? There were springs around the island, Hanno had said, making the salt sea drinkable. It wasn't much of a leap to suppose there might be springs inland too.

He jumped as a great bird erupted from the foliage, chirruping like a rat. It flailed across the path and vanished on the other side, still calling. Yarim's hand had snatched for a belt knife he no longer had, but even in her surprise

Sharabyi had twisted to aim her blade at him, ready if he used the distraction to attack. He didn't, only lowering his hands and watching her, but there was a measuring look in his eyes.

"You'd never leave the island," she told him.

"I know." He stood with feet apart and made no effort to protect himself. "I'm not such a fool."

"Yarim gave me advice once," Mani said. Odd, because he hadn't known he was going to speak. "When I was about to meet the Mad King. It might have saved my life, for all I know. He's all right, for a northerner."

Sharabyi considered and lowered her knife.

"That was a Lonely Bird, if anyone's interested," Tanyih said. "There's good eating on them."

They went on. Sharabyi still walked behind Yarim, and the hilt was never far from her hand.

They climbed at first, up an outflung arm of the central peak. The path brought them to a cleft in the rock as sheer as the narrowest alley and then out onto a ledge with the forest spread out below. The sea lay around it. From here, the water bore a green tinge, and the sky reflected it back. Or the other way around. Blueish sun, almost-green water…but near to the island it turned clear, almost like glass, even from so high.

Yarim came up beside him and paused. "Thank you."

He wasn't looking at Mani, so Mani didn't look back. "For what?"

"Defending me. I don't think I needed it, but still. Thank you."

"We need all the friends we can get here."

"Are we friends?" the soldier asked and then shrugged. "Well, we always need friends, wherever we are. That, or lovers."

He started down the slope. Mani pondered that last comment for a moment, but he really didn't have the energy to pursue thoughts just now. He was full of sorrow and a need to see and learn all he could of this place and the Puradu before they were lost to him forever. Everything else would have to wait. Even the Mad King and his minions.

He headed after the others back down into the forest.

Chapter Forty-Three

AN HOUR LATER, they came to a river, twenty feet wide with steep banks. They were too regular to be natural, and Mani thought at once of the levees that held back the Ranuna between Floods. A wooden bridge led across the foot of a lake to a row of buildings and people gathered before them.

All women, of course, and not many. Two dozen, perhaps. Some were old, the first aged Puradu Mani had seen, with hair turning white and wrinkles around their eyes. There was something odd about their faces, but he couldn't make it out in the strange sunlight until he was closer.

Then he caught his breath.

"Mani, they have—"

"I know, wife," he murmured. He put a hand on her arm and squeezed. "It isn't the weirdest thing we've learned today."

Isha bit her lip and nodded, though she looked uncomfortable. It was odd how someone could accept so many things and then struggle at the relatively mundane. Well, maybe Mani would, at some sight yet to be revealed. He wouldn't criticise.

Scales had invaded the old women's faces, spreading up from necks to cross their jaws. They formed lines and whorls, or patches that spilled across a cheekbone and swallowed an eye. The scales glittered in the sun, red and blue, like lacquer on clay. Conversation among the women stopped. Mani thought they watched the party approach, but too much light was flung back from their faces for him to be sure.

"Don't approach them," Tanyih cautioned. "The Old Ones agreed to let humans land here but not to meet them directly. Let them choose whether to come to you."

Mani frowned. "You're not in charge here? Or Nikkal-Adoyah?"

"We're small fish on land," Tanyih chuckled. "I'm even smaller than she is. No, we're not in charge."

Something splashed in the lake. Mani turned towards it, unable to help himself, and saw a fluted tail vanish into the water. He held himself still, remembering what Tanyih had just told him. He threw a prayer to Eala, swimmer though she may have been, to grant him this one thing, this wish, that he might see a Puradu female in the water.

A head bobbed up, then another. They seemed to exchange words and then ducked under with sweeps of their tails. Mani thought they were more powerful than the males, or perhaps it was a feature of the mating cycle, like a bull becoming more aggressive when a cow was near. He started to turn away.

Tanyih put a hand on his chest to stay him, and a dark head appeared by the shore. A hand beckoned.

"Go," Tanyih said. "Be told, scholar. Harm her, and you die. I don't think you need the warning, but hear it anyway."

"I won't harm her," he said.

He went forward alone. He could feel Isha watching him, and the weight of eyes from the old women was a physical thing, pressing on his skull. The grass was faintly purple here, the water of the pool crystal, so clear he could see currents swirl as he knelt.

"You're the scholar," the swimmer said. She rested her arms on the bank, just like Hanno on the jetty, a world and a lifetime ago. "The one who brought his wife to meet the men."

"Yes."

"I am Demna." A bony head tilted. "Is that her? She doesn't look pregnant."

"She's still early in her term."

"Do you love her?"

"Yes," he said. He fought off the urge to reach out and stroke this beautiful woman's head. "Surprisingly, I do."

"We don't know love," she said. "Not like that. We mate by swimming in a pool where the men have been, and we never know which is the father. The ancient tales say humans are lucky to love the way they do."

Mani smiled. "We are. Love can break your heart, time and again, but you're right. We're very lucky."

"Will you know your children?"

"Yes."

"Love them for us, then," she said, "when we don't know ours to do so. Goodbye, scholar."

Glimmer and splash, and she was gone. Mani had seen that happen so many times, but he found it hard to make himself stand. His feet felt heavy as he trudged back to the group. Tanyih smiled radiantly, but it was Isha he looked for and found.

"You're weeping," she said. "Why?"

"They can't love their children." Mani scrubbed at his eyes. "It doesn't matter. Let's keep walking."

§ § §

There were skinks in the trees and crabs the size of dogs foraging where fruit had fallen. Tanyih said they were Robber Crabs, more at home on land than in water. *Like Puradu women,* Mani thought, but didn't say. He wasn't sure if it was true anyway. He had the sense that the women longed with all their hearts to be back in the water, able to swim deep and long with a swish of the tails they no longer owned.

They lived their years longing for what was lost. Mani thought of the lagoon, empty forever of the Puradu, and tears were near again.

Low down the forest sweltered. They passed through it into an area of stone and clinging grass. The sun had begun to sink to the west and the sky was tinged green. There were rock pools full of things that slithered and crawled, and birds hopping across the shallows. They pecked in grass and stood poised on shores, long beaks ready to strike.

Beyond them fingers of stone ran out into the sea. Water rushed between them, in and out, except in one place where rocky strands surrounded a bay. Mani saw figures there.

Sarru-kin, of course, and the four guards who accompanied him everywhere. Also of course. Shusikil with her stern face fixed in its habitual frown, and Tauth close by her. In the brighter light of this sun Tauth's axe of a nose stood out like a bruise on pale skin. Nikkal-Adoyah was there, standing a little way off with a cluster of Puradu, most armed with bows and knives. None of the women looked comfortable. They were out in the naked sun, far from shade. Their eyes must be full of pain.

There was a boat in the water. Only a small one, enough to carry half a dozen people. It was made of wood. Mani knew almost nothing about boat building, but he noted how the planks curved and saw the plugs of a different wood hammered into the hull. Why different? Did that wood swell less when wet? Did it swell more, and hold the planks together?

A thousand tiny crabs scattered as the little party approached. Sarru-kin turned to them, and he seemed to glow in the sunlight.

"Scholar," he said. "You did what you promised."

This was the man who would take Isha away from him and their child. "I didn't promise you anything."

"But you did. You said you would bring me to the swimmers' island, if you could, and the means by which I would become immortal. Here I stand. Do you see now that the gods want me to become one of them? Do you understand how long they have guided me?"

"Guided you?"

"I knew when you came to Labaš that you were the man I needed. I did not know why, but it was plain to me that you were important."

"Then why was it Shahan you bought?"

"I bought him because I could." The Mad King seemed not to understand. "But he was a tool to be used and thrown away. I would have killed him had he not fallen overboard. A man who will turn against one lord may well turn against another."

Mani made sure not to catch Tauth's eye. "And me?"

"You were something more. I could not tell why. I had barely begun my journey to godhood, and I saw only through veils. But I knew. I knew you would matter, and you did."

"You're insane," Isha said. The words were unexpected, and they jarred Mani's ears. Sarru-kin turned to her, his beatific expression cracking for just a moment. "You're deranged. When you talk, flies enter your open mouth. But Fate walks behind you and always catches you in the end."

"It does not catch gods," Sarru-kin said. "I will remember your words, woman, and you should remember mine. Fate does not catch gods."

"Your gods are a lie," Nikkal-Adoyah said.

She had joined them, all her followers in tow. Fingers held bowstrings ready, but nobody made a move to fight. Sarru-kin only smiled at her words, face shining once more.

"The first of them was a Puradu. Anath-Eala Sisi came among humans to teach them, and the city they built was Aš-alam. Later other people built more cities, and they wanted gods of their own." Nikkal-Adoyah made a dismissive gesture. "They were created from wishes and dreams. The gods aren't the fathers of your people. They're children of your imagination."

"What would you know of our gods?" Shusikil grated. "I have spoken with Eala. I hear her voice when I pray, when she blesses me with her presence. Your stories are the lie, not her."

"So human," Nikkal-Adoyah said. "You see the first city, built by a marsh where Puradu live, and choose to believe they had nothing to do with it. Instead, you invent a myth and say the swimmers, the gods you can see, must be the lie. That's what Belessun did. She had listeners then and you have them now, because your people always want to believe the easy thing, the comfortable thing, and never the truth."

"I want the truth," Mani said.

The Puradu woman nodded. "I know. In all this, I feel sorriest for you, scholar."

"No need," he said. He was trying to sound brave and thought he might even have succeeded. "I've seen your home island and females swimming in the birthing pools. I know the story of Anath-Eala and how Aš-alam began. I spent my life dreaming that one day I might stand here and listen to wisdom. I've done so."

She smiled, which was when Sarru-kin broke into the conversation, his smooth voice as welcome as a raven's croak.

"I will answer your questions when I return," he said, "as a god myself. Enough talk now. You, Nikkal-Adoyah. What must I do?"

She looked at him with distaste. "What you want to do is impossible. Even most Puradu die when they swim so deep."

"So, one of you could fetch it for me?" he demanded.

Time seemed to slow. Mani turned to Nikkal-Adoyah, watching her lips part and words begin to form on her tongue.

"No," she said. Breath burst from Mani in a rush. "The plant you need grows in fresh water at the bottom of the sea. Bring it up through brine and it dies. It must be plucked and eaten on the sea floor or it's useless."

"Then one of you *could* bring it up. Carry down a pot, put the plant in that, and bring it to me still in fresh—"

"No," Nikkal-Adoyah said again. Sarru-kin stopped talking, shock clear on his strained face. Nobody had dared interrupt him for a long time. "The plant must be eaten at once. Plucked, it shrivels to nothing."

"So, I must dive to it," the Mad King mused. "Yes, Azaq, I should have seen it. Such a prize must be gained by my own hand, not another's. Of course it would be so." His eyes snapped back to the Puradu woman. "Very well. Describe this flower to me."

"Even though you'll die?"

"I have not come this far to baulk at the last," Sarru-kin said, "or to be dissuaded by you. Tell me."

"We call it Old-Man-Young," Nikkal-Adoyah told him. "It's a small flower, the yellow of buttercups, with a white heart. It grows in deep water near the fresh springs where brine can't reach. Usually, it's found under overhangs of rock, out of the strongest currents."

"I just pick it?"

"If you can. There are no thorns, no poisons in the leaves. There are riptides, though, where the sea floor is split by fissures. Water races through them whichever way the tide is running. Tonight, this evening, we are between tides. The water is as calm as it will ever be."

"Then where do I dive?"

Nikkal-Adoyah pointed. "There. You see the two rocks, shaped like the horns of a bull? Good. Take this boat. Throw a rope around those rocks and moor there. Then dive."

"Follow," Sarru-kin said. His looming bodyguards turned as one towards the boat.

"You really will die," Nikkal-Adoyah said. The Mad King stopped, head half turned to listen. "Don't think I'd regret that. There isn't a Puradu who would shed a tear for you, and precious few humans in Engiru either, I expect. It doesn't sit well with me to send a man to his death without one more warning. You'll die, king of Labaš. Understand that."

Mani saw the edge of Sarru-kin's smile. "They call me the Mad King. Do you know why? No? Because I do things other men do not understand. I do things they believe impossible. Cities fall to me in an hour, and soldiers abandon their oaths and follow me. I will not die, fish woman. I have done the impossible so often it has become ordinary."

He walked on. The boat was grounded on a shingle beach, from which Sarru-kin gathered handfuls of pebbles before he climbed in. The guards pushed the little craft into the water and clambered in beside him. It wallowed low, but none of them took any notice of that. Two unshipped oars. They turned the boat, a little awkwardly, and began to stroke out of the bay.

CHAPTER FORTY-FOUR

H OW SURE ARE you?" Yarim asked.
Nikkal-Adoyah watched the boat recede. It moved through clear water encircled by the heads of Puradu, watching from a distance. "That he won't come back? I'm certain."

"He has done things nobody else dreamed of," the soldier said. "Sarru-kin is right about that. He's conquered half of Engiru in one summer with hardly a fight. I've caught myself thinking he really must be part god to know the things he does. Like Kammani." His voice caught, and he swallowed. "How did he know about her? How could he?"

"Who's Kammani?"

"She was head priestess of Labaš," Mani said when Yarim didn't answer. "Sarru-kin poisoned her just as we left to sail here."

"That sounds like him," Nikkal-Adoyah said. "Well, I don't know what happened there. I do know the rifts under the sea. No human can dive that deep and survive."

"What about half a god?" Yarim asked. His face was white.

The Puradu woman turned to face him. "If he's half a god, then it means all your deities are real. All your ridiculous, wish-spun fancies have come true, in some way I don't understand. If that's true, soldier, then anything is possible. You might as well say your Mad King could reach out a hand and pluck the sun from the sky."

"So, he *could* do it," Yarim said.

Mani didn't think the big man was listening. Yarim was bewitched by what Sarru-kin had done before and now couldn't quite believe anything was beyond him. The Mad King wasn't a god. Mani had never really been sure he believed in Eala and all the others, and what he'd learned this last month had hardened that doubt into cynicism. The gods of Engiru were illusions. They had never been there.

Since that was so, how could Sarru-kin be half a god?

"Sometimes immature Puradu dive for Old-Man-Young," Tanyih said when the silence stretched. "Males, nearly every time. We tell them not to do it, but there are always some who will. We find their bodies when we are lucky. Sometimes the current carries objects to the shore."

Even Puradu couldn't reach the plant. Mani watched the boat recede. Sarru-kin had reached back to unclip the sickle sword's sheathe on his back. His movements were calm, unhurried. He was going to dive. He might be half a god, might be deluded, or might be just a man who believed in himself and got lucky, but he was going to dive.

The world hinged on what happened next.

"What if he comes back to the beach?" Yarim asked.

"He won't come back," Nikkal-Adoyah said.

"But if he does?"

"He won't—"

"What if he does?" Yarim shouted.

Dozens of heads had gathered around the little boat now. They moved in circles, some one way and some the other, rising and falling like porpoises. Late sunlight flashed from what might be a blade or a spear point.

"We will not kill him for you," Nikkal-Adoyah said.

On the boat, Sarru-kin was tying something to his shoulders. Bags, Mani realised. They must be weighted with the stones he'd taken from the beach. The Mad King had prepared for everything again. *A man who believed in himself and got lucky.* Maybe it wasn't just luck.

The boat reached the rocks. It was only a shadow now, silhouetted against the lowering sun. A figure stood up, paused, and jumped. Water splashed and the figure was gone.

Nobody breathed. The sun touched the horizon, and blue twilight spread across the sea. The peaks behind Mani were still in daylight, but he didn't think anyone else looked at them. It was a beautiful sight, something no human eyes had ever seen, but it didn't matter. Not now.

The water was dark. The Puradu men might still surround the boat, but Mani couldn't see them.

"You won't have to," Mani said. The sound of his voice surprised him.

Yarim's head turned like a cog on a wheel. "What?"

"He isn't coming back."

"Why," the soldier began. He broke off, his stare intent. "Scholar. What have you done?"

"Watch," he said.

Something exploded from the water, right beside the boat. There were shouts of alarm carrying over the sea. Water fountained and fell, and one of the men in the boat was hanging over the side, his comrades trying to drag him back. Then something pulled and he was gone, as fast as that, pulling another man over with him.

Another eruption of water, and this time Mani saw a shape in the middle of it. Like a fresco, a warrior with spear raised and muscles bunching, only this time the fighter had a tail instead of legs. The spear thrust, someone screamed, and the Puradu plunged back under the waves.

There was one man left in the boat. He was on his knees, praying perhaps, when a swimmer rose out of the water behind him. Lips drew back from teeth, a very human gesture, and a spear moved. The man collapsed. Then there was only the boat, bobbing gently against its rock.

"Scholar?" Yarim asked very quietly.

Isha was staring at him. They all were, Tauth and Shusikil white in the face, like bodies laid out for sky burial. Mani looked out to sea.

"Sarru-kin always planned ahead," he said. "He bought Shahan years ago, and the traitors in other cities, too. Strength cannot keep pace with cleverness. The Mad King's gift isn't as a warrior. It's his brilliance. But I'm clever too."

The boat bobbed. Over to their left the sun was nearly down, low enough to pick out the tops of waves and what Mani thought was a body floating among them.

"He wanted to come to this island," Mani said. "So, let him. He was impossible to harm in Engiru, wasn't he? But here, he was just a stranger. He didn't know the Puradu, or care about them. I knew very little, but it was more than him, and I had a friend among the Puradu as well."

"Hanno," Isha said.

He nodded. "I spoke with him, the day Sarru-kin made me ask for passage here. Hanno told me about this plant. I had an idea." He turned to Nikkal-Adoyah. "Thank you. I know it couldn't have been easy."

Muscles shifted in Yarim's neck. "What did you do, scholar?"

"He asked us to lie for him," Nikkal-Adoyah said. "To say that Old-Man-Young must be eaten at once, on the sea floor. The truth is that it can be brought up through brine."

"I don't understand."

"There was no need for Sarru-kin to be the one to make the dive," Mani told the soldier. "Any one of the Puradu could have done it for him, but they would have refused and sent him away. And then what, Yarim?"

"He would have killed you," the captain answered. "Kept your wife as a bed slave and murdered your child."

"And back home the slaughter would have continued," Mani said. "He would have looked for other ways to live forever. The fire demons of the west, maybe, or the gods of the plateau. The trick, Yarim, was to make Sarru-kin think he had won, that he'd forced us to his will, because then his arrogance would lead him out there, and he'd dive and never come up."

"You couldn't be sure of that."

"Yes, he could," Isha said, unexpectedly. "Hanno."

Mani nodded. "Yes."

"They killed him," Yarim said. "Didn't they?"

The boat was drifting towards shore. Pulled, perhaps, though Mani couldn't see for sure in the twilight. Something moved down at the end of the beach, where rocks plunged into water. He moved a bit closer and saw it was a Puradu, young, his head smooth and a spear in his hand.

Mani hesitated and then went to kneel on the shore.

"Is that what waits for all of us?" he asked. "Are we going to die here?"

"Death waits for everyone," Hanno said. "But not here. Not for you, scholar. Don't fear that."

"I'm not afraid for me. It's for my wife and child."

"I know." Hanno gestured with the spear. "None of us know who our parents are. But you humans do. You know your children, and that's a precious thing."

"You're a wise man," Mani said, "for someone so young."

"You've taught me a lot." Hanno grinned. "I'm known now. The wives speak of me as an adult, though not always with favour." The smile faded to a grimace. "They blame me, I think, for bringing this suffering to the island."

"I'm sorry," Mani said.

"Sarru-kin is dead."

"Ah," Mani said. "You did it?"

"No. We would have killed him if we'd needed to. He was told how dangerous it is down there. I dove near to him, Mani. He'd weighted bags with stones. It was all I could do to keep up with him. He went straight down. The current caught him, dragged him around, and he started to trail bubbles."

Silence on the beach.

"He went under a ledge," Hanno said. "There were no bubbles by then. I waited and then came back."

Sarru-kin was dead. For all that the Puradu had said, Mani hadn't really been able to bring himself to believe it would happen. Part of him had expected the Mad King to surface again, with stains from the yellow flower on his teeth. Sarru-kin had seemed invulnerable. It was hard to be sure he was gone.

"Thank you," Mani said.

The young man ducked his head under and came up streaming. "You brought us your wife. You don't owe me thanks."

"I didn't know how significant that was."

"Of course you didn't," Hanno said.

They heard footsteps behind them, and Nikkal-Adoyah said, "You have brought us great strife, the two of you. More even than most males."

"I always try," Mani said, trying for irony, "to be the best I can at everything."

She glowered at him and then at Hanno. The young male's smile was gone, and he flipped over to look at her upside-down.

"From shallow water one can look up and see the sun," Hanno said. "Goodbye, scholar."

With that last cryptic comment, he pushed off the rock and was gone in the surf.

The tide had begun to rise. Mani rose, brushed off his knees, and walked back to the group. They watched him without speaking as he came to a halt.

"He's dead," Mani said.

There was silence. After a moment, Yarim moved away, towards the beach, with the points of a dozen arrows tracking him. He climbed down the rocks into waist-deep water, where he caught the bow of the boat as it washed into shore. His arm vanished inside. It came back out clutching a sickle sword in a black scabbard.

"To prove he's dead," Yarim said as he climbed back up the beach. "Too many of the men back home wouldn't believe it, but they know Sarru-kin would never leave this behind. It's the symbol of the king of Labaš." He hefted the sword. "Now they'll believe."

"Can you hear a god?"

Yarim shook his head. After a moment he bared an inch of blade, and Mani put fingertips on it. He felt bronze, the metal surprisingly cool. That was all. No voice in his head.

"He really was mad," Mani said.

"Did you doubt it?"

"There must have been a time when you did."

"Yes," Yarim said. "Once. Not for some time."

He sheathed the sword and slung it over his back. Some of the Puradu women lowered their bows. Evidently, they thought the danger had passed with Sarru-kin's death. Nikkal-Adoyah was the only one who moved, coming up to join them by the strand.

"We'll have your water casks refilled," she said. "We can give you some fruit and bread, too. Be ready to sail in the morning."

"In the morning," he repeated. Too much had happened. He was numb, beyond sorrow or pain.

"Males will guide you to the door to your world," Nikkal-Adoyah said. She turned and went away. Most of the Puradu archers faded away with her, lost in the twilight.

Isha helped him to the grass, where Mani sat with his head on his knees. He was aware of Yarim moving away, leaving the two of them alone.

Isha touched his arm. "Are you ready to leave?"

No. He wasn't, and he never would be. This was the land of his dreams, the place he'd always longed to see. He could never have enough of it. Already he'd learned so much. How Puradu had their children, how they moved across the seas between stars, and how Aš-alam had been founded. He could learn more if he stayed.

He looked at Isha, who carried his child, and who he thought he loved. "So much of my heart is here. If the Puradu would have me, and if it wasn't for you and our child, I'd stay and go with them when they leave."

"I know."

Mani breathed deep, the air of another world filling his lungs.

"Yes," he said." I'm ready to leave."

Chapter Forty-Five

THE ISLAND WAS behind them, detail fading into a peaked blur of green. "Don't think of the things you could have learned," Isha said. "Think of what you did learn."

"I am," Mani said. He couldn't hold in his chuckle. "Is there anything you don't see?"

"I see you," she told him. "I see a good and noble man, who tried to do his best by everyone, even when he was swept up in something terrible."

He didn't reply to that. The world's blue sunlight made the island's outline very sharp. He thought he could pick out the lakes, if he concentrated, though the effort ached his eyes.

"I wanted to find the answers," he said, "to so many questions. I had dreams of Aš-alam transformed, though I couldn't really imagine how. I wanted to find out. It's all gone now."

"Not all of it," she said.

Mani frowned at her.

"Tanyih told you about steam machines," Isha said. "About iron and compasses. She didn't tell you how to make them, but you know they're possible now. What do you think a clever man might do, now that he knows what *can* be done?"

"I'm not an artisan."

"No," she said. "Husband, I love you, but you're not the only clever man in Aš-alam."

Puradu swam around the ship. There had been a hundred when they sailed out of the bay, as though every swimmer had come for a glimpse of the humans before they left forever. A score remained. Mostly they were shadows under waves, but from time to time one would breach and turn in the air to look at the ship before splashing back down. Mani wanted to watch them, drink his fill of the sight, but he also wanted to watch the island. Whichever way he looked, he felt he was missing out.

"What will you do?" she asked.

He shook his head. "I don't know."

The sun brightened, and he shaded his eyes with a hand. He'd barely done so when the light returned to normal. Real normal, sunshine without the tinge of blue, and the island was gone. There was just ocean, rolling with long waves that caught the ship and tugged it around.

"Sarru-kin is dead," Isha said.

Mani nodded. They were back in their own world, and the Mad King wasn't with them. It might have been necessary for that to be true before he really believed Sarru-kin was gone. He was, and it was over. Isha was safe, their child was safe, and it was over.

Behind them voices came from the upper deck, Yarim talking with the soldiers. The sickle sword Azaq was slung on his back.

§ § §

"What will you do?" Tauth asked.

Mani shook his head. "People keep asking me that."

"Do you have an answer?"

"Not yet."

They were at the prow of the boat this time, heading north. Heading home. There had been times when Mani didn't think he'd see Aš-alam again, and others when he'd been afraid Isha and their child would be lost to him there, but he was coming home. Ra'im might still be trapped in the Immaru Temple, the northern army might still be in the streets at the heart of chaos, but Mani was coming home.

"Will you tell the king?"

Pointless to tell her he didn't know. He'd only be repeating himself, and the *zami* never listened.

He could see better in the light of his own world. His eyes were used to it, he supposed. The ache behind his temples had gone. He stood at the prow and strained towards the horizon, eager for home and the end of this journey. The end, at last.

Except it wouldn't be. He was the scholar Sarru-kin had picked out, the only one who had ever travelled to the island of the Puradu. The other scholars would want answers from him. What the island was like, how the Puradu spoke and lived, and most of all why there were no swimmers in the lagoon anymore. Mani would have to tell them. He could imagine their faces crash as he spoke—Darsal, Hitti, Tash-Yal, the men he'd known for so long.

They would pick at him, the way they had all picked at the Puradu for so long. Probing, asking the same question in a thousand different ways, all to tease out a snippet of information they had missed before. Mani would answer, even if it took years, because he knew the loss in their hearts and the grief. It would be in him, too. He was going to ruin their lives.

Actually, it was Sarru-kin who'd ruined their lives, but it would be Mani who brought the news. Men were hated for less.

Most of all, there was the other thing he knew. How Aš-alam had been founded and by whom. News that would shatter the priesthood in a day, if he spoke it.

"You deserve what happens to you," he said at last. "As payment for your lies."

"Whose lies?" Tauth asked. Her nose made the words nasal, like the whining of a child.

"You know very well. The Temples. The *zami*."

"I was never a priestess," she reminded him. "I couldn't master my letters. Are they my lies?"

Mani was silent.

"Look," she said. "Most of the *zami* don't know the truth. Probably most of the seniors don't. You can blame the Temples, because the organisation has known all along, but don't blame the lesser priestesses. They've been lied to just as much as you."

That might be true, not that it changed anything. Tauth wasn't finished though. "And then there are the people. Ordinary men and women, who believe what the *zami* tell them, because who else are they to trust? They rely on the priesthood for truth, for hope of a good life in the next world, and also for life in this one. Don't forget that, scholar."

"Life in this one?"

"The Temples maintain the ditches. They organise all the irrigation systems, everything on our side of the river. On the north bank the ditches all link together, Tibad's with Piqash's with Shurraš', so the Temples work together to share the work. What will happen there if you break the power of the priesthood?"

"I don't have a quarrel with the Temples of other cities."

"Then don't pick one," she said. "Scholar, if you destroy the *zami* in Aš-alam, you'll deal a blow to those in other cities as well. It only takes one unrepaired ditch for half the water a city needs to drain away again. People will die. Real people, who've done nothing wrong."

"Yes," he said. "I know. The choice is that, or to let you continue to lie as you always have. I've spent my life searching for truth. Lies don't sit well with me."

"Or with me," Tauth said.

"I wouldn't have thought dishonesty would cause any problems for a murderer," Mani said.

She grimaced. "I didn't enjoy doing that. You know it, I think."

"Shahan is still dead."

"Yes, he's dead. He betrayed Eala, and I'll make payment for what I did when I stand before her, I suppose. I'll tell her, then, that Shahan deserved to die. He *needed* to die, because he betrayed her. Don't confuse the Temples with the goddess, Mani. The first has lied to us all. The second never did."

"Because she isn't real," he said.

Tauth laughed at him. "Then tell the people that and see how they receive the news. Be realistic, scholar. Too many people believe too deeply for you to shake the faith. You might be able to rock the Temples. You'll never destroy belief in Eala herself."

That might be true as well. It probably was, in fact. There was the question of why he'd want to wreck that belief, too. What would it achieve? People would just adopt one of the other gods or create a new one to replace what they'd lost. Gods grew out of almost nothing, like a part-scaled Puradu swimming out of the marsh to stand on two new feet and looking at what she saw.

"Think about it," Tauth said. "The Temples hand out food to the hungry, scholar, and clothes for children. Don't make the desperate pay a price because you're angry."

"Tauth," he said, as she began to move away. She paused to study him. "I don't blame you. For Shahan."

"Really?"

"I'd never have believed he could do what he did," Mani said. "It was unforgivable. He put my wife and child in danger, and so many others. I don't think I could have killed him myself. But perhaps someone needed to."

"Thank you for that," Tauth said. The beak of her nose shifted upwards when she smiled. "Remember it, scholar. Before you put other men's wives in danger by what you say about lies."

§ § §

An hour later, he saw a smudge on the horizon. Engiru, not much more than a line along the edge of the sea, but home.

Yarim was at the rail too, back in leather armour with knives in his belt and the sickle sword on his back. He let out a breath at the sight of land, and Mani asked, "What will you do?"

Today's question, it seemed. Isha had asked him, then Tauth, and now Mani was asking it of Yarim. The big soldier didn't look away from the land.

"Do you know what I want to do?" Yarim asked.

"No."

"I'd like to dive for that yellow flower. However certain it is that I'd die, I'd like to make the attempt. If I somehow managed it," he hesitated, "I'd come back here and put the petals in Kammani's dead mouth and see if they gave her life again."

Mani was silent.

"Makes me as big a fool as Sarru-kin, doesn't it?" Yarim leaned on the rail. "Trying to defeat death. But Mani, that woman made me feel…well. Being alive like that, even for an hour, is better than immortality. We're not gods. Maybe there aren't any gods, as those fish women said, and maybe there are. I don't know. But if they exist, they're more than we can ever be."

That was more words than Mani had ever heard from the soldier at one time, and Yarim was right. Mani tended to think the gods had been created by humans, not the other way around. He always had, even as part of him believed in the blessing of Eala. A curse of education, he supposed. He couldn't see things in simple ways anymore.

There was one thing he had to ask. The same thing Tauth had asked him, really. "What will you say, soldier?"

"About the island?" Yarim's hands flexed, though Mani didn't think he was aware of it. "I will say what I saw. Sarru-kin dived for the flower. The swimmers killed his guards, and he never came up."

Mani swallowed. "Thank you."

Yarim gave a big-shouldered shrug. "It's in my own interest, too. I've decided I'm going to be king."

"King?"

"There aren't any Elders left in Labaš. Nor their families. Sarru-kin had them all slaughtered when he seized power. I helped carry the bodies out of the Chamber the day they were butchered." He grimaced. "The head priestess is dead too. So, there's no one to rule, except the army, and most of the old generals are dead. I'm as well placed as anyone—and I have the sickle sword."

"Does that matter?"

Yarim laughed. "You're a clever man, scholar, but you don't know people. Symbols are important. Especially to soldiers, who are as superstitious as anyone. At least," he added, "anyone except sailors. The crew of this boat are half crazy with odd notions."

"I understand symbols," Mani said, stung. "We went to the island. That will count for as much as anything back home."

"Yes, it will." Yarim studied him. "You don't have a living any longer, do you? Not now that the swimmers are gone. You could come back to Labaš with me. I'll need advisors with nimble wits."

"Leave Aš-alam?"

"There's not much there for you now, scholar."

"Well," Mani said, "you might be surprised."

CHAPTER FORTY-SIX

THEY HAD REACHED land too far east. Ludari turned the ship, and they caught a current that ran along the shore with a brisk wind behind. By late morning they turned into the mouth of the Ranuna, and later nosed through a bank of reeds and reached the marsh.

"Easy," the steersman said through twisted lips.

Mani still found sleep hard to come by. Isha slept without moving, exhausted by nausea and stress, while next to her he twitched and wriggled every moment. He was nearly home, and that proximity worried at his mind. Close, and nothing to do.

Nothing but think. He chased ideas around as the night grew old. Mani thought he knew what to do, but he couldn't make himself believe it was right.

Near dawn he fell into a fitful sleep. He woke to find the bed beside him empty and smoke rising from a fire on shore.

"A signal," Isha told him when he came on deck. "Yarim thinks so, anyway."

"Sent by whom?"

"The army," she said. "Sarru-kin's."

Mani watched the smoke thoughtfully. Probably Yarim was right, but there were other possibilities. The signal could be meant for the Mad King's enemies as easily as for his allies. That could mean many things. Some of them hinted at surprises in Aš-alam.

They rowed on. The wind had died, leaving the lagoon still. Nothing broke the surface. No fish, no reeds waving in a breeze. No Puradu splashing in the deeps. They would never be here again. Mani knew it, but his eyes kept searching the water, hoping for a glimpse of a crusted head or fluked tail, or a shape arcing in the air like a porpoise.

There was nothing. He began to understand, finally, that there never would be again.

He wept a little then, silently, so no one noticed tears drying on his cheeks. He thought of Hanno, allowed into the mating pools on the island to dance and play in the water. Alone, of course. The females would come later, and Hanno would have children but never know them. An ache in his heart that would never fade. Mani looked up at the sky and tried to make a place for that ache, somewhere it could live without leaving scars.

The ship angled north. The afternoon peaked. Ahead of them they saw the shore, thick with reeds, and behind them the raised banks, levees to keep the water back. Now they were crowded with tents with soldiers around them.

"Whose are they?" Isha wondered. Nobody answered.

§ § §

By the time the ship tied up at the jetty, soldiers had gathered there in thick ranks, and it was obvious they were outlanders. Mani recognised none of them. If they'd been Aš-alam troops, he'd have known some faces here and there. He scanned the banners and saw the emblems of Labaš and Balih, the war god, but nothing else.

No flags from Piqash, none from Tibad. Mani squinted towards the city, but it was too far to make out details.

"I wonder who's in charge there," he murmured.

The crowd was restive. Some of the soldiers shouted questions as the boat was tied off. Most only watched and waited, but they did so with a tight look to their faces, ready to explode.

"Where is the king?"

"What happened?"

"Show us Sarru-kin!"

They went silent in an instant, as though their tongues had been cut. Mani twisted around to see Yarim standing on the upper deck, the sickle sword slung over his back.

"Sarru-kin is dead," the captain said. He rested big hands on the rail.

"Impossible!"

"How?"

"He dived for a flower that would make him immortal," Yarim said. His voice cut through the noise, stilling it again. "There wasn't any deceit. Nobody struck him or betrayed his trust. The flower was too deep."

Silence, for a moment. Yarim came down the ladder and went to the boarding plank. "I saw it happen. Sarru-kin carried bags filled with stones to take him down to the depths. Down he went."

There was more he could have said. Words that touched on betrayal and a trick that had lured the Mad King to his death. Mani waited, Isha beside him, the pair of them still as old bones.

Someone pushed through the crowd. Yarim turned towards him, hands on hips. "What about his guards?" the newcomer demanded.

"Those, someone did attack," Yarim answered. "Swimmers killed them as they began to row for the land. I saw it myself, Zammash. The swimmer men killed them in the boat rather than have four angry men wreaking havoc. I don't blame them for it. But Sarru-kin is dead."

He let them absorb that, and then said, "What's the situation in the city?"

"No one's been allowed inside for two days," Zammash said.

"Allowed? Sarru-kin left you an army, and the enemy holed up like rats in a cellar. Some captain you are." It was said with a smile, patronising as a grandma, and the other man's face went dark. "What happened, then?"

Zammash didn't answer, so someone else moved forward. "The allies left right after the king did. The Piqash guys went north, through the Flood. Said they could make it in two days without sleeping. The Tibad lot sided with Aš-alam. When they did that, we decided to get out while we could."

They'd had nowhere to go but here, the bank at the edge of the marsh. Nowhere else was dry within fifty miles, except inside the city walls. They might make it to Piqash, but the city would be closed against them, the king back in power. Labaš was too far away, and now they had no Sarru-kin, no god-touched lord to lead them. No Elders, no senior priestess. Mani could imagine the doubt in their minds. Once they made the choice to wait, it would have become almost impossible to change their minds and act.

Here there was food, if they could catch it with spears and makeshift nets. Water was easy to find, and not the muddy swirl of the Flood, but clear and fresh from the lagoon. So they delayed, waiting for someone to tell them what to do.

Mani looked across at Yarim.

"Time for a meeting of captains," Yarim said. "Call them here to this boat. We have no Elders, and no king either. There isn't even a head *zami*. We need—"

"You're not in charge," Zammash broke in. "You weren't even here."

"That's right. I was travelling with Sarru-kin, where he trusted me to be." Yarim paused. "You *were* here and didn't do much. We can discuss that at the meeting, if you like."

"You don't have the right to call the captains," Zammash snapped. "And all we have is your word that the king is dead. How do we know you didn't murder him? Or stand aside while the fish devils did?"

"We can discuss that, too. Look." Yarim went down the plank, hands spread. "We don't need to fight. We'll talk, no?"

"I never trusted you," Zammash said. "I still don't now."

Those were the last words spoken in a life.

Yarim leapt, up and forward at the same time. He drew the sickle sword in mid-air and struck sideways. Zammash had time to begin to move, to draw back, but then his neck was cut almost through, and his head flopped to one side as he collapsed. Blood sprayed sideways. Men stumbled away from the corpse with a torrent of curses.

Yarim levelled the sword and turned in a slow arc. "Does anyone else want to call me a liar?"

Nobody moved. Wind stirred the reeds, and somewhere a heron cried out.

"Call the captains," Yarim ordered. "I will wait for them here."

This time men scrambled to obey. Yarim turned to Mani and grounded the point of the sickle sword in the earth, a pose so reminiscent of Sarru-kin that for a moment Mani was afraid. The big soldier looked at him for a moment, face expressionless.

"You'll need a chariot," he said.

In the end he gave them two. There were Shusikil and Tauth to consider, though Mani had only thought of himself and his wife. Soon they were ploughing down the road to the city, while water sloshed around the wheels and washed over their feet. Birds dived behind them, picking out fish disturbed by the chariots' wake.

"I didn't think," Isha said after a while, "that we'd come back alive."

"No. Or if we did, it would be to a life with you as Sarru-kin's slave and me to no life at all."

"I would have killed him in his sleep," she said. The charioteer glared at her from the side of his eye. Love for Sarru-kin went deep among his army. Some of them, anyway.

"He would never have allowed you a weapon."

"Who says I need one? I carried jars of ale for years, Mani. I piled tables at the end of the night so the floor could be swept. I can't arm wrestle a soldier. But I can pull a cord tight and hold it, however someone struggles." Her smile was thin enough to cut. "I've done it, a couple of times when a drinker wouldn't behave. Once the line is around his throat, nobody can pull free."

He frowned at his wife. "Did you kill them?"

"Of course not. But him…I'd have killed Sarru-kin. For so many things."

"Who would have thought," he said presently, "that day in the Spilled Salt we'd learn to love like this?"

"The gods would," she said. "Eala would. But no mortals, because we're not meant to see."

The gods, and Eala. If they existed. When Mani thought of the goddess now, he saw a woman walking awkwardly on new legs, a trail of scales fallen where she passed. She was weak, like a chick newly free from its shell. Yet there was elegance too, the grace of a swimmer, and the promise of strength to come. Hair was a frizz on her head, webs still clung between her fingers, and she was not human.

"Could we have been anything," he mused, "without the Puradu? Humans, I mean. I wonder if we would ever have moved out of our straw huts and learned to build and watch the stars."

Isha smiled. "Oh, husband. Do you think the savages in their huts didn't watch the stars and dream?"

They must have, he realised. It was obvious once Isha said it. Those long-ago men sat in the night and looked up, marvelled, and begun to tell tales of what they saw. How these stars were a scorpion, cursed to scuttle in the dirt of the sky to atone for ancient cruelty. How these were a dancer and those a bull, each with their own stories, animals and emblems spread across the twelve houses of the sky.

Men had learned, before the Puradu came, to build straw huts. They'd found how to make rafts from reeds to float atop the annual Flood and made spears to fish with or to kill lions. The world had begun to bend to human hands when Anath-Eala Sisi had not yet been born.

Aš-alam was drawing closer. Mani could hardly believe they were back and safe. Or nearly so. One thing remained to do. He could feel Shusikil's eyes on him from the chariot behind, glaring at the back of his head.

"We would have learned," he said. "But slowly."

She shrugged. "Or more quickly. How much have the *zami* held us back with their lies?"

That was a question they could never answer. Time moved in one direction, and it only passed this way once. It passed, and was gone, the path never to be retrodden. There was so much that could not be known, even by the Puradu. The thought of it made Mani want to scream in frustration. Generations of scholars had only scratched the edges of what the Puradu knew, and even they had learned so little it was laughable.

"I wish the gods were real," he said, "so I could find a way to make them tell me everything they knew, all the secrets of all the stars, and I wouldn't have to wonder anymore."

"No," Isha said. "But you'd be as mad as Sarru-kin, and fate would destroy you as it did him." The driver glowered at her again. "Look. We've arrived."

CHAPTER FORTY-SEVEN

THE SCAFFOLDING WAS busy again.

A building had burned just inside the gate, by accident it seemed. Scorch marks spread from inside the window but soon ended. Someone must have lit a fire inside and lost control of it. It was lucky water was so close.

Across the street a frame had gone up, and the top floor of a house had been dismantled. Another was already taking shape, pale new bricks in neat courses on darker old. Mani could see the spaces where windows would be. Men in loose tunics leaned on the scaffold to look down at the new arrivals, murmuring to each other.

A few citizens paused to stare as well and then went on their way.

"It's like we never left," Isha said.

It almost was. A few burnt bricks aside, the gate was the same as it had always been. The city too, if a glimpse could be trusted. And of course, some things never changed.

"Be wary of what you say," Shusikil grated behind him. "Words have consequences. Just as actions do."

He turned his head. "I'll say what I choose to say."

Her mouth worked, and then she strode away. Tauth hesitated, looking at Mani. She had knifed Shahan and thrown him over the side, what felt like years ago. Once she'd wanted to be a priestess, and she might have become his wife if things had been a little different. Only a little. Small changes, and the world becomes a different place.

She walked away, though not after Shusikil. To her own house, Mani supposed, that had once been Shahan's. She had nowhere else to go. For her everything had changed. He felt a moment of pity and shook it away. He had his own concerns.

"Home?" he asked.

"Home," Isha smiled. She took his hand.

The streets hadn't changed, at least no more than normal. Sarru-kin's men had done very little damage, it seemed. There were always labourers on scaffolds, bricks being replaced, and streets overlaid with a new layer of mud. Without constant work Aš-alam would sink back into the plain, worn away by the lapping of the annual flood.

There was no more work now than before. Men called to each other from the heights and whistled at women as they walked below. Shoppers walked with bags of meagre goods, culled from markets nearly bare of stock now with the

Flood here. Some stared at Mani and Isha in shock, those few who knew them by sight.

"Word will spread quickly," he said to Isha.

"It already has," she told him. "Listen."

He did, bending an ear to snatches of conversation half-heard as they passed. Twice he heard his own name, once Isha's. Three times someone said *Sarru-kin*, and then on a street corner Mani heard *the Mad King is dead*. So much for word being about to spread. It already had.

They came to their house. The garden gate was open, but the yard wasn't damaged, and the back door stood intact. Inside everything was tidy. Dust from the street had settled on every surface, but there was no damage. Nobody had raided the house, and no soldiers had slept on the divans. Mani closed the door and sighed.

"Well, we're home," he said, "and safe as bats."

She guided his hand to her belly. It was still flat and would be for some time to come, but Mani almost thought he felt a flutter under his fingers, the first beats of a forming heart. Wishful thinking, of course. It would be months before he could feel anything. Isha's hand laid over his, holding it there.

"Don't be a fool," she said. "We're not safe yet."

He smiled ruefully. "I know that. I was hoping to make you feel a bit safer, that's all."

"Thank you. I'll feel safe when this is over, and it's not, Mani. Not yet. The Temples want you silenced."

"Do you think they dare touch me, now?"

"I think they tried to kill my father," she said, "or maim him, over a petty dispute that was nothing to do with him. I think that when all their privileges and power are threatened, there's not much they wouldn't risk. Your death would cause a scandal. But just now, with the Mad King gone and his army disintegrating, they might think Ra'im wouldn't care too much."

"That's probably true."

"Then remember it. You might also remember that the Temples don't have to hurt you today. They could wait a year, or ten years, and then maim me instead of you. Or our child."

That stopped him. Amazing, how he could care so much for someone whose face he'd never seen. Someone still growing into life, safe inside his mother. Or her mother. Eala's footfalls, he didn't even know! He pressed his fingers against Isha, feeling for that flutter again.

"I'll be careful," he said.

The door opened behind him, and he turned, heart in his throat and mind full of thoughts of Sarru-kin returned or soldiers out for bitter revenge.

"Kassu-Mani?" the man said. He *was* a soldier, short sword at his hip. The shadows of more fell across the doorway. "The scholar?"

"I am," Mani said. The man's face was familiar. Mani didn't know him, but he thought he'd seen the fellow around. Walked past him in the street a few times or sat at the next table in the Spilled Salt, maybe. He was a man of Aš-alam. If that meant anything.

"The king wishes to speak with you," the man said.

Mani didn't move. "My best friend turned out to be an agent for Sarru-kin. How can I trust you?"

The soldier's expression changed. "You took the Mad King away to his death. Today, scholar, every soldier in the city would die for you. By Eala, I swear I won't harm you."

"Words," he said. "The palace is a slippery place, filled with distrust, and these are just words."

"Perhaps you'll trust mine," another voice said. The soldier stepped aside, and there behind him was Ra'im. The king was unharmed, as far as Mani could see. Confidence came off him like an oxen's sweat. Mani started to gape.

"My lord," Isha said. She knelt on the rug.

The king caught her hands and drew her back up. "You don't kneel to me today, lady. No more than you did on your wedding day. If the rumours are true, you've done this city and all Engiru a service beyond words. Both of you have."

"Rumours?" she repeated.

"That Sarru-kin is dead," Nahal said. The Overseer of the Army had to sidle past the soldier to fit inside. Mani's house was decent enough, but it hadn't been built to hold five people in one room. "Is it true?"

He aimed the question at Mani, who found his tongue again. "Yes. He died at the island."

"Will you tell us what happened?"

"Yes, of course."

The king beckoned over his shoulder. "Bring us wine and water, and something to eat. It doesn't matter what. Now sit, Mani, and you too, Isha. Sit, and tell me your tale."

§ § §

It was unfair, in a way. Unfair and unsettling too, because king though Ra'im was, he was no Sarru-kin.

Mani's mind told him this was what a king should be. Strong but considerate, wielding power but not shaped by it. The way kings had been in Engiru for all the decades of peace. Still, something in him compared Ra'im to the Mad King and found him less magnetic and not so compelling. In a room full of people Ra'im was just a man. Sarru-kin would have dominated it.

He hadn't been immortal, but he was never merely human, either.

Mani told the story as simply as he could. It occurred to him that the other scholars would be angry with him for speaking to the king first. They'd say he should have gone to the Guild before he went anywhere else. A scholar's first duty was to what he learned, and nothing else mattered until it was recorded and stored in the Hall of Tablets.

Then he remembered there were no Puradu in the marsh and no need for scholars anymore.

Shusikil slipped into the room halfway through the telling. The soldier had to leave to make space for her. Mani saw her but went on speaking, though his heart began to beat harder. When he finished, he took a swallow of wine, sitting back in his chair.

"Well." Ra'im had taken the divan, of course. "I've never heard anything like that before."

"It's true. Others saw much of it," Mani said. "My wife, or Yarim. Shusikil can vouch for it, too."

He nodded to the *zami*. Her stone expression never changed, and she didn't nod back.

"I'm not doubting you, scholar. I said it before and will repeat it now. What you did for Aš-alam is a service beyond anything I could have asked."

Isha leaned forward. "There's one other thing you should know. Nahal, as much as the king. The captains of the Labaš army are meeting out at the marsh. It's likely that a man named Yarim will be chosen as the new king."

"Yarim?" the overseer repeated. "I don't know that name."

"He's the officer who went with Sarru-kin to the island. He came back with the sickle sword."

"Ah. That's the symbol of kings in Labaš." Ra'im stroked his beard. "And he's moving to consolidate power before anyone can make their own plans? Clever. He'll bear watching."

"He's got an army less than a mile away," Nahal said curtly, "a lot of whom are angry. Of course we'll watch him."

There it was, the difference between Ra'im and Sarru-kin. No one would have dared speak so bluntly to the Mad King, or even in the same room. Men kept their eyes down and their tongues still if they wanted to live. Even if they saw their lover killed before them, like poor Yarim.

"Well then, scholar." Ra'im put his wine cup down and regarded Mani over the table. "You're an odd kind of hero, you know. You don't carry sword or mace. You haven't slain the fire monsters in the west so we can cut cedar trees. A hero's what you are, nonetheless, and heroes are given rewards. You'll be a wealthy man, scholar."

"With your permission, my lord," Mani said, "it's not wealth that I want."

A blink of surprise. "Then what?"

His heart was thumping now, but this had to be done if he was to claim any integrity at all in the days to come. He was going to have children who would need to know right from wrong. How could he teach them that in honesty if he slunk away when truth and right mattered most?

"First," he said, "I want to tell you another story."

CHAPTER FORTY-EIGHT

I S THIS TRUE?" Ra'im asked.

An hour had gone by. The plate of dried fruit and bread was long picked to crumbs, all the wine drunk, and the water jar down to the dregs. Nahal was white behind his magnificent beard.

Shusikil's cheek twitched, much like Lamsi's always did. "The truth is that Eala loves us. This city most of all."

Ra'im smiled at her. "I'm sure she does. I've always put my faith in the goddess. Before I was chosen king, and since."

The twitch went away. Shusikil inclined her head, a queen accepting what was due by right.

"Eala is not the same thing as the Temples," Ra'im went on. "The truth of the goddess need not be what's spoken as truth by her *zami* here in Aš-alam. I'll ask you again, priestess, and remember this. I can send men to your Temples to read the tablets you keep in the darkest crypts. I can open all your secrets to the light of day, and I will, by Eala I swear it, if I even think you dissemble or lie to me. Now. Is it true?"

Shusikil hadn't been smiling, but as her face changed Mani had the sense of a smile slipping away, replaced by a mask over fury. "If you—"

"Don't tell me I wouldn't dare, *zami*. I'm king of a city I thought I might never rule again, and today I think Eala has blessed me and all my people. She gave her blessing in the form of Kassu-Mani, who told me what he suspected before he sailed, and on the island of the Puradu learned yet more. So, for the last time. Is it true?"

Her lips worked. "Yes."

"Eala was a Sea-Goat?"

"Yes."

"She was a Sea-Goat, and the Temples knew this. They have always known it, and generation after generation you chose to lie?"

"We chose to protect the people," she snapped. Evidently, she couldn't hold back any longer. "The truth would have destroyed them. We needed something to unify us, in the early days, and later something to hold us together. First, we had Temples, and then we had kings."

"You think kings owe their places to you?"

"No, I meant—"

"Enough." He waved his hand to cut her off. "It's true, which is enough for now."

"You can't tell the people."

"I'm king. On this day, I can do as I please."

"She's right, though," Mani said. Both stopped, surprised into silence. "I don't like to admit it, but she is. Making this public would cause riots. We can't afford that. Especially with the city so fragile."

Ra'im pursed his lips. "There's truth to that."

"So don't make it public," Mani said. "Let things continue as they are. At least outwardly."

"And inwardly?" Ra'im asked. He'd started to smile. Maybe he saw where Mani was going.

"I don't like lies," Mani said. "I spent my life until now searching for truth, and I found it. Truth matters. The Temples need to be shown that they can't lie without consequences."

"Eala's footfalls!" Shusikil snapped. "Do you think you can threaten the Temples like that?"

"Patience," the king said. "I believe the scholar has a suggestion. Don't you, Mani?"

He nodded. "I'm not a scholar anymore, by the way. There are no more Puradu. My profession isn't needed now."

"Your suggestion?"

Isha leaned forward again, wine cup forgotten in her hand.

"There was a woman on the island," Mani said. "One of the Puradu. She had scales, here and there on her skin. Puradu women grow more of them as they grow older, you know. It might be because—"

"Scholar," Ra'im said. "To the point."

Mani blinked. "Yes. Of course. Nikkal-Adoyah told us some of the things her people can do. Simple tricks they might have taught us one day. How to burn coal to boil water and use the steam to turn wheels." He had to stop for a moment, remembering the beauty of the island in the setting sun. "She said we could use iron instead of bronze and make sharper tools. Compasses with a needle that always points north to guide wanderers and sailors home. We spent a thousand years trying to learn from the Puradu. It's time we began to learn for ourselves."

The king's smile was wider now. "So, one day we can build a door in the world that leads to another. So we can see them again."

"Perhaps." Mani looked up at the ceiling, so any tears would run down his throat. None came. "That will be long after you and I are dust, my lord. When no one remembers Aš-alam, or the *zami*, or the Puradu themselves."

"The Goddess is eternal," Shusikil said in low fury, "and while she lasts, so will her priestesses."

"I am of half a mind to order you banished from the city," Ra'im said. "You, and the other senior *zami* who knew. You've lied to me, and to better kings than I will ever be. The people would weep if their faith was shaken, but how many would weep over you, Shusikil? Just another dried-up crone of the Temples, feared and hated as much as anything. Take care, woman. Guard your tongue."

He turned back to Mani, leaving Shusikil white-faced by the wall. "What are you suggesting, Mani? Some sort of school?"

"Exactly that," he said. "A college, staffed at first by the scholars who now don't have anything to do. They're clever, they're educated, and they have the talent. Tash-Yal would be great at geometry, for a start." The idea made him grin. "We can find gifted children the way the Temples always did when they were looking for young scholars. Let's try to work out what coal is, and how we can burn it to boil water."

"Before Labaš does," Isha put in. "Yarim heard this on the island, my lord. How long before he begins to wonder how it can be done?"

"And as for funding," Mani said, "whatever the kings spent on the Guild will do. There are no more Puradu. No reason for the Guild anymore, unless it's to study and learn. In effect, it won't cost you a thing."

"Very neat," the king said. "It's hard to argue. Although I don't have anyone available to lead this College, of course."

He said it with a small smile and an arch of one eyebrow, and Mani was sure the king knew exactly what was coming. Ra'im was no fool. He'd never have been chosen as king if he were.

"I did remind you that I'm not a scholar anymore," Mani said.

"You want a new job?"

"If I might venture to ask," he said. Shusikil made a strangled sound in her throat.

"Well, you're a clever man," Ra'im agreed. "And you're owed a reward. Are you sure?"

Mani nodded. "I've had time to think about it."

"Then I agree. We can—"

He broke off, a polite man, and turned slightly to face Isha as she leaned forward in her chair.

"Am I due a reward too?" she asked. "I do hope so. It seems unfair to keep rewards for the men, I think."

Ra'im grinned. "You can ask, lady."

"Allow women to study in the college," she said. "The only path to independence for women has always been the Temples. Since they've shown themselves untrustworthy, I think women should be given another choice."

"Suffer in the ash!" Shusikil shrieked. She was on her feet, bony finger flung at Isha. "We give women a chance to make their own way!"

"Priestess," Ra'im said. Something in his tone silenced her. "You can accept this, or we can tell the people the truth. All the truth. So decide. I want one word from you. Yes or no?"

Her jaw worked. No words came out, but she did start to make a whistling sound, like a bird at the marsh.

"Yes or no?" Ra'im repeated.

Shusikil rasped something. The king raised his eyebrows and she spoke again, biting off a single word. Mani thought it was yes.

"You may go," Ra'im told her. "Prepare your Temples for the announcement, *zami*. It will come tomorrow. Your other privileges will be left intact, of course."

She gurgled inarticulate words and departed. She slammed the door so hard it bounced back off the latch, and Nahal got up to click it shut.

"Well," Ra'im said, "you two are brave as mountain lions. Unfortunately, you have the sense of goats."

"It was clever, not foolish," Isha said. Her gaze on Mani was admiring. "I'll grant you, that was clever."

"Thank you, hot limbs," he said. He was delighted to see her blush before she ducked her face away.

"It was clever," Ra'im agreed. "Kings and Temples never rest easy next to one another, and I don't like the *zami*. I'm glad to see their influence reduced, without causing riots. Yes, it was clever. But have you thought it through?"

Mani frowned. "My lord?"

"We can't have something as important as this College run by a mere academic," Ra'im said. "No, you would have to be an Overseer, I think. Perhaps Custodian is a better title? Yes, I think so. You would be an Elder, of course, part of the councils of the King."

"What?" Mani said.

"And this house is simply unsuitable," Nahal said. "It's much too small. We'll find you somewhere bigger."

"Bigger?" Isha repeated.

Mani started to laugh.

You couldn't hold the highest ranks unless you were in the council around the king. Mani didn't really want to be there, in truth. He'd made enemies of every priestess in Aš-alam now. Well, he'd had to, or betray what he believed in. But they wouldn't forget it. The *zami* were well able to wait a year or more, as Isha had said, and then arrange an accident in the market or a little alley, and Mani's children would no longer have a father.

This was protection. The *zami* would still be livid with him, but he didn't think they'd dare strike against an Elder. Ra'im's ideas made sense now Mani thought them through. Even the new house, and servants to go with it, as though Mani was a lord, someone of importance.

His laughter faded. He *was* someone of importance now, whether he wished it or not.

"I'm going to have to learn subtlety," he said, "if I plan to survive the slippery floors of the palace."

Ra'im smiled behind the curled beard. "You will have allies. You have a lot of goodwill, scholar, for what you have done. And it seems you'll have wealth after all."

"Yes," Mani said. "I suppose so. Though I never cared for that."

"An odd sort of hero," Nahal said. The king's words, spoken earlier. "I think you'll prosper in the council, Mani. It's not swords and maces which matter there, but wits, and you have those."

"Sometimes he does," Isha put in.

The king laughed. "No man ever prospers without a wife behind him. You're lucky in yours, Mani. Tell me, you did only marry to prevent the *zami* choosing you a wife, didn't you?"

"Yes, I did."

"At first," Isha said. "It's become more than that."

"Fate is a dog that walks behind us," Ra'im said. "Only the gods might understand Fate or know how love comes to be. Mortals never can. That thought was beyond the Mad King, I think."

"He didn't understand much of anything," Mani said. "Except power and how to hoard it."

"Engiru has had enough of men like that," Ra'im agreed.

There was a rap on the door, and the soldier came back in. "Pardon me, my lords. There's a visitor at the palace."

"A visitor?" Ra'im repeated. "But the land is flooded. Who can—" He broke off, understanding on his face.

"He says," the soldier told them, "that he's the king of Labaš."

Chapter Forty-Nine

R A'IM WENT INTO his own palace by a side door, like a thief sneaking past the guards.

"Tell me," the king said. "Who am I dealing with?"

"Yarim, I think," Mani answered. He felt out of place here, surrounded by Elders and guards. He'd have to get used to that, he supposed. Isha had stayed behind with two men to keep her safe. Aš-alam was free again, but no one could rest easy yet.

"You'll have to learn how to listen to Elders," Ra'im said. "I meant, what is he like? What should I know about him?"

They went up a series of steps, painted red and green. Diamonds of sunlight broke through a lattice to their left. There were excited voices somewhere ahead, and more to both sides. Nahal stumbled on a step and swore under his breath.

"He was a captain in the army. He told me he helped carry bodies of the Labaš Elders out of the chamber when Sarru-kin had them slaughtered. He was only one captain of many then, I think. He didn't really make a name for himself until the war."

"He's not of noble birth?"

"No. According to him, all the high families were wiped out. Sarru-kin didn't want to leave anyone to plot revenge."

"Hmm," Ra'im said. "A captain loyal to a Mad King, then. Nahal, how many guards did he bring?"

"Eight," the other man said.

The king slowed. "Only eight?"

"Perhaps he doesn't want to seem a threat."

"Wait," Mani said. Part of him tried to babble words of caution, but he pushed them away. If he was among Elders now, then let him be one of them and speak his mind. "Yarim—if it really is him—wasn't all that loyal. He was in love with Kammani, the head priestess of the Balih Temples. I think they expected Sarru-kin to sail away and be lost, at which point they'd take power and put everything back the way it was."

Ra'im smiled cynically. "Everything? The priestess would have given up her new power, then?"

"Maybe not," Mani conceded.

"All right. We have a gifted captain who was clever enough not to follow blindly, and wily enough not to let that show. And he seized power the moment his chance came, which means he must be decisive too." The king caught Mani's eye. "What, Custodian? Did you think only the scholars knew how to be clever?"

"The palace," Nahal said, "is a slippery place."

They entered the throne room, from a door behind the dais. Soldiers lined the walls, which on another occasion might have looked imposing, but their weapons didn't match. Some were missing their shields, and one even had no sandals. They'd been assembled in a rush, and it showed. Nahal scowled at the man nearest the dais—the captain, Mani assumed. The man gave no sign that he'd noticed.

Ra'im settled onto the throne. "You stand one step below me, Mani, on my left. Nahal will be on my right. When our guest is shown in, let me know if it's Yarim. Cough if it is, be silent if not. Is that clear?"

His mouth was dry. "Clear."

So much for the danger being over. The king was behaving as though there was as much threat as before. Mani had the sudden thought that this might be life among the elite, a constant game of move and counter move, with danger lurking behind each one. Maybe he shouldn't have asked to join them. He might have been better running a tavern.

Ra'im nodded to Nahal, who nodded to the captain. He made a gesture, and two soldiers swung back the doors to let a single man walk in.

It was Yarim. Under the circumstances, not a great surprise. Mani coughed discreetly, and the sound drew the soldier's eyes to him. Yarim blinked and missed a step. It would have been funny, on another day. A moment's surprise, and then Yarim continued to the foot of the dais. He looked at Ra'im and inclined his head.

Kings didn't bow, or kneel, but they did nod to each other, equal to equal. Someone sucked in a surprised breath.

"You're welcome to Aš-alam," Ra'im said. "Though I doubt it's the first time you've come here."

"I was less welcome before," Yarim replied. "You're gracious, my lord. Thank you for that."

"You claim to be king of Labaš?"

"I *am* king," he said. "Named by the council of captains, which is the only power left to our city now."

"I'm surprised," Nahal said. "Officers aren't usually in such quick agreement. Was it unanimous?"

Yarim's eyes moved to him. They were both big men, Yarim perhaps a little broader in the shoulders. "There was one man who might have objected. A senior captain from the time before Sarru-kin, named Zammash. He sadly met with an accident. The scholar was there. He can verify it."

Everyone looked at Mani, whose dry tongue said, "I'm not sure that was an accident, in fact."

Yarim shrugged. "Perspective changes how we see things."

"My perspective says that was fortunate for you," Ra'im said.

"No soldier turns his back on good luck," Yarim said.

Everyone knew the truth, of course. They weren't even bothering to hide it, just talking in curves around it so that everyone understood without a single explicit word. Zammash had been a threat, and he'd been killed for it. The other captains had fallen into line. It was easy enough to follow.

Mani thought it meant that Yarim was not secure on his new throne. He had the sickle sword and a little time, and that was all. He needed something to show his men, an achievement to make them follow him further. Gain that, and he might reach Labaš with his soul and body still attached to each other.

Servants entered with cups on trays. Ra'im indicated with a hand, and one went to Yarim with a bow. The captain—the king—took a cup. "Thank you."

"What are your intentions?" Ra'im asked. After the deft prelude, he was blunt as a hammer.

Yarim smiled slightly. "If I planned war, I'd hardly say so here, in your hands, would I?"

"You'd be free to leave. I promise it."

"Well, it's not necessary. I mean to take the army of Labaš home, when the Flood ebbs enough to allow it. We won our battles but lost friends. Labaš needs peace now."

"We all do," Ra'im said. He rested his chin on one hand. "Can I trust what you tell me, I wonder?"

Yarim shrugged. "Ask Mani, there. The scholar heard me speak, back on the boat. We talked a little."

This was the man who knew how Sarru-kin had died. Only he could speak the truth of that. It would destroy him, but it would make Mani a target too, someone all the Mad King's resentful followers would long to kill. When eyes turned to Mani he nodded. "It's true. The captain had no love for Sarru-kin. He did love Kammani though, who the Mad King murdered. Yarim struck me as a decent man, although he's no captain anymore, and I'm no scholar."

"Are you an Elder?"

Yarim was quicker than Mani had thought. "It seems so. Custodian of the Royal College, I think."

"What College is that?"

He smiled. "Give it a year and you'll know, my lord."

Yarim grinned. "We've risen like the spring sun, you and I, though neither of us wished it."

Yarim had wished it, at least a little. He and Kammani had planned to rule Labaš together when Sarru-kin was gone. Mani decided not to mention that.

"You're right, and you did say you would return to Labaš. The war was Sarru-kin's, not yours."

"The war was the Mad King's," Ra'im said, "but it was men like you who made it possible to wage."

"Yes," Yarim said. "Yes, that's true. I've been a soldier all my life. There was a boy in the back streets, long ago, who thought that war was the only way he could build something for himself. That's how Engiru has always been, isn't it? Well, the boy is a wiser man now. In war a few men make their names, but too many others lose their lives."

"You have an answer for everything, it seems."

"For everything? Hardly. All I know about kingship is what I learned watching Sarru-kin, and Rassuni before him. It's not enough. I need to learn a lot, very quickly."

"Can we help?" Ra'im asked. The question came slowly, dragged from a reluctant tongue.

"Yes," Yarim said. "But it's a lot to ask. My lord king, I'll understand if you say no."

Ra'im's mouth tugged at the corners. "My lord king, I won't know what to say unless you ask."

He had called the other man a king. Mani felt his eyebrows start to climb and schooled them to stillness. One thing about Elders, they let nothing show on their faces unless they wanted it there. Even the little lift at the edges of Ra'im's mouth was probably calculated.

Perhaps that was a problem. It might be that hiding thoughts and feelings became so much a habit that nobody questioned it, or wondered what it was that lay hidden. Thus, a Sarru-kin could arise, cloaked in the manners and guiles of an ordinary noble until he gained power, and only then show his true self. It would be better to be more honest.

Except when had scholars been honest? There had always been politics there too, a gentler game than this but no less subtle. The palace was a slippery place. That was a byword in Aš-alam, a proverb as true as hot summers and the slow rise of the Flood. Honesty was laudable. In the council, it might get Mani killed.

"Then I wonder if your Elders have sons who might want to come north with me," Yarim said. "Or daughters. Third children, perhaps, nobody who will ever inherit rank here. But someone who might marry a Labaš merchant's daughter, or a landowner's son, and begin a new noble line."

"I understand," Ra'im said. "You don't have any Elders. Sarru-kin slaughtered them all."

"And their families. There might be by-blows hiding here and there, but nobody with a firm claim to noble descent. I need a new council, and quickly, to counter the power of the Temples. They'll choose a new head priestess soon enough and leave me enough power to choose my own tunic in the morning and not much else, unless I'm careful."

Ra'im almost smiled again, hiding it with a stroke of his beard. "If you take the sons and daughters of Aš-alam, you'll forge links with us as well."

"Instead of the anger that follows war," Yarim nodded, "and often leads to a new one. Yes. I thought of that, too."

"And Piqash?" Mani asked. "Tibad and Kindar? The other conquered cities might want links as well."

"I have also thought of that," Yarim said.

Ra'im and Nahal looked at one another. The king gave the smallest hint of a nod.

"I believe I have a nephew whose talent is rather greater than his opportunities," the Overseer of the Army said. "I could speak with him. He might be persuaded."

"Abamuta has four daughters," Ra'im said. "He's Governor of the River March, from a very old family. In Aš-alam, that makes it as old as any. The youngest is called Lamassa-Na. A pretty girl. She could be willing to move north, given a suitable husband."

"Don't look at me," Mani said. "I need twenty years before my child will be old enough. And even then, I'd have to ask my wife."

Yarim laughed. It was the first time Mani had heard him laugh properly, without an edge of sadness beneath it. "I've met your wife, scholar. Custodian, I mean. I don't think I'll ask. It wouldn't be fair to you."

"Thank you," Mani said.

"No. Thank you. I never thought I'd come back alive from that voyage, but I did, and I seem to have a future. A lot of that is because of you." He looked back at the king. "Thank you all. The other cities will probably follow where Aš-alam leads. By agreeing, you've given me a chance to put my city back together again."

"To put Engiru back together again," Ra'im said. "I'll have food sent out to your men at the marsh. We have spare, and I don't want hungry soldiers raiding reed platforms before the Flood goes down or farms after it has."

"Again, thank you."

"Was there anything else?"

"I'd like to speak with Mani, if I could," Yarim said.

"I don't mind," Mani said when his king glanced at him.

"Come back here when you're finished," Ra'im said. He stood, began to move away, and then paused. He turned back to Yarim and inclined his head, one king to another. Equal to equal.

§ § §

"It's going to be all right, I think," Yarim said.

"I think so too."

"Did we make it out because we were clever, Mani? Or was it luck, or the gods smiling on us?"

He couldn't answer that, even to himself. One moment he thought it was pure luck, the next that Fate or Eala must have been guiding the steps of the dance. Never mind that the goddess had been a Puradu who learned to walk. *Someone* had to be looking down on Mani, sheltering him in a benevolent hand. He was a scholar; he didn't like thinking that way…but the idea wouldn't leave him.

They were in the corridors, walking back through the palace. Mani was already lost. He was going to have to learn his way around.

"Why can't it be some of all of them?" he asked.

"Always the clever one," Yarim chuckled. "Tell me one thing, at least. Were you told what waited for Sarru-kin on the island? Did you know he was going to his death?"

"We all knew," Mani said. "The Puradu told us—told him—again and again. He just didn't listen."

"No. He was never good at that."

Yarim had reclaimed the sickle sword and his eight guards. They walked in a tight group, men who knew they were in a city of their enemies. Aš-alam soldiers waited at the doors to escort them out of the city, but even they could be a threat. Yarim's men walked as though expecting an ambush. Only Yarim strolled unconcern.

It must be something to do with kingship. Give someone a crown and he became confident, even when he shouldn't be.

"I want to ask you to come north," Yarim said. "Not now, and not as a new noble for Labaš. There might be no swimmers now, but I think you'll want to walk by the marsh sometimes and remember. Still, I'd like you to speak to our learned men. Tell them what happened on the island and what we saw. You came before, and they know and respect you. After what happened in the ocean, they'll respect you even more."

"I'll be glad to come," he said. "After my child is born and I've established the College. It will be a year at least, I'm afraid."

"You've found something to occupy all those scholars with nothing to study, haven't you?" Yarim was unsettlingly quick, and he didn't wait for an answer. "And I thought I'd moved fast to establish my power. I might see if I can use this as precedent in Labaš. The *zami* have too much power there as well."

"I know they do," Mani said. "I met Kammani, remember?"

They came into the sunlight at the top of the steps with a crowd gathered below them. Yarim's men drew their circle tighter, ready for trouble.

"I loved her," the new king said, very quietly. "I loved her, and nothing feels the same anymore." He faced Mani then, sunlight full on his easy smile as he grasped the other man's arm. "Be well, Kassu-Mani. I wish for Eala to be real and to smile on you and your family."

He left Mani no time to reply. With the words he was gone, he and his guards clattering down the steps to the street below. Mani was reminded of Sarru-kin, flanked always by his four burly protectors, wards against a knife in the back. But only for a moment.

Yarim stumbled and nearly fell on the last step. He didn't look down even as he fought for balance. Something in the crowd had him transfixed, and Mani thought *a knife in the back* once more. But Yarim went towards it, whatever it was, not away. The Aš-alam soldiers swerved to follow him, and he didn't seem to notice. He halted at the edge of the throng and then just stood there.

"Did you want something?" a familiar voice said. Smoky, like charcoal smouldering in the ashes of a fire. Mani blinked in the brightness and realised Elessa was at the front of the crowd.

"Yes," Yarim said to her. "I didn't know it until now…but yes, I want something."

"And what is that?"

"I want you to walk with me," the king of Labaš said, "while I tell you about life in my home city."

Her smile was slow and beguiling. She half turned and cocked her head, inviting him to follow. Yarim went with her into the parting crowd, two steps only, before the next thing happened.

A man pushed through the crowd, towards Yarim. The guards let him through. The new king listened and then turned. He looked up at Mani in the sunshine.

"A matter for you, I think," he said. "My soldiers have seen something in the lagoon."

Chapter Fifty

ANI REACHED THE levee at a flat run, came to the bank of rushes, and halted.

Soldiers of Labaš stood around him, hundreds of them. A moment ago, they'd been jostling for position, but now they were still, waiting. For him, of course. To see what he did. He heard some mutters and realized they knew who he was—the clever man of letters who had somehow led Sarru-kin to his death. There would be knives in belts in that crowd. Someone might think of revenge.

Mani found he didn't care. He stepped down to the gap in the reeds, and ahead of him the water shone, bright gold in the sunshine.

"Go on," someone said.

He only noticed then that he'd stopped again. His feet felt rooted, like trees on the Puradu island.

"Go on, scholar," a different voice said. "Talk to it."

Something bubbled inside him, anger or joy. Maybe both. "They're not *it*. Not animals. They're people."

The soldiers drew back when he glared at them. They were afraid. Well, so was he, frightened in his bones and the flesh that clung to them. If he went along the pier and there was no Puradu there, Mani thought his heart might wither and Death would take shape at his elbow.

If there was a Puradu? He shivered, thinking what that would mean, and who it must be.

He went down to the pier through the gap in reeds. Some of the planks had been taken to make firewood, and in one place Mani had to step from the top of one post to the top of the next, like a rope walker at Festival. Then he looked up and saw something bobbing in the water, out across the lagoon. It might be a head. A hairless skull, with bones that curled like horns beneath the skin.

He walked on in a dream, hardly feeling the boards, and if more had been missing, he might have fallen and broken his neck.

The head vanished. Mani came to the end of the pier, beside the bell, and sat down. His feet hung in the water, and after a moment something surfaced before them, water streaming from a smile.

"Scholar," Hanno said.

The Puradu he had thought he would find, the only one it could possibly be. Mani felt dizzy, overwhelmed, but then he had forgotten his hat again.

"Hanno," he said, as gravely as he could. Tears were close.

"I thought," the young Puradu said, "that we could learn some more together, you and I."

Mani bowed his head. "Only you?"

"Only me, scholar. The others would have stopped me if they knew."

"How did you get past them?"

"I hid myself in the reeds under your boat," Hanno said. "At the back, where the water is most disturbed. No one came to look for me. They had no reason to think I was there."

Breathe, breathe. "Why are you here, Hanno?"

"To be near you and other humans. To speak with you."

"But Hanno—"

"You told me once," the Puradu said gently, "that you longed for the chance to stay on our island forever. Do you remember? Even alone, the one human there, when the wives took the island away. Mani, what I have done is what you wanted to do."

"Hanno," he said. "Hanno. Hanno. You must go home."

The smooth head shook. "I want to learn about humans. I want to see the world as you see it, with no water to filter the colours and make them shimmer. And it's too late, scholar. The door is closed."

"The door?"

"The way between worlds. The island is gone. It's too late."

Mani wept then, just a single tear from each eye. Enough to make colours shimmer. Hanno reached up to wipe them away with a webbed hand.

"Don't cry," he said. "I wanted this, Mani. I want to talk to you and the other scholars, openly now. I tell you of my people and you tell me of yours. There's only one thing I ask for."

He nodded. "What is it?"

The water rippled, a thousand vibrations as Hanno laughed in near silence. "Can't you guess, scholar? Your wife. I want to speak with your wife, and to see your children when they're born and as they grow. Can you do that?"

Mani pushed himself forward. He slipped into the water at Hanno's side, making the Puradu wriggle away in the middle of more ripples. Mani reached out a hand.

"We can do that," he said.

Epilogue

A DAY SPENT buried in reports," Mani said. "Suffer in the ash, I've turned into a clerk."

"You wanted the college," Darsal reminded him. "Besides, there's been good news today."

The sun burned the fields around them. Last year the Flood had turned the whole plain into a swamp, even the little bumps of land that usually stayed dry. There was no sign of that now. Earth crumbled to dust under every footfall, and air clogged in the throat.

"Tell me the good news," Mani said.

"The lad from Piqash had decent results from his new furnace. Taribet, remember? You spoke to him last month."

Mani frowned. "Cross-eyed fellow?"

"That's him. The one who said he could smelt iron ore by double burning marsh reeds."

The mad one, Hitti had called him. The ancient scholar was still alive, still clattering about on his twin sticks. He didn't have much to contribute now. Time and change had left Hitti behind, and the young man from Piqash was just one example of that.

"Did it work?" Mani asked.

Darsal wiggled a hand in the air. "Sort of. I went over to watch him a few days ago. He packed reeds in flat bundles, very tight. Then he laid them over embers, with sods of earth over the top except for a tiny hole. That lets the fire burn, but very slowly. Yesterday he uncovered the fire, and the reeds had burned down to black lumps. Those are what he says will burn hot enough to smelt iron ore."

"And do they?"

"Sort of," Darsal said again. "The ones he's made so far turn ore into a glittery sludge. Taribet's product is mostly iron, at least, which is better than anyone else can manage."

"Hardly a breakthrough, then."

"I think it will be," Darsal answered. "If you want more good news, look at the girl from the villages. Nitanu says she's as clever as any student we've had through our doors."

That was two lots of good news, in truth. Nitanu himself was the first, a young would-be scholar who had proved to be a very good tutor. Then there was the village girl herself, Ahatiwa. Mani had only met her once, but intellect had gleamed in every shift of her eyes. She was interested in maps, although *interested* wasn't really the right word. Obsessed would be better. She had made Mani think about himself, years ago, so entranced by the Puradu that he hardly thought about anything else.

"Yarim is starting a college in Labaš," he said. "The idea has begun to catch on, Darsal."

"But they won't teach women there."

"No. Only we do that." Mani nodded. "Aš-alam was the first, and we'll be the best. Anyway, it makes Isha happy when we teach women."

"Did I hear my name?" she asked behind them.

Tanyih dashed past a moment later, all coltish legs and flying hair. Seven years old now, though sometimes it seemed she had only been born a few mornings ago. Other times it seemed she had always been there, and Mani's life before his daughter was just a dream, the memories of another man. Behind her came Nikkal, smaller than her sister, running hard but never able to catch up.

Then Isha was there as well, smiling under the brim of her hat. She took Mani's hand and guided it to the swell of her stomach. Two babies had changed her figure, but this plumpness was new, the proof of another child. A son this time, perhaps. Not that Mani really cared. He wouldn't swap either of his girls for a dozen sons.

"Come on!" Tanyih called. "Hurry up, or he'll be gone."

"Gone where?" Mani called. Tanyih only laughed and ran on, towards the bank that marked the edge of the lagoon.

"Your hat," Isha said. "Put it on, Mani. Last month the sun burned your bald spot red, or did you forget?"

"I tried to." He crammed the hat on his head. "You won't let me."

They reached the bank. The air changed there, full of the scents of water and mud, and the whisper of reeds. The girls raced down the path, Mani and Isha behind, Darsal bringing up the rear now. They went through the rushes, and there the lagoon shone, bright and beautiful in the sunlight, the reeds around it impossibly green.

Tanyih rang the bell. From so far away Mani didn't even hear it. Both girls had stripped off their dresses and were in the water by the time he arrived, splashing each other and laughing. Nikkal took a breath and dived, one thing she did much better than her older sister. She came up ten yards away, pushing hair back from her face.

"You know there's nobody else in the city who could do that?" Isha called.

A moment later the water erupted. There was a shape in the middle of it, tailed but human, flying over Tanyih's head. Hanno hit the water and popped back up again next to Nikkal, both laughing out loud.

"Nobody else anywhere can do that," Darsal said softly. "You know what an incredible thing this is, don't you?"

"The last Puradu in the world," Mani said. Hanno and Nikkal dived together, and Mani sat on the edge of the pier, feet in the water. "I know what it is."

He remembered an island, pools of water shining in the sun with forest all around. Women stood there, arms bare, their skin a-glitter. He saw a man, flush-faced, sure that eternity stretched before him like a promise, a destiny to be seized. All of them gone now, too far for anything but memory to see. Gone, and lost.

The last Puradu and two daughters. Eternity enough for anyone.

Acknowledgments

A lot of people have helped bring this novel to publication. I was given some good feedback by my writers' group in Barnstaple, England, so thanks go to Gill, Ruth, Rebecca, and all the other members.

Thanks also to Sandra Tirado, the first editor I've ever worked with at a traditional publisher. She showed me how to knock my book into shape, and was always helpful and clear, exactly what a first-time writer needed. Finally, thanks to Ken Tupper, the lead editor of Divertir, for believing in me and giving me a chance.

The Altered Manuscript
Ellen Taylor

The accidental discovery of the narration device completely changed entertainment and proved too dangerous to use without strict laws in place. Junior understood the reason behind these laws, which is why Bree does not know she's a character in a story. When a rogue narrator hacks into the system and begins creating chaos in Junior's story, does Junior continue to follow the laws to keep herself safe, or does she risk it all to protect the characters she loves?

The Knight of Innocence
Julius Brown

Young people are being killed by the dozens. The police are baffled by the dismembered bodies and missing persons reports. With Baltimore about to become a playground for demons, the communities turn to the one man in the city sworn to defend them. Armed with a magical sword, a desert eagle—because he can't hit a target—and a network of friends better suited for the job, can Michael Franklin White prevent a wizard from opening a portal to Hell in his city?

Time Starts Now
Michael Walsh

Professor Cal Sutherland's research on time travel elicits only snide remarks from fellow philosophers and rejection notices from journals. Even Cal would admit that time travelers probably aren't real—until he encounters one inside his neighbor's burning house. Cal soon learns that, while the past cannot be changed, there is much a time traveler can do in the past. Unfortunately for Cal, this includes the possibility of dying there…

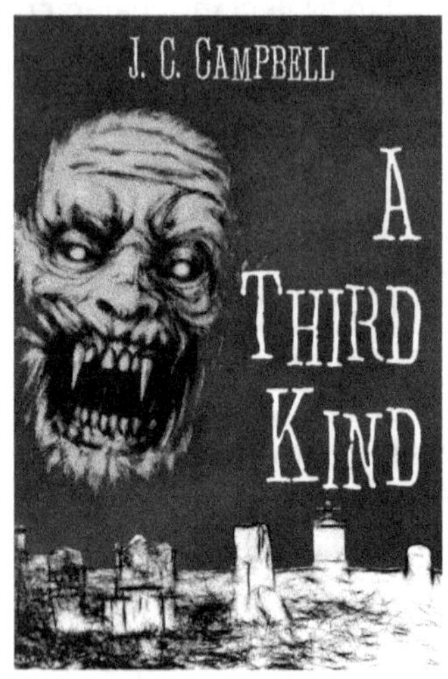

A Third Kind
J. C. Campbell

He was to have been an immortal undead, to have power and strength like he'd never known in mortal life. The Vampyrs lied. When he awoke he was some- thing else, a creature so foul they abandoned him to die alone in a crypt. When the local ruling Vampyr clan realizes what is living in their midst, they come in force to destroy Kaleb and wipe every last trace of his existence from the face of the earth.

The Adventures of New World Dave
Chris Cervini

In the spring of 1519, Hernán Cortés arrived at the shores of Mexico to conquer the Aztec Empire and claim its gold for the glory of Spain. That's what the history books tell us. But sometimes, right in the middle of the history we know, somebody goes and does something to change one important detail, and the world is never the same…

The Entropy of Knowledge
Mark Dellandre and Britton Learnard

We've all had moments when we felt like we were surrounded by idiots…
Babylon Briggs feels that pain every day because his town, his planet, even his galaxy, is jam-packed with the most thick-headed simpletons imaginable. So when his home world is invaded by a group of equally clueless conquerors, it's up to Babylon to save the day. The only question:
Is he smart enough?